MISERY

PAULINE S. FLYNN

Published by

DolmanScott

www.dolmanscott.com

To the past, the present,
and future selves.

Desdemona
N
NW NE
W E
SW SE
S
Forgotten Isles
Ortulunae
Endolas
Vison
Fort Zira
Scarbra
Delwae
Crossidius
Old King's Port
Newmont
Port Nesmo
Klaedo
Ortusolis

CONTENTS

Chapter One 1

Chapter Two 19

Chapter Three... 26

Chapter Four.. 34

Chapter Five 40

Chapter Six 49

Chapter Seven 58

Chapter Eight... 68

Chapter Nine 74

Chapter Ten 80

Chapter Eleven 92

Chapter Twelve.. 101

Chapter Thirteen 108

Chapter Fourteen 117

Chapter Fifteen... 127

Chapter Sixteen 136

Chapter Seventeen 148

Chapter Eighteen 157

Chapter Nineteen 165

Chapter Twenty 178

Chapter Twenty-One 196

Chapter Twenty-Two 207

Chapter Twenty-Three 221

Chapter Twenty-Four.. 235

Chapter Twenty-Five... 246

Chapter Twenty-Six.. 254

Chapter Twenty-Seven 263

Chapter Twenty-Eight 272

Chapter Twenty-Nine.. 281

Chapter Thirty 290

Chapter Thirty-One.. 301

Chapter Thirty-Two.. 310

Chapter Thirty-Three 317

Chapter Thirty-Four 327

Acknowledgments 334

MISERY

The ill-fated series.

By Pauline S. Flynn

Newmont, Desdemona. 1353 – A W

CHAPTER ONE

Screams echoed all around, trailed by iron clanging in the distance. Ear-piercing howls followed and filled the breaks between the clashes of turbulent chaos.

I look frantically around for my father, shouting his name. No words fall from my dry, split lips. As the haze-like world around me shrieks with noise, I am silenced.

Alone.

Nothing but black mist. My hands were shaking as I scatter the ground around me for some stability, my fingertips brushing against invisible objects. I would reach further to grip whatever was there, only for my hands to meet empty space. I desperately needed something to hold on to. My legs were numbing, I had been kneeling on the ground for far too long. I could still – just register, feeling twigs and stones wedged into my kneecaps.

I could not still my mind, anxiety cracking the walls I had built within. Thoughts of the earth splitting open, and I'd begin to freefall into a never-ending dark abyss.

"Hecate"

My head shoots up, to the voice calling. Scanning the barely visible space around for someone – anyone.

Black and grey shadows continue their dance, tauntingly, a reminder of how alone I truly was.

"Hecate, wake up you lazy cow!"

I jolted awake – eyes wide open. Regret slaps me in the face as the sun burns my eyes. I struggle to sit up as my vision steadily returns, my body felt heavy. My arms feel like jelly as they prop me up, from behind.

A tall man stands, arms folded, leaning in the doorway.

Not entirely sure of my wits, I look around the room for anything to prove to myself otherwise, heart pounding so violently.

"Father wants you dressed and downstairs, now." His raucous voice rattles within my aching skull.

This is real, I am not dreaming… I'm drenched in sweat, the bedding damp, probably from sweating through the night. I try to lick my lips, but my mouth is unbelievably dry. A grunt draws my attention back to the doorway. That man – my brother, impatiently tapping his finger to a bicep, frowning. "Morning to you too, Alastor." I croak out, my throat burning for just a drop of water.

He turns his back to me, his white tunic without a single crease. "I tire of repeating myself to you. Stop reading those books." He spoke over one of his wide shoulders.

We are starting this already? "Whatever, I stayed up a tad too late last night– "

I am not able to finish my excuse when Alastor rudely cuts me off. "Bad dreams after reading bedtime stories? You are a child, Hecate, grow up!" He barks back, disappearing before the damp pillow I launched, could reach him.

I hastily grab one of the other pillows decorating my dishevelled bed, screaming into it – or try too anyway. "Are all brothers dicks, or just mine?" Grumbling some more, I attempted to drag my tired body out of bed.

Not even a step away from my soft sleeping haven, my big toe painfully jars something. The throbbing under the nail, confirming that I was indeed awake, and present. Glancing down, I notice the book I was reading in the night. I throw a few curses at it, before bending over and picking it up.

The New World.

A book of narrations, how our island came to be, more fiction than not.

Tales of the 'mythical' first gods and how Desdemona became an island. Ravaged by war, magic, monsters, and God–like beings.

I had stumbled upon it in the family library yesterday, it looked completely out of place, worn and tattered unlike all the glossy spines on that shelf. I had never noticed it before, which is why I grabbed it. The irony of the narrations to the legends and myths our nannies told us, to scare us into behaving. I found it a real page turner.

I glimpsed into the vanity mirror, only to be spooked by a pale looking ghost of myself. My eyes–dull, evidence of a restless night's sleep.

Placing the monstrous book down, I decide to start with the rats nest that accumulated during the night. Brushing the few stray hairs mangled by sweat, stuck to the back of my neck. I braced myself for the pain, from the hairs being pulled from the scalp.

I hate pain, hated feeling weak over something so mundane.

After detangling, I placed the brush down. Attempting to massage the bags now occupying the space under my eyes.

The maids must have already been.

A silver washing up bowl waited for me, on the corner of the ivory dressing table. Scooping the water up with my hands, I splash my face. I was thankful no one else could see me in this state, I needed to make myself seem more presentable, before joining father downstairs.

The second week in a row... Perhaps I should listen to Alastor and switch up my reading material. I throw on a robe hooked on the back of my bedroom door, contemplating.

Light bombarded me as I exited my room, which was found on the third floor of the home, the brightest floor of the estate. It was also much brighter than the sunshine that poured in through my bedroom window. I blink numerously, waiting to see the familiar hall adorned in famous paintings and tapestries from overseas. This floor had many large-arched windows, and a medium-high ceiling, allowing light to fill even the darkest of corners.

My nostrils filled with sea breeze air, the balcony doors opposite the corridor, wide open. Sounds of chatter from the staff outside providing me with reassurance.

I am home.

Our family lived rather comfortably, one of six families owning larger parts of the west that lead to port. Ours, 200 acres of stunning gardens and training grounds, followed by the Smithes' with their 100 acres just down the road, and so on. Each of the lands owned in Desdemona by lords born or selected by the kings to govern.

Desdemona is a large island divided by mountains and rolling foothills, with a king ruling on each side.

The south has eight towns, governed by seven lords and the southern king ruling in the east. Each town divided by meadows, plains, and scenic forestry. Whilst, the north has four towns and their northern king, ruling far north to the western seaside. The dense forest of the mountains stretching and hiding those four towns, from outsiders. North of the mountains is dangerous territory for us southerners. Full of savages, and endless stories of a boogie man, whispering in the northern king's ear.

Twelve official towns, two official kings owning the kingdoms.

My father – one of those lords, was awarded Newmont. Our king – King Jonathan - owned everything south of the mountain's boarders before the vicious sea.

My fingers intertwined with a stray thread hanging off a tapestry on the wall. An image of my father glade in armour, deep in those mountains, standing victorious over a battlefield. "One of the Twelve," I read the gold-plated plaque, beneath the colourful cloth.

A light agitates my eyes yet again, the sun reflecting off Alastor's silver plaque. Youngest recognition award, no tapestry of his own yet. The space above the plaque calling to be filled.

My brother, Lieutenant Colonel of Newmont's battalion, Alastor Crosse. A near splitting image of our father, following close with his own high achievements at twenty–five years of age. Future Duke of Newmont. I rolled my eyes as I walked past his plaque.

I ran my fingers along the high–white trim, their edges of complicated designs. Admiring the stretch of gold, red, and white colour scheme of the corridor. My heels dragged slightly on the maroon rug that stretched in centre of the white marble floors. I loved the cultivated paintings filling the spaces between each arched window. Each like their very own story, if you just looked long enough at them.

The Duchess had a wonderful taste in fine art.

I slow to a stop when my reflection off the windows halts me, just before the descending staircase. *I must be the splitting image of my mother then?* Fidgeting with the necklace around my neck, I pondered this.

I was young when my mother died, pneumonia they say. We do not discuss her – ever, or Alastor's mother, the Duchess. Conversations of them are taboo anywhere you go. Rooms once filled with chatter, die. Alastor storms off and becomes volatile for the following days.

I do not think anyone could really blame him, they say his mother went crazy, and could not live with life anymore. Others say, her head got too sad when father was committing adultery, thus my very existence. Whenever we used to attend social gatherings together, audible whispers and pitiful stares whenever something was remotely brought up.

I learned my lesson a long time ago, avoiding invites and lounging round the estate was just less of a headache. It was a safer choice than being out there with those social two-faced monsters.

I fill my days with reading and helping the gardeners around the grounds and arguing with Al. Finding new ways to annoy him, for research purposes. When I really needed to get under his skin, I usually mention, Katrina.

Katrina's name holds power against my mighty douche-bag brother, my trump card in arguments.

Kat as I have gotten accustomed to calling her.

Skipping off the bottom step, I make my way to where father was waiting, the conservatory attached to our home. This place is full of quiet life. Explosions of colours from the flowers reflecting and bouncing off the glass surroundings.

Purples from the Hesperis matronalis, reds from the begonias, and yellow tulips, complimenting the purples. I planted them all myself and was quite proud of this section of our home.

This is my number two spot of comfort, a change of scenery from my number one – the dark library on the first floor. It was a routine father and I had adopted. We have had our morning tea together there since I was nine. It is a peaceful place to muster the energy for the day ahead.

As I neared the conservatory, I overhear Alastor's deep voice complaining to father, for being too easy on me. I was shocked to hear him over here, well aware of his disgust for this area.

Entering, I curtsy. "My Lords, what a fine morning this is." Daring a cheeky peek, at them both.

Alastor looks less than impressed. The indents of his t–section, between those thick eyebrows, deepening.

Father has that mischievous glint in his deep blue eyes, flicking his chin for me to sit. "Good afternoon, you mean."

Cringing from embarrassment, I subconsciously reach and fidget once again with my necklace. D*amn, afternoon already.*

Lifting the local paper, he continues, "we need to have a little chat."

"Double damned." Slips out, earning me a look from both men sitting.

"Hecate Crosse, mind your tongue." Alastor visibly relaxes, and smirks, hearing father reprimand me. I waited, sticking out my tongue, when our father looked more focused on the paper, and Alastor's signature frown reappears.

I begin my mental tally for today. *Hecate 1 – Al 0.*

"I'm sure you'll hear the gossip, but I want you to hear it from us first."

I tense at those words, sipping from my teacup. Concealing that his words had any visible effect on me.

"There's been a group of rebellions as of late, creating chaos all over the ports, and even so far as the town centres."

He is going to advise we – well me, to stay out of trouble.

"I want you to stay out of trouble young lady, do not be going into town unnecessarily. If you must go, I will assign you a guard for when you leave the estate."

"SHE DOESN'T EVEN GO OUT, ANYWAYS!" Alastor's sudden outburst has both of our full attention, "She literally does nothing here at home, at least bring in a teacher for her."

Now it was my turn to scowl, his words leaving a bad after taste in my mouth. "Listen, I don't interfere, or make opinions about what you should, and shouldn't do." Placing my cup down, I point at him. "So, I would appreciate that you. Butt. Out."

He matches my scowl, leaning forward, the weight of his arms causing the table to groan beneath them.

Father folds the newspaper onto his lap. "That is enough. The both of you," his voice getting quieter.

We both, ceasefire wisely, backs eventually pressed into the support of our chairs, not once breaking eye contact. This was something we mutually agreed upon, a quiet father- was a scary father.

"Alastor does make a good point, perhaps it's time for you to start lessons again... To aid our family as the only lady of this household," he said with a small smile.

I blink quickly, stopping myself from rolling my eyes. I had never been good with people, let alone having to pretend to be something I was not.

I catch Al from my peripheral view, smirking once more. Plastering a smile on, I slowly nod my head. "I do not need to host floosy parties, do I?"

Father chuckles, "No dear, but what you'll learn will help you. As well as aiding your brother and I." He reaches over and pats the back of my hand. His calloused hand rough, and much larger than my own.

Father works for the high council now. After his many years of servitude – a mediator of peace for the two kingdoms, and us. In his youth, he was Captain for Newmont and Port Nesmo guards, just west of our home. Later, leaping ranks to General – for ending the ten-year war.

Recognised not only by the king, but by the temple for his contributions to *'the realm,'* he was appointed as Duke. The title was just the King's way of keeping a hold onto my father. A feudalism, a title for continued work... or a leash...

He is a busy man, on top of leading the household and managing the western's first army. Everything we have today, was earned solely by him. It does not go un-noticed, more and more each day, the greys creeping upon his neatly combed hair. The whimsy grey patches of facial hair that box in his chin, or the deep wrinkles near his blue eyes. I remember a time father was just as stalky as Alastor. Now that he does not have to swing a sword, all hours of the day, I am conscious of the shrinking figure.

Time catches up to us all, eventually. My father was looking at me with such love that guilt settled over me. *I should get along with Al, at least for Father's sake.*

Alastor jeers as I am in thought, "She needs friends first to hold parties."

"Ah yes, I'm sure Kat could help me with that." I turn my fakest smile to him, batting my dark lashes.

Alastor falls deadly silent, turning oddly pale before excusing himself, to father.

We were always like this, cat and dog, hot and cold. *Why do I always have to be the one to compromise?*

When we were younger, it was not so bad. I blame puberty, mainly. Ever since he shot up like a bean stock with his head so high in the sky. His 6'4 to my 5'6 did not mean squat. I could always make up the height difference with a tall attitude as well. I found it hard sometimes fighting with him, he was father's look alike, except those eyes.

Alastor inherited his mother's eyes.

His hair, chestnut brown, neatly combed to the back. A square shaped face, scattered with freckles a shade darker than his skin tone. His skin – sun kissed, from endless hours under the scorching summer suns, giving his arms and face, a bronze shine. It was his eyes that set him apart from father, cinnamon-coloured eyes protected by enviously long lashes.

"He's hard on you because he expects the most from you."

I roll my eyes back to my optimistic father, "We are talking about Alastor, right? Lord of, I'm too cool for fun. Or – I would rather die than say anything encouraging to my little sister. That one, yes? Or do I have another brother around, I have yet come to meet." I flip the table linen up, looking under it for dramatic effect.

"Hecate...." Father sighs, "He just wants to see you succeed, I want to see you succeed. You are both such strong willed and opinionated. I am not saying you do not do anything... I know you have your hobbies and I love that for you... I just think you can do much more, for yourself. You do not think I have noticed, have you?" His face morphs into a look of concern, like Alastor, deep creases appear near his eyebrows. "Your brother has noticed as well... you need to do more... mentally."

I swallow down my words, fidgeting with my necklace... I did not want to sit here and start the day arguing with him now, too.

"We should get ready..." Father murmurs before rising, "we shall finish our talk another time." Giving me that all-knowing look. "We've already missed morning prayers."

...

The carriage ride was quiet, wheels turning on the cobble stones, horses trotting along. The silence was welcoming, Alastor was riding ahead, and father was looking over his paperwork.

I was adjusting the straight cut skirt that raised mid-calf when sat, feeling uncomfortable in my worship clothes. I peer over to father's tidied suit – envious the men did not have to dress in such manner.

When all the ladies and children were gathered, anyone unfamiliar with our customs would assume we were some... cult. The south had this funny dress code for us attending the temple, and attending is a must. A by-law to prove there were no demons among us, the only exemption to those currently on guard duty around the towns. Something about these demons catching fire the moment they stepped inside the sanctums of worship.

We are made to dress in these pure white kaftans, embroidery on the chest down to the un-restricted waist, in soft brown beads and threads. Similar to what the priestesses wore, the browns replaced with gold embroidery and different shades of red jewels. Their hoods however, completely embroidered in gold and red threads, a sign of devotion to the new gods.

Many of the fine clothes we wear today is created by Katrina's mother, Lady Grace. She is one of the lead tailors in Newmont. She was the one who explained the importance of wearing these kaftans, a sign of purity and devotion. Not just to the gods but to our neighbours, a united front, a kinship of man. Which seemed contradicting to me, considering the men themselves were not required too.

I am pulled from thought when the carriage comes to a stop, father begins to put his papers aside before the carriage door opens. I tuck my necklace inside my kaftan, groaning as father extends his hand to help me out.

I hope I burst into flames, then I will not have to sit through these old geezers preaches.

"Teeee!!!!!" A cheerful squeal penetrates my eardrums, as I am nearly toppled over. "I'm so glad you're finally here. How dare you show late, punctuality makes a lady!" This is the one and only – Katrina Smithe, my very dear friend.

She has medium-long blonde hair of curls, and bright-blue eyes on her still round, baby face. She is about the same height as me, when she is not wearing heels, or has her hair up in the ridiculous latest trends that are going on in Ortusolis. Today, she was dressed down, as were all women and children.

I wrap my arms around the blondie, laughing, "Sorry we're late Kat, I didn't want to come."

We both start snickering and my father's eyes warn me to watch my mouth, here. Loitering near us, he greeted other lords, keeping a watchful eye that I did not try to slip away again. I was placed under probation by father last time, for self–reflection, he had said. Luckily for me, my attendance was taken before I had done so, those caught slipping away or not attending, were slapped with hefty fines.

Kat's arms slacken a moment later, I catch her cheeks colouring pink. Turning my head to Kat's line of sight, I spot my brother Alastor, dismounting his horse.

...

After everyone is seated, and the check in proceedings are completed, the afternoon's lengthy sermon began. The head Hierei at the stand ahead of us all, had his arms wide open. *"In the beginning the gods of old, gave life's children many gifts, they lived in harmony and prospered. All were equal, all were loved. Love, however, was not enough for some. Desire festered, temptation leading sinners to make deals with devils. Greed was born, with greed came envy. The children turned away from their gods, hungry for more... Then came the war. A war separating monsters from man."*

I was beyond bored, fighting a yawn I could feel building in my jaw, and the back of my throat.

"The people were slaughtered needlessly and cried for their gods. In one last attempt to help, a mighty strike from above, separated the world that we know today. Before vanishing from our plains. Our forebears fought for the lands we call home. By the grace of the new gods..."

A nail piercing pain jerks my eyes open. "I'm awake!" I whisper–yell to my seated attacker. Kat retracts her small hand, smiling slightly – not once looking away from the front.

"The warriors of light…. Our ancestors!… Fought day and night to vanquish the beasts from these territories."

I rolled my eyes to the dramatics – we heard these stories time and time again. Warnings of demons and deals. Of gods who abandoned the people, and people rising to godlike status with unfathomable magic power.

Desdemona did not welcome sorcery anymore, magic in the blood of mere men was seen as the devil's work, and a threat to the royal families. Sorcerers, witches, and wizards were seen as evil beings, power hungry villains. Anyone suspected of sorcery was imprisoned by the temple and dealt with.

Magic was commercialized now, through safer methods.

It was harvested from the earth through rocks, known as mana stones, only authorised individuals were allowed to wield them. They required years of studying, and undergoing rigorous tests in the capital, before even qualifying for their certificate. These people were known as Mana-Handlers, they usually aided the armies and police sections, under specific circumstances.

I once dreamt of pursuing this career but spending twenty-to-thirty years of studying, before I could even touch one fragment of stone… Shattered the dream for me.

The black market too had their own mana stones. Being caught with unauthorized items, or forged paperwork, could easily have you imprisoned, or worse… executed.

So much for a 'kinship of men.'

I laughed, not realising I had done so out loud. Many eyes turned to me, bewildered. I slammed a hand over my mouth. Judging by the stunned Hierei turning the script, he had just got to the part about the 'heathens', butchering the ancient queen.

I slowly sunk down in the pew, as the row of folks –one by one–
spun back forward. Kat's beat red with embarrassment, probably
wishing, I really had not come today.

Thankfully, the sermon continues about the 'perfect world' we
lived in and the creation of the new gods. I did not dare look in
father's direction, I could feel his eyes, burning a hole in the side
of my head.

I was certain, that I had used up all his warnings by now....

...

After a painstaking couple of hours of book readings, wine sharing,
and blessings we were able to leave the temple. I am relieved
leaving the grand dome structure behind, wiping off the ash
smeared on my forehead. The late afternoon air was nippy, the chill
on my warm cheeks, sensational. Fall was right around the corner,
quicker than it was last year. I briefly heard Kat mention shopping
for furs beside me, aware she hated the cold. My attention was
elsewhere, her voice was smothered out by shouting in the
distance.

The commotion earned much attention as people began
gravitating toward the disturbance, much like a herd of cows. Kat
and I shared a look of curiosity, linking arms, we decided to follow.

We barely managed to weave through the groups of people, to
where all the noise was projecting from. There, stood a barefoot
man in rags, grabbing people as they approached. His clothes
torn and mangled. His rags were that bad, I could not make out
the fabric's original colour. The smell of piss wafting with each
sway and swing of his arms.

*"They are here! D'you hear me, they are coming! Damned is
the day! A debt to be paid!! They are here!!"*

Katrina's arm tightens around my own, uncomfortably.

His eyes were bloodshot, skin grey, the man looked sick. How he was still standing was beyond me. With every move, the tears in his clothing would reveal just how under-weight he was. There were shades of purple-blotching areas visible to the naked eye. Indicating, obvious signs of abuse around his protruding ribs. What gave me the chills, were the near black veins covering and stretching over his torso, and the gangly scar around his neck. It had me reaching and rubbing my own throat.

My brother and the local guards tried to defuse the situation, not a moment after. The man seemed startled by them, lashing out violently. How he could grab one of the guards and hysterically shake him, was baffling to all those on looking. The man looked frail, like the wind would snap him in two, in comparison to the armoured men surrounding him, like wolves.

Pointing around at us, hysterically, he started screaming. *"Desdemona is damned, you hear me? The darkness has begun sweeping over the lands –"* He is gagged, his hands yanked behind his back. He was thrown to the ground after, a knee to his spine, while the other guards placed iron cuffs on him.

Gasps resound, people begin scurrying away, like they would catch whatever sickness he had. His bulging eyes found mine, almost pleadingly. A part of me felt unnerved by how roughly he was being treated, there was no need for such brutality. I do not know when my father approached us, but his hand gently covered our eyes. "Come now, let us leave this place." He gently led us away from the muffled screams of a madman.

...

Zoned out the entire travel back, I barely acknowledged the fact the Smithe's were joining us for dinner. The man's words echoing inside my mind.

Who are they – What darkness?

Questions upon questions, interlapping with the man's words –a spiral of internal dialogue. Twirling the circular pendant that hung around my neck every day, I carelessly spaced out, staring at the floor.

Father gives my knee a little tap, and I jump to attention. "Penny for your thoughts?"

I continue to stare at him absent-mindedly.

"Hecate, my dear, you've gone pale again." He removes his dark gloves, placing the back of his warm hand to my forehead.

I brought his hand down from checking, holding them for a moment in my own. "What was that all about..."

Father sympathetically nods his head, humming. "Rebels." He then started shuffling things around and swapping seats to sit next to me. A sturdy arm outstretches, pulling me in, closely to his chest. "It's alright, Stinks." Soothing me as though I was still a child. He gently rubs the side of my head, caging me to him with his other arm. "This old man of yours will protect you."

We quietly arrived home, to my regret.

I exited and watched Kat's carriage settle behind ours, the doors flying open. She leaps out grinning ear to ear, to whatever her mother was saying, twirling her curls around a finger.

Lady Grace approaches me, while I waited patiently at the bottom of the stone steps leading to our stained oak doors. Her hand slipping to the back of my neck, placing a kiss to my forehead, her plump lips lingering. I hear her, mumbling a silent prayer, for us all.

We finally got to the dining room, the atmosphere normal, as if nothing happened. I could not forget, my thoughts like waves getting bigger. *Was a plague coming?* I try to rationalise it all, saying a simple yes or shaking my head, to not rudely ignore our guests.

"Young lady, you've hardly touched your food."

I am neglective, staring at the simple painting of a forest in our dining room.

"Hecate!" My father's voice echoes.

I blink a dozen times and look to him. "Sorry Pa, you were saying?"

"Hecate, Lady Grace was speaking to you."

I turn my head to apologise to her, when she speaks up. "Eat your greens Hecate, let go of this afternoon's excitement, crazy is as crazy does."

The dinner continues, my slip up forgotten. Kat and her mother were talking about the latest fashions in the capital. Katrina was gushing about how charming the young prince was becoming. Mean-while, father and Lord Smithe spoke in hushed words to my left, I found my attention more drawn to that. They kept leaning closer to each other, eyebrows jumping up and down, with their quiet words.

Alastor finally joins us not to late into supper, sitting to father's right, filling the empty seat between us. I try to listen into their conversation, seemed more appealing than fashion, and who the princess would have on her arm during social season.

Alastor places the dinner napkin on his lap, "The second one now, and that's not counting the ones that have come off ships, sputtering madness." I wince at Alastor's grip on the napkin, strangling it.

Father was rubbing his groomed chin at the head of the table, completely ignoring the roast beef on his plate. Lord Smithe grumbles, across from Alastor, "If we do not somehow stop these random outbursts, order will collapse! "

"Gentleman." We all turn to Lady Grace now, sitting poised on the other side of Katrina. "Talks of work are meant for studies and offices. Not for dining room chatter." She raises her chin and confidently stares them down.

The men apologise and talk about the weather. I pick up a piece of tomato on my plate and aggressively pop it in, once they leave this table, there will be no chance of having my curiosity satiated. Dinner finished, dessert came and went quietly, Katrina invited herself for the night. Not that I was complaining, I wanted to see if she had any insight from her social circles. To say I was nosey would be an understatement. Perhaps my love for a suspenseful story would be the cause of this.

CHAPTER TWO

KATRINA

Katrina was washing up in one of the guest rooms on the third floor, at ease in the lavish bathtub filled with rose petals. One pale white leg hung over the side, her head back, daydreaming.

A faint knocking disturbs her moment, it was a servant to assist her, Anna. She was Katrina's favourite, few years older, short rusty coloured hair. Katrina found her boring to look at, but that made her easy to blend in amongst the others. Anna always came and assisted Katrina during her visits, with so much to gossip about. Usually, they prattled on about Alastor.

"Miss should have seen the way he took down the others in his training yesterday. A three on one training match, he was unstoppable, our future duke is indeed a dependable one!" Anna sighed with her eyes closed. Katrina faintly smiled as she listened on to Anna's stories.

Anna excused herself shortly after, as Katrina prepared to exit. She wrapped herself with the pink-cotton robe Anna had laid out, damp blonde hair dripped onto the floor. Her attention was snagged by the painting hanging in the attached dressing room.

The Crosse estate had an expensive collection of paintings, and sculptures in every room. All thanks to the late Duchess, collecting art was her hobby.

This image in particular was a beautifully painted garden, blooming with an assortment of colours. Odd materials were used in this painting, making it appear as though it was coming out of its frame. One lone black bird, sat among the flowers. It reminded Katrina of how she had met Hecate, all those years ago.

It was the week before the summer festival, the Smithe's were heading over to the esteemed Crosse estate. Her mother had to deliver the duke's suit – her father came along as well. They had been friends since boys, telling Katrina, she would get along great with the duke's two children.

Everyone knew of the Crosse's, but most importantly, of the young miss and her mother.

The other little girls talked about her, and the adults, the highlight of gossip. A little beauty, the result of an affair, her gypsy mother was branded a home wrecker. The mistress who came out of nowhere and seduced the faithful Duke.

The illegitimate princess, that was Miss. Crosse's nickname.

When they arrived, Katrina could not believe the luxurious sight, her little heart was convinced a family of royalty lived here. The gardens twice the size of their own, and flowers she had never in her life, seen before. The home itself three times the size of theirs, vines twisting around pillars growing up and over, towards balconies on the other floors. Pink and yellow flowers in bloom upon them. Trees planted strategically around walkways, giving an elegant feeling to the front terrace. A huge fountain with a knight statue at its centre, just where the carriages rounded and dropped off, on nearly white cobble stones. Stepping out of the carriage the air itself was fragrant, each inhale a new scent, depending on which way the wind was blowing.

She spotted Hecate as she spun around looking over the sight. She was outside, dressed in simple attire that could not dull down her shine. Even from where Katrina stood with her parents, Hecate radiated this prestigious air.

She was on her knees, hands deep into soil helping the servants in the gardens. Her shining black hair braided back, decorated with a deep green bow. She wore a matching colour dress, and a brown apron on top of it, Katrina could hear a melodious voice carry from her direction. Chattering away about some little weed, and all the benefits it offered. The next moment took Katrina by surprise, when the old man went to pick it out of the garden.

"Mr. Spencer!" Hecate frowned. Her cheeks puffed up, while she threw her stinking hands on her waist, ruining her dress completely. The old man laughed along nodding his head, apologising to her.

Katrina was anxious. Would she get along with this hot–tempered princess?

A little boy appeared from around the side of the home, and it was like time stopped just for him. The wind stopped gently blowing, if only not to offend and ruin his neatly combed hair. He wore a suede jumpsuit, a white blazer with blue patterns at the collar, and a matching suede topcoat. A wooden sword resting on his little shoulders – a prince straight out of a fairy tale.

His face though, not very princely, it was identical in fierceness to the princess. She knew he was fighting with her, because the next thing she witnessed was them at each other's throats. Even though Hecate was slightly shorter than the boy, she put up a mighty fight. Grappling him, trying to bring him to the ground.

The old man jumped up, swooping them both up into each arm. It halted their sibling throw down, and they both erupted into infectious laughter. It was a strange place, filled with strange people, but the strangest thing was the feeling of wanting, growing in Katrina's little heart.

Her father mentioned there were two children of the house, she assumed he was the other. Judging by their fierce attitudes, and the fighting spirit they both carried themselves with.

Later, they were finally introduced, confirming they were in fact, the Crosse children.

They were forced to sit with snacks together, while the adults went to settle the accounts. The young master never spared Katrina a glance, he sat there elegantly drinking his milk, Hecate too. It was awkward for her, and nerve racking sitting between them. They were all about the same height, but between the two of them... Not even the large room felt big enough, Katrina felt like she was shrinking into her seat, between these two preying cats.

A panther and a lion.

Alastor got up without a word and left the girls. Giving his sister the side eye, head held high, leaving.

Hecate stuck her tongue out to his back, before addressing Katrina. "Want to go outside and play tag?" She extended a hand grinning. Her teeth were extremely white in contrast to her dark hair, her green eyes sparkled like jewels in the sun.

Katrina cringed thinking back... Whatever possessed her to speak next, would forever haunt her.

"I wish I was as pretty as you," she felt her face pale as the words left her tiny mouth.

Laughter froze her, Hecate's head was tilted back, hands on her belly. Not like the other little girls Katrina often spent time with, Hecate's laugh was free, not trained or toned down.

"Papa says beauty is only skin deep. It's what is inside here, we should all work on." Hecate pointed a long finger to Katrina's chest. Young Katrina titled her head in wonder as she continued, "You're adorable by the way, so I don't think you have anything to worry about!" Hecate grabbed Katrina's hands without apologies, *yanking her up. She did not use any etiquette, as young ladies their age, should have.*

That afternoon was the happiest day she had experienced in a while.

Hecate was civilized yet wild, young yet able. She never made comments for the way Katrina spoke, never told her what she could and could not do. She was able to be herself completely without guard, without judgment. Hecate was a nurturer, she encouraged Katrina to be braver and dared her to have fun, the rules be damned.

That was how their friendship started. Hecate became the big sister, Katrina wished she had...

Katrina was making her way down the hall towards Hecate's room, reminiscing of how much they had grown up. As she reached for the doorknob, Alastor came charging out, and Katrina fell flat on her bottom. Alastor never stopped, to her disappointment. He stepped over her with his thick long legs and a frown, disappearing down the hallway with great strides. All she could do was stare dumbfounded at his vanishing figure.

Pattering feet came to her quickly. "By the realms Kat, are you okay?!" Hecate took a deep intake of air and Katrina braised herself for what was to happen next. "YOU REALLY ARE A DICK, ALASTOR CROSSE! MAYBE YOUUU– SHOULD BE THE ONE TAKING LESSONS!!" Projecting down the empty corridor. Her friend finally helped her up, fussing over her like a mother hen.

Katrina's nose hurt entering her friend's room, Hecate was burning something, once again. She looked around, pinching her nose. A plate, with a smoking bundle of plants, laid upon Hecate's vanity. *Urg, she is burning that stuff again?!* It was an overwhelmingly strong scent, one that Katrina knew would induce a headache. She opened Hecate's window, fanning her hands out, trying to push the scent out. It completely overpowered the smell of the fresh flowers that were displayed on the bed sides, and the sitting table in the corner.

"Hey Tee... I was thinking, maybe tomorrow we could go into town..." Katrina was fiddling with the rope to her robe, facing the window still. "I heard your brother will be taking part in the tournament coming up. I wanted to get a few things for good luck..." Katrina looked back to Hecate with her head slightly down. Trying her hardest at puppy dog eyes, one she knew, would sway her best friend to do whatever she wanted. Hecate loved dogs, loved the way they expressed themselves with their personalities.

Hecate grimaced, looking at her with a pained expression. There was a brief silence, only the birds chirping as the sun said it is goodbye to the day. She was contemplating something, before holding her index finger up. "On one, condition."

"Yes, yes, of course what is it!?" Katrina jumped on her, grabbing that finger before Hecate could change her mind.

Hecate tilts her head back, waist long hair cascading off her shoulder, exposing a slender white neck. "Your friends with the captain's son, right?"

Katrina was momentarily lost, trying to figure out what he had to do with her request... "OH! My goodness, are you interested in Jack!?!"

Her face contorts into disgust at Katrina's words, "Eww no. I'm asking if maybe you could get some information for me?"

"Why don't you ask him, I hear Jack fancies you." Giving her finger a tad squeeze, hoping she could persuade her friend. Katrina was scheming to get Hecate back out in the social circles anyway, she missed her friend's companionship while out in public. It just was not the same anymore, without her.

"That's precisely why I cannot." Hecate pulled her hand from Katrina's, gently massaging it, "He will expect something in return. Whenever you ask, he does not do that!" Her eyes flashed with amusement. "Don't you feel like something bigger is happening around us? Something straight out of a book!"

Katrina only caught half of what Hecate was jabbering about, momentarily forgetting the difference between them. Men of their age had always seen Hecate as a woman. Drooling over her unique features, and voluptuous figure the older they got. She had always been the talk of circles, men and women alike, good and bad. Katrina grabbed her own breasts, giving them a good squeeze, her attention drawing down.

Hecate's eyes widened, laughing at her strange action. "What are you doing?"

"Just wondering, if I should start stuffing these?" Katrina mumbled.

Her mouth closes into a tight line, as Hecate pulled her best friend into a tight embrace. "Kat, don't start changing yourself for anybody, you're perfect just the way you are, okay?"

Katrina nods her head, clenching her fists at her side, until her knuckles were ghostly-white. That was not what she wanted to hear.

CHAPTER THREE

HECATE

We were tucking ourselves under covers with our separate books, abandoning the thought of questioning Kat for any information. She was easily irritated as of late, my brother's attitude towards her probably the cause. For as long as I can remember, Katrina yearned for Alastor. My brother, however, has never reciprocated those same feelings.

Their relationship soured even further, two years ago, at the time of Kat's coming of age. Teasing Alastor by using her name, really begun around then too, he was never one to easily rattle... But something changed with them, and I took full advantage of it, when I needed the upper hand against him.

I glanced over and noticed Katrina had another romance novel, she only ever read gushy stories. "He loves me not?"

She smiled sadly to me, "I can really relate to the female lead, she loves this guy who does not love her back.... It's just comforting..." She brought the red novel to her chest, hugging it tightly.

I shake my head, opening my book to where I left the marker on it, last week. Deciding on my better judgement, and not commenting any further. *Why does she waste her time obsessing over this?*

Unless the guy was a fictional heart throb in a fictional story, written by a woman, then I did not want any part in it.

Kat leans over, "Tales of Old, oh what's that about?" She blinks a few times. I could practically hear her thoughts churning.

"It's tales of royalty, monsters and mythical lands that once occupied pixies!" Wiggling my eyebrows at her.

She looks at me briefly, uninterested, "Is there any romance in it?"

"Well, there's a tale about a princess who kisses a frog, and he turns into a prince." I flipped back a couple pages to find it.

Her eyes widened the size of saucers, "I do not care how handsome a prince might be, I would not kiss a frog. That is so unhygienic, eww, think of the slime and warts!" She ducks under the cover, head completely covered.

"I think your mixing up frogs with toads," I point out.

She grumbles, surfacing briefly, "It does not matter! The point being it is gross!"

That was the end of that, we had vastly different tastes in books.

I had been reading for some time after Kat fell asleep, the candle on the side completely gone out. My eyelids were heavy trying to finish the chapter, I closed them briefly for a reprise...

When I opened my eyes, I was not looking into the book on my lap. I was greeted by white bark, hands pressed against a tree. The area around my vision, hazed with black mist, creating a tunnel effect ahead.

Dreaming, I shudder, my dreams lately consisted of this.

I pushed off the tree, trying to take in my surroundings. I could barely make out the flourished tree branches above, shiny gold leaves rustling with the chilly breeze. It is hazy and too quiet. My previous dreams were chaotic and gore sounding, but one thing similar, the black mist that shrouded my sight.

I am standing in a yard, the ground beneath me of soft mossy grass, broken up by stone pads leading away. The cracked stones had weeds shooting up from them. It is hard to make out the building made of stone behind me, as it seems to go on forever, standing tall and wide. I deduce I am clearly outside, as I look up to the sky of different shades of pink and orange.

A feminine voice of silk, whispers around me, while I was taking everything in. A language I was unfamiliar with, crept into my soul. "Dal haras ellath." The hairs raised on the back of my neck, as goose bumps spread all over my body. Whatever the voice was saying, it was reaching deep parts of me, that I could not even explain. "Si haras ellath." My feet began to move on their own, spinning me around, hands reaching back for the tree.

I am only able to shout out, inside my head. No–no–no, *stop!* My mouth flops open and closed, like a fish out of water. I was a marionette, to whoever was pulling the invisible strings.

Black mist descends, completely blinding me. Releasing me from the hold, that yanked me to do their bidding. I tried fanning my arms around me, the mist thick as sand now, levitating in air. I struggled to breathe, coughing as I inhale mouthfuls of it.

Panic sets in, *what happens if I suffocate!?* There is a flash of light that dissipates the darkness, before I can even finish that intrusive thought.

Now, I was standing in an unfamiliar stone hall, feeling motion sickness from the quick shifts. I look up to lofty ceilings, inhaling deeply – pausing on a gem-stoned chandelier decorated with candles. Pillars were reaching high around the great room, one wall completely covered in stained glass windows. White candles adorned the pillars around. Wax dripping down, painting the stones below.

Drip – Drip – Drip

I slowly pivoted on my heels, observing.

Jumping back, I fell hard, scrambling even further. There were huge dark-grey creatures everywhere – staring! My back suddenly hits a solid wall, my heart in my throat.

They were frozen in place, but their glinting eyes followed me, like a creepy painting.

Pointed ears sat upon their heads, those heads proportionally smaller than their ginormous hunched bodies. What was even more alarming, was their huge paws with overgrown nails. Similar, in size to the long yellow canines, hanging down from their top jaws.

They are not breathing, the only noise from the dripping candles, and my nearly hyperventilating breaths. Shaking like a leaf as I try pinching myself, I was screaming internally to wake up.

Swirls of the mist begin to grow, just before my feet, spiralling up. A lump form turns into a humanoid shape, darkness reaching toward my face. A distinct-hoarse voice coos, "Don't cry, madam." As a hooded man appears before me, leaning over. The same mist – thick as sand – surrounds him, covering him like a cloak of darkness.

I am challenged by silver feline eyes, pupils dilating. I see my own pale face, reflecting in them. Fear grips hold of my soul, whether the darkness swallowed me, or the creature at my feet did. Throwing my hands up in defence, I shout, "Go Away!" A quaint sensation spreads from my palms to the tips of my fingers, a pulse of force ripples through the air. My voice reverberating off the walls, the chandelier swings violently from the impact of my words. My lungs burn, as though I had been holding my breath for ages.

The hooded man leans back, silver smouldering within the darkness. The bottom half of his face just visible, his lips move. "Dearie me, what a clever little thing," growling at me. The corner of his lip rises, revealing an unusually long fang. His left arm raises too, displaying a large white hand, veins bulging.

Snap – He snaps his fingers and I lurch awake.

Greeted by the purple draped canopy of my bed, I swallow back a violent scream building. I cover my mouth with my hands, palms warm and covered in sweat, as scepticism creeps in. That dream unlike any other I ever had before, far too vivid. I wipe the beads of sweat that formed on my brow and turn over, face to face with a sound asleep Kat.

I was not alone.

I hold my breath as I reached, pulling the cover up more to her neck. I carefully turned and swung my shaky legs off the bed. Leaning over, I fist my hair into my hands, trying to control the shakes. A breeze licks my tear-stained cheeks, and I shiver in response. My window was wide open still, the skies were clear tonight, the new moon on display. I wobble my way to the window when silver eyes flashed before me. The hooded man's voice rattles my bones, causing me to stumble back.

What a clever little thing.

I stare at my feet, wiggling my toes, deluding all thoughts. I was not ready to unpack tonight's dream, looking back to the book on the bed, I make a clear decision. I would take a break from the stories and take up father's advice. I needed a change, mentally.

The breeze picks up once more like an un-seen touch, turning my chin back towards the sky. I regard something further out in the estate below, thinking it to be a fox or rabbit. The shadow moves again under the shield of night. I squint, only to see a dark figure snooping round the archery grounds, instead.

My worries leap out the window, as I am rushing out on shaky legs. Quietly as I can, not to wake our sleeping guest. I close the door softly behind me, and sprint down the hall, racing down the stairs. No thoughts about my slippers. Our home is quiet and dark, no doubt most asleep at this hour. I grab an umbrella from the rack, as I scamper through the back door.

I'm gasping for air once again, the fastest and most I had ever run before. Inwardly cursing myself, for how unfit I had become. Holding the umbrella, mimicking a stance I had seen the soldiers do. My eyes searching for anything out of place, outside. Fuming that someone would dare sneak around our home at this hour.

"What the actual fuck, Hecate!" I flail to my left. Gone is the umbrella, as it flies towards the voice. Al's standing there, averting his eyes. All while removing his coat, not even aware of my pathetic attempt to hit him. "Put this on will you, you're in nothing but under garments!"

I swipe the coat from him, "Sorry, w-w-wait, hold on!" – fumbling over my words, I remember why I'm out here in the first place – "I saw someone creeping around the yards from my window!"

Alastor looks at me gravely, brown eyes leering out to the terrain. "Go back inside. I'll deal with this." Unsheathing his sword, he steps sideways.

"I'll come with you!" I quickly throw on the oversized coat, rushing after him.

"Don't make me laugh" – he continues forward, not sparing me a moment - "Go inside now, it's dangerous."

"I know where they were, I'll show- "

"Hecate!" He spun around quickly, I wobbled to a stop, "For once in your life, bloody listen to me. GO. BACK. INSIDE!!" He bellows, some emotion flashes in his eyes, but vanishes before I could place it.

The bushes far out, abruptly shake. My eyes are drawn to the same figure I had seen from my window, behind him. Scurrying further away. "THERE, THERE!"

Alastor takes off, sword in hand, after the assailant. I debate on following still, when some of the night workers start appearing from all over the place. Alerted from our shouting, likely.

He'll be fine, right?

Father's office window is thrown open with a rattle of glass, head leaning out. "Young Lady, what on earth are you doing outside, and dressed like that, at this hour!?"

Our grounds keepers whistle sounds off in the distance, alerting the guards of an intruder. I ignore father, standing on my tiptoes, looking back in the direction my brother ran off. My brief look away had them lost, I consider going out further, to investigate.

"Get inside this instant, young lady!" My father's shouting now, too.

People start approaching me and I am shoving hands away trying to grab me, my eyes scanning for the whereabouts of my brother, or the hooded figure. Faint glowing lights begin illuminating the grounds, but I still could not see where they ran off to. Strong hands grip my sides, startling me. "Unhand me!" I squeal. I am lifted and thrown over someone's solid shoulder.

"Apologies my lady, orders." The guard, sternly states.

I'm put down moments later, father rushing over, fully dressed. "Escort her to her room, I want the estate locked down, two guards at her door!" He orders, disappearing out the door we just came in from.

I leisurely walked back to my room, two men walking behind me. Upon entering, a very sleepy Kat is rubbing her eyes, "What's with the noise?"

I was hesitating by the open doors, when one of the guards gently pushes me in, closing it. I am quick to steady my fumbling feet. "Oi, how dare you!?" I'm fuming, hitting the door with closed fists, "What is your name?"

A mature voice replies to me, "Trevore, my Lady."

"Well Trev-ore" - drawling out his name, "prepare yourself for a scolding tomorrow. You do not push people around, especially not the lady of this house!" I listen intently, hoping he would retort.

"Tee, what's going on?" I turn to Kat, who is nervously getting out of bed.

"We have a trespasser"

She gasps, "Are we safe?"

I point my thumb behind me towards the door, "With dumb and dumber there, we should be." The adrenaline I was feeling moments ago, wanes, rationality sets in. I stumble forward to my bed. *What exactly was I thinking...?* Face palming myself, physically.

"Tee, is that Alastor's?"

I do not look at her, feeling a wave of embarrassment wash over me. I pick at the sleeves of the coat for some invisible lint. "Um yea, I kind of thought I could run off in nothing and catch the intruder." It sounded far worse now, that I had said it out loud. Shrugging off his coat, I leave it on the bed as I head towards the window. The previously quiet yard is brightened by many lit torches, guards marching every inch of it.

By the gods, my sense of adventure could have gotten me into some serious trouble.

My father is in the distance, hands closed behind his back, tapping his foot. I recognise who he is speaking with, the Grounds Keeper. Someone is in trouble for a crack in security, and I do not envy whoever is on the receiving end. A shiver ripples through me with that thought, I am next on father's list of punishments... For my little stunt.

CHAPTER FOUR

KATRINA

Katrina snatched the coat, eyes gleaming similar to a starved animal, with Hecate's back turned. A strong smell of sandalwood filled her senses, swinging the coat around herself, she envisioned Alastor's strong arms.

I will approach him tomorrow and return the coat for Tee! Her toes curled with excitement. She had a valid reason to approach him, envisioning the possible outcomes of their encounter.

Hecate mumbled something under her breath, swinging her leg slightly, sitting on the edge of the window. She was curiously watching whatever show was happening below.

Katrina pondered if she should approach Hecate about the incident that occurred earlier... When she was awoken to Hecate talking in her sleep, whispering weird words. "Haras ellath," over and over. Hecate's face looked to be in pain, she guessed her friend was having a nightmare.

We have a trespasser. She decides not to mention it, curiosity brewing someplace else, "Tee?"

"Go back to sleep, everything is all right. I'm sorry I woke you." Hecate's voice was low, not even paying attention to Katrina.

"What made you think you could run out in nothing but your underwear"– Katrina points out– "to catch whoever was out there, might I ask?"

Hecate turns to her frowning, she goes to open her mouth, but then closes it. Shrugging as she turns her attention back out the window.

Katrina scoots, fixing her posture like her mother does. "Tee, we are ladies, we leave the heroic stuff to the men. That is what they train for… What if the trespasser was armed? What if this, was some ploy to kidnap the esteemed daughter of the duke? You… You could have gotten hurt!" She paused, careful with what to say next. "I would have been really sad if something happened to you. I worry about you sometimes –"

"Kat, do you ever feel like, there's more to this life than pretty dresses and boys?" Hecate asks melancholically.

Katrina's face drops into a frown. *And what's wrong with that?*

"Do you ever imagine more? Breaking the mould that society bounds us too?" Her ethereal eyes glow under the moonlight. "I feel… out of place, you know?"

Katrina was stunned, Hecate who had always been seen strong, faltering. She did not know what to say or do to make her feel better, so she sat there in silence. Not knowing how to handle the situation. Hecate was the emotional stabilizer. She was the one who knew what to do or say, in these situations. Hecate usually had the answers she needed, not the other way around.

Neither of them had spoken for some time, an uncomfortable silence fell between them.

Katrina began chewing on her thumb nail. *I don't get it, she has it all. Looks, money… What was she lacking that made her feel out of place?* She stared at Hecate, as if she was an unsolvable puzzle. Looking her over, to see if she was missing something, physically.

Hecate's faraway look struck an idea in her. "Hey, were going shopping tomorrow! The fresh air will do us some good." She grabbed the book off the bed, shaking it. "You really need to get out more, reading less of these fictional fantasies. Experience more of the reality we live in… Oh, I know! How about we go check out the new café on high street?"

Hecate gives Katrina a look of resignation as she slugs her way back to bed. "Yea sure, whatever…" She lifts the duvet before plopping herself under the covers, back turned to Katrina.

"It'll be fun." Reaching over, Katrina squeezes Hecate's shoulder. Shopping and outings always cheered Katrina up, "Get some sleep Tee, we have lots to do tomorrow." She retightened the coat around herself, orchestrating how they will spend their time and money.

Tomorrow we'll deliver the coat to Alastor, cheer Tee up and everything will be right as rain, again! Katrina could feel herself fall back into a blissful slumber with a smile on her face.

…

A stream of bright light burns Katrina's eyes, waking her up. She rubs her eyes still heavy with sleep, readjusting to the brightness. She says through a yawn, "Morning Tee." Stretching her limbs out.

Hecate does not answer, and she remembers that her friend is an early worm, already getting dressed. She takes the moment to herself to retighten the coat around her, smelling the sleeves. Alastor's musky scent still on them.

Just then, Hecate walks in. She's dressed in a deep violet dress, complimented with lilac frills on the shoulder, continuing across her full breasts. The dress train drags slightly at the back, lilac peeking from under the front slit, opening and closing with every step. Highlighting, long legs from knee to slim ankle. Deep-tanned boots tied up just under her knees, curving out and in at crucial points. Her earlobes glinted from the sun pouring in, decorated with emeralds the size of a grape, bringing attention back up from her mature attire. Her hair as usual, down, and free from anything that may restrain it. She stops with a click of her heels. "That's boarder line creepy, you know?" giggling at her friend.

Katrina realises what she is still doing, "That's so pretty!" Scrambling out of bed.

"Thank you, I had the maids prepare a few dresses for you in the powder room. I will help you dress. It has gone noon." – she unfolds a lilac fan in her hand, with black foreign writing– "What is it you say about punctuality?" Hecate bursts out laughing this time.

Katrina hurries to the attached room, complaining, "Why didn't you wake me!"

...

Hecate was braiding Katrina's hair into a crown around her head, and they agreed on a duck blue – ankle high – dress. Her closet always had such fine clothing, most of them hand made by Katrina's mother. She noticed some other bits and pieces, foreign, envy sets in as she thinks about how the duke dotes on her. Katrina looks at her through the mirror in front of them, Hecate was never one to care for the finer things.

She is ever so gentle with Katrina's hair, as if pulling too hard might hurt her. Placing clipped flowers in an arrangement here and there on the braided parts, leaving curled strands, free by her ears. Katrina admired her skills though, she was able to do her hair in trend setting ways, which is why she allowed Hecate. "Did the servants teach you, how to do hair?"

Hecate's reflection gives her funny eyes, "No, I have always done my hair myself. Other than father, no one touches my hair."

It never once occurred to her, thinking back to all their nights together. Hecate was always awake before her, and whenever the rare chance she got up with her, the servants usually came in and left quietly, even in her home. Hecate did not have a lady in waiting with her, like most women of her position. She really was independent, just seemed like unnecessary challenging work, to Katrina.

"There, all done." Taking a step back from Katrina, Hecate gestures her hands to another mirror.

Katrina bolts up, looking at herself in the body mirror, comparing their outfits. Hecate always looked more mature than her age, and her attire usually aided that. Her dark over all style – to her very bright one. She points out to Hecate, sniggering, "We're night and day."

After a couple final additions of makeup, they finally made their way down the stairs. Katrina practically skipping down, excited. They step off one of the landings, just as Alastor was going up. Dark circles under his eyes, head down.

Katrina's heart flutters, clutching her dress. "Good afternoon, Ally!" He pays her no mind, as expected. "I have your coat! I'll have it pressed and cleaned for you. What day works best to delivery it?!" Her cheeks flush, words flying out of her mouth nervously.

It's only then he looks up, glaring at Hecate. "Why does she have my coat?"

Neither of them gets a word out, he passes by furiously, deliberately on Hecate's side. "Burn it when your done with it, Hecate. I do not want it back after that thing has touched it!" He barks behind them.

Katrina could feel Hecate about to explode next to her, and as if right on cue, her eyes water. "Why are you always so mean?"

Hecate immediately starts rubbing her back, trying to drag her away.

Boots screech the floors. "Why... WHY!?"

"What is your problem?!" Hecate's snapping now too.

Katrina anxiously waits, her eyes meeting his finally. However, to her dismay, utter contempt looks back to her, hissing venom. "You repulse me."

CHAPTER FIVE

HECATE

I barely slept, after Kat fell back asleep, I just stared at my ceiling till my eyes shut. Thinking of our conversation, she made a valid point. Everyone lately was making valid points. I would take father's advice, my decision final, so when I got out of bed, I got straight to work.

I was brushing my hair when the maids entered, asking them to arrange a couple of choices for Kat to choose from when she finally woke. Knowing she would want options. Having a room full of clothes and nowhere to wear them anyway, at least they'd have a use with her.

Once I was presentable, I straightened up and left my room to speak with father. "Good morning, my Lady." The guards addressed me in unison.

"Morning." The same two from last night, I note. "Do you guys ever get exhausted?"

"We're trained for this, my Lady." Trevore speaks up, I knew that voice, and did not forget the warning I gave him last night.

"Hecate is fine, you can drop the formalities."

Trevore's lips parted but it was the other one - whose name I never got – replying. "Apologies my Lady, it's proper decorum to address the young madam, respectively." That stern voice, the one who carried me over his shoulder, last night. I studied him for a moment, an older guard, guessing he was in his mid–thirties. I had seen him a lot around Alastor, brought in from outside with the increase of disturbances, I presume. He fit the bill – this was someone Alastor preferred to keep around. His eyes focused, alert, and ready.

I regard Trevore next, who shuffles his feet, straightening his spine, with my attention.

Trevore was taller than me, but not as towering as my brother, nor as beefy. Noting the well–kept uniform, Alastor was strict on appearance when representing our family. Our family insignia – the cross wrapped in thorny vines – on a button at the collar. Undeniable proof of service. I trail up to the stubble on his jaw, not a lot of facial hair but not exactly clean shaved, he had a small white scar to his right. His skin was also spotted with freckles, few here and there, scattered on the bridge of his nose reaching under his hazel–eyes. Random strands of copper hair were touching his brows, stubborn hairs that would not stay pushed back, my hand flinches. I did not know if I wanted to push the hair back or rip his hair out.

I catch a growing grin on his face. Quickly looking back to guard number two, embarrassed for blatantly staring. "What was your name again, I do apologise for my rudeness. Long night as you know." He nods his head and introduces himself as Gregory. There wasn't anything striking about him, blue–green eyes that stayed focused ahead. His short sandy blonde hair, un–styled, his uniform immaculate. I respected the way he carried himself though. Nodding my head in acknowledgment. "I'll be in your care then, Gregory." I start to set off, but it wasn't Gregory who followed. Copper hair reflected off doorknobs and windows from behind me. I turned the open spaced corridor, aiming for the stairs, rolling my eyes.

I make my way to father's office on the second floor. I was going to have a chat with him about a few things, Trevore being one of them.

The second floor was just as nice as the third, decorated with blues, silver, black and the occasional white. This floor was considered the men's floor, it screamed sophisticated masculinity. There were two more rooms on the second, than the third, a total of nine closed and probably locked doors. Each painted black with the silver outlines and silver doorknobs. My brother and father's rooms located across each other at the furthest end, looking over the front of the estate.

The first rooms across from each other, as you step off the stairs, were their offices. I slow when I see the head butler – Spencer– patiently waiting at my father's office doors. "Is father available?"

He smiles gently at me, announcing my arrival before opening the door. Trevore stations himself outside as I enter.

Father's hands were clasped together under his chin, elbows propping them up. "Oh joys, I was just about to summon you, sit." I swallow, he must have been up all night too, there was this dreadful look on his face. He looked to be chewing on what he was to say. I gasped after realising I just walked myself willingly, into the gallows. I should have waited a few days until he calmed down.

"Don't doddle Hecate, sit down."

...

I returned to my room defeated and helped Katrina get ready. As we were coming down the stairs, Alastor lost his lid on her. I could see he was not himself, exhausted, I tried to get Katrina away, and failed.

Kat's eyes are casted down the entire time, quiet as a mouse after that. All my teasing really got to Alastor– I had never seen him so on edge. I couldn't help but feel at fault. No, I knew I was the culprit to blame for it.

We exit the front doors, a dark blue carriage is stationed, accented with golds and black. Our family's insignia in gold on the doors. The colour design like the second floor of our home. Four black horses attached at the front – ready for our trip.

The skies turned cloudy this afternoon, matching the mood we were all feeling. The scent of rain on the wind, I prayed it didn't start, not while we were out anyway. I preferred rainy days indoors, where I did not have to be wet. My steps slowed, spotting Trevore waiting for us, opening the carriage door. I squint at him, Trevore is standing there giving me a lopsided smile. A look of triumph on his smug profile.

We are going to be such good friends.

That's what his stupid face was saying to me. I knew he heard father's raised voice, disciplining me with a lengthy lecture. He chewed me a new one, for last night, punishing me with Trevore after hearing my protests. I had a sneaky suspicion that Alastor may have suggested him, if only to get back at me. The fact Trevore was up all–night guarding us too, not even evident. That irritated me even more for some reason. I just did not like this one, whatsoever. I stood there squinting, he stood smiling. Neither of us standing down, Trevore was my karma.

Gregory comes up, giving Trevore an elbow jab, whose face flinches from it. I turn and give Gregory a genuine smile, before taking his hand, helping me enter the carriage. I could feel Trevore's eyes following me, but I kept my chin held high entering the carriage with Gregory's help.

"Hey, you alright?" Kat startles at my words, quickly relaxing her face, she smiles bleakly. She turns her head back toward the carriage window, obviously avoiding the conversation. I decided to let her be, I did not want to force a conversation she was still processing.

I too had a few things to rationalize. Reviewing the new development in my dream.

The woman's voice, the man, there was so much to organize. Silver eyes blaze in my mind, my finger's flinched for my necklace. His voice was contradicting to his hooded, villain-like appearance. Just as soothing as the feminine voice I had heard previously to his arrival... The beasts, that was also new... I vaguely recall seeing something similar in a book...

Where had I seen them before? I just couldn't remember which book it was now.

...

The carriage gradually comes to a stop, Kat, and I both begin to gather ourselves to un-board. Gregory and Trevore stationed few paces back, as per father's orders. Giving us space, but also in reaching distance in case they needed to intervene.

Katrina was twiddling her thumbs, slowly walking next to me. She's still quiet, which is unlike her, I decide to break the ice. "Hey... I've been meaning to say this for some time now..."

She huffs, as if she expected this. "If you're going to tell me to give up on your brother, Tee- don't."

"Kat, I just think you should move on from him. You know my brother can be a bit of an -"

She turns her nastiest glare to me, "Hecate, I know you do not think highly of him, but I love him. I will not give up, he's focusing on himself right now, and that's okay, we are still young!"

I open my mouth to explain, but Kat storms off. "Katrina!" I knew I had touched a sore subject for her, and an angry Kat meant an afternoon of misery for everyone.

I spend the afternoon waiting on Katrina, hand and foot. Positively sure it would brighten up her spirit, she loved to be spoiled. She took full advantage of it, dragging me around to all the stalls, even ones she seemed less then interested in. I am silently celebrating when we finally stop at the new café she mentioned, my feet were ready to fall off. These boots were too high for lengthy period walks, regretting many choices made today.

It was a nice café from the outside, looked more of a boutique with all the vibrant colours. To attract attention by those shopping, presumably. I could faintly smell chocolate and vanilla, as the doors swung open with people coming and going.

Hmm, I do like chocolate.

As we enter, the loudest cackles reach my ears. My celebration – ruined – pinpointing who the cackles belonged too. A sickly-sweet tone, beckons us, "By the gods... Is the sun going to rise over Ortulunae next? Our lovely Katrina, and our own mysterious princess!" Beatrise and her little pose began waving for us to join them.

Do it for Kat... I steel myself, following a cheery Katrina, to the table.

Beatrise Langly, Penelope Thorpe, and Emily Karenn. The wicked witches of our society, very much like their monster–mothers. The gossip queens of Newmont. Dressed in the puffiest, frilliest, and brightest dresses – walking cupcakes.

I knew this was going to turn into a battle of words, and even though I stopped attending socials, my daily squabbles with Alastor kept my game strong. I just prayed this would be over with quickly.

"Ladies!" Kat squeals sitting in one of the empty seats next to Beatrise.

I was stunned by how fake she sounded, but I schooled my facial features swiftly, not giving anyone - anything on me. High society was just as dangerous as sword play, where words were used as weapons, and daggers hid behind smiles. I was already drained sitting next to Emily, the biggest snob of them all, luckily for me, she was the silent judger. At least I did not have to listen to her chat my ear off.

"What brings our local princess out of her castle and into our humble abode?" Beatrise asks, smirking.

She's mocking me, and I bite. "Charity visit." Grinning back, I look around pretending to admire the scenery.

Penelope and Emily both choke on their tea, Kat's hiding her smile behind her cup.

Hecate 1 – Bitch-rise 0

Beatrise's lingering smirk transforms into a full-blown smile. "You don't say?!" – her tone rising higher in pitch- "Here I thought you were too busy for us..." She brings her gloved hands up, clutching her chest, in an exasperated gesture. "It turns out she is working ever so hard! You really are something else, Hecate."

"Lady." My façade drops, "Correct me if I am wrong... Ladies of Society, Lesson 23. Unless you were of higher ranking than me, it is Lady Crosse. Furthermore, since my family are nobility, only kin and intimate friends should – could, address me informally. What was your family ranking again, I ignorantly admit, I cannot quite remember?" I feel the power of my words as the café falls silent. The giggles and murmurs cease completely. I hated playing the status card, but I hated nothing more than being looked down on for not 'fitting in the mould.'

Alastor always made sure to remind me. When people tried to bully me with words, squash them with only weapon I had in my arsenal. My family's power.

Penelope speaks up first, fanning herself. "Lady Crosse, there is no need to be mean or aggressive. Bea was just teasing you. You still do not know a joke between friends, it seems."

A pulsating sensation builds in my temples, knowing I had reached my limits. Today was exhausting but not as exhausting as these three. I looked to Kat, who is tight lipped, eyes looking down at the teacup in her hands. I find myself further annoyed that my 'actual friend' was not saying anything in my defence, pretending as if she was not sat here, present to the conversation.

I turn to Penelope, countering. "I am not mean, nor am I aggressive. I am assertive and honest, and I act accordingly to those around me. Oh, and personally, I love a good joke. I sat down with you all... no?" I didn't bother waiting for Kat, excusing myself. I gathered my skirting, not wanting to fall on my face, and act a fool after the airs I just put on.

This was why I preferred to stay home.

Once outside, I took a deep breath, letting the air fill up my lungs till they could not hold anymore. The smell of cow faecal from the fields, was an improvement from drowning in ladies who practically bathed in perfume. My head didn't feel so bad.

"Tee! Tee– wait up!"

I spun back, "What the hell was that?!"

"They were just playing..."

I damn near explode at Katrina, and like the earth felt my wrath, it begins to shake violently, windows around us rattling. Loud booms, like canon fire, crashing to the ground or into things, dust rising in the distance. Screams of the town's folk close to the square following the outburst, we pause. People stopping and looking in the direction of the library's tower to the east. The guards assigned to us are in position, with a flash of silver.

Trevore's sword is drawn, his eyes alert assessing the situation. "For your safety my Lady, we're leaving." His free hand light as a feather, tucking me behind him, blocking my sight ahead. They start herding us back to the carriage when chaos erupts, all over.

Roars ensue in all directions, my eyes instinctively shut tight. Roars I thought only haunted my reading induced nightmares. My body trembles, from head to toe.

This is not happening...

My blood runs cold when a voice responds to my very own, in my mind. *"Oh, but it is happening!"* Purring back to me. A strong gush of wind blows, my trembling form sways. The roars begin to go quieter, getting further away, as the wind carries them – or me from it all. I reach forward to grab Trevore for assurance, only snatching air.

Daring a peek, I crack one eye open. The town, the people, everyone is gone.

I stand alone.

The ground shifts slightly under my feet, I notice I am knee deep in calm water. There is a full moon illuminating the surface of it. Mist hovers over the water, stretching and whirling around. The air is heavy with moisture, and a strong stench of must. My reality feels warped, I can no longer separate what was real. Heart pounding, I swallow the constant watering of saliva as my tongue rolls back – fighting the urge to be sick.

Wake up, wake up!

That voice proclaims in the emptiness around. "But you've only just arrived, would be a shame if I didn't entertain my guest?" A hint of amusement coating his words.

Something causes the water to ripple towards me. I spy what resembles a bony spine, dive back under the dark water. Few meters from where I stood.

CHAPTER SIX

Back to yesterday morning

ALASTOR

"Common Lieutenant Colonel, drink up!" The lads erupt with cheers, slamming their glasses together. Foam sloshing and soaking the wooden benches even more. This place was a shit tip. I had more than enough for my fill, brushing off the ales handed to me. My vice persuaded me, into joining him for 'a couple of pints' with some of the soldiers.

A couple my ass. A couple turned to a few, a few into more. Now I sat among drunk idiots, trying to play me into drinking to oblivion. "Unlike some of you – lazy sacks of shit, some of us, have duty charge tomorrow." I stand up quickly, the bar in the squadron's quarters drifting back and forth.

"Sir!" Trevore's smiling, displaying that toothy grin. That very same toothy grin that had ladies gushing and fretting over him for. I was going to recommend him to father as a potential guard for my sister. She hated guys like this. His three arms and three hands point to a window. "You mean today, it's just broke dawn, sir!"

Shit!

I had an hour, to get into bed, sleep off the alcohol and get my never-ending list of shit to do, done. I remembered then, why I do not go out with these fuckers anymore, there wasn't enough time in the day – or night – for this.

I wave them off and excuse myself, staggering out of that stinking place. The wooden door creaks loud when I make my exit, my boots just missing the step directly below, and I latch onto the railing. I stumbled my way back unseen and unheard, or the guards on duty were seriously slacking. I repeat over and over again on my journey, to make note, and check in with those on duty.

I throw the covers off the bed, face planting into my clean linen sheets. That was the fastest yet slowest walk, of my life. Harping on my door has me grumbling, "What..."

The silver handle turns, and Gregory stands, stern faced. "Apologies for disturbing you, sir, the duke commands your presence."

Not bothering to lift my head, I dismiss him. "Got it, you may go." Gregory closes the door as swiftly as he opened it, I make a slow attempt to move. I needed to wash my face, brush my teeth, and at least change my clothing. If I dared to show up before my father, reeking of alcohol, he would have my balls.

...

"You wished to see me, sir?" I stand steady, clean in father's office.

He does not look up from the documents on his desk. Holding papers with one hand, the other stroking his well-kept beard. Something I hadn't seemed to inherit from him, to grow facial hair. At least not very easily, my sad efforts took months, never coming in full or glorious like his.

"You will join us for tea, this morning."

I was far too hungover for this, so early, "Hecate will have a fit if I crash your bonding time."

My father looks at me, tossing the papers to his desk. That same look he gives my sister when he's chewing on words. The man can never say what's truly on his mind. "You'll be there regardless, Alastor." He shakes his head slowly, hands tucking behind his back. Mumbling under his breath, about how we are just as bad as each other.

I follow with dreaded steps, hating where he was heading. The glass conservatory.

Father had it built for my mother, a wedding present, before I was even born. She used to dream of tending it together with future daughters throughout the seasons. Only to let that gypsy bitch have her filthy hands all over it, when my mother was on her death bed.

I throw a hand on my head, completely messing up my hair. I should have had Spencer bring me a tonic before I decided to take today, head on. We turn the corridor near the piano room, leading to the fully glassed building, my nostrils are assaulted with flowery fragrances. My stomach starts summersaulting, I begin debating whether to ditch, and summon Spencer immediately. It had been seven years since I last vomited all over myself. I would not embarrass myself in father's presence.

"Believe it or not. Hecate will take this more seriously if she hears your input on this, as well. You know she's a curious cat at the best of times, so let us satisfy her curiosity before she goes snooping around, where she should not be." I stumble back at my father's words. Wondering if he really knew Hecate. The same Hecate that would threaten to shove my opinions, right up my own ass. Or if I was still drunk and hearing things. "Just you being here Alastor, she'll understand the severity of this." He gracefully sits at the round table, that easily sits six. Immediately going through letters and notes on the wooden tray, set next to his seat.

I sit in the chair to his left, staring at how different this place was. The chairs were unpolished, hand crafted – tree looking. Stumps of trees carved into chairs, after examining them closer. The seats complimented with creamy cushions, matching the unpolished wood table, laid with a creamy tablecloth in the centre of it. A glass bowl of water and a white flower placed on the table, growing up and over.

This place used to scream – wealth, but now... *Hecate maybe?*

It had been three whole years since I last stepped foot in here. I used to feel anger and hostility, and I am dumbfounded at the change. Not only for the scenery but how relaxed it made one feel. Felt as though I was sitting in the forest far away from the hustle and bustle of everyday life.

Poking and probing the plain dish wear, unaware of how much time had gone by. One of the maids excuses herself, whispering something in my father's ear. His face scrunches up, sighing, and he starts to rise, hands down flat on his lap. I'm quick to act as he is about to step away from the table, and I volunteer to go up instead.

I needed to see for myself, anyways.

I knock on her door with three loud thumps, and she does not answer. "Hecate." I did not want to shout too loudly, lest father's bat–like hearing was to assume the worst.

Still, silence.

I turn the gold encrusted knob and enter cautiously, the windows drawn open. Things were scattered round her four posted bed – no doubt knocked over and off during the night. A squirming figure catches my eyes under the sheets, she's thrashing her arms.

Another nightmare – I confirm.

I'm slightly concerned she's still in bed, not that I would ever admit it to her. You'd usually find her wrists deep in the gardens, harvesting her herbs at this hour any other day, or drying them at least. I could draft a book of things to call her, but a late riser was not one of them –unless she was unwell. The last couple of weeks she had been having a lot of later days, and I was clearly aware of father's zone outs during town hall meetings. Father has always reacted uncharacteristically when it involved Hecate's well–being.

Trying again, "Hecate..." I waited for her response. She doesn't, still violently thrashing. "Hecate, wake up you - lazy cow!" The thrashing stops, her hands gripping the sheets she was battling against a moment ago.

Never misses a chance to fight back.

Perspiration glistens off her forehead and shoulders as she slowly sits up. Still not all there, fear adamant in her green bulging eyes. She's paler than she was yesterday, but she's breathing... Standing at the threshold of her room, I grow impatient. I advise her to stop reading those children books, if father seen her in this bad of a state, he'd burn the library down, and somehow it would be my fault.

We begin our usual banter back and forth, and I know full–well she's back to her usual self. I take my cue to leave and re–join father downstairs.

"Is she alright?" He asks quickly, I am not even a step through the glass doors.

Retaking my seat, I voice an idea. "Father, sister is now twenty-one, don't you think it's time she started doing more?" My father raises his brow at me, I should have worded that differently. "Staying cooped up all the time, isn't doing her much good. With how things have been lately around town, learning some self-defence with a teacher, or taking up archery lessons might help with–"

"Let her be, Alastor." He shuts down my proposal immediately, not fully hearing me out.

"Sir, excuse my rudeness..." I place my palms down on the table, "But don't you think you're far too easy on her?" They say the devil comes if spoken about, and exactly at that moment, Hecate enters.

Fan-fucking-tastic.

The conversation goes as predicted, but my temper gets the best of me, during an exchange of words with Hecate. I see the smugness in her eyes when she throws Kat into our head-to-head, so I leave. I make my way to my office and slam the door shut, leaning against the solid material. A growing pressure in the centre of my chest causes my breathing to labour. Concentrating, in through the nose and out of the mouth, stilling the mind of any thoughts. A trick the former commander taught me after my first kill. The panic and guilt of taking a life nearly consumed me.

How pathetic.

I waltz over and pour myself a glass of whiskey, sitting on the edge of my mahogany desk. The spice from it warming, as it slides down my throat, curing my hangover as well. I place the glass down next to the stacked – never ending – paperwork.

...

I greet the captain of the guards on arrival, watching carefully as our family carriage stops near the temple. Watching every single person in the crowd outside, ready to pounce at any unexpected occurrence.

My family enters and I slowly prowl my way in, making sure I am last, eager to linger by the doors. The priest does his sermon. As I'm surveying the crowd, noting fresh faces, dismissing familiar ones. The great hall silences, the only sound coming from the swinging of the gold hanging lamps can be heard, the gold chains making a slight creaking noise with each sway.

Heads turned back, looking at my sister, she shrinks down trying to disappear. I fight the urge to laugh at her, noticing my father further down the pew staring daggers at her as well. Cursing myself for missing the comedic moment.

Service ends and I'm first out the doors, scanning the whereabouts of the eerie-quiet afternoon. Nothing suspicious seemed to be lurking around. I quickly to do a perimeter check around the religious sanctum and the old tombs, everything checks out. I am making my round back to the front, noticing people were gathering further into the shops sector.

A man's voice is heard spouting in the streets, the nearer I got. Few local guards looking my way, I nod at them to carry this out. The sooner we contain and isolate the situation, the better.

I stand by and watch these four armoured men struggle to contain the individual. Not surprised, like the other instances, I note similarities. Sickly, maddened looking, the individuals shouting about a darkness. The only thing I could not figure out, was where they are coming from. No eyewitnesses, as if they appear out of thin air before the commotion begins.

After the incident, they throw the haggard into a cell, waiting for the local police to take over their duties. Interrogating civilians here was out of my job description. I just needed the reports that followed for widespread investigations, things weren't adding up lately. On top of the monster sightings that have been increasing, our spies say we are not the only ones going through it. Villages as well as another town were hit, scavenged by huge dog beasts. Word of mouth is civilians of the south have named the creatures – hellhounds. Appearing on a gush of wind, smelling of decay. Ripping places apart, killing our soldiers. The tolls slowly climbing, missing persons reports too. Compared to when I signed on to aid five years ago, the incidents increasing more frequently. Numbers keep jumping with the sightings of these creatures. It was going to be hard to keep panic from rising too.

King Jonathan was up all our asses for answers and solutions, fearing things were beginning to spiral. One of the commanders from the east, beheaded under the king's temper, he did not like incompetence. He also avoided taking any accountability, throwing blame to anyone with the slightest bit of dirt on their record. Hypocrisy at its finest. What was the point of an autocratic sovereign when those who are born to a role of responsibility could not rise to said standing – morally even.

I am leaning against a post, waiting outside the station for a report. My train of thought is broken, overhearing a conversation between the younger recruits. I glance quickly, seeing the captain's boy swaggering with the group of lads not far off.

"See that pretty little thing earlier?" The young guards gossiping like women, I hear my father's title in one of their mouths. "Yea, she's the duke's girl." I pause, ready to dismiss their words, I was used to the rumours of our family. "Just one night with her I'd have her calling me– "

I launch toward them, seeing red, acting on impulse. Grabbing the weasel by his throat and slamming him into a nearby wall. The dagger from my boot in hand, pointing for his eyes. "Finish that sentence and not only will I cut out your tongue boy, but I am going to carve out your eyes, and send them to your mother. How does that sound?" Practically snarling like a monster, myself.

He is struggling for air, and none of the others budge to make a move. Eyes tearing up, the young guard's hands are scratching my forearm holding him in place. Even a kitten had more strength. I hold him a second more, before releasing, watching as he folds in on himself. I turn to the other lads who were idly standing by, watching their comrade just get man handled. "Want some?" – They hastily shaking their heads at the kind offer. "Then fuck off back to your posts!" They scrambled like bugs, abandoning their 'friend'. This was meant to be the new generation of soldiers, knights even...

I take one last look at the scumbag at my feet, etching his face into memory. He wraps his arms around his-self, asking for no more.

CHAPTER SEVEN

ALASTOR

The horse gallops, deafening any other noises. I'm able to recollect the events, the similarities to them all happening across the south. It's a quiet ride tonight, *a calm before a storm,* I thought. Once home, the butler hesitantly informs me of our guests. I now wish I had stuck around in town, rumbling with hoodlums rather than being in there – with *that* family. I desperately needed food though...

Dinner dragged on and the Smithe family did not seem like they were leaving anytime soon. Myself, and Lord Smithe joined my father in his office, since we were unable to discuss matters earlier.

"But what does this all mean?!" Harold's pinching the bridge of his nose, Lord Smithe was a good friend to my father, but useless regarding politics. He was also really bad with money, from what I knew, his wife oversaw the finances of their estate. That was why he never advanced far like my old man did. He was a viscount, all thanks to his wife, behind the scenes.

"Alastor, the report?" I glance over to my father, he sits in his chair, relaxed into it. Swirling a glass of bourbon in his hand, waiting for me to answer. The sun was setting, casting shadows around him, reminding me of a gladiator, waiting for his match.

"I rode back after the suspect was booked in. With these incidents, there's a rise of petty crimes, the authorities are neck deep in back logs. Hopefully, it's done before the man drops dead and we get no answers..." Father looks less than impressed, with my answer. Laying his head back he releases a deep sigh. I find myself quietly, swallowing.

We discussed necessary steps, father tasking me to find out more about who 'they' were. If we were dealing with a foreign attack or not. He was writing a letter to send to the lords up north, for intel on their side. They only seemed to communicate with father when it came to politics, insulting our king.

The only thing we had to go on at the present was hellhounds, scavenged towns, and these unidentified persons appearing. The casualties, soldiers doing their jobs. What was even more concerning was at least one or two women were missing after the attacks. We were dealing with human trafficking too?

I left father's office, planning to have a word with Hecate about classes. Even if father did not agree, I would rather be safe than sorry. I saw Anna making her way to a guest room, so I slid into Hecate's quick, keeping the door behind me slightly opened. Walking in further, her room had a strong burning scent. My sister is sat at her dressing table, "Uh, can I help you?" Her back to me. Her face reflecting in the mirror ahead, brushing her long–poker straight–hair. Smoke passes by her reflection, giving her an eerie outline.

Is that why she dries herbs? I stand there for more than a few moments, and she gives me a pressing look. "I was telling father earlier that you should take lessons."

She rolls her eyes and places her brush down before turning to me. "I heard as much. Why do you care so much about what I do, you'll be the one inheriting father's duties, not me." Shrugging her pale shoulders, she questions, "Why do I need lessons?"

Her attitude has my jaw clenching. "That's not what I'm suggesting!" I take a deep breath. Hecate fed off energy, if I came off aggressive, she'd match it. "You know if you channelled that energy into something more useful- "

"Oh! I am sorry!" My sister and I both snap our heads, eyeing up the maid who walked in silently. Anna curtsies, head down. "I didn't mean to intrude, but Lady Smithe is finished with her bath."

"Fuck!" I curse out, startling the red-faced maid.

Hecate stands up brushing off her lap, "Thank you Anna, you may leave. Al, we'll finish our conversation tomorrow, unless you want to stick around, and say hello to my guest."

I didn't miss the jab there, squaring my shoulders, I give her a piece of advice. "First lesson for you, just because they hang around you, and laugh with you, doesn't mean they are your friends. People pretend well."

Hecate's hands fly to both sides of her hips, her signature pose when she was ticked. "What the hell are you on about?"

I continue, hoping to get through to her, "At the end of all days... real situations expose the fakest of all people. So, pay attention!" Leaving in a huff, I knock something over on my way out.

...

I returned to the station, hoping they had some news for me. I also hoped to kill time and avoid an unwanted guest staying over too.

I wanted to tell Hecate to take up some defence classes, it wasn't unheard of for some women to learn how to wield a sword or shield. Women from the continent did, even if Desdemona was a bit misogynistic, I'd support my sister if she wanted too. Hell, I would teach her myself if we got on a bit better. I'd heard in the last decade, even women up north were beginning to train in the basics. Though it was assumedly rumours.

The chief comes and hands me his findings, the report is bleak, same rambles as all the others. I eventually return home again, empty handed, with no more of a lead.

I was lost in thought as I approached the stone patio that circles around to the back. The patio lined with rose bushes my sister and the lead gardener pruned themselves. Giving credit where it's due, she took diligent care of our home's grounds. My mother would have appreciated her care. She always had a touch with nature, more than I did.

As I step up the stone, I'm alarmed by my sister, indecent outside. Nearly breaking my own neck, I quickly avert my eyes. "What the actual fuck, Hecate!" *Think I too, will start having nightmares!* "Put this on will you, you're in nothing but under garments!" Shoving my coat to her.

"Sorry, w–w–wait, hold on! I saw someone creeping around the yards from my window!" She's huffing and puffing for air, overly excited.

I'm momentarily startled, "Go back inside, I'll deal with this." I draw my sword, hungry for some action. I hear her behind me, offering to help. "Don't make me laugh." I make eye contact with her, hoping she understands how serious this is, "Go inside now, it's dangerous."

"I know where they were, I'll show– "

I appreciated the fact she wanted to help, but she could be so dense, sometimes. "Hecate, for once in your life, just bloody listen to me. GO BACK INSIDE!!" Snapping at her, she falters for a mere second before her eyes glow with excitement again, unfazed by my temper.

Jabbing the air in the direction behind me. "THERE, THERE!"

I pivot, a hunter ready to kill.

Focusing in on the figure she spotted, trying to flee. They zig-zag, trampling through wild-flower patches, jumping over the fences that caged in groomed vegetation. Desperately trying to evade my pursuit.

A whistle sounds off, people realising the breach too late, for my standards. The hooded figure was two steps ahead, every inch I gained, they took it back- and then some. As if they had planned this, mapped my family's home, knowing where all the sharpest corners of the estate were. That fuelled my fury more, I felt my speed pick up.

They don't get much further before our estate guards bring out the dogs. We finally corner them near one of the lookout towers that meets two joined walls, only a few yards from our weapons building. My lungs were burning, but I felt good. I looked forward to getting answers, I would gladly lose another night of sleep, torturing them.

The figure drops to their knees, back still to me, the dogs snapping their teeth toward them. I eagerly approach and grab their hood, yanking it down, revealing our trespasser.

The dogs silence, ears instantly pulling back. A few surprised grunts from the men holding the dogs. The cloak collapses in on its-self, a black mist rises and dissolves into the air, smelling of rot. None of us say anything, staring at the pool of fabric. I push it around with my sword, looking for remnants of mana stone, but find nothing. A disturbing discovery. The only thing on all our minds, the only way this was remotely possible... magic.

Sleep would not come for me tonight, for a whole different reason. I report my findings and the events to my father, who stares off serious. He walks over to his mantel piece, hands behind his back, "War is coming..." His voice certain, staring at the magnificent sword displayed there.

More things to add to our never-ending lists of investigations. I depart from my father's office, closing the door, feeling beat.

Spacing out as I make way to our library down on the first floor. Realising how unqualified we were– I was, against a force with little knowledge on. Magic was merely a myth – wives' tales nannies use to scare the children with. There were beings in faraway continents capable of this, but we had not had dealings or run ins with their species for centuries. Desdemona had its freedom now for over a thousand years, they would be declaring war if they were behind all this chaos.

Lighting candles, I begin searching for anything with insight. Spending the entire night skimming books, going over scrolls, anything that mentioned magic. An idea drifts through... *Hecate has read most of these books...* The chair creaks as I shift, debating. I didn't want my sister getting involved, but she would be more useful than spending hours or days in here.

The sun beams into my eyes, bringing me back to the present, I conclude to sleep on it. A clearer mind would help. The trek back to my room was hell, my body fought me with every step. I slowly lift my feet up the stairs, very aware how heavy they felt. I turn on the mini landing towards the last fourteen steps to my floor. My sister was making her way down.

I hear what sounds like nails on a chalk board addressing me, talking about my coat. Snapping at Hecate to burn it, the tiredness, the stress, everything boiling over.

"Why are you always so mean?"

I speak to Katrina finally, her eyes watering – unable to hold myself back anymore. "You repulse me!"

Hecate stares at me, like she'd never seen me before, Katrina begins bawling. I turn and practically leap, skipping three or four steps with the last of my strength.

Fleeing to the safety of my private space. I slam the door shut, the pictures on the walls rattling. Locking the door before going and collapsing on my bed. I'm depleted, there was so much to do, and I couldn't help but feel like we're running out of time.

...

I woke to someone shaking me, not knowing who, I grab them and flip them under me. Forearm on their throat.

"Young master, it's me, wake up!" My father's butler – Spencer, blue, struggling to breathe.

False alarm. I grumble an apology, so exhausted I had forgotten head staff had keys to our rooms. He exclaims the town is under attack, groaning as I get off from the bed. I don't even know how much sleep I got, but I could have used more.

Spencer drops something on me, waking me up, instantly. "Our lady is in town..."

My stomach plummets, my feet immediately take off through the house. I'm yelling at everyone as I pass by, to get in gear and move out.

My horse was galloping with everything the brown mare had to offer, while I focused on the dark smoke rising in the distance. The screams begin getting louder, accompanied by deafening roars. Debris cluttering the ground, I had my horse leaping over it all. My eyes scanned everything. People cowering in and under things, the crying of children, pools, and smears of blood – painting the once vibrant town, red.

I'm hit off my horse while distracted with the carnage. The mare neighs, toppling over and trapping me. My lower half is crushed with a yell, unsure if I have broken something. I struggle to push her off.

Gangly nails appear one by one, and I am faced with a tooth. Hollow crimson eyes, a yellow fang hanging over its long snout, saliva drips onto my face. The thing was bigger than my horse, and it oozed, death. I'm pinned, unable to reach for my sword to defend myself, when something strange happens. It looks at me and leaves, discards me as the dead horse.

I finally pull my body from under it, no time to grieve over my faithful steed. The urge to find my sister stronger, my eyes catch sight of our family carriage, in pieces. Two guards unconscious and bleeding, Trevore was near it, while Gregory was slunk over by a destroyed wall.

I couldn't see black hair, or a purple dress, among the debris.

Anxiety grips me, as I begin swinging my sword cutting down anything in my path. My eyes never leaving the carriage's insignia, I limp and swing recklessly.

Dark and dense mist prances around this once peaceful street. No matter how fast I tried to move there was this feeling of an invisible force, trying to hold me back, gripping the pain in my legs. My ankles felt shackled, an un–seen opponent pulling me further away from where I needed to be.

"Hecate!!" I holler hoping she was there, among the debris, hiding.

Another beast blocks my path, snarling. I think of nothing more pleasing than driving my sword through its head. I swung and swung, drunk on the adrenalin till I was practically covered in its innards. Hacking at the creature, I probably killed it after the first few blows, but did not relent. It was in pieces before me, and bits of it on me, when I finally stopped my attack.

For a moment all sounds stilled, the mist pulling away before the ground begun to rumble.

I'm thrown off balance, bouncing on the ground floor with everything else. The dancing mist thickens, swallowing up objects and people in the distance. A laughter fills the air over top the screams and roars that begin once again.

"We've only just begun!" The laugh turned into a taunt, and with a gust of wind it was gone.

The beasts, the mist. All that was left was ruins of our town. Shop's roofs collapsed in – windows shattered... Struggling to my feet, I needed to search the area. I was throwing the debris away, hardly recognising Trevore, his right shoulder gashed. His eyes barely open, "Where is she?!?" I shake him. His skin is pale, lips turning blue. Trevore's pulse is faint, his lack of awareness has me frustrated.

I let him go when I spot a bloodied – brown boot.

...

My office was in no better state than the disaster of the streets, scrolls and papers scattered. A chair in pieces from being thrown earlier, into the wall, a flipped desk from rage. A tribute painting hung above the fireplace, it was the only intact, and undamaged thing, with in the once neat room.

I sat on the floor, back up against the wall. Bottle in one hand, the other fiddling with a stone. I was waiting for father to return from Port Nesmo, to break the news to him, myself. I stare at my mother's painting above the fireplace, a tsunami of emotions inside. The stone in my hand heats up, almost as though it was trying to comfort me.

Blue Calcite – Hecate had told me. A gag gift she had given me for my coming of age, the next best thing to coal.

It'll help with your time of the month!

Her laughter was swirling into the chaos of noise inside my head. I could hear her repeating those words to me, like she had done that evening, before giving me my actual gift. A dagger, decorated with our family insignia at the knob of the handle, the very same one I had tucked away in my boot every day. Similar design to my father's battle sword.

I could never bring myself to get rid of the stone, the blues, and whites of raw rough edges, reminding me of the waves that splash up against the rocks. One of Hecate's favourite –yet dangerous– hiding spots. The stone was a reminder for me, of the pain we both understood, a pain no child should have to endure.

"I want my mommy..." She said between sobs.

I remember her devastated face like it was yesterday. Knowing what it was like to lose a mother, I sympathised with the pain she was going through back then.

I looked out to sea, it wasn't safe to be here, the tide would soon be coming in. Father had the guards searching high and low for her, for two days she had been missing. She ran when father told her of her mother's passing that morning. Her head was between her knees, hands covering her head, shaking. As much as I hated her mother... she was still my sister, and she was hurting.

Now, she was gone too.

CHAPTER EIGHT

HECATE

I ran, pushing the water out of my path, trying to stay on my feet. My instincts screaming at me, that if I stopped, if I fell, I was done for. Sheer horror unlike anything I had ever felt, utmost certainty, that death was following me, playing with me.

Something was under the water, enjoying the game of cat and mouse. Sounds of clicking from whatever monstrosity lurked. I caught glowing eyes peer up at me, drawing closer, then hanging back. Not wanting our game to end too quickly. A skeleton-like fish tail, slapping the water if I kept my attention off it too long, as though it was displeased with me.

I needed to get out of here, with no end in sight, no structures of buildings or worlds end. That voice laughing at me, offering his advice. "Are you sure you want to go that way? I wouldn't if I were you!"

I tried to run a different direction, keeping my pursuer behind me, with only the moon – lighting the way. The water below dark, my feet grazing nothing, no obstacles to slow me down. No signs of any other life. Clothes-soaked clinging to me, hair too, sticking to every inch, like I was a fly stuck in a spider's web. I trip over my own feet, stumbling. My face slapping the surface of the water with a sting, as I try to control my balance.

"Dearie me, does someone have two left feet? You must not be a particularly good dancer..." He laughs at me. "Perhaps it is time our little show comes to an end."

Something below grips my ankle with inhuman strength. Screaming, I was pulled down. I'm gasping for air, but no water fills my lungs. Everything is dark.

Am I dead?

Katrina begins whispering to me. Warmth gripping my cold hands, "Tee, Tee are you okay?"

"K–Kat, I can't see..." My words coming in harsh gasps.

"Shh keep quiet, you'll attract their attention..." She's sniffling, trying to soothe me.

My head is a mess, memories flooding in. I see orange light appear and disappear – my back pressed to a firm surface. Wherever we were, seemed to be moving, I could feel the area sway. "Where th–the hell are we?" I felt so cold.

Kat sobs quietly, "We've been taken Tee, those things – those monsters... They killed so many... You went down, the guards went down – there was blood, so– so much of it... I... I don't remember anything else..." I interlock my fingers into her shaking ones, mine too also trembling. *Those monsters...* I remember the roars, the very same ones that echoed in my dreams. The mist, the voice – a cold sweat takes over my body from my revelation.

"We're going to die!" Another voice squeaks out from across the darkness. Followed quickly with more 'shushing,' something jars the floor sending us jumping and hitting it. More yelps and weeps resound. I realise we are not alone. Four, maybe five other women, were here with us too.

"They're going to eat us!" A younger voice muffles out.

I try to sit up, the moving of whatever we were in, making it hard to stabilize. It smelled of wet wood and dirt, the floor was definitely wood, my feet catching splinters. We came to a sudden halt, causing us all to shout out and jolt completely sideways.

"We camp, here!" A raspy voice proclaims outside our dark box. I try focusing on the other voices, no growls, or roars outside. Just men with foreign accents, not local ones. "We should move with the cover of night...." Is what I catch, the voice drowned out by movements and banging.

"Hey- hey, did you hear that? We're camping here, we can make a run for it!" I whisper to the sniffling girls.

"What are you talking about?" Kats miraculously still holding onto me.

"They said something about moving at night, now's our chance!" Keeping my voice low enough so only they could hear. I figured we must be a couple of hours away from Newmont, calculating we have been missing few hours by the darkness around. If we ran, I would be able to navigate us back to town. Many streams and creeks ran through and around our district, all flowing directly to sea, we could follow it home. We just needed to successfully escape.

The sniffling stops, I could hear shuffling from the furthest corner.

"Tee... W-What do you mean? You cannot ..." Kat's hold loosens. I feel her gently pulling away from me.

"We don't have time - if we act, we act now!"

The darkness illuminates, that orange light shines in. A tall, shirtless man – with scars riddling his hairy torso - stands at the entry, torch in hand. He starts waving the flame around, checking us. I see from the side, the girls squishing into each other, trying to occupy the corners, farthest away from him.

He stops on me, "Who grabbed the hag!?" I squirm back, away from the flame. "The lord said maidens, not hags!"

"Watch who you call a hag, you fiend!" I scream back at him. I had been called many things growing up, but this was a first. I found myself feeling outraged, despite the current predicament.

His eyes grow wide, his face then twisting into one of disgust, "You speak the mother's tongue?"

I look back to the others, all eyes on me, fear adamant in Kat's big blue eyes. Movement has my eyes back at the scarred giant. Another man appears next to him, just as tall, his skin much darker. Markings of red and blues covering his chest, leading up to a shoulder and down an arm. The red as glossy and dark as his eyes, reminding me of blood. Thick black hair brushing his shoulders, just like the other one. "What's going on?"

"The crone here speaks…" The other one, tilts his butt chin up, pointing it towards me.

The red eyed one hums, looking to the others. "Can anyone else, understand?" Shaky breaths fill the silence. His eyes slowly drag to me, voice calm and unnervingly smooth compared to the raspy barbarian. "Are you a witch, hag?"

My head shakes immediately, words forsaken. Some primal instinct within, telling me to comply.

"We should kill her, the Lord wanted maidens, not hags!" The barbarian speaks again, staring at me as though I was the monster here.

"No. We follow what the Lord Commander orders, this one might be of use to us…" Those blood eyes squint, I lean back, flattening myself to the wall behind me.

"The Lord… might find this one entertaining…" He places his ginormous hand on the hairy one's shoulder, before they both leave. Leaving the flap of fabric open, I behold our captures. Many bonfires lit, men – half naked men – scattered around. I figured we were stuffed into the back of a wagon.

I let out a breath I didn't realise I had been holding.

"Tee…. what… what happened?" Kat hesitantly asks, I notice she's on the other side of the wagon bunched in with the other girls.

"Did… Can you–"

She shakes her head quickly, "Tee, they were speaking gibberish… You– You were speaking gibberish!" She swallows hard, eyes watering.

My breaths become short, everything starts spinning faster and faster.

KATRINA

Katrina held herself back from rushing over to Hecate, who passed out, body leant over. She had just witnessed her friend converse perfectly with the demons. Switching between English to gibberish without a moment's notice. She watched Hecate's chest rise and fall but couldn't move a muscle to check on her further.

"She's one of them…" One of the women close, whispered.

Katrina shook her head, "That's impossible, sh–she was born and raised in Newmont. I've known her my whole life!" Despite her words, some growing suspicion had Katrina's mind and heart conflicted. *She has been inside the sanctum, she cannot be!* She willed herself to go to Hecate, moving dubious, she flinched every time a sound escaped Hecate's lips.

"Don't do it!" The little brunette grabbed Katrina's sleeve. "She may be infected with the madness!"

Katrina recoiled, shuffling back to the other girls. Her mind drifting back to the rumours and the man in the streets. She stares at Hecate's neck, watching, waiting to see anything out of the ordinary. "H-Hecate..." She called out to her friend, too afraid to approach.

"Hecate?!" A short haired women squeezed forward. "You mean – THE Hecate, Hecate Crosse?!" Her face lights up.

"Y-Yes..." Was all Katrina could say.

"Blessed be... You hear that, there is no way in the seven rings of hell, would the Crosse family not come for her. They'll save us all!" Tears begin falling from her face, hands together in silent thanks.

That's right... They will come for us... Katrina instantly sobered up, she crawled quickly to Hecate. Collecting her limp body into her arms. "They'll save us Tee, hang in there. They are coming."

CHAPTER NINE

ALASTOR

I sat tapping my foot in the council hall, around a large table. Listening to the local authorities, other lords, and my father, debate every microscopic thing. I was peeved, with every moment spent bickering in here, we lost out there. The sun gone, we now had to take in account other manner of beasts.

There was currently a search team, consisted of dogs, knights and mana-handlers— with limited supplies of mana-stones – conducting it. Using mana-stones embedded with specific spells, searching for traces of magic, while the dogs sniffed out trails of the beasts and the missing women… Admittedly, I couldn't care about the other two also missing, but my sister… Regret gripped my guts so hard, I thought I had been stabbed.

Voices erupt all around the table.

"This is a ploy, they want us defenceless, I say we stick to it my Lords!"

"We need to retaliate!"

"We shouldn't waste resources on measly captives we need to- "

"How dare you..." My father stands up slowly, his hand – reached behind his back – on the handle of his claymore. "Measly you say? MY DAUGHTER WAS TAKEN!"

I stare down the half-witted baron, who flinches hard. My hand also on the handle of my sword. Tension was high, everyone was on edge, waiting for the first person to draw blood.

"I am Duke of Newmont, me! We have been attacked – my people have been personally attacked!" My father's yelling, the vein in his forehead pulsing. "We counter, we engage, we will find those bastards and slaughter every – last one of them! I don't give a single damn about how much resources it takes!"

Many of the others begin nodding their heads, Lord Smithe was fuming beside my father. Katrina too was also on the missing list.

"Sir, I meant no disrespect, but we have to see the bigger picture– "

Sling

My father unsheathes his claymore – Wrath. The magnificent sword that stayed on his mantel, above his hearth, unless he was going to war.

The captain stands up next to me, "Our Duke, Lord Protector of the People has fought in more wars than our very own king. He has bled for the people, prepared to die for our people! If he declares we fight. Then we fight!"

Men in unison rise from their seats, swords also drawn and raised, chanting. "For the people – by the people – WE ARE THE PEOPLE!"

...

I rode with two knights, a mana–handler and fifty of our best soldiers from our estate, up north. My team tasked of tracking and running them down if they were headed for the mountains.

Gregory suffered minor injuries, knocked unconscious in the attack, when he was thrown into a wall. He was aggrieved to have failed protecting my sister and her friend. Begging to be brought along, or killed for his sin, to atone. The man was a good soldier, loyal to our family. I didn't waste a moment when I told him to saddle up, we rode ahead of our company looking for signs of large group disturbances.

My father and his group rode south of Newmont, across the southern river that ran down, south-west. Two other squadrons split east and west.

The nearest town a couple of days ride east, Delwae. A hawk was sent out to alert, a speed stone attached to its leg, it would have arrived within the hour. With no reply, we decided not to wait any longer. Guards were also alerted and on standby at Port Nesmo to ride and secure the coast, no ships in or out. Our district was on complete lockdown.

We would find her– it was only a matter of time.

"Lieutenant Colonel! Over here, I got something!" The handler – Marcus, calls for me across the small creek. The older man was on his knees, digging through the bushes.

I rode through the waters, swinging my pained leg over, before recklessly jumping from my still moving horse. "What have you found?" There was a lightening shock up my leg, toward my hips, I did my best to brush it off.

He was moving around a decent sized reddish stone, glowing even brighter red, whenever it brushed up against them. "We've got traces of magic!"

I was eager, "Anywhere else?!" My usual character broken. I was running on adrenaline, guilt, and pain today.

"Whoever, we are dealing with here... I have a firm suspicion, they are shapeshifters." His bushy grey eyebrows rise like mountains. "It's unbelievable, I've only experienced such energy during my travels through the continents, to think that such beings were here." He stands up, waving and following the direction the stone would glow. He checks his trinket in his other hand. "Your gut was right. They are making way for the mountains. Probably thought the rivers and creeks would wash away any traces." He smiles before adding, "But the earth never lies."

"It's a few days ride to the foothills if we ride straight on." Gregory trots up beside us, still mounted, eyes north. I thanked whoever was listening, for this small piece of hope, they could not be more than 4 hours ride from us. "We cannot be certain if it was the same group who attacked the town, there's other things that lurk at night, and the nearer we get to the mountains, the worse we'll encounter." Gregory's honest input shakes my hope.

I make large strides for the horse that stopped a yard away. "It's all we got, and that's good enough for me!" I was betting on them to camp, I *needed* them to camp if we were to catch up.

I swing back and pull Marcus to sit behind me, Gregory shoots a flaming arrow straight up to alert the following group of our direction. The three of us carefully ride north, we would have to stop and wait for the squadron to catch up before we crossed the next river. We were dangerously close to monster territory...

KATRINA

Katrina sat legs crossed, still holding an unconscious Hecate. The women with her seemed to have quieted down when the local proclaimed who Hecate was. One however, kept a good distance from them all, eyeing up Hecate.

"So, you're from Newmont then?" Katrina opened her eyes to that angelic voice, only nodding her head. She wasn't in a mood for idle chit chat. "Your friend there, I think the child over there was right." Pointing a finger from the darkness to the little brown-haired person gripping the lady beside her.

Katrina looked down at Hecate brushing her hair out of her face. "She doesn't look sick..." She examined Hecate, not seeing any signs like the man she saw before.

"It's not a physically seen sickness." Eyes stare daggers at Hecate, "It's one of the mind... then the body."

"She's been like that since we've been here..." The lady next to the brunette scowls at her. "Paranoid of everyone."

"Won't be long now till they skin us all alive." The lights outside reflecting off her only visible eyes, completely hidden within the shadows.

Katrina tensed – she would not let those words unnerve her. *She's simply scared....*

"I'm Anna," one lady says to Katrina.

She looks to her and smiles softly, remembering one of the Crosse servants named Anna... "Katrina... Tee here, calls me Kat." Her voice wavers as she thinks about the comfort of home.

Anna pulls the brunette into her more, "This one here is Olivia... she's my little sister."

Katrina smiled at them both and pulled Hecate closer to her. "I had a sister too... She was older than me..." Her smile faltering, the tears in her eyes falling onto Hecate. "She was killed many years ago, when I was just a small girl."

Anna's face falls, "I'm sorry..."

"Are you going to hold hands and pray together next? Everyone dies, it's the only thing we have in common..." The one in the corner sputters at them.

Katrina's head snapped to her, and before she could open her mouth and retort, Hecate began mumbling. "Dal... haras... ellath..." Hecate was speaking gibberish again, then it struck her. Hecate spoke those same words before...

Olivia squeaked, "See... your friend is sick..."

CHAPTER TEN

KATRINA

K atrina could not deny it, the signs were there. She pushed Hecate off her, laying her body in front, further pushing her with a foot.

"Mat!" The girls all startled when the taller scarred one appeared, yelling gibberish as well. He threw down a plate, hard bread bounced all over the place. He eyes up Hecate laying before Katrina, sniffing the air. "Mat... Mat" Bringing his large-scarred hands to his mouth, repeatedly.

A dirty hand emerges from the corner, snatching the nearest piece of bread. The man shakes his head, and points to Hecate. "Faran?"

Olivia squeaks next to Anna, "Please don't hurt us..." Who quickly tucks her little sister, behind her.

He grunts and rolls his eyes again, "Faran?" Choking himself, head tilted - eyes closed. He waits for them to respond when Hecate begins mumbling the same thing as earlier. He leans forward, his thick eyebrows bunched together. A look of surprise crosses his face, he says nothing, turning and rushing off.

Within moments the marked one appeared with him. They spoke quickly, eyes and fingers pointing at Hecate. Katrina wanted to hide in the dark corner away from Hecate, just like the other girl. She didn't like the scrutinizing looks on their faces, fully believing Hecate was unwell.

The marked one slowly crept in reaching for Hecate's ankle, causing the girls to lose their minds.

"No don't come any closer, just take her! Just take her!" Katrina was practically climbing up the wall behind her.

The man lets out a frustrated growl, his ears hurting from the high pitch screams. He drags Hecate from the wagon, careful not to expose anything above her knees. Throwing her over his shoulder he pays no mind to the others, walking away. The scarred one grunts as he follows them. None of the women knowing what just happened or if they'd return for them next.

"You're no friend of hers..." Eyes stared daggers at Katrina now. "You better pray they kill her, quickly."

Katrina was shaking uncontrollably, bile threatening to come up. "Go to hell, wench!"

Teeth appeared in the darkness, smiling at Katrina, "I'll see you there."

HECATE

I had a pleasant dream, I walked in light, warm radiating light for ages. I could not explain this place, I assumed I was now walking the path to the afterlife. So much had been happening, I felt a pain of remorse.

I never got to say goodbye to papa...

A sweet melody played, echoing through the empty plain. Notes played from a woodwind instrument, so sweet I wanted to dance. I let my feet wonder, basking in the warmth on my skin.

"Si haras ellath."

I slow my swaying rhythm when I hear that voice. Repeating back what I'd heard before, "Dal... haras... ellath." It felt foreign on my tongue. I was not even sure if I was saying it as beautifully or correct, as she did.

Floating orbs of peach lights materialised, flickering one by one, showing a way to go. I felt compelled to follow, and so I did. Every time I neared one, its light would vanish, just before my fingertips touched them.

I felt no cares, no worries... Just peace.

I swayed along listening to the tune, until I reached a lake, mountains surrounded this lake, resembling a crescent moon. I had never seen anything so breath-taking. The water was calm, not a ripple or disturbance, the smell of honey suckles wafted into my senses.

I snuck up, daring a peek, peering at my reflection. Only, an old lady stared back, with the same green eyes. Her thick hair grey and dull, up in a messy bun. Her skin saggy and textured, I reached up to my own face and the old woman mimicked my action. I watched and played with the reflection for some time before voices pulled me away.

"I heard her say it, crystal clear!"

I knew that voice somehow... I looked around and found no one nearby. *Huh weird...*

Another voice I had somehow heard before, begins as well, sounding as though they stood with me. "And you're absolutely certain that's what she said?" That voice was smoother than the other, and much calmer.

I called out to the sky, "Hello?" Waiting for an answer, but no body spoke to me. I went back to playing with the reflection, tilting my head back and forth, fascinated.

The reflection stops following my moves, her mouth moving even though mine wasn't. She was shouting, I couldn't read her lips, she seemed upset. The water's surface began distorting. Two old hands broke through the surface of the water, grabbing me by the shoulders of my tattered dress. I'm broken from my trance as she pulled me in.

I lurch awake, still screaming.

"Evenin." There's a man sat down – he barely turns his head to my acknowledgment. I flip over, falling off some cushioned bench. Scrambling to my wobbly knees, I try to make a break for what I think is an entrance.

"Whoa – whoa! Slow down ma'am!" He crosses the room faster, grabbing me.

"Unhand me, help! Somebody please, help!" I'm lashing out as he lifts me from the floor.

He's ginormous too, taller than Alastor by a few inches, I was a baby lamb in his arms. He laughs at me, his voice strangely soft, "That's what I'm tryin' to do ma'am. You're seriously de'ydrated and in need of some medicine, you've gon' and caught yourself the nasty bug." He places me gently on the bench I was on earlier, I try escaping again from his arms when his hold loosens. "You're like an ol' cat! Just sit still will you. You don't want those two fellas comin' back in ear' now?"

I stopped trying to break away hearing – those two fellas – and realised that the one holding me, was one of them too. *You speak the mother's tongue?* We were conversing, and I had a feeling it wasn't in my native tongue. "How?" Mumbling to myself.

Though, the friendly giant responds. "Ma'am de'ydration happens when one doesn't drink enough fluids to keep the body going. When your immune system is shocked it's rather easy to catch anythin'." He lets go of me and begins filling a cup with water. "I thought your kin was all into that science."

I stare, my adrenaline plummeting, my stomach was aching, the water looked amazing. Saliva began pooling under my tongue, watching it pour into the cup like a waterfall.

"It won't kill you, quite the opposite actually. Ear' drink."

Fingers shaking, I take the large mug from his incredulously large hands. His fingers twice the size of my own, spotting clean kept nails. This one had long dark hair too, seemed to be a trait among them. His hair was gathered back into a very neat bun, the left side above his ear, shaved with symbols. Double taking when I glimpsed the ear – a long pointed ear – dazzled. A tiny gold bar pierced across it, I spot what looks like pendants of arrows sliding on the bar, with his movements. His skin was flawless too, not a scar or freckle. His eyes amber and round, hidden behind thick lashes.

"See somethin' you fancy?" He smiles big, his teeth straight, except one that just about over laps another on his bottom row.

No unusually long canines at least... "What are you..." I hug the mug to myself. Positive my face wasn't one of admiration.

He brings his hands together, sitting down at a work bench to the left side of me. Head tilting, an eyebrow raises slightly at me. "Interestin'... Can I ask you somethin' ma'am?" He leans back, slender legs stretching out, one crossed over the other.

He was fully dressed unlike his companions, brown leather trousers, and a soft blue tunic underneath a leather vest. His demeanour of hospitality slowly disarming me. I nodded my head carefully, cautious still. *These people... are not human.* That much I knew.

He smiles again, "You realise you are speaking to me in my people's tongue?"

I sniff the water, daring a sip. Squinting at him, "I was made aware...."

He nodded once, "I presume you know what language we speak then?" Thumbs tapping together, his body language reminded me of an old professor.

I start to move, suddenly stopping myself, "I answered your question– so, so you must answer mine!"

He makes a funny face at my words, "You are also aware, you need to be careful exchangin' words with my kin..." Holding a hand up, he is counting on his large fingers. "You are also able to speak fluently, the accent is..." He kissed his fingers in a weird gesture, eyes closed. "But, even with these, you 'ave no idea?"

"You're not answering the question." I say through gritted teeth, "I wouldn't be asking if I knew." I was beginning to feel aggravated. I knew men believed women to be stupid, they even took advantage of it. I was also anxiously aware, that one wrong word, and he could – would, snap my neck with swift action. I had to tread carefully.

"Strange... Very, strange..." He turns away from me, writing down in a notebook.

I don't move my head from him, though I side–eye the entrance a few times. *I could just...*

"You could try, even if I choose not to chase you." I snap back to him, his attention still on the notebook. "There are twenty–eight more, right out there. Those ol' legs of yours are no match."

Silence followed, the sound of scratching on paper so loud to my ears. *Did I say that out loud?* I fidget with the necklace around my neck, running my thumb along the symbol. Eyeing up the quill in his hand, a sharp object to tuck away, for later.

"Why did you not inform me, she was awake?" I jump in my own skin, head twisting to the tattooed one strolling in.

"I thought ye' might've 'eard her screaming moments ago." The seated one stops writing long enough to address him.

My knees come up to the mug, tucking the necklace into my cleavage. I wanted to make myself as small as possible, praying they would not pay much attention to me.

Red eyes stare me down. "What is your name, hag?"

I didn't want to talk to this one, no, I wanted nothing more than for him, to go away.

"Your mama ever taught you to talk to ladies?" The other stands up from his work bench and approached him. They shared a look before walking outside the entrance.

I could not see the quill on the work surface anymore. I sighed frustrated and take this moment to look around, for something else. Thick poles holding up fabric – a makeshift tent. I'd been in plenty during the social hunts to know I was inside one. There were two makeshift beds, I was currently occupying one. Crates and barrels around the tent, used as tables, some weird glowing light hanging above, lighting the space up. Other than the work bench and a shelf with bottles and plants, it was quite bare. Nothing of use to me.

My head starts swarming with questions, wondering where the other girls were taken, if there were other tents or not. A breeze cools my heating body, from my right. There's a draft coming in through a tear in the fabric, big enough for me to slip out. I weigh my options, not knowing when those two would return. Placing the mug down on a box, I inch toward the side. Trying to see what was beyond it. Murmurs from the entrance have me scrambling back to my spot.

"Let's try that again, more civilly ya?" The dressed one walks in first, heading straight to the work bench. The other, lingering by the entrance. "There's no need to tell you my name ma'am, though you can call me, Doc. That is my profession and what these 'ooligans call me." He's sitting again, legs stretched out, a placid smile as he speaks to me. He gestures to the tattooed one, "That's Arrus over there. Now he may look mean, but he is not gon' hurt you, not unless you give'm reason. Savvy?"

I feel sweat trickle down my back, looking to Arrus. His arms are folded, biceps bulging, his tattooed arm of blues and reds making his arm appear even bigger looking. He looks to his arm, flexing it a couple times. Then back to me, "What is your name?"

"Beatrise." I lie quickly, spitting the name out.

Doc and Arrus share another look, Doc shrugging it off. "Right then, I believe, I owe you an answer."

KATRINA

Katrina was rocking back and forth, eyes assessing the groups of men. She did not see where they had taken Hecate, she heard no screams either. She found it alarming she heard no other noises outside the wagon. Not even the sound of the men, around the blazing fires.

"It's magic..." The last women with them, who had been quietest, spoke up. Katrina looked at her stupid. "We witnessed them fighting each other, yet we couldn't hear them destroying their surroundings." The stranger's eyes full of sorrow, "Our village was attacked days ago, I think. I was taken with another... she killed herself..."

More bile rises in Katrina's throat. "W–What happened to her body..." She saw no bodies other than the still warm ones, present.

The woman's reply does not help Katrina's anxiety, "I don't know..."

Anna sobs, clutching Olivia to her. She could hear the little girl's words from earlier on repeat. *They're going to eat us!* Katrina eyeballs the hidden one, in the other corner. "How long have you been here?"

Eyes like an owl slowly meets hers, "No idea... the nights mesh. You arrived but maybe you've been here three days already. This place is enchanted, like she said."

Katrina's faith waivers, but she continues – only to keep her sanity, "What is your name?"

A laugh responds, "Does it matter... no one will remember it when I am gone. ... There's a bucket over there by the way..." The sound of nails digging into wood, follow. "They won't let you leave, not even to relieve your business." Katrina cringes, she tries spying further into the darkness to see the girl. Only eyes reflected, the rest of her a shadow. "My name's Selene... satisfied?"

Katrina nods her head, "Where are you from, Selene?" The girl's voice was lovely, if not for her attitude.

"North... like the others. My town was hit, some time ago, I think."

Katrina faced back out, watching the fires as her vision blurred. Her hope for a rescue, dwindling.

HECATE

"Fae." I had no idea what to say to that, not knowing what that even was. None of my readings or education, mentioned these fae beings. I wanted to ask, though I had a feeling they would keep me in the dark as much as possible. For their own benefits, and my lack of knowledge could be a weapon to use. "Well, that settles that, my debt is done." Doc claps his hands together, standing up. "The patient needs some rest. Can further questions wait, till she's least had somethin' to eat?"

Arrus's calculating look goes back and forth between Doc and I, he nods his head once and turns. Speaking as he leaves, "Make haste."

Doc opens a crate, pulling bits and pieces out. I scope out an apple and few other fruits, easily fitting in his one hand. My stomach growls demandingly, I clutch it quickly to stop the sound.

He smiled again, offering me the apple. "I've got some bread in ear' as well."

I nod my head, my cheeks burning. I could not recall when I last ate, and if I were going to escape, I needed anything I could get. He slowly reached out, I too slowly took the apple, careful not to touch him. He goes to the shelf next, pulling out things wrapped in leaves.

"Ear' you go." He approaches slowly yet again, mindful not to spook me, I guessed.

Regardless of what they were, I wasn't without manners. "Thank you."

Grinning to himself, he returns to his work bench. "Ooh, a thank you. How refreshin." Flipping through the notebook, he pulls out the quill he tucked away in his vest's inner pocket. Facing me, he gives it a wiggle.

My face burns hot, I dart down quickly to the food in my hands. *Was I too obvious?* I sneak a peek at him. He's back to scribbling away. I quickly bite the apple in thought, the juice overloading my senses, I just about moan. *Was fruit always this delicious?*

"Slow down there, wouldn't want an ol' lady like you choking."

"Do I look that old to you?"

"Grey 'air, saggen skin – not even the ancient of me kin look like ye. Your kin ages somethin' fierce, if you don't mind my saying so."

It all clicked – the names, the dream... I would use this opportunity to my advantage. "Why are you taking the young girls of the south?" Figuring out how this was possible, was for another time. The most important thing at this moment – they wouldn't know who I really was.

"Can't tell ye, not my business."

"What do you mean not your business!!" The injustice of the recent events burst out of me, exploding at him.

He puts the quill into his pocket, fully turning to me. "Look ear' ma'am. As I've already tol' you, I'm the doc. I fix these 'ooligans up and send them on their way. That is my business, nothin else." I go to open my mouth, but he continues, "If you really want answers, wait for Arrus to return. Remember though, a question for a question."

My mouth shuts instantly, biting my lips as I suck them into my teeth. He shakes his head, pulling out glasses from another pocket. I look to the tear in the fabric, I would be better off...

"Go for it, though I can assure ye, you'll only find yourself back in that stinkin' wagon with the others."

The others... Now I knew where they were.

"Prepare for an attack, soldiers to the rear!" Some massive man with shiny grey markings barges in, nearly scaring me to death. I dropped the apple, and bread, flinching hard.

Doc stands up quickly, gathering his things. Before I could even think of moving, he strolls over, "You're with me." Grabbing my arm. I try to squirm from his firm grip being dragged outside the tent, that's when I see.

Men everywhere, melting into puddles of shadows, those shadows then growing into things.

"No, no, no! Get off me, let me go!"

Huge paws, massive canine fangs, eyes glowering, they were exactly as I dreamt them. The smell of decay turning my stomach, snarls filling the night. Some eyes followed as Doc dragged me towards a wagon, the only wagon around. Lifting me by the arm, he makes quick to toss me over his shoulder.

Suddenly a horn sounds off in the distance, a horn I had heard throughout my childhood.

CHAPTER ELEVEN

KATRINA

Katrina eyes burned, fatigue, and all the crying had her struggling to keep them open.

Thud – "Ow! My kind is practically made of bones, you prick!"

Her eyes shoot open. "He–Hecate?!" She didn't know if the enchantment of this place was messing with her. She seen Hecate sitting near the entrance, rubbing her arm, scowling.

Bright green eyes looked back to her, "Kat, are you alright?!?" A tranquil tone chasing away the shadows in Katrina's mind. She scurried quickly to Hecate on all fours, tackling her. Hecate wrapped her arms around Katrina, she could hear Hecate's strong heartbeat within.

Katrina wailed, she let everything in the recent hours come out, finally.

"Shhh, shh, it's okay. Help has come!" Hecate looked around to the other girls. "The soldiers have come!" Tears welling up in her eyes as well.

"What?"

"By the gods, were saved!"

Olivia too began to sob loudly.

Katrina lifted herself up and grabbed Hecate's face in both hands, "What do you mean!"

Hecate smiled through her tears, "The battalion's horn sounded off just before I was tossed into here..." Cheers and sobs combined, filled the wagon.

Selene peered around, "That's if they don't all die first, trying to save us."

"The attack of our town was a surprise. Mark my words, they will regret this day for what they've done." Hecate proclaimed proudly, "My father will kill every last one of them and stand victorious over their cold corpses!" Even as a tear ran down her fierce face, her eyes radiated with confidence. Her words were dark for a lady of her calibre but said with such conviction.

Something in Selene's eyes wavered while she took in Hecate, quickly cowering away from her. Hecate pulled Katrina into another hug. "We'll be home before you know it, and this too will all be but a nightmare..."

Katrina wrapped her arms around Hecate, basking in the warmth and security they provided. "Tee did they do anything to you?"

Hecate was staring out the exit, waiting, "There's so much to explain and things not even I could explain..." She takes a deep breath through her nose. "They're Fae." Katrina sat up, the girls in the wagon listening intently to Hecate. "You know all those preaches we're told Kat. I think... I genuinely think some of it might have been true... There is a huge part of it, I think, they are also not preaching to us."

"What is fae?" Olivia asks curiously, her voice just above a whisper. Hecate shakes her head, she had not the slightest clue, herself.

"They're beings of the gods." Selene's small voice counters, "One of the many first, loved by them."

Katrina whips around to her, still hiding in the corner. "How do you know that?"

Eyes appear again, "I'm just like her..." those eyes going straight to Hecate.

"What do you- "

"You can understand their language?" Hecate cuts in.

"I thought they'd kill me if they knew..." They hear her suck in a sharp breath.

"Coward!" Katrina yells. "You taunted us with threats of what they would do, you – you could have said something when they were taking Tee away?! Instead, you hide in those shadows!!"

Her eyes snapped back to Katrina, glowing brighter, "That's grand coming from you, princess!"

"Oi, don't you dare talk to her like that." Hecate pulled Katrina back to her, protectively.

"Girls calm down," Anna tries to intervene, "We need to stick together, if we're to get through-"

"Which one of us is the coward here, hmm? My silence for survival? Or you, shouting for them to take your so-called friend!" Selene spits back, fully immersed from the shadows of the corner. Her hair purely white, her doe eyes -violet. Even covered in dirt and dried blood, she was stunning, on par with Hecate.

The wagon goes silent, Hecate inching away, examining Katrina. "What does she mean, Kat?" Katrina shakes her head vigorously, not answering her. Hecate examines Selene next, "What do you mean by that?"

Katrina stutters out finally. "I-I was scared, I f-freaked out when he reached in f-for you!"

Hecate was in disbelief, her chest tightening. She doesn't get a moment to process what had happened when the wagon violently moves, tilting almost sideways. Sending the girls tipping and crashing into one another.

Wood planks bent and broken inwards, on one side of it suddenly. "It's begun."

HECATE

Katrina was stuttering, I watched her lips flap but heard nothing further, my ears ringing. My chest felt compressed, threatening to crush my heart with it. I try to pull away from her when something crashes into the wagon, nearly sending us over. We're slammed hard into the wall, Katrina landing with me.

The noises outside even louder than before, roars erupting on all sides of us now. The barbarian's voice booms, "They're circling us!" Morphing into a roar.

"It's begun." The odd eyed one says, pulling herself up, right as I did. Our eyes connected – she was telling the truth. I could see the awareness in those amethyst–coloured eyes. I wanted to be angry but a part of me understood, I would have done the same too if it was not for my big mouth. The main thing now was our escape.

Another horn sounded off, I painfully crawled for the exit. I had hit the other side of the wagon hard, my shoulder taking most of the impact. I don't see any of the creatures guarding the wagon, so I slip a leg out.

"Where are you going?!" Katrina grabs the back of my dress.

"We can make a run for it. The soldiers are circling the area. We should take our chances out there."

The woman holding the little brunette shouts, "No! Its suicide, we should wait here, it's safer!"

"No." I wasn't going to wait around and be saved. "What do you think pulled the wagon because I didn't see any horses. We wait here and allow them to take us, or –" I point a finger out, "We go out there and take a chance while they're distracted!"

Katrina's eyes widen so big, I swear they would burst from her sockets.

White hair gets closer to us, "I'll take those chances..."

"WE'RE LADIES TEE!" Katrina attempts to pull me back, "Leave the heroics to the men!"

I yank myself free, Katrina falling back hard. "Then stay here!" I holler at her. I look to the four remaining back, behind Katrina. No one else moving to come as well.

The white haired one comes right next to me completely swinging her legs out. She gives me a not-so-confident nod, "I'll follow your lead."

I felt better knowing I wasn't going alone. "We'll come back for you." I promise the rest, my eyes lingering on Kat. I leap out quickly before my courage ran away, a thud sounds next to me, the woman indeed following. "Under the wagon!" We both crawl, the ground was moist, dirt clinging to us easily. We yelped at the dead beast, whose arm is partially under it, a spear through its side.

That explains that.

"Selene."

I glanced over, "What?"

Those odd eyes with different shades of purple, meet mine. "You are Hecate, I am Selene. I think we should at least know each other's name if we are to die, together."

"We're not going to... die." My words came out not-as-confident, as I wanted them to sound.

"Yea, sure. Now what?"

That dark mist started creeping into camp. The fires now gone – we could hear the battle but could not see anything.

"Mist…" I whisper, crawling to the front, Selene following beside me. I look around before getting out from underneath the wagon, a part of me wanting to scream for my father. The other telling me to keep as silent as the grave. A hand slips into mine, Selene was trembling but still following. Her grip tightened immensely– face paling deathly white. I'm about to protest when I hear snarls ahead.

One of those beasts, emerge from the mist, stalking toward us. I grip her hand in return, "Run," and take off. Paws upon the earth, sounding of thunder, chasing us. I could feel Selene slow slightly, guessing she was looking behind, over her shoulder. "Don't look back!"

It would catch us if we didn't act quickly, I start to zig–zag around bushes and trees quickly appearing, careful not to let go of the hand holding mine. I prayed our size difference would make all the difference with spontaneous docks left and right.

A horse appears through the mist, hooves up in air, neighing. "Ahh," we scream in unison, falling back. I let go of her hand for a brief second, to aid my fall. Selene's gone before I even hit the ground, the mist swallowing her. "S–Selene?!" I'm grabbing air next to me, looking for her.

"Did you think it would be that easy? tsk – tsk." That distinct voice returns, as if it had been watching the show unfold.

Fury has me screaming, "Damn you!" Into the darkness around me, so hard my lungs burn. I continue to yell for Selene till my throat is hoarse, crawling on all fours.

Silver eyes accompanying a sickening grin, flashing in my mind every time the area rumbled with his laughter. My hands feeling the ground in front of me. I couldn't see anything – I couldn't even tell where I had just come from.

Shadows dancing around tauntingly, my sanity was fracturing.

Screams echoed all around, trailed by iron clanging in the distance. Ear-piercing howls followed and filled the breaks between the clashes of turbulent chaos.

"Papa!!" A broken cry rips out of me. "Papa!!" My knees ached – my head throbbed. I was alone again, afraid, and at wits end. "P-please..." I cried – "Somebody... Anybody..." My voice giving out, along with my will.

"Hecate!"

My head shoots up, to the voice calling. Scanning the barely visible space around for it. A white horse breaks through the shadows, galloping like a beacon. Chestnut hair bouncing on the rider's head, blood painting his silver armour.

"Papa!"

ALASTOR

We had tracked down a group, unsure of their actual numbers. During our hunt we had minor run ins with monsters along the way. Creatures of all teeth and legs, giant bats and one big spider. *I fucken hate spiders...* Silently complaining as I rip off pieces of webs still attached to me.

Marcus equipped us with stones for the raid. Educating us with how strong these creatures really were, their weak spots, and how some could even use magic. He had a suspicion of what we were dealing with. All of us raid leaders received a stone to attach to our belts, this would break through the magic barrier, and protect us from whatever manipulation spells were being used. Smaller stones were given to the rest, battle buddies selected. The more fragments together, the stronger the counter spell was.

You could feel the atmosphere changing the closer we approached. Abandoning the frightened horses, yards back, we crept on foot. The group had tucked themselves in a cove between a riverbank and heavy forest. Many fires were lit, groups of men around them all, not a hellhound in sight.

This was one of many rivers flowing from the mountains.

Silence and the element of surprise was the upper hand today, and we needed it to get as close as possible before we launched our full-scale attack. Our company broke off into four sections, we would surround them before we ran them through.

"There's a wagon, sir." Gregory hands me a monocular scope.

I get an eagle's eye look inside the camp, spotting the wagon he'd spoken of. The wagon was a prison carriage, a massive wooden box. The windows where there were usually bars, planked down. Whatever was being transported, hidden from the light. From where we were, I could only see the front of the wagon, no rider or horse attached.

"Once the teams are in place, we strike." I notice the men begin to act strangely, gathering their things, some even putting out fires. "Fuck! We lost the element of surprise."

Gregory sounded the horn, alerting all units to act now, I book it back for my horse.

...

Dark mist descends on us, shrouding our vision to a minimum. My stone vibrating on my belt, glowing so bright that I was surrounded by a bubble of light.

"Damn you!"

I pull hard on my horse's reins, trying to decipher which direction that came from. Swearing I heard my sister cursing. I send the horse forward, galloping blindly, dodging trees rapidly that appeared.

"Don't touch me!!" A scream startles my horse, throwing me off. I hit the ground hard, the wind knocked from me. Staggering quickly and recovering to fighting stance, I face forward. A girl cowers on the ground just ahead, in a fetal position. One of those beasts were towering over her. Its attention drawn to me, jaws foaming.

I dash forward, it peels itself off her, pouncing in my direction. Manoeuvring to my left, quickly, I swing my sword up, sliding the sharp blade across its throat. The beast flies past, sliding into the ground behind me.

Taking a knee, I watch for its movements. Blood soaks the ground around its head, pooling it. Side–glancing the girl opposite and the beast, for activity. I stand, going to her after observing her leg twitching.

I lift her up like a paper weight, "Where is she?!" Careful not to break her bony arms.

Her eyes bulging, she begins to thrash. "Get your hands off me!"

I yell again, "Where is she!" Shaking her.

She spaces out, examining my features, "Who?" She's trembling, dried blood down the sides of her face.

"Where is my sister, where is Hecate?!"

Violet eyes begin to roll back, "She's gone." Is all she chokes out, going limp in my hands. I could feel the air around changing again. A dark laugh circulates, one I wished I could hack to shreds. I pick up the girl, throwing her on the saddle as I mounted the horse.

She had to be near, Hecate was tenacious, she would not go without a fight. "HECATE!?"

CHAPTER TWELVE

UNKNOWN

"My liege, the extraction team is being attacked." A shadow of a being, bows low.

"I'm aware." A hooded man stands on a cliff, watching the waves splash against it. Toying with a pendent in his hand. "Lovely sky tonight." Completely unbothered.

"My liege, orders?"

Silver eyes drag to the one still bowing, he clicks his tongue. "My, my... How the mighty have fallen... Can they not deal with such low-life scum, on their own?"

The shadow flinches under the cold gaze on them.

"You've ruined my mood, be gone or I'll have your head instead."

The shadow flees, swirling off the ground, soaring away.

He slowly saunters away from the cliff, tossing the pendent up like a coin. The end of his cloak dragging along behind him, a trail of dark mist in its wake. His hood was nearly covering the entirety of his face, with only a menacing smile peeking out. "I was growing bored anyways."

ALASTOR

I kicked the horse forward, one hand holding the unconscious stranger. Bodies and parts of them, littered the ground floor. These things were powerful, we'd lost quite a few. A shadow rushes towards us, bringing my sword up, I slash down through it.

"Papa!"

My heart drops into my stomach when I emerge through the shadow. I see my sister on her knees, wheezing. Clothes torn, knees bloodied, not a shoe on her feet. Her hair tangled – lips dry – she looked as if death was calling to her. I wouldn't have recognised her without those gleaming emerald eyes.

I leap off the horse, and rush for her. "Hecate!"

She's staring at me – through me – calling for our father. "Papa!" Latching on to me, her body starts convulsing, a broken wail rips out of her throat.

"I got you... I got you." I repeat, not sure which one of us I was trying to convince.

"Well, isn't that a tearjerker!" Shadows form together – swirling – growing. The mist parting and encircling us in an empty ring. Hecate's head whip lashes towards it, unfathomable fear in her eyes. I bring my bloodied sword up, ready for the next fight. "That would do you, no good, boy." A hooded man steps forth, silver eyes smouldering from under his hood. "Mighty valiant, I must say." He purrs to us, his eyes creeping to my sister, a sickening smile reaching those ethereal eyes. "Found you!"

"Eyes on me, fucker!" Using my body as shield, I give her a moment to escape. "Run to the horse Hecate, go!" She's frozen in place, a broken shell of her previous self. When she stood next to Katrina on the stairs of our home, where she had been safe.

"Hecate, is it? I'm sure you told them, Beatrise?" He laughs more, that same infuriating laugh that haunted our town. The very same one guilty of destroying the livelihoods of our people. "Naughty thing." His eyes drag back to me, "Here's the deal boy, I get the women, the hag included, and you get your life. Sound good?"

My blood boils at his audacity, "I'm going to enjoy killing you."

He raises his hand, examining his long-pointed nails. "Boring." That hand flicks forward, shadows exploding from behind him. I attempt to block them with my sword, when the stone at my belt explodes with light, shielding me instead. He seemed momentarily surprised by it, "Oh that's fun, do it again!"

All sounds drowned out, as though it was just him and I in the ring of mist. The light shielding me, pushing back inches from his onslaught of power. I could feel the shadows push the shield back, feet threatening to give out from where I had rooted myself. "Enough with the tricks!" I desperately shout, I felt stuck in a windstorm. "Fight me like a man!"

The force pulls back suddenly – I, nearly falling forward with it. Shadows lurching back to the spawn of evil, lounging where he began his assault. He asks me annoyed, "And how do men fight?" He whips his hand down, "Like this?" – an unprecedentedly long-sword of darkness appears. "It seems mine is quite bigger than yours." The sheer insolence of this demon, winking at me.

Rage erupts from my soul, charging him with heavy swings. He effortlessly dodges every swing and slash, dancing round my lifelong training efforts.

"My turn." He swings his sword finally, clashing against my own. The solid blade of my sword, vibrating on impact.

HECATE

He came for me... I hold him with all my might, afraid I'd be alone again, if I let go. *Papa came for me.* "Well, isn't that a tearjerker!" My hope crumbles with every syllable spat out. I heed the shadow of a being that plagued me. Same silver – feline – eyes.

I wished I could wake up from this nightmare already, I wished I woke up, and was still in my bed. Under my warm covers, feeling the sun on my face. I wanted to wake up and have tea with father, I wanted to tease Al. I wanted to dry my herbs and read my favourite book for the hundredth time in a row.

The world around goes quiet, that sinister smile baring its fangs at me. "Found you!"

Something blocks my sight, murmuring to me to do something.

"Hecate, is it? I'm sure you told them, Beatrise?" My blood running cold from that cackle. *He knows my name now...*

Sounds of swords clashing breaks me from falling deeper into despair, I see a swift shadow battling my brother. *Alastor?* I look around for my father, who was holding me moments ago. "Papa?!?"

"Hecate, run for the horse!" Alastor yells to me, my awareness returning.

He was losing, much slower than the hooded figure spawning quickly around him, spontaneously. Time seemed to have slowed down to a snail's pace – inch by inch – I watch as Alastor is kicked to the ground. That shadow looms over him, a long dark sword raised to strike. Alastor's sword out of reach, defenceless, as the dark sword begins to descend.

"No!" I reach my hands out for Alastor, screaming. Purple energy ruptures through the earth and air suddenly. The shadow is thrown from my brother, the mist pushed away from us. I could see everything again, in real time. Soldier's body parts scattered, dead beasts, and the wagon.

My brain pulses painfully, an excruciating pain shot down my spine, just before my head hit the dirt.

ALASTOR

I sit up quickly, reaching for my sword that was knocked from my hands. An insane force rocks through everything, saving me from death. Purple light brightens my vision, my enemy thrown hard into a tree. I see him staggering up far from us, hood down.

He was just as tall without the absurd hood, hair jet black. His face symmetrical, except one dark dot under one of his striking eyes. He watched Hecate, amusement shown in his face, "You want to play as well!?"

Soldiers were riding to us – more horns being blown.

His head twitches to me, his striking eyes fuming. "This is far from over," growling towards me. He explodes into darkness, fleeing, the mist gone with him.

Turning for Hecate, I see she's lying face down, unmoving. I scrambled quickly to my aching feet, "Hecate?!" Sliding next to her, uncontrollably. Her skin is burning to the touch, her heart racing.

"LIEUTENANT COLONEL!" Gregory comes galloping over covered in blood and fur. A look of relief when he sees Hecate in my arms, "They're fleeing sir. We've secured the wagon and the women!"

It takes me a second to really let that settle in. We'd won.

...

The travel home was a blur, riding straight back through dawn's first light. I was there, yet I wasn't – my mind was shattered, my body ached all over. Sounds felt more far away, people were taking Hecate away when we arrived. My father switched from his warmongering demeanour to an old mess of a man.

He was informed before we launched the attack, Gregory had the handler do whatever voodoo to do so. Father was just riding through Newmont, like a bat out of hell with his company, as we were returning.

I stood at the doorway of her room as people of all sorts, touched and poked her with different tools. A heavy feeling of regret in my heart. My father summoned the best doctor in town to look after her. I stopped the man, as he was exiting her room, "Is she alright?"

"She is comatose. I cannot tell you what exactly is wrong, son." He turns back, studying my sister's still body, puzzled. "I imagine she has been through a lot... we must pray for her recovery."

I would pray for her, not that I believed some magical sky man would help, but I would try anyway. I am reliving a nightmare again. The state of my father brings me back to a time I fought so hard to forget.

"Father, where's mother?"

Victor looks down, attempting a smile. "Your mother's tired, Alastor, be a good lad and go with Mr. Spencer."

I watch men with funny tools enter, and exit, mother and father's quarters. Day in, day out, a new face – same words. She's tired.

I was anxious always hearing the same thing, tired too, of waiting to see her. That evening I remained hidden, until the funny dressed men and my father left her alone. Giving me a chance to slip in. The door squeaked open, I lingered to see if anyone else was inside, just in case I needed to bolt away. When all was clear, I tiptoed in, where she laid. She was motionless under the red duvet that swallowed her up.

"Mommy?"

I could hear her funny breathing as I crept forward. Her face covered in perspiration as she gripped the duvet, nails digging in. I tried again, whispering, "Mommy, are you okay?"

Barely even tall enough to see above the side of the lifted bed, I climb onto a chair for leverage. My once beautiful mother laid there – her brown eyes closed. What I thought was strange breathing was in fact whispers. I could not make out the gibberish. Only catching bits and pieces of English. "Child... Hecate."

"Mommy, it's me. It's Ally." Holding onto the arm of the chair with one hand, so I wouldn't fall and hurt her, I leant over. Her once soft hair, dry and fading. Her once full cheeks, sunken. It was scary, that pasty woman hardly looked like my mother.

"What are you doing in here, young master!?!" I'm startled, nearly falling. My sister's mother rushes over in panic, dragging me from the room.

That was the last time I'd seen her. The last memory I had of my mother, as she whispered another child's name. "Hecate..." I'm brought back from my flashback to my father's wavering voice.

Watching as he slightly rocks on the edge of the seat, holding her hand. Whispering words to her I couldn't make out, from where I stood. I run a hand through my grime infested scalp, standing around doing nothing was not going to bring justice for our people.

CHAPTER THIRTEEN

ALASTOR

The other women were brought back to the estate as well. Lord Smithe, however, took Katrina away to be treated at her own home yesterday, not long after we had arrived. After finally getting some sleep, I was back to our investigations. Tasking Gregory to aid the authorities with the local family's welfare and contacting the other towns with an update.

The captain assisting me in his stead. "Our three check out, we have two from Delwae, one from a village near Scarbra, and another from Fort Zira. There was an eighth, but I was informed she's deceased, hailing from the village near Scarbra as well. Ages ranging thirteen to twenty-seven, all names check out to the missing persons." The captain's holding a stack of papers, giving me a report.

"Did you say, Fort Zira?" I didn't know if I had heard him correctly. Fort Zira was north of the mountains.

"Yes, sir. The strange lass, Selene, no last name recorded."

I begin marking the map from the towns given to me. It made no sense from a glance, once I connected the markers with string, it formed a slanted 'J.' *Is this supposed to mean something, or a coincidence?* I follow up, "How long have the girls been missing?"

He starts flipping through the papers. His patchy dark eyebrows jumping up and down, silently skimming. "The one from the north, Fort Zira, had been missing seventeen days. Then..." He flips more papers, "The girls from the village, eight. The girls from Delwae, four, and then..." He peers up to me, apologetic.

"So, they started here." Pointing to the furthest marker, Fort Zira. We both stare at the map for some time, puzzled. *How did they infiltrate Fort Zira? The entire North-East coast was suicide cliffs...* "Do we have the northern report of attack that day, or surrounding areas that may have been hit?" Captain shakes his head to my question. "Send a letter to the mayor and find out."

He firmly nods his head once and makes haste from my office. I continue to stare at the map, deciding whether I should ask father for his opinion on the matter. He hadn't left Hecate's side, choosing to sleep in the chair, monitoring her. I did not want to involve the civilians any more than what they had been, but if my father was still adamant on not leaving Hecate. Then I didn't think I had a choice...

...

Hecate had been unconscious for five days now, father was in pieces, barely even functioning at this point. I stood in her doorway yet again, watching them both. Father rocked on the edge of the seat at her bedside, my sister laid there, unmoving.

So many times, I'd watched them from afar, observed my father learn to smile again as my sister grew up. As much as it hurt, as much as I hated it, I endured. It didn't help the growing resentment I held for them both. I wasn't like Hecate who could absorb and adapt to change quickly, who was compassionate and sometimes... No, most of the time, a pain in the ass.

I sniggered thinking back to some of our fights, how her groomed dark eyebrows would curve bat-like upon her small smooth forehead, when she'd scowl. How she would make this awful face when mocking me, crossing her eyes like an idiot. She thought she was this small mighty badass.

A noise slipped from me, and my father turned. "What news do you bring?" His words dull.

I inhaled deeply, "Unfortunately not much we don't already know. There was another town attacked in the east, as well as a village yesterday... We cannot confirm if it's the same group. Seems this path of destruction is heading towards the capital now. They are more frequent too. We've sent a letter out to the north as well, forewarning them..." I held his gaze, he slowly nodded in approval, turning back to Hecate.

"That's good..." I wait a moment, but he doesn't offer any opinions. I was nowhere near ready to take up his position, and with the uncertainty happening all over, we needed the duke.

Mr. Spencer approaches quietly, clearing his throat. "My Lord, it's time to go." Father doesn't budge. "The carriage is ready, sir."

My annoyance festers once more. I wanted to be patient with him, but for five days, myself and Spencer have been going around doing his errands. We needed all hands-on deck right now. "With all due respect, the others need you as well. You'll change nothing just sitting there watching her, we need you – "

"I left your mother alone that night, when she needed me..." I choked mid-sentence, not finishing my point. My father spoke even quieter. "Don't hate this child too much Alastor," he turns to me, eyes glossy and red. "She didn't ask for any of this, nor did Melena." My mother's name came with a voice crack, his hand covering his mouth.

That suppression in my chest returned, tightening even further, suffocating me. I leant back, holding the door frame for support. This was the first time since my mother's passing that father openly spoke about her. "I–I'll stay with her..." There was something lodged in my throat, while I tried to offer an alternative to him.

Spencer softly speaks, ushering him away. "Let's get you cleaned up..."

I stand there staring at Hecate's sleeping form, long after they had left. The sun at its highest peak in the sky, shadows casted over her. I walked to her side, "You can't die..." wondering if she could hear me, "It would break him."

Not a single twitch of the face. Her long hair, pulled down along each side of her, head bandaged like she was a fragile piece of glass. My hand shook while I reached for her slightly upturned nose, checking to see if she was breathing. I feel warm blows on my fingers and whip it back right away.

This scene all too familiar, the room smelled of medicine. An unmoving body, swallowed up by the duvet. I pull the chair closer, sitting in it, listening to her uneven breaths.

HECATE

I was back at the tree, or so I had thought. The tree was different, no gold leaves swayed on it, these branches were barren. I picked up a silver leaf from the ground, near its groovy trunk, thick roots diving into the earth. Rubbing it between my fingers, I caressed the leaf, enjoying the velvety texture. Silver residue painted my tips, sparkling as if the stars themselves laid upon them.

I looked beyond the thick branches above, the moon behind larger than I've ever seen it before. I wanted to climb the tree and reach for it. The sky here was different as well, shades of purples and dark blues. I was most drawn to a translucent green light dancing across it, reaching everywhere.

I called out, "Are you there?" I don't know who I was expecting to reply, only the wind answered, whizzing by. I walked around taking in the new sight. There was a huge stone building, similar to the other I'd seen. Trying all sorts of doors around the stone building, unfortunately, all were locked. Wherever I was, near the sea, dark waves crashing against extremely high cliffs.

I could stay here forever, the sky was astounding, but it was freezing. My breaths coming out in clouds, my teeth on the verge of chattering.

I found an open door, at long last, wanting to get out of the cold. The iron handle creaked loudly as I turned the circular latch. I poked my head inside, "Hello?" The stone corridors were quiet, my words bounced off the walls, down it. I rubbed my shivering arms and dared to venture within, torches along the walls, flickering.

Armour was displayed here and there further down. Armour of distinct designs, colours staining some of them, many looked old – outdated. The hallway branched out eventually, many others like it. I decided to keep going straight, lest I got lost.

"Si haras ellath." I would repeat this time to time, beginning to like the way the words rolled off my tongue. Half expecting that beautiful voice to respond if I said it enough.

I eventually walked out into an open room, two wide staircases leading down, opposite each other, connecting to the same landing. Even more stairs lead from the massive landing, wider than the stairs at my bare feet.

A ballroom? Soaring ceilings in the great hall, small chandeliers placed around a gigantic one at the centre. I guessed it was a ball room from the open concept. Designed to hold hundreds of people, I could faintly imagine phantom figures, twirling around down below.

I held the paint-chipped railing, making my way down. The stairs bore no rug and was cold under the pads of my feet. "A castle..." I breathed in awe. I had always wanted to visit the capital, if only to walk in one. History fascinated me, castles had long histories, and history meant stories.

There were huge paintings covering some of the walls, red dusty curtains concealing them. I pulled a yellowish-brown tassel hanging beside the biggest one on the landing. Dust fell towards my face, I sneezed from the surprise. Closing my eyes, waiting for it to settle. I was breathless from what appeared before me. Thick silver frames, framing two people painted.

One of a naked man, reaching toward a clothed one. Their index fingers nearly connecting. The naked man laid on grass, dark claws gripping and scratching his one outstretched leg. The colours dark and gloomy. The one in the sky, clothed and bearded, he was being carried away by other naked people. All the colours used there, bright and inviting. "Amazing..." I wanted this painting. I wanted it displayed among the other paintings at home. Periodically, my eyes were drawn to the dark claws. Beasts' eyes and teeth flickering through my mind.

I spun quickly, scoping out the empty hall, there was nothing but marble floors. *By the realms...* I put a hand on my thumping chest, as a head rush came over me. I sat down on the top step, going over what transpired earlier.

We had been taken... I pinched the bridge of my nose – I somehow was communicating with our captures too... I reached for my necklace, subconsciously, but my hand felt nothing around my throat. No delicate silver chain. I leapt up, my *necklace?!* Wasting no time to retrace my steps, sprinting down the corridors.

It was the only thing I had left of my mother, something she had given to me before she died. I ran out the door that I had come in from, sprinting for that tree. Throwing silver leaves around, seeing if I had dropped it here, and it blended in with the silver below.

"And what do we have here, hmm?" My muscles ceased. "Do I have a pesky rodent problem?" I inched my head behind me, silver eyes watched, unimpressed. "Ah, a child... my apologies." He bowed his hood, "Tell me child, how did you get in here?"

I could not respond, squeezing my diaphragm. I was either going to be sick, or piss myself, the latter being more likely.

"Are you afraid?" I nodded quickly, betraying myself. His pale lips pushed forward, "Those eyes... have we by chance, met before?" I shook my head this time, feeling my cheeks jiggle from the quick action. A black leather boot stepped forward, and I threw myself back. He paused, boot not fully down, silver irises on full display. "Is it the hood – it's probably the hood, children frighten easily over something so silly." His large hands removed it from his head, and a beautiful face revealed.

Everything was proportioned perfectly, nothing too big nor too small. A beauty spot ruined the phenomenon, under his left eye. His lashes dark, accompanied by strong cheek bones and an even sharper jawline that went down to a strong chin. His hair shining from the moonlight, framing his face. I was deeply troubled by that near perfect face. How could someone so glorious, be so despicable? I always imagined villains in stories I read, to be ugly and old. I expected a hideous face to be revealed.

"See? I am not so scary, now." He crouched down where he stood, speaking softly to me.

Is he fucking with me? I didn't believe the façade, not when I had seen first-hand him trying to kill my brother. Not forgetting how he tormented me through my previous dreams, that face be damned!

He tilted his head, "What is your name?" Layered black hair that reached his jaw and cheek bones, swayed. A white pointed ear peeked out on the other side of his head. My mouth struggled to open – my jaw full on chattering, by this point. "Come now, don't cry." He moved slightly, and I scrambled back even further.

I could feel the thick roots diving into the ground with my cold fingers, the tree would stop me from moving any further back. "P–please, d–don't come any c–closer!"

His hands went up in protest, nails peeking over fingertips. "Alright, okay. I'll stay here." He moved idly, sitting on his back side, "Is that better?"

Wake up Hecate!! I was screaming at myself.

"My brother sent you, didn't he?" His thick black eyebrows bunched together. He ran his fingers along them, smoothing them out. "Bastard..." A deep vibrating sigh released from his chest, I felt it in my own. "I'm not going to touch you, relax. I do not know what horrible things he said to you, though, I can imagine..." His head flicked to the side. "I'll show you the way out." He got up, brushing at himself while stepping away. His cloak followed, dragging behind him, reminding me of the villain in the mist. I was extremely conflicted and paranoid, waiting for him to turn that fake kindness into a malicious grin, or sneer.

He paused his steps, "It's this way, you won't wake up otherwise. I will send one of my men to retrieve you from whatever torture chamber he has you in." Wobbling, I followed, a great gap behind him. He seemed satisfied enough to proceed forward.

He walked to a cliff, his dark hair wildly flying back, edging toward hidden steps. "Careful, the steps are steep. There is a rope, so hold on. Dying in the dream world is just as painful in the real one."

I swallow hard. *A psychopath... That's what he is.* I didn't need to know what manner of being he was, his character was telling enough.

We scathe the side of the cliff, into fog, down to a small shoreline. The tide somehow – magically out, just here. The scene tranquil, waters calmer, as appose to the wild crashing waves when I was up there. He waits, hands in pockets - that I didn't realise he had - by a cave entry. I let go of the rope, hopping down into the sand, the last step was crumbled to nothing. Warm white sand seeps through my toes on impact.

"Just head on in there, keep going through the dark. Eventually you'll see a light, that is unless the room is dark. In which case, just keep going. You get the drift." He pivots quickly heading my way, straight back toward the steps.

I quickly sidestep, keeping a distance, sand kicking up. "H–how do I know... my impending d–doom doesn't wait for m–me, in there?"

He does not stop, "Children are a no-go for me, I'm not like him." Waving his hand, goodbye. "One of the shadows will be along shortly to retrieve you, I suggest you make haste. Unless you enjoy that bastard king's company." I watch as he begins his ascend back up the stairs, I shuffle backwards to the cave entry, keeping my front to him.

"Ah, you never told me your name!?"

CHAPTER FOURTEEN

HECATE

"Ah, you never told me your name?" Leaning forward dangerously, one hand one the frail rope, he shouts down.

I shout back, "P-Penelope!" Trying not to be suspicious.

"You don't look like a Penelope!" I can briefly make out a smile, white teeth gleaming. "Take care Miss. Penelope and do find better company!"

"And y-yours?!" *This could be vital information.* I thought.

He laughs, not that maniac laugh I had heard so often. This one was sarcastic, sad even. "It's no one of importance, I am but extra parts!" He waved one last time, his ascending figure getting higher – disappearing into the fog above.

Damn it... Once I was sure he was gone, I entered the cave. It was dark as he said, I stumbled forward blindly. I walked in darkness for hours. My feet were sore, my knees, my back – everything ached.

"You can't die... It would break him." I hear Alastor whispering, and slowly as the mad man said, I began to see a light. I pressed on further and further. *Oh god...* The light took me to a room, I opened my eyes to a canopy. Purple cloth draping down - out of focus, I could see double.

"Urg, my head..." I lifted my shaky arm, feeling something tightly around my forehead.

"My lady?!"

I lift my head next, looking left, a woman in uniform rushing out of the room. I could hear her shouting, I let my head heavily fall back, hitting the pillow. A man rushes through the doors, followed closely by another individual, next. I thought I saw relief on the individual's face. "Hecate... my girl."

My head throbbed so bad. Words felt like blows to my fragile skull.

He rubs my cheek, "Relax Hecate, you are home now, you're safe." A shaky smile grows on his wearied face. Deep blue eyes, glinting with joy. *Papa!!*

I look to the other one, remembering that he is my brother. This was my room – my home – my family.

"You've been unconscious days now," he calmly states, arms folded. Whatever I thought I seen on his face, gone. That signature frown replacing it. "We should let her rest." Alastor marches up to father, placing a hand on his shoulder.

Father doesn't move though, staring at me. His eyes darting back and forth between mine. I give him a weak nod, assuring him I was all right. He gently takes my hand, kissing the back of it, "We won't be long." All I could do was watch as father left, I had only just woken up and was exhausted. Alastor lags behind, one hand holding the door, sparing me one last look.

I closed my eyes again, only this time no dreams found me.

...

I woke with a stretch, head tilting to my side, surprised by my visitor. Alastor sat at my bedside, quietly reading in my chair. Clearing the phlegm from my throat, "Morning." I greeted him.

Cinnamon eyes look up from the page. "Evening." He had one leg crossed over the other, a black belted boot swinging slightly. His boots were polished so good the room reflected off it. His hair relaxed for once, not brushed back or even combed to the side. His attention went back down to the book in his hands. I recognized the lengthy thing, for I was reading it before everything happened.

"Thank you, Al."

He closes it, giving me his full attention, "For?"

My words next came shaky, "Coming for me..." I repeated mentally, not to cry in front of him. He would only tease me later.

Those thick eyebrows turned down. "Do you think I would be so awful to let my sister die?"

How many times have you told me to take a long walk off a short cliff? Is what I really wanted to say. "No."

"Then, do not thank me for doing what I should be doing. You are my sister, even though some days – I want to strangle you... I will always save your neck. Cannot have someone else, taking away my right."

I coughed at his words. "Did – Did you just make a joke?"

He didn't smile, slowly rising from the chair, but those browns sparkled. "Who said it was a joke?" He tucked the book under his arm and took my hand. Placing something from his warm pocket, into it. *My necklace!*

"Spencer removed it when they cleaned you up, it's been polished."

I brought it to my mouth, kissing the symbol. The symbol was a stick person, its torso a waxing crescent moon. It was by no means, fancy looking, but it was mine. The only thing left to me, the memory of my mother. *May it be a reminder of how strong and capable you are, carry it with you always... You have and will always be the light of my life. Guide others with that light too, Hecate.*

"Father should be returning soon, there was a meeting... I need to do my rounds on the others recovering." He made quick work towards the door, I just caught what he was saying over my mother's voice.

"Wait!" I screamed at him. "Are the others alright? Are the guards, okay?" I quickly put the necklace on, I had so many questions to ask, and everyone disappeared before I could do so.

He rubs the back of his neck, hesitantly speaking, "Gregory will never walk again and Trevore... " His face pained, "He died." My gut twisted, the tears I tried to keep at bay, rushing forward... "I am kidding. Trevore woke up the other day, he's on the mend. Gregory is currently working his ass off." Alastor's head tilts back, smiling a rare smile.

I try to launch one of the pillows, "You jackass!!" A pathetic attempt as it just barely leaves the bed, "That's not even funny!"

He does not respond, leaving with a shake of his shoulders.

Father visited me before bed, and again in the morning. Giving me a run-down of what's going on, and plans moving forward. The king has subpoenaed all the high-ranking lords to the capital in a fortnight's time. They were currently working on the travel route, and all the other nitty-gritty stuff. The girls rescued were all waiting to be taken back to their hometowns, finally. The recent attacks causing delays in travels, so they would travel with them.

The last girl, the northerner – I found out – didn't really have anything to return too, she was homeless. So, they didn't know how to approach her situation. I offered to speak to her.

I walked through the halls, heading toward the visitor wards on the first level, near our library. Walking seemed like a chore, even with all my rest, my legs were tired. I saw two of the girls from the wagon, snuggled together, reading on one of the lounge chairs. Their heads briefly glance up and double take. The older of the two, rising and curtsying to me. "Well met my Lady. I am Anna, this here is my sister, Olivia."

I pull my robe tighter around myself, nodding my head at them both. "Greetings, I hope you have been treated with the upmost care."

Olivia smiles wide, I see now just how young she is. "You live in a castle!" Her face lighting up as young children do. Anna's face reddens, she softly scolds her sister's remark.

I smile at their interaction, "It is unnecessarily big for our small family, isn't it?"

Anna checks back to me relieved, returning a smile, "Thank you, for everything..." Olivia peeped up again, defiantly to her sister's warning. "It was hard to see you in the darkness of that wagon but seeing you now – wowwee miss! You must be beating the boys off with sticks!"

"OLIVIA!!" Anna was trying to cover her mouth, Olivia laughs, running from her.

I too find myself giggling with them. Our chat was short, but I was glad to see colour in their cheeks, and light in their eyes. It was relieving to know, that even after everything they had been through, their spirits were not broken.

I knocked on the last door of the hallway, Spencer had said this was where Selene was staying. She had all her meals brought to her room, not daring to venture further. Unlike the others who have been out to stretch their legs, walking our gardens.

I knocked gently. "Miss... Selene?" I heard a bang, and then feet shuffling to the door. "It's me, it's Hecate," I announce myself.

The bronzed handle turns, her violet eye peering at me, "Can I help you?"

"Am I disturbing you, I can return later. I just wanted to see how you were faring?" I stepped back, not wanting to make her feel uncomfortable.

She watches me for a second, before opening the door further, glancing down the hall. "The others are not going to be joining, will they?"

"Uh–" Before I answer, she grabs me, yanking me inside. She pushes me further in, slamming the door. I recover quick, about to berate her for her actions.

"The others won't leave me alone!!"

I blink, unsure how to respond. Her white hair is braided back, large doe eyes framed within snow white lashes. She was a completely different person all cleaned up, odd, but in a refreshing way. "So, you've woke then?" She asks me, and I realised I'd been staring too long. Her arms go around herself, defensively.

I look around the room, averting my eyes conspicuously. "Well, I'm standing here aren't I... I was going to ask how you've been treated, but I take you feel slightly harassed, by the others..." I glance out the window, the other girl from the wagon, was smelling the roses below. "They don't seem so bad," I mumble out.

"Your so-called friend has been by a few times while you were sleeping. Asking me a bunch of questions. She seems like a real treat!"

I whip my head to her, those violet's aggrieved, even if her face wasn't. "Kat is.... Kat." I think back to the wagon... Selene looks away as if she wanted to give my thoughts privacy. I spin back toward the window, fiddling with my necklace. Father never mentioned Katrina visiting me while I was out, nor did Spencer... My eyes stung – some kind of dynamic seemed to have changed with us.

"What were they like?" Selene was talking behind me. I shook my head, shaking the spiralling thoughts with it.

How was I to explain this... "Scary... Kind... Different."

"Did... Did they hurt you?"

I thought back to Doc, how 'professional' he was. "No. I was taken to their camp doctor, I think. Or that's what he called himself."

"What did they say to you?" Selene pries for more information.

Knock – Knock – Knock

I spun to the door. Selene had her back up against it, one finger up to her mouth, "Yes?"

"Tee, are you in there?" An all too cheery person resounded on the other side.

I rapidly shook my head to Selene, who regarded me gladly. "Why would your friend be in my room, she has her own, does she not?" Selene says against the door, that snazzy attitude in her tone.

I had heard from father once, northerners naturally had attitudes. They usually lived secluded lives, so their way of speaking, came to offend others who were not used to their tones.

Katrina mumbles something incoherent on the other side, "Just open up." Her tone flat.

"Last I checked, Miss. This guest room was for me. Go away, I tire of your visits!" Selene raises her voice, I stare at her, wondering just how much she detested people.

"I'll have you know! I am the future Duchess of Newmont. Watch your tone with me, wench!"

I was bewildered, so many questions ran through my mind. *Did she just curse – she was future what?*

"Big talk from a girl, who the young master, seems to avoid." Selene begins mocking, her eyebrows reaching for her hairline. My head was going side to side, between their interaction. *The hell did I miss?...*

"Oh, so brave hiding behind that door you are... Remember my warning. Stay away from my man, scavenger!" Katrina yells one last time, clicking of heels stomping off.

Selene finally looks to me, back pressed against the door, still. My face must have said what I was thinking, as she spoke. "Sorry – not sorry, but your friend's a bitch."

I nod slowly, jabbing a finger behind her. "Want to explain what the hell that, was all about?" Our voices low.
She sighs, head against the door, "Where do I even begin..."

ALASTOR

Spencer stands at my office door, exasperated. "Young lord..." I noticed how he's tapping his thumb to his thigh, he only ever did that, when he was fed up with something.

"What seems to be the matter?"

"It's Lady Smithe, Miss Katrina is here again..."

For the love of God. I get up and pour myself a drink, offering one to Spencer, we all needed one as of late. The eyes he gives me, saying he wished he could. I nod and pour him one anyways, "We'll keep this between us, you've more than earned it."

He strides up, "Shall I send her away again?" Downing it in one go.

"No, I'll deal with this, thank you Spencer."

He bows, excusing himself. I sit at my desk, braising myself for her entry.

Click–Click–Click–Click

Heels tapping on the floor get louder, Katrina enters - curtsying - a sickening smile on her. She wore heavy makeup on her face. Lipstick too dark for her complexion, smeared on her lips. My stomach churns, clowns gave me the heebies, and standing at my door was one.

"Good afternoon, Ally. How's Hecate doing?"

She's playing this card again. "For all the times you've visited... I find it strange, not once, have you gone to visit her."

"A lady needs her privacy during her recovery."

"Cut the shit." I cannot stand to hear her voice or see her face. "Why are you harassing our guests?"

Her lip twitches, but she quickly schools her features. "Whatever do you mean?"

"Don't play coy, you may have my sister fooled, but not I. I know what kind of fiend you are."

Those theatrical tears return, "Ally, you're hurting my feelings..."

I clap my hands, loudly, she really could have been an actor. "Bravo, now state your business and fuck off."

She smiles, pulling out a handkerchief and dabbing the corners of her eyes. "Always straight to the point... Stay away from the northerner, the scavenger is sick with madness."

"And who are you to order me what to do? Are you an officer? A duke? The king?"

"Ally... I'm just concerned. Speaking of concern... The reason I have not visited Hecate is– "

"Hold your tongue!" I slam my hands down, my patience well ran out. "Spew your lies elsewhere, I will hear no more. Leave."

She huffs, clearly not amused I didn't allow her to finish. "There is something wrong with Hecate, she can speak the devil's tongue!" Her non-existent, thin eyebrows angle downwards. "I saw her converse with them with my own eyes, she's infected with the madness too!" She spins to leave.

"Katrina Smithe."

Her gloved hand pauses on the doorknob – the doorknob I'll have replaced the moment she's gone.

"If I hear anything about my family – my sister... and they spin back to you... well..." I toyed with a blade in my hand, pulling it out when her back showed.

"Well, what!?" She's fuming, turning back to me.

"Well wouldn't it be a shame if the young lady who is heroically saved, befell some tragic event only weeks after..." I bring the blade up to my neck, gliding the dull end across my throat.

She pales and with clicking of her heels, disappears out my door. I feel grimy just having her in my office.

There's something wrong with Hecate, she can speak the devil's tongue...

My suspicion grew after the battle when I recalled Hecate shouting... That energy that soared from her direction... There was a time when we were younger too, when her mother died, that purple energy... I pour another drink going over all the information I had gathered.

The other women gave similar statements to each other, the place was enchanted and played with all their heads, I didn't have much else from them. I wasn't satisfied, my intuition telling me there was much more. I tried to get a statement a couple of times from the northerner, but the most I got from her, was a door slammed in my face. She was even moodier, and odder than my sister.

Katrina 'came to check in' and flew into a fit, seeing me visit the woman. Shouting outside the guest's door, I walked away not wanting to deal with her. Since then, Katrina's been visiting every day, not once seeing Hecate. I noted today, Katrina had gone under some sort of identity crisis since then too.

I was glad we were leaving for the capital. A change of place and people was welcomed. Father mentioned Hecate was coming as well... Even if he had to drag her kicking and screaming.

I smiled to myself. *I'd love to see that.*

CHAPTER FIFTEEN

ALASTOR

It had been over a week since the attack and rescue, the town was slowly rebuilding. I sit on a horse, watching from a distance, people working hard together. The skies were clear, chatter and banging from the town carried to where I was positioned.

Horse hooves hitting the dirt from behind, has me alert of someone approaching. "Good morning, Lieutenant Colonel!"

"Didn't the doctor say you had a few more days in bed–" I pull the reins, "Lance Corporal Barnes?" Greeting Trevore, galloping up. He was looking stronger than he did yesterday.

"That's what I said to him, sir. The young buck doesn't listen!" Gregory, hot on his tail, pushing his older horse to keep up.

Trevore brings the horse up alongside mine, "If I continue lounging around, I may be seen as unfit for duty!" He had lost some weight in the week, but he was up, and on his feet, that was a good sign. His over-energetic self, brimming to the rim. His hair was all over the place, his uniform in disarray.

Gregory's usual stoic face was frowning, "That's because you are unfit for duty!"

I watch their back-and-forth banter, neither standing down from their points of view. The attack of our town just a memory of healing wounds. "What news do you bring?" I cut in, guessing Gregory only found me because he had some.

He strokes his horse's braided mane, "The units are ready to be mobilised as ordered, sir. The duke wants to set out first thing tomorrow. If all goes well, we should arrive at the capital on schedule."

"Sir! I wish to be brought along!" I eyeball Trevore, he's determined, the sergeant next to him looks ready to chew him one.

"You're still on the mend, Lance Corporal." Reminding him of the doctors' orders.

He rolls his eyes at me, a look I would have punched anyone else out for, but Trevore was a good lad. In the last year or so, he'd grown on me, the same way he had grown on Gregory. I found his antics amusing most days. It was hard to believe he was a year older than my sister. He didn't act his age...

"I was given' orders to guard our Lady, and I am determined to see it through, sir!"

Though sometimes he surprised me. I glance over to Gregory, if it were his choice, Trevore would have been signed off years ago. Too reckless, he claimed. The truth is, Gregory worries about him.

Trevore starts again. "I'm ambidextrous, sir. I am still able to fight with my left, you know this."

That determination would be the death of him, I had to agree, "There are still jobs to be done here..." I try to persuade him, leaning more with Gregory.

"Please... I won't fail her again."

I sigh, we all felt the sting of failure this week. I failed her too, failed to be a decent brother while training to become the duke. "Fine..." Gregory slaps a hand to his face, clearly not happy with my decision. "Everyone deserves the chance to redeem themselves...

but mark my words, Lance Corporal. Anything, and I mean anything, happens to my sister under your care..." I kick my horse to begin our ride back. "You better die this time, because I'll do much worse to you."

Regardless of the threat, Trevore's toothy grin grows, "Yes sir!"

Gregory catches up to me, "You sure about this?"

"Hecate blames herself for what happened to you both... It'll give her something else to think about." I glance back to Trevore, following. He's still smiling, straightening out his top. "Besides, I want to see her first-hand, put him, into his place."

Gregory and I share a look, the corners of his mouth twitching upwards, "Not bad... Not bad at all."

HECATE

"No. Absolutely not!"

"Hecate..."

"I don't want too." I sit up quickly, slamming my book shut. I was revising my studies earlier, looking into the family logs of accounting. My father came in with tea, for a visit, he claimed.

Apparently, I was going along on this trip with them to the capital. He almost got me, the idea of seeing the old castle, however those things were still out there. I had finally started having proper dreams, dreams of flowers and sunlight, not nightmares. No beasts, or dying soldiers, and certainly no silver eyes. I had forgotten what it was like to have a proper night's rest, and it was glorious.

"I won't." I pull the cover up, "I'll help Mr. Spencer manage the estate in your absence."

He leans back, stroking his beard, "I'll make you a deal." Pointing a finger at me, he continues. "You come along, where I can protect you myself, and I'll grant that girl's requisition with us."

I squint at the low blowing old man.

"Or, I drag you along with us, in other case, I do not grant your request for her."

"That's not fair." I really did not want to leave the house again.

"Life isn't always fair my dear..." He stands up, leaning over, kissing my forehead. "We leave tomorrow, I want you packed by tonight..."

I call out to him walking away, "And if I don't?"

He halts at my door, grinning mischievously, "Then you'll have to make do with your brother's clothes..." My jaw drops. "Either way stinker, you're coming with us." He blows me a kiss, leaving me gawking at the empty doorway.

I got out of bed, still in my pyjamas. Stomping my way over to Selene's quarters, just next door, now.

Harping on her door, she answers it, not impressed either. I storm around her, sitting on the bed. "We're going to the capital!" I blow out.

"How can I help you my Lady, oh of course you can come in, don't mind if you do... Isn't there usually a conversation, and an invite, before people enter?" She complains, plopping down next to me. "The capital is heavily guarded, be much safer there for you, anyway."

"Us." I point out.

"Us?"

"Yes, you're coming. If I must be dragged along, I'm dragging you too."

"No. No." She abruptly stands, protesting. "The agreement was, I would stay and work for my board, since I really have nothing else to return too. AND we would figure whatever was going on together! How we can understand the tongue, and why we both have premonitions of similar events – "

"SHHHHH!" I run to the open door, throwing my head out, luckily – no one eavesdropping. I carefully close the door, "Say it any louder will you?!" Whisper yelling at her.

Now she's sitting on the bed, arms crossed, sulking. "Do I really have to?"

I want to tell her she looks like an angry rabbit, but I refrain. "You can officially start working, traveling with us. It'll be easier than sending letters back and forth." She falls back onto the bed, and an un-lady-like sound comes out of her. "Besides." I add bashfully, "I could really use a friend."

Her head comes up, understanding deep in her gaze. "Fine... Fine! But I want a decent salary!"

A smile climbed my cheeks, "We only pay, the top salaries around."

Father agreed to me bringing Selene, since I decided to voluntarily cooperate with him. Selene was anxious, because I made a big order with my father then too, having clothes made up for her. She had told me she was homeless, so she needed clothing anyway. As her lady, it was my job to take care of her.

We packed Selene some of my clothes for now, unfortunately they would be loose. Her weight seriously lacking. I do not know if it was too soon to say, but I really liked her, I couldn't explain the instant connection I felt. I trusted her enough to tell her about the dreams the other day.

The look on her face when I did, had me regretting my rashness.

After a few regretful minutes, she too in fact bore a similar burden. She nervously told me about how she was plagued by night terrors; the stranger thing was what followed days or even hours after them... At first, she thought them to be coincidences.

I felt better having someone to confide in, I had not realised how lonely I was, till I let down my walls a little. I withheld the information about the silver eyed bastard, nor did she mention dreaming of anyone in particular.

That's when I offered her a job. At first, she was hesitant, but I also asked for her help with figuring out how we could understand these fae people. She was curious too, so we struck a deal, one that would help both of us.

I offered her all sorts from my jewellery box while packing and gave her free range to my shoe collection. Thankfully, we shared a shoe size.

She didn't take much, other than some boots and slippers, saying she'd make do. Whatever she wanted, she would buy with her own hard-earned money.

...

The morning arrived quickly, I stood in the front foyer taking in our home, while some of the staff were carrying the luggage out. With everything happening, I prayed this would not be the last time I'd see this place.

Alastor was coming down the stairs as I was etching every nook and cranny, into memory. He was in his silver armour, polished, our family insignia in gold on both his shoulders. "That look on your face, one would think we were going off to die, at war... We should be back in a month's time, no need to be dramatic."

I ignored his teasing, hoping he'd quietly let me go. We were going to be stuck in the same breathing space for a week, I was going to do my best to get along with him. He strolled up beside me, turning to stare as well. "I remember you pushing me down these stairs."

"I beg your pardon!" I tried to shove him aside, "You pushed me down those stairs!" He doesn't budge, scoffing at my hand still trying to move him. I try using both my hands to push him, and he still doesn't budge.

Father appears, walking in from a side room behind me. "If you two weren't trying to race and ride the railings down, neither of you would have fallen. I thank the gods above, no one was seriously hurt, other than some nasty bruises." He stops on the other side of me, hand going around, resting on Alastor's shoulder. We both leaped on our heels, attentive.

"The best thing about this foyer, is the memory of two little people who came racing in, to welcome me back." He sighed in thought, "A house is just stone and lumber, and a whole lot of useless furniture. It's the ones inside, that make it worthy of calling it, home."

Alastor's brushes off his hand, "What is with the dramatics with you two, today?!" Quickly escaping. I am curious about his red ears, as he shoots off, out the door.

"You're first long-distance journey is always a little nerve racking." He squeezes my shoulders. I smile in thanks for his comforting words. "Though I must warn you, the road is long and not at all comfortable. Get used to washing up in a river and eating mediocre food."

My smile dropped, "Oh, so now you tell me this?"

His head tips back, a proper belly laugh erupts from him. I watch as he leaves out the doors, still laughing. I take one last glance, before following them out as well.

I'm with some of the strongest company in the country... We'll be alright. I reassured myself.

As I step out the doors, blonde hair immediately catches my attention. "Tee! How exciting, we're going on a trip to the capital! Just like we always dreamed!" She's bouncing up and down, next to her mother. Their carriage is pulled in, a few wagons behind, the ones our staff were currently loading.

I leisurely descend the stairs, frowning at my father, who returns me a stupid look. Alastor's eyebrow shoots up, watching us closely, I didn't care what look was on my face.

Katrina skips up towards me, "Shall we ride together, bestie?"

I hardly acknowledge her, "I'm still rather tired, my lady in waiting will ride with me." Nodding my head toward Selene, who's fluffing the cushions inside the carriage we were to ride in.

She's wearing a fuchsia pink dress from a few seasons back, something the maids found at the back of my closet. Turned out, that was before I put a little weight on my bones. The dress really complimented her skin tone and hair, she reminded me of a pink tulip with snow on its petals.

The look on Katrina's face was unreadable, "A-A lady in waiting?" Her head shot to the carriage – her eyes nearly launched from their sockets.

"Excuse me." I brushed past her, Alastor's scrutinizing our interaction.

My father and Lord Smithe walked off with some of the higher ranks present, so I couldn't even ask him when this development happened. I was trying to keep my temper under control, when copper hair terminated my steps. Walking up to assist me into the carriage. "My Lady." Breathing became hard while I took him in, he was exactly as he was the day we went into town. Smiling smugly, his cheeks seemed less full since then, but that punch-able face all the same.

"Glad to have you back." Was all I could get out.

He seemed dazed by my greeting, offering a genuine smile. "It's good to be back, my Lady." He offered his hand to help me in, and I took it with gratitude.

CHAPTER SIXTEEN

UNKNOWN

Screams rang through the cells. "Where is she?" The hooded man asked, peeling back flayed skin.

A stranger with grey hair, cried, "I don't know, I don't know!"

"Do you take me for a fool? I know you helped her escape... Who else helped her, hmm?" He did not stop, peeling back a layer, and then another. The aging man thrashed against the holds, iron cuffs holding him down to a table. Blood dripped onto the stone floors, creating puddles. "Your suffering will cease. All I ask is your compliance..." He paused, giving the hostage a chance, his fingers glimmering red.

"She asked to be taken aboard a ship... That's-That's the last time I saw her! I swear, I swear!" Blood oozed from all sorts of places, cuts, and bruises all along his torso.

"Tsk... How disappointing..." He flicked his hand, one of his nails lengthening dangerously long. "Then it appears, I have no use for you." A swift flick of the wrist, the hostage's head was severed, rolling off the table. A frustrated sigh followed the thud, the head running away even in death.

A shadow forms, swirling up behind, the hooded one. "You summoned me, my liege?"

Silver eyes contemplated, "Yes… tell His Highness, I will be returning… First, I want this one's head reattached, then I'll take him with me, and drop him off somewhere nice. I'm sure they're wondering why things have gone quiet. Wouldn't want them disappointed."

"I'm sorry my liege. His Eminence has asked, that you return to him, first."

Boots scoffed the stones, blood splashing up his trouser pants, "Oh?" The shadow spreads out, more emerging from the depths of its darkness. "An escort is this? I'm flattered!" He laughs, maniacally to the entourage. "Come then, we mustn't keep lord brother waiting any longer."

...

The walk through the dark halls seemed endless, the hooded one strides up to a wall entirely of dark doors, followed by the shadows. Two stone creatures were guarding the door, watching the approaching visitor.

"I've come to see His Highness." A coy smirk playing on his pale lips.

The doors groaned open. A dark rug ran across the great hall, toward grey stone stairs. Pits of green flames beside the stretching rug, lighting the path forward.

He marched in, the shadows unable to follow further than the threshold of the doors. Nails running along rock, echoed along with his steps, creatures of flesh and claws, crawled across the high ceilings.

Silver irises stopped at the steps, leading up to a monumental dark throne, mocking a bow. "I greet the darkness between Heaven and Hades. Long may he reign and corrupt the souls of all."

A being sits on the throne, his hair long and black, secured down by a dark crown. Golden irises, scorching like the sun, looked upon him. "Welcome Prince, Lord Commander of the Legions. You were summoned to my presence days ago, why have you delayed?"

The hooded prince is forced by the king's immense aura, to hold his bow. "I was... preoccupied with duties... my King."

HECATE

"You're quiet..." Selene was playing with the ends of her braid, speaking to me.

"My heads a mess..." I sigh, almost growling, "As usual."

"Is it Piss-head?"

I straighten up, "Piss-head?" Wondering who she was talking about.

"Your friend, the squawking duck, pisshead. That's what her hair looks like to me." She shakes her head as if that were something obvious.

"One, never call her that, least not to her face. You would get into trouble, and as my lady in waiting, it'll fall to me. Two..." She stared, listening for me to go on. I lean back, "There is no two..." I didn't want to fight with anyone today. Katrina joining our journey was a huge surprise. I was hoping to organise my thoughts and feelings, before returning home, and confronting her. Plus, seeing Trevore made me feel emotional, and triggered, all at the same time. The last time I was with them both, everything kicked off, I couldn't help the ominous feeling in my gut.

"Listen, she is not a particularly good friend to you. I know first-hand what folks like her are like and seen how she discarded you the moment that man reached in at us."

I considered Selene's words. "My brother once said – just because they laugh with you, doesn't mean they are always your friends... real situations expose fake people... Or something like that..."

"AND HE'S ABSOLUTELY RIGHT!" I gawked at her outburst, a fist slamming down against her palm. "Been there, done that. I get you must be civil because of your position or whatever. That doesn't mean you have to tolerate her shit either. That air you put on before entering the carriage was awesome! You looked like a scorned queen, girl."

"My Lady..."

She tilts her head at me, "What?"

I laughed at her confusion, "Make sure when it's not just the two of us, you address me as, my Lady... We really need to work on your speech too."

Her cheeks flushed, puffing up. "Yea I know, I know... I must stay quiet when you're addressing someone of higher rank, I must..." She began mumbling over what the maids were telling her earlier.

"I owe my brother an apology."

She stops her list, mouth still open. "We all make mistakes, Hecate. I think recognising them, and learning from them for the future, is a very mature thing to do..."

I nodded my head with her words, "You're right... your council is appreciated... Did you ever go through something similar?"

Her head slightly shook, "I was alone, I was forced to grow up fast... See things first-hand, and most of the time, it isn't sunshine and rainbows." Her hand found her hair again, twiddling with the ends. I realised when she was uneasy or unsure about something, she fiddled with her hair between her fingers.

"Hmm." Her words made sense, "Off topic, I know... but how old are you, if you don't mind me asking?"

She paused, thinking, "I think twenty-five, twenty-six... I don't even know my actual date of birth, just that I was born during a long winter."

My heart ached for her, father always made my birthdays special, everyone deserved to be celebrated. "Pick a day, any day. Moving forward I'll be sure you never forget. We can even throw a winter party for your birthday."

She smiled, it was an awkward one, but a smile all the same. "I... I would really like that... Thank you... my Lady." She picked up her notebook and continued practicing her writing. It wasn't terrible, but for her position she needed to improve it. I was oddly proud of her for really giving this everything she had.

The carriage ride was quiet, I used the time to think about how to approach things, and what were my priorities. "Hey Selene?" She looked up from the notebook, pen in hand, her tongue sticking out between her thin lips. "What does my hair look like to you?"

She snickered at me, without hesitation, "Raven feathers."

...

Selene woke me up with a gentle shake, "Hey were stopping, I think your boyfriend said were camping for the night." I must have drifted off during the ride.

My neck was achy, sleeping funny, "My what now?" I rubbed my face, wondering who she was talking about this time.

"Coppertop, he's been riding alongside us this whole time. Every now and again I'd catch him throwing you longing looks." She stealthy pointed out the window to Trevore, dismounting his horse. The back of his shirt was riding up, I caught a glimpse of his bandages.

"He is not my boyfriend." I scoffed, "He is our guard, besides my father would murder anyone I even dared, thought about." I was trying to see more of the bandages, face close to the glass. Then my eyes met Trevore's, he threw me a wink, before going to secure the carriage. "What the hell was that?!"

"Uh huh, sure, not your boyfriend, you say." Selene goes for the door, just as it opened, my father is standing there.

"What did I just overhear?" His face, disturbed. *Oh my god, kill me now...* My father helps Selene out, offering his hand next, for me. He holds my hand a little longer, pulling me closer. "Boys are gross, never forget that."

"I'm not a child anymore, father!" My head whipping around for anyone listening. "Besides, you and Alastor set a pretty high bar to be achieved!"

A smile replaces his tight lips, pleased with my answer. "Stretch your legs, we're having stew, shouldn't be long. You and your lady in waiting..." He nods his head to her, standing by, "Will sleep inside the carriage, I don't want either of you leaving this facility." He gestures around the group of soldiers making camp. "And keep two metres away from the men."

I roll my eyes to his defensiveness, Selene's fighting a smile. Katrina's mother exits her carriage from the corner of my eye, I grab Selene's hand and begin walking the opposite direction. "Where are we going?" She grips my hand back.

"Stretching our legs over there!" I was evading any run ins, knowing Kat, she moaned to her mother about me. I really did not want to know what she may or may not have said, my heart was feeling fragile.

We weaved around men in all sorts of different uniforms, some wearing the Newmont symbol of crossed swords, others the Crosse insignia. I spot Alastor giving instructions to an armed group, near a makeshift canopy. Gregory standing shoulder to shoulder with him. I decided to linger near them, I didn't know what exactly to do with myself, otherwise. I snuck a glance back to Katrina's carriage, and Trevore's body was blocking my sight. A lopsided grin on his face.

Tonight's going to be a rough night.

Just as I was in thought, a scream filled the cool setting sky. Everyone grew quiet, another shrilling scream followed, a banshees shrill. Selene tucked in closer to me, Trevore suddenly at my side.

My brother booms across the camp, "There are many things we all need to be aware of. Keep to your duties, stay within the group, and do not stray into the darkness. Anything suspicious, cut it down! We are to take no chances. Do I make myself clear!?"

"Yes sir!" The company shouts in unison, I flinch from not covering my ears fast enough.

Trevore warns us next, "If you need to stretch your legs then please stay close, ladies." He flicked his head toward the fires, "They fear the flame and the light it provides, try not to go further than what the light reaches."

I apprehensively ask, "What happens if it rains..." I did not see any clouds in the sky above, but things could easily change, the weather was never certain.

"Can we go back to the carriage?" Selene's hand trembles, whispering to me. I nod my head and begin quick steps back, Trevore tailing close. He opens the door to assist us and Selene flies in so fast she was a blur of white and pink. We both look at each other stunned – his hand still offered out.

I accept it instead, taking a step up. "If you want someone to read you a bedtime story –" I whip my hand out from his, that smug look plastered on his face.

I speed up, "Goodnight!" Slamming the door without thanking him.

The night was rough as predicted, Selene and I both barely slept. We peeked out through the curtains, as the men outside took turns, some sleeping, others patrolling. I was flabbergasted by the fact they could sleep at all. Not by the fact they slept on the ground, but for the noises that taunted us all night. Not a single animal noise, father visited late into the night, saying that's how you knew something far more dangerous lurked near. When the animals themselves were quiet. It spat through the night too, Selene and I deciding to sit closer to each other, watching each window. Once the sky began turning pink and shades of orange chasing away the clouds, that's when we finally rested.

Her head on my shoulder, my head on hers.

I woke to constant shaking, my head snapping up. I laid across one of the box seats, Selene the other. Two thin travel throws covering us. Selene was grumbling in her sleep still, bouncing up and down. The sun was high in the sky, not a tree in sight, Trevore riding along side. Wondering who and when we were moved, praying it wasn't him.

I sat up, running my fingers through my hair, scratching my scalp. A basket on the floor, piqued my interest. Opening the basket for further inspection, fruits and sandwiches laid inside, a canteen of liquid too. I screwed off the lid, drinking the water. I rummaged through the basket, picking out a sandwich and an apple.

Selene sat straight up, like a tree bent back and released, frightening me. I nearly choked on the apple I had bitten. She was covered in sweat, her amethyst eyes bulging, white lashes twitching. "Are you alright?" I inquired, handing her the canteen.

She stared at nothing, rattled by something. "Selene?" I reached for her knee, shaking it lightly.

Her eyes snapped to me, "I... I wasn't alone."

"It's alright, I'm right here." I rubbed her knee, reassuring her.

Her eyes started rolling, "Silver.... Eyes." Before falling back, unconscious.

ALASTOR

We had been lucky on our first night. Father and some of the senior officers took first shift, separating all others into the three rotating groups. With fall around the corner the nights were getting longer. I was placed on second rotation, I blonked myself down after a hearty bowl of stew and bread, getting ready to sleep.

Most of us were used to this.

I watched our family carriage, seeing Trevore pace back and forth. I was glad he was taking his job seriously, more surprised he didn't try to make advancements toward my sister. A part of me was eager to see Hecate bloviate the ladies-man ego. She had a gift for humbling men, especially when they thought they could slide into her lane. I had witnessed her first-hand, making a grown man weep from a single sentence, one eyebrow sky high.

Red glints in my peripheral view, father was making his rounds, Wrath strapped to his back. He had put his armour on, prepared for combat, his red butt cape swinging with every step. His cruises and greaves making his legs look thick and impenetrable. The man's pauldrons had always been my favourite, they extended his wide shoulders even further, more platinum than my own. The family insignia on his left one, black fur around the back of the neck making it appear as though they were inter-connected. I pitied the fuckers who'd have to face off with him, the man looked like the devil, especially when he had his horned helmet on.

Another snarl let loose deeper in the darkness. He altered to its location, unsheathing his sword, and planting it into the ground before him, waiting. This was the reason we were able to sleep, this was the Lord Protector of the People.

When I opened my eyes next, Gregory was kicking me for my shift. I stiffly rose, "I ought to knock your teeth in." Rolling my shoulders back to ease the stiffness.

He sniggered at my miserable state, "Time for switch out, I've knocked off Trevore, I'll take the carriages."

I inclined my head to his report, standing. The night was quiet, clouds blocking out the stars. The smell of rain carrying on the air. "Fuck..." If it rained and those fires were put out... I put my suit on, preparing for the worst. There was no need to worry about the what ifs, we just needed to expect the unexpected.

I walked over peering into the carriage quickly, careful not to spook the girls inside. They had the curtains closed, but the sound of sniffles could be heard. Hecate was probably fuming for having been brought along.

My shift was quiet, no other sounds of life outside the camp.

When it was time to rotate again, I found myself unable to sleep. Rain began to spit, nothing heavy fortunately, that would douse the fires. Nonetheless, I was on high alert, fearing the rain would come down harder, any second.

Many others awake too, feeling the same. Father was among them, he checked on the girls when it begun. Placing himself within leaping distance of their doors, sat, watching the flames. I sat down on a log across from him. "Get some sleep Lieutenant Colonel." His intense stare down, never leaving the fire.

"I've slept enough, sir." I studied him carefully, the flames roaring in the reflection of his pupils.

"Help her, Alastor." He amended, hands running through his hair. "Teach her a way to defend herself..." I choked on air, and he looked to me, a serious look.

"I thought – "

"I know... I know... The older I get the more I realise, I won't always be around to protect her... I have been too easy on her, as you have said. I fear now what that may cost me..."

"I do think she should know the basics of self-defence..."

A small smile crept up his face, "She does... Kick them where it hurts." I grimaced, *by the realms,* my hands covering my crotch. My father chuckled, "Your mother would be furious with me for the way you turned out."

"Don't start this now, of all – "

"You're a lot like me in my youth, hard-headed, and always trying to take the world on alone... But you're not alone my son, we're all here for you."

I stopped protesting, "Are... Are you dying or something?" Keeping my voice low enough, not to create panic.

"Heavens, no" He cracked up, "I've been so busy these years, it's like I've blinked and you've both grown up... I've been asking myself lately, where has the time gone." He shakes his head, "Or perhaps this old man of yours is getting sappier with age." He rose from his seat, walking past me, patting my shoulder. "I'm proud of you..."

I sat there, staring at the fire as he did, till the sun peeked over. I went to the carriage again, this time opening it. Both girls were asleep, holding hands. Selene had tear-stained cheeks, they looked equally uncomfortable.

I tried to be as quiet as possible, the floor of the carriage ratting me out, groaning from my weight. I moved my sister to the other box seat. Her eyebrows frowned, those bat-like arches appearing. I battled the laugh brewing in my chest, a miserable git even when she was sleeping. Once they were both laid out, I pulled a couple blankets out from the sliding compartments underneath and covered them.

I would try with Hecate, just to ease father's mind.

CHAPTER SEVENTEEN

ALASTOR

We were back on the trail again, units spread out, we had crossed one of the three main rivers that flowed down to sea. Now just a day's ride from Delwae' s rendezvous-point, we brought along the women needing to return, a tactic group would meet us as we rode through.

We approached an endless plain, stretching far, a green tree line way in the distance. This was how we would spend today, riding east to reach that tree line. A unit from Delwae would meet us along that and take the women back to Delwae the following morning.

As we inch through the never-ending land, a green bird circled above. "Duke! Message inbound!" One of the soldiers alerts, a whistle is blown to signal the bird to land.

A bird whose feathers mimic all shades of green to hide among the trees. Its wings with six black markings, two bigger ones and four smaller ones. As the bird's wings were down, one could easily mistake its wings for a spider's face, by the way the dots and feathers coordinated. Nature's natural shield to detour predators from hunting it. A bird that was easily trained as a dog, and could grow to the size of a goat, its wingspan tripled its body size. A Fechin.

It swoops down, diving straight for the bird handler. I ride up to get a closer look, the bird's magnificent brown beak tagged with a small insignia. A mini bird soaring, the symbol of Klaedo. The handler removes the letter from the bird's brown claws, handing it to my father who rode down to join us from the front. "Klaedo's been attacked, following another madman incident..." His tone is grave.

"Sir!?" One of the higher rank officials speak up, "Klaedo is down by the shore, wedged between our last major river crossings."

Father looks back to our company, and then ahead, the path east. "Indeed... We make camp earlier tonight. We need to plan an encounter." Tucking away the letter, he addresses those present. "Some of you have battled these sons of bitches, were counting on you now for intel. Move out!" He spins his black stallion, racing for the front.

I instinctively look for our family carriage, riding for Trevore. "You may get your chance at those bastards yet." Lowering my voice as I came next to him.

His nonchalant face, turned fierce, "Understood." I galloped forward – this was why I liked the kid.

HECATE

I dabbed a cloth to Selene's forehead while she was out, monitoring her. When she woke again, I gave her time to collect herself. She was dazed for a while, paler than usual. Like the version of her I met in the wagon.

I came clean about the silver eyes, starting the conversation first. I don't know if it was to clear my conscience or to help her. I told her not only did we encounter him when we were taken, but I had nightmares about him on two occasions. Which coincidently stopped around the time Selene came to our home.

"He asked about Hecate, the crone... He wanted to know where the hag had gone."

It was startling but I pressed on, explaining the pleasant dream when I thought I had died. The woman in the lake, and somehow even the fae-people saw me as an old woman.

"An enchantment..." Was all she whispered, listening carefully to my story.

I finally told her about the latest bump in, when I met him again, he saw me as I was. I told her I called myself Penelope in the dream, and how different his demeanour was.

She continued to stare at me, her face greening, "Hecate, if he finds out..."

"I know...." I knew the possible consequences, but I didn't know why, why they were taking women. Why any of this was happening, so many damn whys. I was beyond stressed and on edge.

Selene and I cleaned ourselves up, trying to be as normal as possible. The carriage slowed briefly, shouting about a bird inbound, outside the moving box.

"I'm a witch..." Selene's voice was quiet, no more than a whisper, tears filling her eyes. "That's why my family abandoned me at the orphanage, my very existence was the devil's work. I'm sorry..."

She looked scared of me – of my reaction. "I didn't ask for any of this, I don't want to die for being born this way." Her face went into her hands, her shoulders shaking uncontrollably.

Goosebumps took over my arms, "Do... Do you think all witches have these dreams?" The energy I had felt in the forest, imprinted on my spine.

She lifts her face from her hands, liquids dripping from her nose now too. I pull the handkerchief from my pocket, offering it to her.

"You think maybe– "

"Yea..." My words break off. Too many things to be brushed off as coincidences anymore... "And were heading straight to the capital of all places..."

"Let's run away!"

I shake my head at her quick solution, "We won't make it long out there..." The truth was hard pill to swallow.

She curled up on the seat and sobbed quietly into her hands. I covered her with a blanket, telling myself repeatedly I would not cry, crying would not solve this... Alastor flies up to Trevore, quick words were exchanged as he kicks off forward even more.

You are my sister, even though some days – I want to strangle you... I will always save your neck.

"We need help..."

...

We made camp earlier, the sun barely even begun its descent. Selene was in no mood to stretch her legs, so I decided to put my plan into action alone. I stepped out of the carriage, Trevore quickly marching up. My feet hit ground before his hand reaches out to assist me, I return my own smug look to him. *See, I can do it myself.*

We were posted in the middle of a field, the grass long and yellow. Uneven ground in patches, huge pieces of land rising-up in some spots. We stopped in an area – I'm assuming – they could use the higher grounds as lookouts, giving us the advantage for attacks. I watched the men carry boxes and crates around, some building canopies, others starting fires. I was looking for my brother, head bobbing about, my ponytail swinging heavily.

"How can I be of assistance, my Lady?" Trevore stands next to me, with his arms folded.

"Do you know where my brother is?"

His head looks out, chin flicking forward, "Probably in the middle of a briefing." I curse, and Trevore lightly chastises me, "A lady shouldn't curse." A toothy grin on his face.

I roll my eyes at him, "Thanks dad." Strolling further into camp, my boots crunching the dry grass. It slipped my mind while I was preoccupied with my plan, forgetting another issue at hand. Katrina. She comes bee lining for me, with a look on her face...

"Hecate!"

I slow my steps, side eyeing her. Trevore questions my body language, "Shall I intervene, my Lady?"

"No... I cannot keep running away from everything." I meant to keep that to myself, but he tilts his head, repositioning himself back.

She throws a tantrum right in my face, "Why have you been avoiding me, you know how upset you've made me?!" Many men look over, some dismissing it quickly, some frowning.

I school my facial features, I was aware my eyebrow liked to wonder, and there were still eyes on us.

She wore a distinctive style of dress than what she normally did, this one pushing her chest up to her chin. Her hair down, curls free of restrains. I barely got a look at her when we left the estate, the last time I had really seen her, we were in the back of that wagon. The dress she was wearing now, dark, not as fluffy or structured as her usual attire. There was a slit right down the middle, exposing her long stockings.

I crossed my arms, the same way Alastor usually did, finger tapping my bicep. "Avoiding? What a presumptuous thing to say..." My tone firm, back straight.

"Hecate!?"

"Katrina Smithe, I am standing right in front of you. You will lower your voice when addressing me."

I hear Trevore choke on something behind me, Katrina's face faltering with my firm attitude. "Tee, I – "

"Since we're on the topic of..." I quoted my fingers in the air, "avoidance, shall you start first as to why you – have been avoiding me even before we set off for this trip?"

She wobbles in her spot, stiff eye lashes fluttering quickly, she had layers of mascara on. A striking resemblance to spider legs, "You were recovering, Tee, I – "

My hand comes up, stopping her, her head pulls back at my action. "I've heard quite enough... If you'll excuse us, my guard and I have business to attend too." Trevore steps forward to my side again, Katrina steps back, anger washing over her features. She turns quickly, stomping back in the direction she came from.

I exhale deeply, a pain striking my chest. Eyes turn away, some nod as they carry on with duties.

"Well done, my Lady." I try to brush off Trevore's words, it felt wrong acting that way towards someone I considered a good friend. Trevore carried on, "There's a time for being friends, and drawing the line as a superior. You handled that well."

That pain worsened, like my heart was breaking, "Well it doesn't feel nice..."

"No, I suppose it doesn't." He says no more, gesturing for us to maintain our direction. I raised my chin, walking towards a dark canopy made on the other end of camp.

So many swords, and other weapons, I hadn't realised how much the men were armed. Some in full on armour gear, that confidence I had slipping. I felt small among the armoured giants. My attention was snagged by a wooden crate of stones, an assortment of colours. I redirected my path toward them.

A grey bearded man sat inspecting them, pulling more out, and using a magnifying glass on them. When he was done with the stone, he placed it in one of two piles.

"Mana-stones, my Lady." I twisted to Trevore, stopping quickly, causing him to collide into me. Arms fly around my waist to keep me from falling back from the force.

"S-sorry!" I quickly remove his arms and gain my composure. His face and neck as red as the hair on his head. I cleared my throat, "Mana-stones, here?" Trying to revert to what I was going to ask him.

The gentleman behind me, speaks up, "Would you like a closer look, miss?"

I turned, approaching him, carefully. Keeping my fingers glued to my sides, the itch to reach out, strong. My face must have said what was going through my mind. "These are not the typical gems and jewels you're used to, ugly stones here, but effective. The colour of them, is the reaction to the magic they are holding."

That's awesome... I breathed out, "Like colour schemed?" I met the man's eyes, I thought they were brown from a distance. Looking closer, they were the colour of seaweed, his eyebrows bushy, resembling squirrel tails.

His eyes examined me just as carefully as the stones, "Correct."

I held my own hands now, fingers interlocked, a temptation to fidget with something. "Can you explain the concept of them, and what the colours mean..." I sat down on another crate placed by, eager to know more. "Please?"

He sat straighter, "Certainly."

I found out the man's name was Marcus – he was a certified mana–handler. Something that took years of his youth to acquire. Not only did I listen and learn about the stones, but I inquired about his travels through the continents. He spoke with such passion about the stuff he learned and experienced, I was shocked to learn he was well in his seventies, he did not look his age.

I felt comfortable conversing with him, not once annoyed with the many questions I randomly fired at him. He snickered, calling me a curious cat. Someone brought us snacks at one point, and I ate quietly as he showed me the uniqueness of each stone and the species, they correlate too.

"This right here..." A dark red stone was in his wrinkly hands, "Was what aided us in tracking that group down."

"Because it's enabled with tracking spells, yes, the red?" I leaned forward.

"Yes, and no. Remember the colours associated are not just the type of magic, but species they derive from."

The sun had quietly set while we spoke, it wasn't until a soldier approached Marcus that our conversation ended. I had no idea how long I sat there, my mind clearer from the information he offered.

"It's a rare thing..." He spoke, collecting a few stones to place around the camp.

"What is?"

"We live on an island surrounded by a sea of ignorance. As we inquire more knowledge, the shore of our ignorance, grows..." He tosses a stone, catching it. "Seeing someone of your youth, be so inquisitive and understanding, about something others see as taboo, is refreshing. As the years go by, we all lose sight of what really matters, allowing fear from the difference between us, to divide us further apart."

I spoke up, finishing, "Fear is the real enemy... Born of ignorance..." I knew those lines from somewhere.

He smiles so wide I notice one of his premolars missing. "And she has a good taste in literature too." He laughs, "It was a pleasure conversing with you, my Lady."

I shot to my feet, curtsying, "The pleasure was all mine, Sir."

When I raised my head to bid him farewell, Alastor was sitting on another crate, leaning toward us.

CHAPTER EIGHTEEN

ALASTOR

"We cannot be sure if it was the same group, but what we are sure about is, even in small numbers, they are a unit of raw power." I pointed to a rough sketch, showing them the weak spots, we were shown. "Their size is intimidating but also their weakness. Get past those dagger–like claws, and teeth, their neck here, is the easiest way to bring them down." I moved the stick to the underbelly, "Find yourselves unfortunately under them, slash down and open them up. Kills them slower but does the trick."

"Surely a sword to the head can effectively bring them down?" Harold inquires, hand raised standing at the back of the group.

Gregory speaks up, "Eventually sure, their skulls are tough as stone. You'll only blunt your blade, leaving you defenceless to the next."

Lord Smithe covers his mouth with that raised hand.

"Not to mention some of them can use magic, our town seen first–hand how they come and go like the wind. Mana–stones must be attached to your belts, shielding you from manipulation of the mind." I folded my arms, making eye contact with many, "If the silver eyed sorcerer appears, your mana–stone is literally the difference between life and death."

"By the realms..."

"This is futile!"

My father pushes off a post walking to the front, the men quieting down with his every step. He glares at the paper, as though the beast were right here with us. "We have no intel of their numbers, but we do know that fifty of our best fought them, and had them fleeing. Even with that sorcerer among them." He pulls a blade from his belt, stabbing the paper on the board. "They've got double of us to deal with this time."

Everyone filed out after the briefing to resume duties, Gregory and I were going over inventory checks, coming across Trevore standing by.

"What are you doing here, Lance Corporal?"

His head flicks forward, "On duty, sir."

I follow his line of sight – my sister was eagerly chatting away with Marcus. She was in a long ankle skirt of grey, a turquoise long sleeved dress shirt, tucked into her skirt. A white bow hanging around the neck, her hair for once put in a high pony tail, a smaller white bow tied into it.

"She's a chatter box when she's piqued by something, almost as bad as him." His head gesturing to Marcus. I double take when I catch a weird look in Trevore's eyes. His pupils massively dilating observing my sister.

"To be honest with you, Trevore. I'm surprised you haven't tried wooing her off her feet."

Colour explodes over his neck and cheeks, he shifts to me, offended. "Sir, I take my duty very seriously, sir!"

Oh?

"Since, uh, when?" Gregory barks next to me, peering up from the sheet. Looking flabbergasted from Trevore's statement. Trevore's face flushes a shade darker even more, if we pushed more, I was sure his head would explode.

"So, what does purple mean?!" My sister's excited voice draws my attention back to them. Gregory and Trevore's voices – bickering next to me, fade off, as I tune into her conversation.

"Uh good question!" Marcus picks up a stone, identical to a plum. "Purple has many meanings, ranging for the magic itself and whatever being! Purple signifies physic ability and power..." Marcus inhales a deep breath, prattling on, "Divination, spirituality, and enchantment!"

Purple energy throwing the enemy off me, flashes through my mind. I observe my sister's eyes widening, my feet take off on their own. Sitting down within ears distance, learning as well.

Marcus was spewing out so much information, my brain was melting, but Hecate was absorbing it all. I sent Trevore away, swapping our shifts, I would watch over Hecate tonight. I did so discreetly. My sister's eyebrows would bunch then rise, her eyes shadowing over then sparkling. She was a sponge, soaking in ever little word thrown to her.

"They called themselves Fae, when we spoke." My ears perked up, she never mentioned them speaking to her, or vice versa.

Katrina's voiced echoed. *She can speak the devil's tongue!*

Marcus nods his head, "Fae are old beings, and they live long lives too. Ranging from shape shifters to sirens and so on. We are dealing with the dark fae species."

"Dark fae?" Hecate leans forward, intrigued.

"The fae, like us, have families, or more so houses and courts. Their language derives from different dialects of the old elvish language. They claim it to be the tongue of the gods. Dark fae are said to be born from the House of Darkness or Court of Death, feared by the elvish ancestry. Dark fae have interbred their kind for maximum magical spectrum... This right here..." Marcus picked out a dark red stone, I remember him waving one similar, around. "Was what aided us in tracking that group down."

A soldier pulled Marcus away, Hecate stood up and jumped when she finally noticed me. I rose slowly, she looked to be contemplating something, straightening her back, she marches up to me... Then swerves around my side, heading straight to her carriage.

The hell?

She fled to her carriage and hid away ever since.

...

The rendezvous was a success on our part, the tactic group picked up the women and left as planned. We travelled for two days and camped two nights undisturbed after that. We were now only a day's ride from our next major river crossing, the halfway point. Father wanted to camp before the river, so we wouldn't have to camp between them. Not a single person disagreed, it was our safest choice.

Hecate hid away, hiding from Katrina and her mother as well, when they tried to visit the carriage. Trevore intervened on their behalf claiming the girls to be travel sick.

I saw Hecate for a moment yesterday and she took off scarce. Avoiding all interactions, she considered unnecessary. I was beginning to think I was the paranoid one, over thinking all this.

Anger bubbled inside me, *they called themselves fae, when we spoke.*

Yesterday I pulled Marcus aside, drilling him with questions next. Was being able to speak to them something you learned, a born quality, or a sickness. My ears were abused with the information next. Turns out most people had to spend years of their lives learning the language like any other, and even then, that took decades as the tongue was a complicated one.

The only other exemption, beings with specific ancestry. The mana flowing through their souls gifting them to be able to adapt to their surroundings, the gift of absolute truths. Also, life's river that flowed through all our chakras or something else. I clued out after hearing what I needed to know from him.

"Can I offer you a little advice, Lieutenant Colonel?"

I turned to Marcus, what more could he have to say?

"There are reasons, people hide this sort of knowledge. Fear. Be kind and open minded, we live in a society that condemns those for being different." The man raked me over, as though he was ready to throw down, depending on my answer.

A sinister smile grew on my lips, "Is that why you decided not to bring this to my attention, Marcus. Do you think I would condemn, my own sister?" I was hissing at him.

His head nods off to the side, "Not everyone feels the same... Others may see you as biased, for the sake of saving face." I nearly grabbed him, but he never allowed me to state my opinion on the matter. "If it's any consolation, she's a good child. The world would be a different place with more people like her... My lips are sealed." He tucked his hands into the cloth of his sleeves and wondered off.

I saw the old man in a new light.

Hecate never mentioned speaking to them when I took a statement from her, nor did she mention anything to father. I was not going to rely on a statement from Katrina, she was a rat, a pest in need of ridding. I rode along, mind swamped with so many questions, I had a gut feeling that if I kept investigating, things would finally make sense. All the answers were there, I just needed to reach out and take them.

Our entourage made camp as planned, the sound of the river roaring in the background. I stalked from the distance, for one of the girls to exit, but Trevore was speaking to them quietly through the door. His head was leant against it, a soft smile tugging on his lips.

Oh ho. This was a new development, I wondered how much Trevore knew. My target now in sight, I would get this briefing over with and corner him next.

HECATE

I chickened out speaking to Alastor that night, the look on his face was deadly, just as I neared him my heart screamed – abort mission. I fled to my carriage, Trevore was sleeping when I tripped over him, camping near our box.

"My Lady? Where is the Lieutenant Colonel?!" He sprang up from the ground, scrambling for gear.

I lied, "He'll be along, sorry for waking you. Goodnight!" I scurried inside quickly. Frightening Selene, who was drawing.

"How'd it go?" She closed the book, waiting.

I sighed defeated, "I couldn't do it..."

Understanding shown in her clear eyes, she seemed better than when I left her earlier. The next morning, I popped my head out, finding Alastor asleep. The sun far away from rising.

Trevore scares me, "Why are you sneaking around?" I nearly tumbled out of the carriage.

"I am not sneaking! I am just being mindful, to those sleeping!" I lied, again.

"With all due respect my Lady" He held the door, standing before me, I was still on the top step, towering over him. *"The corners of your lips twitch downwards just before you tell a lie."*

"They do not!"– *"They do."* – *"They do not!"* – *"They do."*

"How would you know?!" I was whisper yelling, glancing, and checking Alastor's movements.

He leans putting all his weight onto his hip, *"I'm watching your every move."* That signature smug look on his mug.

I covered myself, giving him a once–over, *"That's creepy."*

"Uh–wait" – he stammered – *"that came out wrong!"* His hands up, fussing.

I slammed the carriage door.

The next time we camped, Katrina and her mother visited, or tried too. Trevore fed them a story of how we've been road sick, asking for their understanding while we rested. Father visited after hearing we were unwell too, I felt bad for going along with it... He brought light snacks to eat but left us alone mostly, I could see guilt in his face when he was speaking with me, about the rest of our journey.

That night, a nightmare came over me, beasts jumping at me, clawing for me. Those silver eyes high in the sky, watching down on me from above, I woke making noises. Selene woke alarmed but was quickly at my side, and Trevore swung the carriage door open, alert for the intruder.

That was embarrassing enough.

I could not fall back asleep after all that, too scared to close my eyes, cabin fever hit me hard. I dared a venture out for air, Trevore was waiting, leaning against the side of the carriage.

"Shouldn't you be sleeping?"

I countered his question, with my own. "Shouldn't you?"

He considered something, his hazel eyes slowly blinking. "Do you and the Lieutenant Colonel not get along... Pardon me, if I'm prying?"

I shook my head, "It's fine, you'd be surprised how many people ask me that actually..." He helped me out and I sat on the steps, not gutsy enough to go beyond.

He sat on the ground next to the steps, gazing around the camp, "My sister, hates my guts." A small chuckle coming out.

Curiosity got me, "You have a sister?" I knew he was making small talk. I appreciated the attempt to distract me.

"Yea, my twin, Anna. She's one of the maids in your home." He glances, head tilting up to me, his hair falling to the side.

"YOU'RE SIBLINGS!?"

He chuckled more at my ignorance, I didn't see the resemblance there, other than the hair and freckles. Their personalities opposites. I was about to fly off with questions when he brought something to my attention, rising quickly. "Lieutenant Colonel, approaches."

I made eye contact with Al, before disappearing inside once more.

I knew I needed to try, even I was aware of my suspicious behaviour lately. Al wasn't stupid, he noticed things most people didn't, that was why he was Lieutenant Colonel at such an early age.

CHAPTER NINETEEN

HECATE

Tonight, was the night. "I'm going to do it!" I slapped my cheeks.

Selene gave me a crazy look, "Don't force it, my Lady." She was sewing together pieces of fabric, making herself a vest.

I was impressed with her creativity and stitching, she liked to keep her hands busy. From drawing, to fiddling and now sewing. She had a gift with those hands, I wasn't exceptionally good at that kinda of stuff. No, I wasn't good at most things...

I was trying to steal my nerves. "We can't delay, won't be long till we're in the capital."

We made camp just before the river, Trevore was telling me the plans through the door when the carriage came to a stop finally. "Thank you, Trevore."

There was a skip of silence, "Of course, my Lady."

I stood up, "Are you going to stretch your legs, you're going to go stir crazy in here."

Selene glanced out the window, "I'm not ready yet, I was in the back of that wagon for weeks... I think a few days inside this luxury box will be fine."

"Do you want me to get you anything?" My concern for her was growing increasingly.

She made light out of the situation, returning to her sewing. "isn't it I, who should be retrieving things for you, milady." She tried mocking Trevore's accent.

"We're friends, are we not?" Her eyes shoot up to me, still standing, waiting on her. She awkwardly smiles and nods. I really liked it when she smiled, she reminded me of the fairies in my books, back at home. "Then never forget as your lady and as your friend, if you need anything, I'll help you. Okay?"

Pink spreads across her cheeks, her head going down, "Thank you."

I let her be, exiting the carriage. Trevore and I walked a few laps around camp, I asked him about his relationship with Anna and why she hated him. He looked embarrassed to say, telling me she didn't like his personality, I had a feeling there was more but I wouldn't pry further. He clearly didn't feel comfortable talking in more detail about it, his hands in and out of his pockets, not being able to keep them still. The air was doing me good, and the company wasn't terrible either. Trevore wasn't as bad as I made him out to be in my head, however that smug look was still punch-able.

I saw Alastor leaving the dark tent, we both paused, waiting for the other to make a move.

Now or never! I mentally cheered to myself, marching straight up to him.

ALASTOR

I was just stepping out from the camping brief, I caught sight of Trevore's copper hair, then my sister, staring me down. *I don't like that look on her face.* She didn't spin and run, no she physically marched herself right up to me. Like an angry black cat, back arched stalking towards another cat. Attitude flew up from where she placed herself, "Can I have a word with you?" She didn't seem happy about something.

"Speak, but if you don't lose the attitude, I'm walking that way." I pointed my finger in a random direction.

She frowns, "I don't have an attitude..." She then randomly slaps her cheeks, and I'm taken back from the strange behaviour. "I don't mean to have an attitude, maybe the journey is taking its toll on me."

I held in the laugh for her weirdness, my lips twitching, she frowned again. "We've still got three – four days of travel, at best." I pointed out.

"By the realms... Wait, wait... I need to speak or else I'm going to chicken out..." She looks around, "Can we speak privately?" Turning to Trevore, she commands him, "Return to the carriage... Please."

He nods his head, regarding something between us. "Yes, my Lady."

My curiosity festers as well and I begin walking towards her carriage behind Trevore, she grips the back of my tunic. "No, Selene... Just not there... Yet."

"Fine?" I take a deep breath, trying to keep my patience. "We can use one of the wagons." I squint at her.

She gestures for me to lead the way, we begin walking side by side, passing the Smithe's carriage. Katrina pops out, as though she was watching and waiting for Hecate. My sister averts her eyes swiftly, acting aloof.

"What's going on with you two?"

"I don't want to talk about that." She tries to storm ahead, evading.

I then grabbed her arm, spinning her to me, "What did she do to you, Hecate?!" Aggression rising to the surface, I was done with her running away.

"Can we please just go somewhere private..." Tears brimming in her emerald eyes. A memory surfaces, and I itch to pull out my sword. "Al, please..." I break from my trance, Hecate searching my face.

We round one of the furthest wagons, somewhere less likely someone would eavesdrop on us. We kept the tent equipment in this one, empty, it had space for us to sit.

I notice her pathetic attempt to jump, no upper body strength to pull the rest of herself up. "Here." I put my hands down as a step, assisting her.

"Thank you."

I don't know if the recent events have shaken her, if that tramp did something to her, or the travel was hitting her hard as she claimed. Hecate wasn't acting like the Hecate I was accustomed with. My suspicion was in hyperdrive. I swung a leg, boarding in next, choosing to sit across from her on the wooden floor.

She brings her knees up to her chest, fixing her skirt to cover herself. "I'm sorry..."

"For?" I wonder where this is coming from.

"Being a horrible sister..."

"Hecate – "

"Wait... Let me finish..." She was on the verge of hyperventilating. "Oh god, just get it over with..." She quietly spat it out, "I think, I'm a witch."

"Mhmm" I was suspicious recently, and Hecate's behaviour and actions had me leaning this way anyway.

She was trembling, "Alastor I'm serious..." her voice still low.

"Thank you." I stop her from leading astray, "For saving my skin, when I was trying to save yours."

Confusion crossed her face, and then realisation, "You knew..."

I shrugged, "I suspected some-thing... does it change the fact you are a miserable head on the best of days? No. Does it change the fact you're my sister? Also no. You are what you are Hecate, a bitch, a witch, whatever. It makes no difference to me." I wanted to get to the topic at hand since she was finally opening up. "What I want to know is... why you decided to withhold some pretty important information, pertaining to your kidnapping." I felt the frown take over my face, I couldn't help it. I didn't believe she meant to with malicious intent, but it was vital information that could help us. "So?"

She explained everything, how she could understand they're language, she also added the fact that some kind of enchantment made her appear old in the Fae's eyes. That was something we needed to investigate. I listened, she spoke low, pausing when someone made a round by. She mentioned Selene and that too wasn't a surprise, Selene's over all appearance was odd, but the way her and Hecate became partners in crime quickly was a tell-tale.

I could clearly see all the anxiety she had to deal with, leave her. Then she told me something that made everything just click, like gears falling into place and moving together at last.

"Between those silver eyes or the dreams that are like premonitions, sometimes I fear closing my eyes. Even Selene has been plagued by these sort of dreams..."

All those nights Hecate thrashed the sheets, the times she woke screaming. My mind drifts back to my mother... "No..."

Hecate peered up from playing with a chipped piece of wood from the floor boards, "I'm sorry I didn't tell you sooner..."

I reached over quickly grabbing her face, startling her. "Hecate, I need you to be brave and tell father this as well." A revelation, Hecate's state to my mother's... All the answers were right there in front of us the whole time.

"No..." She tried to squirm out from my hold.

"Hecate – "

"NO!" Her eyes flashed, something within swirling. "I... I don't want him involved... I don't want him to know..." She was afraid, she braved herself to speak to me, after running for days. I could see the terror the moment I mentioned father.

How could she not be scared... Father was someone who knocked out a baron for making a comment on Hecate's legitimacy, his honour be damned. Father was someone who embraced her whole-heartedly. He protected her time and time again, taught her the way of the world himself. He let down his walls, so she could let down hers.

While I belittled her, while I threw hateful comments and nasty remarks, I pushed her away. She wasn't afraid of losing something she never really had with me. She wasn't afraid of my rejection. All I ever did was reject her.

I blurted out the one thing, I never spoke to anyone about, not a soul. Hecate fed off energy... She needed me to be just as vulnerable as her, that was the only way forward.

HECATE

I felt my world begin to crumble. *I couldn't tell Papa... He might...* Selene's family discarded her, I was regretting involving Alastor now. There was no way he wouldn't go and tell father himself. I needed to leave, the idea of running away sounded like the only viable option now.

"Katrina... molested me..."

My head went silent, my heart stilled, for a beating second. Alastor's face was inches from mine, paling. *What did he just –* I don't finish that thought, when his usual steady tone, wavers.

His shaky breaths, hitch. "The night of her coming of age... I went to the guest room made up for me, to sleep off the wine... When I woke to... someone... t–touching..." I felt the sick rising from my stomach. "She... was on top..." He sat back quickly, his head bouncing off the wall behind him, as though he was reliving it. Trying to walk me through that night. His irises shaking, like he could not keep them in one spot for too long, didn't want to watch the assault happen a second time.

The tears that dried, returned, for a completely different reason.

"I've not been okay around women in general, since..." His brown eyes wouldn't meet mine. I didn't recognise the person sat across from me.

I shouted at him, "Alastor why didn't you tell anybody!?" Anger replacing the anxiety in my heart moments ago.

His gaze shot to mine, "Who would believe me? Huh? A man, being molested by a woman?"

I felt my stomach drop. Every time I mentioned her to him, his reactions... I was constantly reminding him of his trauma, of what she had done to him. The tears didn't stop coming, my chin was wet. I really was a horrible sister, that's why he hated me so much.

Alastor was many things, but a liar wasn't one of them. He always spoke truthfully, no matter how harsh or ugly it was.

The animosity he showed since Katrina's coming of age, Katrina assaulted him and he had to deal with seeing her face every time I brought her around. He couldn't tell anyone because he thought no one would have believed him...

"I... believe you."

Surprise fleeted across his face, blinking at me rapidly. "Seems like... Neither of us, have been very good at this... Sibling thing." After a while of silence, he scooted toward the entrance, shaking away the thoughts that tormented him. He jumped out, breathing deep through his nose, before extending a hand to me. "I've got your back, I'll wait until you feel brave enough before we tell father. Alright?"

It was as though my every encounter with Katrina was playing through my mind again, her every encounter with Alastor flashing through slowly, closer. A flip book showing me every missed detail. I felt something snap inside my core, just before I took his twitching hand.

SELENE

I remembered green eyes. A dream I had when I was but an innocent child, still tucked up in bed, in my family's cottage. I recalled, sparkling emeralds, emerging from darkness, offering a pale white hand to those still drowning in it. It was another premonition, my fate.

I was beyond grateful to Hecate, it was impossible to accept there could be more people like me, on this damned island, alive. If the ancestors could see our island now, they would have been outraged. They were slaughtering the very ancestry that fought for our rights. That rose for the sovereignty of freedom, to be who we are. They fought those creatures in the night, vanquishing them, so we could dance under star light.

The moment Hecate woke in that wagon, she was already in action to save those around her. I spent weeks in there and didn't have the courage like she did. Hiding in the corner waiting, for whatever death had in store for me. She was different, she wouldn't leave her life in the hands of fate. She was what I wished – I could be more of. When she jumped from the wagon, taking chance in her own hands. I wanted that, I wanted to be strong regardless of the situation. When they brought me to their home, I understood where that strength came from.

The maids proudly spoke about their masters, to the other survivors. Hecate took care of the home and the people in it, how her brother took care of his duties and the town... How their father took care of every single person, regardless of rank and status, near and far. Hecate had fight in her because she had reasons to fight for...

"I don't have a home to return too, unlike you miss in your fancy house with your fancy clothes. Your oh so perfect life!" I hurled words at her, trying to push her away.

That dark eyebrow raised, and a part of me naturally told me to hide. I was there when she shouted at that fae, calling him a fiend, scorned for being insulted. Yet here I was, a nobody, trying to insult her, so she'd leave me like everyone else did.

"Well... it just so happens... I need a lady in waiting." She shrugs it off, "Work for me, and you'll have a roof over your head, and coin

in your pocket." No pity in her those emerald orbs, she was treating me as a human being. Giving me options where others hadn't.

"If they find out– "

"IF!" She stops me. "What's the point of ifs... Let's focus on the present, now." She points to the floor. "I am way over my depths, but I believe if we stick together, if we work together, we can figure all this out... together."

Why? Did it matter, we'd be liabilities, to each other.

She walked to the window, "Misery likes company." Hands behind her back, her shadow behind her tall.

I watched her intently, "What are you talking about?" She was blabbering, her attitude strange to me.

"I read it in a book..." She turned, her sleek black hair spinning with her movement. Those all–knowing eyes, I found something haunting about them. "The nightmares... The attacks... The fae... It's a miserable world out there. I wouldn't mind some company while I challenged it..."

I accepted the offer, and was immediately showered with gifts. A red–haired girl named Anna, ran me through the basics, smiling and thanking me for assisting her lady. The people here acted like a big family... They gave me clothing, advice, and even told me funny stories about each other while they showed me around the estate.

Later, Hecate tried to give me jewels, I even got boots that were never worn. Hecate offered me everything, I felt bad enough accepting shoes from her. Admittedly, it felt nice to have something on my feet without holes. I had no idea how to pay these people back for their kindness. I swore to myself with whatever I earned, I would buy it myself, I would work hard not to disappoint these people. I wouldn't take advantage of them, the same way others had of me.

I was fed, and given a warm bed, even a bathtub to clean myself in. I officially had a room again, one that was mine. I cried so hard that night, afraid to fall asleep and wake up next to a stranger for some coin. If this was a dream, I never wanted to wake from it.

I occasionally checked the carriage door, in thought. Waiting for Hecate to burst through it, like the other night. She was terrified to speak with her brother, and I couldn't blame her. I noticed red hair bob about, but Hecate didn't return with it. I put my sewing things aside, creeping up to the door, quietly opening it. "Pst. Coppertop!?"

The guard stiffly turns, "Copper... top?"

I don't think he appreciated the nickname. I didn't care, "Where's Hecate?" I wanted to know why he wasn't guarding her. He made a stupid face, and I immediately understood why Hecate claimed his face was 'punch-able'.

"Well, Miss." Hissing his s's at me. "Our lady, is currently talking with the Lieutenant Colonel." He faced forward again, done with me.

I gasped, this was a make-or-break situation now... I brought my hands together. *We honour the moon, and thank you for thy generous light. May the sun protect the day, while you protect the night. From the earth, the sea, the stars, the sky. Keep us from worries and bring us thy lullaby. Your gift to us is kindness, and we praise you for your benevolence. Lead us from catastrophe and shield us from maleficence.*

Coppertop's voice pulls me from prayer, "Miss, should I be worried for her?"

"Hmmm?"

"The look on your face tells me it was a mistake leaving her with him."

"Well depending on how this conversation goes, yea I think I'm worried about me too." His hazel eyes enlarged, his weight shifted from foot to foot, then he takes off rapidly. *Strange guy...*

I close the door, peeking through the curtain, waiting for Hecate to return, or someone to come drag me away.

Hecate did return, eventually, with Coppertop and her brother in tow. The men kept giving each other strange looks, while Hecate's face was blank, but.... I saw the shadows swirling in her orbs, I didn't think I could find her eyes even more haunting, but I was wrong.

The young master opens the carriage door, and I scooched down the seat, side pressed against the other wall. He helped Hecate in, climbing in after her. "Take a walk, Lance Corporal." He orders sternly.

Oh god... I looked to Hecate, her eyes down casted, still swirling.

"Sir, with all due resp –" Coppertop starts...

However, Hecate's brother, cuts him off growling. "That's a command." He closes the door with force, the carriage rocking side to side. We sit in a heavy silence for a heartbeat, until the guard leaves, not looking too happy.

"So." I hear my heart in my ears, the moment brown irises are on me. His voice was pleasing if it wasn't for his scary tone, sounding as though everyone was going to receive their death bed wishes. "Relax, I'm not going to hurt you. Hecate explained the situation." He looked over to her, then jabbed her with a massive elbow.

That seemed to have pulled her from wherever she was. "Huh, oh ya.. Al's on board..."

I found myself trembling, "S–so?" My eyes not leaving Hecate.

There was something even more terrifying... I hadn't realised just how big her brother was until he was crammed inside the carriage with us. I only had peeks through the crack of the guest door and from afar. He was as big as the fae, his aura like second skin.

"For now, we ALL." He side eyes Hecate, "Keep each other informed, no secrets. It's best if no one else knows for now, we are headed to the place where people are executed for suspicion of sorcery. Keep your mouths shut, I'll see what I can find out." I let out a breath, and those brown eyes found mine again. "You two will also take part in some basic self-defence training with me."

Hecate shouted, while I whispered, "What?!" Together.

CHAPTER TWENTY

ALASTOR

Hecate and I were on our way back, "I'm sorry..." She spoke gently, her head down.

I didn't want to keep talking about it, "It's in the past now, it's over." Her legs were much smaller than mine, so I usually had to slow my long strides. Right now, Hecate was dragging her feet, I could see the weight of my confession on her. I slowed my steps to match her's even more, dragging my own feet.

"No, it isn't..." I thought I heard her say something, when a very panicked Trevore appeared, legs moving quick. He scanned my sister head to toe, before taking position behind her. I found his behaviour odd, his hands flexing on his belt, but we continued onward, no words exchanged.

The night was colder, the heat radiating from the many lit fires were just enough to keep us from shivering. This winter would be a harsh one.

We were passing by the Smithe's carriage, I spat on the ground walking by. Discovering after, only I was walking ahead, Hecate was no longer at my side. I rotated and found my sister blankly staring at the carriage, Trevore's noggin going back and forth, clearly concerned.

"Hecate?" I stepped toward her. Creaking of the red door sounded to the side, Katrina stepped out smiling. I double took Hecate's chest heave, faster and faster, her eyebrows pulling forward. My gut telling me to get her away from here, now. "Comon." I slid my hand to hers, engulfing them entirely, they were warmer than usual.

She didn't flinch or pull away, her attention never left Katrina, those pupils pinpointed now.

Trevore tried as well, "My Lady?" He lightly tapped her arm, his touch lingering. I didn't like the idea of her guard touching her, without consent. Hecate was rooted to her place, neither of us able to distract her. Katrina too halted on the steps of her carriage, her knuckles ghostly white, gripping the door.

"Let's go, Hecate." I tugged her little hand, my sister finally followed with a wobble, but those eyes stayed on her target. We got to the carriage, still holding hands. I feared If I had let her go, she would have spun back and done something crazy. I ordered Trevore away so we could speak privately, Hecate never mentioned telling him and I would take no chances until we had more. Not even with Gregory.

The guy tried some chopsy shit with me, I could not believe this chump's one-eighty in the past few days. I was beginning to wonder if assigning him to Hecate, was a mistake. I grounded out to him, "That's a command." Shutting the door so I didn't launch myself at him.

You're just as bad as each other. I could hear my father now and began to understand why he always said that. I hated to admit, he might have been right.

The northerner too looked like she was going to shit herself while I spoke to them, reminding me of a white hare caught in a snare. "You two will also take part in some basic self–defence training with me."

"What?!" Hecate shouted, while her lady in waiting murmured.

"It's decided, tomorrow morning before we set off, you both will meet me outside for an hour." I started towards the door.

Hecate was aghast, I knew she wasn't ecstatic about what came after. Curses were flying out of her mouth. She didn't like pain, that was why Hecate stopped dancing. She had really hurt herself years back, unable to walk for weeks. Painkillers had no effect on her, oddly, so she avoided painful things in general.

"Hecate, I pray you never have to use what I teach you." I stepped out, regarding them. "But considering recent events. Just try… goodnight." I closed the door before she could let off on me, or throw something, she had picked that up while she was bed rested all those years back.

Boots tapping the earth snagged my attention, Trevore was back, leaning on the side… Or he didn't go far to begin with. I walked up to him, fixing his messy collar. "If you ever try to talk back with an order, I'm going to knock that thick skull in, understood?"

His eyes didn't bulk back, moving his neck so I could fix the sides of his collar as well. "My orders are to protect our lady, sir."

I straightened up, "From me?" Inches higher than him, his nose came to my chin.

"Even from you. Sir."

I scoffed at his newfound attitude, "Good man." Leaving to do my shift. I would monitor him, in the next coming days. Something didn't sit right with me…

The night was quiet, save for the sound of the river. The skies were also clear, stars on full display. The hooting of owls sounded off in nearby trees, a good sign nothing lurked near camp. I took in the scents of pine, enjoying the moment of peace. Things finally made sense, as if the skies too understood the clarity.

Father checked in on the girls before he had gone to bed, I waited to examine his face, leaving. He stayed for a long while, exiting just as the next rotation was starting. He found me immediately, jumping down the steps, "Everything alright?" I inquired– his steps quick.

"Is this true?" His words low and rushed.

I looked around, that nervousness from his approach turning into paranoia. "Depends on what you're on about?"

"You tell, no one!" His face had the same look of fear as Hecate's, his lips moved, and I barely made out what he was trying to say. "They'll hunt her."

It was my turn to be surprised, I couldn't believe Hecate told him, so soon. She was terrified when I mentioned telling him together... I inclined my head, reeling it in, "Obviously, and we'll protect her regardless, right?"

Something cleared in his blues, I tried to ignore the gnawing feeling that he thought I'd sell her out. "We've got a lot to talk about... I know a place once we reach the capital, we carry on as planned till then." He marched off just as rapidly, checking over his shoulders. I rubbed a hand over my face, the tension of this journey exhausting as hell. I didn't like surprises, and it seemed like one after another these last couple of days. I dropped my hands to Trevore, gawking at the carriage.

Fuck!

I stalked up, while he stared stupidly, unaware. "Everything alright, Lance Corporal." Hand on the hilt of my hidden blade. Ready to do what needed to be done.

His head twitched to me, face flushing, "UH – SIR YES SIR!" Shouting in response. I hear a scream from inside and the one curtain open, slammed shut. "I D–DEFINITELY DIDN'T SEE A–ANYTHING SIR!"

Relief washes over me, my tense muscles, relaxing. *It's fine, he knows nothing, the man only saw some skin.* I release my hold on the blade, and marched off to find a stiff drink.

SELENE

I woke to a knock at the door, groggily sitting up. "Who is it?" Hecate called out, loud, I rubbed the sides of my head. She was sitting across on the seat, bags under her eyes.

"Common you two, time to get to work." That brassy voice declared. I wasn't looking forward to this so-called training thing. I wanted to sleep for another peaceful hour.

Hecate was already dressed, no longer in that black sleeping gown she went to bed in. I had no idea if she went to sleep after me. Once the duke left and we changed, all the nerves melted away and I crashed hard. "Give us a moment to change." I replied next, to our wake-up call.

Hecate wore loose looking trousers, a string tied around her waist, to keep them up, the loose legs tucked into boots. A baggy tunic tucked in the tied waist, with the sleeves also rolled to her elbows. She reminded me of those boot shining boys from my town, her hair was in another high updo, a messy bun.

I grabbed the canteen and took a drink, "Did you even manage to sleep?"

Those orbs were swirling again, "An hour maybe, I woke because of a dream."

"Want to talk about it?" These nightmares were bouncing back and forth between us.

She shook her head, "It wasn't silver eyes and mist that chased me awake...." I was curious as to what else it could have been, but considering the Duke's reaction last night, I believed it could be several things.

He gave us quite the shock with the face he pulled, when Hecate pointed my situation out next, he said nothing. He was so silent– I was contemplating how quick I could get to the door. I squeaked when the man pulled us both into hugs, whispering to us that everything would be okay. It took everything in my entire being not to cry like a baby. There was a time, I would have wished with everything in my heart, for my father to take it the way he did.

Victor Crosse was born to be the Lord Protector, I passionately believed this now.

I quickly changed, opting for trousers that were set to the side. "I had Trevore retrieve them for us, I don't think skirts will do us much good this morning." Hecate handed me a string, similar to the one she was wearing. "You're going to need this."

I finished changing, and we exited the carriage. Coppertop was waiting for us, and in such a state every time he looked to Hecate. Creepy guy saw Hecate's back last night... Or so we hoped that was all, he held out his hands for us, not looking at Hecate smugly.

The sky was shades of purple and orange, the air was cold compared to the warmth inside. I rubbed my hands together, "You'll warm up quickly with some exercise." Brown eyes watched my movement. *This guy is a freaking hawk.* I put my hands into my pockets and followed the guard, who followed Hecate, who followed her brother. We marched to the other corner of the camp, passing by Piss–head's carriage. Hecate didn't even look once at it. I'd been meaning to ask her lately about her.

Stupid-face stood to the side after, while hawk-eyes instructed Hecate and I through different vigorous stretches. My muscles shook with some of the leg stretches, I was like a thumping bunny. Thankfully to my embarrassment, Hecate was no better. You could hear Coppertop stifling a laugh, it was painfully obvious, Hecate and I were in bad shape. "I think this, might be the thing that kills us…" I breathlessly whispered to Hecate. Her face was red, sweat collected on her hair line, as she grunted in agreement.

We were handed sticks eventually, I stared at it dumbly wondering what for. "I don't fancy having to stitch you two up, so sticks will suffice until your hand to eye coordination improves." Hawk-eyes declared, retaking his position in front of us. I could draw out every muscle under his tunic, the guy was jacked. He'd jab forward with his fancy blade, and I was stunned stupid again, by the muscles upon muscles on his biceps. *Is that even possible?*

Hecate snickered next to me, something else was there in her tone. "What I heard was, I don't fancy having to get stitches because you stabbed me." I tried not to laugh, biting my lips.

"Oi focus." Hawk-eyes surprised me, my hand flew up, saluting. His thick eyebrow twitched at my involuntary action. I was a bag of nerves with this one, and I was certain that he was aware of it too.

He showed us how to stand and the way our arms should move. Our elbows were too high or too low, our feet not far enough apart. Her brother was intensely serious with our training, his eyes focused on the task at hand. Correcting our awkward forms, and even explaining the parts of a dagger. Our hands should always be on the handle and pointy end away from us, that's what I grasped.

By the end of it, my head and body ached. The sun broke over the land, everyone was up and moving things around. "Head to the carriage and clean up, we'll be setting off soon." He looked satisfied with our efforts and that was good enough for me, this training thing might not be so bad. Even though I felt sore, something else felt stronger, within.

Coppertop followed behind us, Hecate was rubbing one of her shoulders, mumbling about her incompetence. "You did well, my Lady." I pulled a face at Hecate, who rolled her eyes. *This guy, he is making it obvious at this point!*

Hecate stilled, Coppertop nearly running into her, stopping on his tip toes. I trailed her line of sight, Piss–head had quietly snuck toward us, moving hesitantly.

"Tee.... Can we talk?" It wasn't the cheery, snobby girl that I came to know, but a shy little lamb.

I looked back to Coppertop, his one shoulder shrugging to me. Seemed like he had no idea what changed between these two.

"Tee?"

"How dare you." Venom spat forth from Hecate's lips. I felt the shift in her energy, Hecate's aura drastically spiked. Now I was wondering, her aggression seemed to have worsened in the last couple of days.

The blondie stumbled back, her face wanting to cry. "Tee, what's wrong."

"How. Dare. You." Hecate stepped forward, her voice louder, now. I grabbed her arm from doing anything regrettable, Coppertop too gently grabbed her other arm, his attention on the blonde.

"Tee, you're scaring me."

"Don't you dare!" Hecate was trying to pull free from us, "I thought you were my friend?" I had to use the rest of my waning strength to keep her from launching. Coppertop placed a hand on her stomach, the other on her arm.

"Tee what happened in the wagon was a mistake, I was afraid – "

"Enough!!" Hecate hollered, something pulsed from under her skin, those breaths rapidly increased. "I'm not talking about the wagon, but you know that, don't you?!" Her green orbs flaring,

Coppertop's face went rigid taking Hecate in. I knew immediately he noticed it too- the situation was getting dangerous.

That annoying girl stammered again pushing Hecate further, "What are you talking about Tee?" Katrina was shuffling back, and then her eyebrows shot up. Whatever Hecate was implying, the girl realised it now. "Tee, I d-don't know w-what he told- "

"Silence!" You could see the air evaporate from Katrina's lungs, her face going a shade of blue. An invisible force struck the girl and lunged back to Hecate.

"My Lady?" I tugged on Hecate's arm, many eyes were looking toward our commotion, and Hecate was ticking to explode. "We need to leave..." I whispered to her. She would be found out, right here, right in this moment.

Surprisingly, Coppertop blocked her, "Please excuse us Miss, my Lady needs her rest." Blonde hair took off with the given opportunity, fleeing for her life.

Hecate's chest proceeded to rise and fall drastically. "Did I order you to intervene?" That venom was now spitting at his back.

He rotated, breathing deep as well. "I'm sorry my Lady." Those hazels confused, that's when the scent hit me.

I could smell the essence of magic surrounding Hecate. It was dark and earthy, myrrh and mugwort whirled off her like pheromones. "Hecate, don't. Let's go." I pulled hard, knowing she could easily turn that energy to me. I needed to get us to the carriage, she needed to breathe and not allow her emotions to take the wheel.

"Hecate!"

The Duke flew to us, from out of nowhere, his face terrified. The guard stepped to the side with a small incline, Hecate's eyes were darkened. Hands found her shoulders, I let go of her arm as the Duke pulled her into a hug, shielding her to him. His eyes telling all other eyes to clearly look away, that's when it happened.

HECATE

I sat and watched Selene sleep, her white eyebrows at ease. The more I looked at her the more concrete my decision became – I would learn self-defence for her. Her arms were still bony, even with all the food I stuffed into her. Her years of hardships, took its toll on her.

The night was quiet, the river in the distance flowing with my nerves. I opened the smoky coloured curtain, to watch the stars in the sky. I dreamt of hands groping me, a drunken smile, slobbering all over my skin.

Katrina molested me.

Scenes of her spying on my brother, her very obsession with him, obvious now. How she used to make excuses to garden closer to the training grounds... How she preferred to stay at mine, regardless of his attitude towards her. How she disappeared that night, claiming she got a bit too drunk, and needed to clear her head. So many signs were there, yet I was blind to all of it.

I could not even begin to imagine his suffering, the dream I had was frightening enough. His broken face recalling the night to me, the best he could, ripping me apart. For two years, every time I ignorantly threw her name at him, the way he recoiled or paled as though I physically slapped him. For two years he battled his demons – her demon... Silently, alone, as I played accomplice in his trauma, relentlessly throwing it in his face. I was just as bad as her.

Hatred brewed inside me, I deserved no sympathy, not even from myself. That's why I told father about me, if he wanted to be rid of my existence, I would have gladly accepted... For everything I had done to Al. Though father being the understanding man that he is, hugged me and Selene, telling us it was going to be okay. I shouldn't have expected anything less from him.

I inched toward the door, "Trevore?"

Boots against dirt sounded near, "M–My Lady?" His shadow appeared against the curtain, hands straightening out his shirt.

I attempted to clear my head from our little accident earlier, praying it wouldn't make things awkward between us, now. "Could you grab some trousers for us?"

"Trousers?"

I smiled at the confusion in his tone, "Yes, any will do. For myself and Selene, we'll need them for training soon."

"Uh sure... Of course! Wait a moment, please." His shadow disappeared, returning moments later. With more than what I asked for. I cracked the door open, the items handed to me, with Trevore's eyes tightly shut.

I found some string later to tighten the loose waist, throwing my hair up next. I had just finished rolling my sleeves up when a knock at the door woke Selene up. She was showing me kindness and concern, still courteous of my privacy. "Want to talk about it?" But I wasn't worthy of any of it.

Alastor's story was not mine to tell, but I wished I could tell her what a horrible person I was. How I could be someone who could hurt her too, unknowingly.

After she had gotten ready, we started the day, Alastor was his usual character. He stood firm, back straight, his hair combed back, and boots polished. The traumatised brother confessing his suffering to me, didn't exist here, before us. His face was alert, focused, he spoke clear and direct.

He gave us sticks after some brutal stretches, commenting about our hand eye coordination. "What I heard was, I don't fancy having to get stitches because you stabbed me." That nagging voice with in, had me commenting. I couldn't blame him– I'd been verbally stabbing him for years.

The session ended, and I didn't feel any better than beforehand. I was sore and feeling valueless, just another thing I wasn't very good at. I was beginning to re-evaluate my whole life's purpose at this point, complaining to my company, when I noticed her.

Katrina.

She wore her usual attire, bright and inviting, no makeup on her face. Something with in me slithered to get out. Her lip was quivering, my ears were ringing, saliva dropped onto my skin with the shaking of her lips. That slobbering – drunken – smile.

"How dare you." Everything faded away, it was just her and I, many scenarios played around us. Our life stories flashed on in the background, white mist swirling around them. Her blue eyes tearing up, acting frightened of Alastor. Her many proclamations about waiting for him, her finding opportunities to approach him... No, she was harassing him. Tormenting him, because he couldn't do anything, say anything about it.

"How. Dare. You." Her foot staggers back, and I stepped forward. *You think you'll get away with this?*

"Tee you're scaring me."

The space around us began to swirl, the scenes clashing together into murky colours. "Don't you dare!" Something was holding me back from reaching her, "I thought you were my friend?"

Her mouth began to flap, speaking about the wagon. That thing inside snapped its tail, a whip to my soul. "Enough! I'm not talking about the wagon, but you know that, don't you?!"

She kept trying to back away from me, I seen the truth in her eyes. The moment she knew, I knew. "Tee, I d–don't know w–what he– "

It launched forth rearing its head, "Silence!!" Her mouth froze, I was dripping with hatred. A force tugged me back again, just as something blocked Katrina out of my sight. She ran away, with Trevore blocking me. Betrayal sank its fangs into my very bones. "Did I order you to intervene?"

How dare you.

The urge spread through my veins with my rage, hissing into my ears. Before it reached my breaking heart, a familiar scent embraced me. A heart beat louder than any heavy downfall, diluting the rush. The push kept coming with every beat in my ears, I clutched my father's chest...

"Take cover!!" Father threw me to the ground painfully, my back slamming against the dirt floor, shielding me. I heard the arrows as they whizzed through air, hitting the earth. Roars smothered out the echoing of the river. The wind was knocked from me, all within seconds.

"BATTLE STATIONS!"

Fire was spreading around the camp, Trevore was thankfully shielding Selene, crouched over her body that hit the ground next to us. My eyes quickly darted around for Alastor, our visibility becoming poor.

Father desperately dragged me to the nearest cover, "Get under there, go!" Shoving me under it.

"Where's Al?!" I screamed at him, then the next attack began. Those black beasts running straight through the camp, on both sides. Debris and people were flung through air, the fire and smoke shrouding more of everything. Then the mist rolled in, so dark, it blocked out dawn's light.

Selene was shoved next, shivering as she bumped into me. Father was cursing, a knife in hand, "You stay here until I return!" He grabbed Trevore next with his other hand, "You protect them with everything you've got. I will not accept your death, stay alive soldier!" Then he disappeared into the mist and flames.

I tried to go after him, "Papa?!?!" But Trevore was quicker, caging my waist, holding me back. "No! Don't leave me!" There was so much yelling, so much noise. Random bursts of lights flashed in the distance. It was absolute mayhem. "Let go of me!" I tried to break away from Trevore.

Claws broke through the flames, advancing our way. Familiar red eyes met mine.

Trevore threw me behind him, unsheathing his sword. "Get under the wagon, my Lady!"

"Hecate!" I felt Selene's cold fingers grip around my ankle, through the leather of my boots.

Time slowed again, as the beast charged for us, Trevore charged for it, like someone was manipulating the flow of time. A vague feeling of déjà vu came to me.

Silver eyes in the sky looked down. That diluted all other noises. "Show me what you're made of!"

That slithering creature uncoiled itself once more... This time, I gripped my control on the familiar rush, I let my heavy eyelids drop.

When they opened, I saw the world through slitted pupils. I felt it rear up to strike, fangs dripping with venom. The moment those silver eyes appeared before me, grinning ear to ear, I knew I needed to let it go.

UNKNOWN

"Woo-eee Sire! If this is what ye back looks like, dare I ask what the other guy looks like?" A man laughs, cotton dapping a fleshy torn back. The well-lit room thick with medicine, and dirtied medical tools.

The silvered-eyed-prince hisses with every dab, "Just shut your mouth and do your job. You're paid to fix me, not question." His fists tightening, nails piercing into his palms.

"Ooh – Always a charmer you are." He fixes his glasses, pushing them higher on the bridge of his nose. "The biggens not pleased is 'e?" He pivots on the stool behind him, pouring a dark liquid into a cup. "Ear' drink this."

The prince swigs the drink back, groaning as the liquid goes down, "That tastes like shit." His voice straining, a cough burning his throat to be released.

"Doesn't taste the nicest, but ye won't feel a thin.' Why'd you leave this so long, should've came and sort it out the moment it happened. Guna have a nasty scar.."

He clicks his tongue to the man's complaints. "And pray tell Doc, why does your voice sound so bizarre?" His words were true, the stinging subsided to numbness.

"I was tryin' the liquid you were just drinkin' then poof, voice was stranger than a ladies laugh!"

"WHAT?!" The prince spun around grabbing Doc by the collar of his shirt. A fist stopping just before connecting to Doc's face.

"Relax, the tonic was fix not lon' after, I'll sort my business when I can fine' the time." He chuckles at the fist there, pushing it away with his finger.

The prince shakes his head, black hair swaying with it, "You're a crazy bastard, Asclepius." Returning to his slouching position.

"Only the best, sire."

A shadow seeps from under the wooden door, swirling towards them. "My liege, I bring news."

Silver eyes squint, annoyed that he can never have a moment of peace. "Get on with it then."

"The merged extraction teams, have reported some mysterious vibrations, coming from west of the river."

"West ye say? They hit few towns west, funny vibrations true. The vibrations came from that ol' missy." Doc was bandaging the prince's back now, chatting away aimlessly.

"Old missy?" The prince countered, his arms up as Doc wrapped him. He'd slipped into many dream states, not finding anything suspicious. He had come across that white haired woman in the dream world, the one accompanying the hag and knight, that night. He had a score to settle with those three, if it weren't for his orders, he'd have preoccupied his time hunting them instead.

"Yes sir, I fix'er up myself that night. Somethin' very strange about her energy. Not like them other women."

He abruptly stood up, Doc tipping back on the stool with a noise. "How far?!?" He had felt that vibration, come and gone with a violent strike. Felt it as it rocked through his very soul, coiling around his core like a snake. Paining him greater, than the whips of their king's power. His breaths came quick with excitement. His black markings of arrows, over his heart, revealed, the bandages falling.

"A day's travel, my liege" The shadow was still holding his bow.

"Rise, my friend!" He made quick strides, clasping the being on its dark shoulders. "I think our king's orders is the hag, I shall receive two birds, with one blood dripping stone!" He spun to Doc, "Tell me more about her and leave nothing out!"

...

The prince marched down dark hallways, leading to doors of pure darkness, tentacles of shadows moved within them. "I need to speak with His Highness!" He stops before the stoned creatures, his cloak flicking forward. Eyes gleam toward him, the doors groan open, not a moment later. He pushed forth, impatient to wait. The green flames roar to life, bringing a different worldly light to the hall.

He stops before the stairs, dropping to one knee. "I greet the darkness between Heaven and Hades, long may he reign and corrupt the souls of all!"

Golden irises appear, from the throne, "Welcome Prince, Lord Commander of the Legions, I do not recall summoning you." Those creatures of flesh prowl down thick pillars, nearing the unwanted guest.

The prince stays bowed, "I have come to seek your most gracious council!" Aware of the empty eyes stalking him, prepared to leap at any given moment.

A deep resonating laugh rumbles through the hall, sending the creatures fleeing for higher sanction. "Your manners have improved, little lord. Rise, and tell your brother what ails you."

The prince rises to his feet, silver meeting gold. "I have reasons to believe, perhaps this is what ails you, my King."

"Go on..."

"That woman who stole from you, I believe she has been hiding in Desdemona all these years. We can cease these useless raids and bring her into custody to pay for her crimes." He waited– the halls grew eerily quieter.

Those golden eyes emotionless, "Impossible. The bargain she struck with me would have killed her years ago. It is the jewel she took away, that is what I seek!!" Hands covered in black armour slammed down on the arms of the throne. The impact so violent, the solid material rattled.

"We have been extracting maidens, yet you say it is a jewel we seek..." Confusion slows the prince. "What... Or who, exactly are we looking for?"

The king sprung to his feet, his aura exploding from him. "KILL THEM ALL FOR THEIR TREASON!" The prince is thrown through the hall from the force, bouncing off the stone floors. "BRING FORTH EVERY MAIDEN. I WANT THE ONE WHOSE EYES ARE GREEN, AS THE UNDERWORLD'S FLAME" Every word roared, hit the prince like an invisible blow to his guts. "HAIR DARKER THAN THE VIODS BETWEEN THE REALMS!" His limp body slides out, tangled in his own cloak. The doors slamming shut with his exit. "THE CHILD VALDIS, BRING ME ASTERIA'S PROMISED CHILD!" Those dark tentacles, latching the doors, sealing them shut.

He struggles to his knees, flipping his head up. Blood drips from his nose, rhythmically, onto the stone floor. *P–Penelope!* A sweet little voice, echoes in his skull. "You!" Anger seethes through him from the deceptive child in the dream, who played him like a fiddle.

CHAPTER TWENTY-ONE

VALDIS

The prince stormed into his quarters swiping everything off his desk. Those green eyes continued to flicker in his conscience, her hair swaying with her movements. He imagined that terrified look transforming into an overconfident grin. "Uraaahhg" An ungodly roar ripped from him, darkness shooting out around, throwing everything smashing into the walls. The wound on his back ripped open more, soaking his shirt through. She was within his reach, mere steps from his grasp.

"My liege, you summoned me?" His head whips to the guest, another shadow trembled by his door.

"Where is that traveling entourage?! I need to blow off some steam!"

"The shadows have heard whispers... their path is for the capital. We can confirm the knight, the hag and the white haired one is among them!"

A malicious smile grew, "Good, very good. I can settle my accounts then. Bring Arrus to me, make haste." He grabbed a stool that wasn't smashed to smithereens, sitting on it.

Those eyes flashed through, taunting him. "You like games, little girl?" He needed to find out how she ended up there, and how much she knew. There was a lot of information he needed, and he was aware the king would not divulge any more than he had already done. There was something else.... Something even the king did not want to talk about, or admit.

Shadows whirl in the floor, a figure projects out of it, hitting the floor with a growl.

Valdis watches the giant, "Captain."

A menacing growl greets the prince, "I do not appreciate being pulled through dark vortexes!"

A dark eyebrow rises, "You get used to them." Amusement in those silver eyes.

"I do not wish to get used to them! What business do you have with me, now?" Valdis gradually rose with his guest's tone. Arrus steps backs, bowing to his offensive manner. "Apologies, my Lord. Forgive me for my rude behaviour."

Valdis stopped his advancement toward Arrus, with a click of his heels. "The team will head west. We will hit that travelling company, the hag is among them."

Arrus raised from his bow, frowning, "That crone is dangerous, her energy alone killed three of my men. Not to mention the soldiers who took out another nine."

"Her magic is juvenile, probably draining her vitality as we speak, she will not be able to make many attacks. I will deal with her. I want that boy and the white haired one as well." He examined his nails, one by one. "You and the others can run the rest through, just dishevel them enough so I can have my play. Our target has changed, the king wants green eyes, black hair. Asteria's child."

Arrus was shocked from the news. "Asteria is with child?"

"Hmm, was, is the word... She's dead now. She made a bargain with the king. I do not know the exact details of said bargain... I only just found out myself... The price I believe, was the child... I'll have to do my own digging for this."

"Do we know the child's name?"

Valdis went to answer him honestly, only to stop. His silver eyes shot to Arrus. "I think I met her – those damned haunting eyes keep flickering in my head..." He smacked the side of his skull, swatting away the thoughts. "Although, I have a sneaky suspicion, she didn't give me her real name."

Arrus nodded, who in their right mind would have given their name to Valdis. "If you return me, I will pass the message along, and begin our plan of attack."

Valdis flipped his hood on, ready for his fun. "The plan is simple, utter chaos. We leave now." Mist and shadows swirled around the room, two beings plunged into the darkness between worlds, racing for Desdemona.

ALASTOR

A wave of arrows hit us, seconds before flaming ones did. We didn't hear or see them coming till it was too late.

I was currently bandaging Gregory's shoulder – he'd taken a direct hit, when the first arrows came down. Rendering his left, completely useless. I pulled the arrow out as quickly as possible, tearing the bottom of my tunic, to wrap it. If that had been more to the right...

He was grinding his teeth as I was tightly securing the bandage under his armpit. "I can still fight, sir!" There was no doubt in my mind that the man couldn't.

I surveyed around, the camp on fire, dark mist rolled in, it was night once again. "You stick close, got that!" Another wave hit us, this time those beasts running straight in.

I grabbed Gregory rolling left, claws clipped my right arm, three jagged knives were dragged across my skin. I yelled out some serious profanity. This was bad, the mist seemed thicker than our previous encounter.

Lights flashed in the direction the beast went, a clearing opening next to us. Gregory and I crouched, waiting. Luckily, I had my dagger, it was better than nothing, but I knew I needed a sword.

This was an absolute, shit show.

Marcus appeared in that clearing, swinging a stick in circles, a stone wedged to each end. "Boys!" He skipped up to us, a heavy satchel at his hip. "Let's go!" His face looked younger, some sort of glow to his cheeks. Few more hit soldiers following him, bleeding from arms and legs.

Something dark came charging through flames, just as he approached us. "Over there!" One of the wounded soldiers yell, Marcus whirled himself around for it. That twisted wooden stick, projecting black light from a dark stone, then twirling it, white light shoots from the other.

The creature's snout just emerges as the double impact hits, sending it and the flames away. Sparks of magic, exploding on impact, "How'd you like them apples!?" He laughed crazily, skipping toward the new clearing made, the other arm in air, signalling us to follow. "Let's go boys!"

Gregory and I shared a look, tailing the old crazy man. Our mini unit cut down and shot anything beast–like near, Marcus was going hams, enjoying the rumble. Glowing red light gleamed ahead of our path, my father geared head to toe, wielding Wrath, slashing through humanoid shadows.

Marcus shouted happily, "Vic! I got your boy!" Swinging his stick around again. White light shot out, clearing the mist, and sending three creatures lurking, yards away. *Where was this guy during our rescue raid?* My brain didn't get a single moment to register everything going on when panic hit me next.

If father was here, where was Hecate?! "Hecate!?" I shouted around the clearing. I could vaguely make out a broken-up wagon. The Smithe's carriage.

"She's on the other side, push forward!" Father raised his bloodied sword, power pulsing through, clearing more space for us. His helmet on, blood splattered upon it too. He had a mini unit of his own, Lord Smithe too, bloodied up and fighting. His family, nowhere in sight.

A sinister laugh filled the atmosphere, we all looked to each other, some of us switched on immediately. "Show me what you're made of!"

I yelled to my father, "He's here!!!" The whites of his eyes consumed black, his blues glowing unnaturally – met mine. In that moment, another humanoid figure dropped from the dark sky.

He was here, for Hecate.

"Hecate?!" I began racing toward the darkness, father hot on my pursuit. We slashed and dashed, pushing, to a clearing.

That hooded sorcerer stood meters away from my sister, that very same ring of mist around them. Trevore on the ground, a sword of darkness pinning him there, Selene nailed to the wagon behind Hecate, her arms and legs pierced through.

My father flew forward, sword ready, when a force sent us both flying back.

VALDIS

"What's this?" Silver orbs dilated, focusing in on the hag confronting some insignificant individual. He watched as the white-haired maiden tried to pull the hag again, observed the red-haired mortal look to the hag with weird eyes. "Interesting..."

"My Lord?" Arrus was wondering what had him so intrigued. "Now?"

"Wait, wait, wait... Something strange is going on... Start the attack, Arrus get close to the crone. Get the red-head mortal away from her, I need a closer look."

Waves of arrows went flying, Valdis released a blanket of his power, giving the fae an advantage for sight. He materialized himself in the sky, further taunting the crone, she was at a deadlock within herself. Arrus was battling the unwanted one to the side, as he dropped down in front of the old woman.

"Hecate, run!" The white haired one, hid cowardly under the wagon behind the old woman.

Valdis strutted up, watching the crone. Her eyes changing, those wrinkly hands at her side, twitching. "You don't know how to use the power within you, do you?" He snickered, amused at his finding. "Come, let me teach you. I would be disappointed if you died too quickly." He mockingly raised his hand, offering it to her. The hag watched him like prey for dinner. "Don't worry, I don't bite...." He continued to taunt.

The white haired one, popped up before the old woman, hands raised protectively. "If y-you want a fight, t-then you g-got one!" She stuttered as bad as she shook.

Valdis pulled a face, "How about, no." Flicking his hand, blades of darkness shot for her. Her hands went up illuminating, those blades evaporated. "Well, well, another witch in the mix?" He titled his head, glancing to Arrus and the red head.

Arrus, do not kill him... I don't know where the other knight is, but he'll do.

Arrus left at once, disappearing into the mist. The boy halted his following steps, turning back. "Watch, little girl, what real power looks like." He flicked his hand down, that long dark sword reappearing, as he flew to the young mortal. The boy barely blocks, Valdis kicks his sword up, round housing him with that opening. A scream resounds behind him, as he continues his assault.

You're not the one I want, but you'll have to do for now. He raised his sword to strike, when burning lights shot at him, scolding his wounded back. He spun, the white haired one still shaking, palms illuminating as bright as her eyes now.

"You vicious little bitch!" His hand shot up, sending more blades of darkness spearing toward her.

She was able to block a few, the others sending her flying and pinned to the wagon. Soaring past the crone, with a painful scream.

"See? That is juvenile, even you could do that." He catches from the corner of his vision, the boy moving for a blade at his belt. Quickly kicking it away, he brings his own sword down, pinning the boy down next. His hands fly up to his shoulder and burned, trying to remove the sword. The boy screams, Valdis twists the blade to secure him further.

"Ah, ah, ah, no touchy." He smiled at his miserable state before stalking closer to the hag, who idly stood there, twitching out.

No one stood in his way now.

He noted the smell, cascading off her. "That's it, just a little more!" He felt a presence appear behind him, advancing with hell's power. He waits, knowing any moment now, and right on cue, she explodes. Purple energy shoots forward, forcing him and everything else flying. He was ready this time, melting into shadow as the energy soars. He materializes moments later, his mist pushed back, "Ha see–" Valdis freezes.

The crone no longer stood there, a young girl with black hair, and haunting green eyes, stared him down. Every vein in her body flaring with that same purple energy. "You!?" In his moment of confusion, she raises her hand with incoherent words, and a bolt of pure mana, connects. Sending him flying, faster and harder than before.

"Hecate!?!" Some-one yells as he hits the ground hard. An armoured mortal, with that hell's power, clinging to him rushes by. His vision shakes, the crone in place where that girl stood. The mortal shields her, "Come at me fiend!" That sword in hand, reeking of death.

How? He staggered to his feet when a blow comes from the right. A boot to the ribs. "Die!" This voice – the knight from the raid.

He catches the man's raised arm, halting the dagger before it even begins its descent on him. "You should really do the shouting after, the killing." He knees him in the gut, sending him stumbling back painfully.

"Alastor!" The armoured one shouts again. "Get to your sister!" Valdis doesn't see the man randomly pop up next to him, swinging that sword, a lightning bolt of red advances. In the last-second, he dodges, that sword catching his cheek, with a sting. Flicking his hand for another sword, he has no choice, but to go toe to toe, with an old opponent.

ALASTOR

"Alastor, get to your sister!" Father commands, his swing inches from beheading the sorcerer. I sprint for her, her body limp on the ground. Selene behind her, unconscious, pinned still too. Her blood ran thickly from her pinned body parts.

I check on my father's position, two swords clashing, sparks flinging from the combat. The sorcerer struggling against my father's relentless attacks, battering him.

Holy shit...

"Those tricks won't work on me!" Father throws off his helmet, his blues consumed by the storm, "It's time to end this." He swings his sword up, his hand gliding along the blade, smearing his blood. "My mercy to you, shall be a swift and painless death heathen!" Wrath ignites, blazing red flames, overtaking the blade.

The silvered-eyed-sorcerer staggers back, "Impossible! Your ilk was slaughtered long ago!" His sword in turn, pulses. Silver flames of its own, igniting with every pulse.

"Not all of us." Father flings himself back into the fight, in tune to the battle dance the sorcerer was displaying.

I picked my sister up, throwing her over my shoulder, shuffling next for Selene. Those blades burning like fire when I tried to touch them. "Fuck!" I pull my hand back, quickly. She was pinned in several spots – I had no idea how to get her down.

A yell pulls my attention behind me, the sorcerer on the ground, my father now looms over him. *Kill him!* I was mentally screaming at him. The sword went down, through the sorcerer's chest.

The whole area blows back from impact, shadows pouring forth. I lose my hold on Hecate, flying back and crashing into her pinned lady in waiting, those blades burning me in several spots. Sounds of roaring, and men crying as I tumble through debris, from the blast wave.

Jamming into a stone, the dust settles, my ears ring at a high pitch. Our camp completely blown apart, people scattered, everywhere.

I crawl from my spot, "Father... Hecate!?" My own voice muffled.

"Retreat!" A tall dark man of markings roars, holding the sorcerer's body in his arms. A dark cloud swooshes through, taking the enemies away. The sky cleared, the sun brightly shining on the destruction.

My vision blurs and clears. I stand to my wobbling feet, limping back towards the centre of the blast. My father on his knees, lifting my sister, red liquid covered her entire face. I tried to rush forward, falling. "Easy there, son." Marcus appears, helping me stand again.

"I need to get to them..." Warm liquid poured down my face, I felt it run over my cheeks like rain.

"Relax, take it easy."

My vision began to darken, the area now whirling red. I fought to keep my eyes open when Marcus whispers to me, "Fume..." and my world goes dark.

I dreamt of our gardens, my mother in the distance, in her coveralls tending to them. She wore a straw sun hat, tied under her chin, in a light blue bow. Her beautiful golden hair in waves around her. "Ally, come here my sweet." Her hand covered in dirt, reaching to me.

I fumbled forward to her, my legs short, my hands small. "M–mommy!" My little legs rushed to her, my tiny hands grasping those warm smooth hands, that I hadn't felt in forever.

"Shh. Don't cry, my brave little knight. Mommies right here." Her voice was as sweet as I remembered it, she was warmer than a summer's day. "You've had a nasty fall, didn't you." I had no idea what she was talking about, and I didn't care, she was here. I basked in the warmth radiating from her. "You need to be strong Ally, protect our people..."

"From whom?" I looked up to her, those brown eyes sparkling brighter than any star. Her mouth was moving, but the sounds drained away.

"Mommy?" She turned to white mist before me, the gardens burning in flames. "MOMMY!" My small voice, much louder and deeper now. My hands covered in blood. Our home engulfed in flames, as black thick smoke raised to the skies. Our town burning to the ground, I spun around repeatedly, or the world was spinning around me.

"Ah" I jolted – my eyes opened.

"Whoa, relax, Alastor." Father's voice settles me, I try blinking away the dark, everything hard to see. "Good to see you're finally awake..."

"W–What happened?" I attempted to sit up, my back aching.

"Oh no you don't. Lie still, you're on bed rest boy."

The room begins to appear, herbs hanging from a ceiling, above the bed. "Where– "

"We're in the capital now, my son." His voice calm and quiet. My eyes dart around for the others, "Calm your nerves, you're going to have another fit."

"Where's Hecate?! The camp?! The– "

"Alastor, calm down!" He shoves my shoulders down, his face above mine. "Everything is alright, back up arrived not long after. Reinforcements from Klaedo and Crossidius came to us. Escorting and aiding us here." He releases his hold on me, sitting back into his chair. "The others are recovering at the castle, in the medical wards."

"And– "

"Hecate is in the garden with Sir Marc."

"Sir?"

My father leans back, something in those eyes shift. Those whites consumed by darkness, resurfaces in my mind. "We have a lot to talk about..."

CHAPTER TWENTY-TWO

ALASTOR

Before Desdemona was an island, the land was connected to the others, known as the first world. For thousands of years many species and races of beings lived together. Many wars were fought over trifling things, as always.

One war stood out in our history above all others. One that happened two thousand years ago, a group of gods band together to stop this great war, that raged on for four hundred years.

Combining their power and divinity in sacrifice, a great power like no other, came down from the heavens. Blowing people and earth apart, separating the lands.

The continents later, fought for this tiny island, the earth soaked with the magic of the fallen. The very creaks carrying the memories of past secrets. Twelve warriors stood above the rest in defending the land from other beings, good and bad. Protecting the sacred land as their predecessors did. These people were known as the Warriors of Light.

"Each town is named after these warriors." My father continues this tale, one so similar yet so different from the history we were taught.

Lady Zira of Kindness, her town Fort Zira. Sir Endolas of diligence, his town, Endolas. Sir Yison the strong, his town of course, Yison. These three make up, three of the four towns in the North.

Lord Newmont the loyal, of course is Newmont, the town you were born in. Lady Nesmo the wise, her town is Port Nesmo, for she knew the stars like no other. Charting the seas for Desdemona.

Sir Delwae the brave, his town is Delwae, just east of Newmont. Lady Scarbra the patient, who was said to be the greatest ally among the warriors, her town in the centre of the South. She kept the warriors grounded.

Lord Klaedo of temperance, his moderation in thoughts and feelings won many battles, allowing rationality when all others let their emotions run away with them. Just like the bird that stands for Klaedo's town, the Fechin. Then, Lady Crossidius the brutal... Her town closest to the capital for she was the king's greatest sword. These six make up, six of the eight towns of the South.

The twins, Lady Ortulunae, and her brother Lord Ortusolis the commanders of the warriors. As well as their younger brother Ortuelen, who was governor of the king's port.

Together they fairly ruled and protected the island, fighting for its own sovereignty, the day they won, that's when this island was named Desdemona. The meaning itself is twisted... Ill–fated, for the past was indeed unfortunate.

The twins were unanimously voted to rule the north and south. Queen Lunae of the North her castle in Ortulunae, and King Solis of the South, his place is our own capital, Ortusolis.

One however was not happy about this arrangement, Prince Elen, having the king's port was not enough for him. His sister even created a port of her own, giving it to Elen... That still was not enough for him. He sought out alliances with those the warriors themselves fought against, plotting to have the queen killed... His own sister. So, he in return could rule in her stead, he wanted a crown, not a town.

That sparked another war, one that condemned those of magic, magic was seen as the root spark for war... In the transcripts the word power was mistranslated to magic...

"What does this have to do with us?" I stopped my father's long history brief, wondering where this was going.

"Uh sorry... Well Lady Victoria Crossidius..... Had a son... Who had a son and so on... after the slaughter of their people, her great-grandson changed their name to protect the future of their heirs."

"Wait– "

"Crosse." His hands clasped together, gazing off outside. "Our ancestors became farmers, protecting the land in other ways... Wrath was once Victoria's, a family heirloom passed down through the ages... Only a Crossidius can wield the demanding sword... It is cursed to our bloodline..."

Wrath contained the power from one of the cardinal sins, immersed in the red stone at the pommel. A family heirloom passed down from generation to generation. The sword resembles a cross, upside down. The handle engraved with thorny vines that stretched out and around the guard arms, some vines engraved into the shoulder of the steel up the edge. The fuller up the steel – deep red– myth be told, the powerful sword thirsted on the blood of its fallen. A brutal sword for the Lady of Brutality herself.

My eyes enlarged from the truth laid before me, I could not speak, my mind was blown.

He didn't stop there, and my once normal life became even more complicated. "Your mother... Melena, descends from the Ortu–family... Her ancestors went into hiding as well... Mana runs in your blood on both sides." He paused, breathing deeply. "She predicted this was to come... Dreams... are powerful things..."

HECATE

We we're attacked, and then everything goes foggy, a white mist fogging my memory. I remember the sorcerer taunting me, but before I could finish him, white mist swept me away.

I walked along a trail of worn-down grass, as though many walked this before me. Trees taller than buildings, old trees. Their trunks thick, bigger than any tree I'd ever seen. They were shades of light browns with markings only on the ones along the path. Un-seen birds sang high up in the green tops, as the sun poured through the tree's gaps. It was peaceful, and that's what I found unnerving.

I constantly peered over my shoulder, following this path. Eyes watched me, but nothing lurked in the open spaces between the trees. I steadily carried on until I found a cottage, the trees circled the cottage, as if it were the final destination. The sky above without any branches, the sun, floodlighting like an arrow.

I listened for a while watching my surroundings, debating to go further. Only the birds sang, tweeting to each other. White smoke raised from the little cosy chimney, covered in moss. I willed myself to investigate further. *Curiosity killed the cat... That's what father always says...*

My steps were shaky, trying to climb up the five stairs before a short iron gate connected to a stone wall, that surrounded the cottage. The smell of baked goods carries from the other side. Movement through a window halted my steps. Someone or something was in there.

"H–hello?"

The movement paused, disappearing from the window. I went to take a step back, as the wooden cottage door opened. A lady stood there, smiling, "I've been expecting you." That voice, the very same one I heard in many dreams, beautiful and enchanting. Her eyes had my hairs on end – silver eyes.

"Y–You know m–me?"

Her smile grew wider, she had auburn coloured hair braided into a crown around her head. There were gold leaves sticking up from her ears, a crown, I presumed. A thick brown animal pelt around her shoulders. "Yes, of course I do, Hecate. Please come in, I was just putting the kettle on." She opened the door wider, disappearing back inside.

I stood there debating, to enter or to flee. Anyone I'd ever dreamt of, usually tried to harm me, and those silvers.... My foot slid back, kicking stones.

"Come on dear, I'm sure you have questions and I too in turn, have mine!" Her silky voice called from within the cottage. Little grey mice scurried across the entrance carrying cheese chunks away.

I was torn, I had many questions sure, but events as of late had my nerves on high alert. She returned to the door, a hesitant smile, "Life has not been kind to you, has it?... There's a table to the side, we can have our tea there." She pointed her finger around the cottage. Wiping her hands on her robes, she returned inside once more.

I step around the cottage in the direction she pointed, and as she said... A little wooden table and three chairs waited, the design similar someway, I'd seen them before... I choose the chair facing to the cottage, she appeared through another door. Barrels of rainwater occupied the sides to this door. She carried a tray with a tea pot and something else, covered with a red cloth.

"I have some snacks as well." She claimed, laying the tray down. I noted her placing three cups down, my head looking round for the other guest. "Selene will be along soon."

My attention went back to her, "Y-You know Selene?"

That smile goes again, "Si haras ellath." Those words had my toes curling.

"Dal... haras ellath." I replied to her hesitantly, the words were like food, to my soul.

She looked to me, silver eyes sparking, "Yes, yes you have..."

White hair bobs up over the stone wall, shyly. I shot to my feet, big violet doe eyes stared around at the scenery, in awe. "Selene!?"

"Come darling, we were just about to have tea." Our host sits, hands under her chin, smiling happily.

Selene looked just as surprised as I felt, she hastened her steps, joining us. "I know that voice..." She mumbles, watching our host.

The woman nodded, "Yes, I've been calling to you two for some time. It's taken awhile but we're all here now." She stood up, gesturing for Selene to sit. "You may wish to sit down before I answer your questions..."

"Do you first mind, telling us, whom exactly you are?" I was suspicious over her overly friendly attitude toward us. If she was another witch or not, I needed to know how she knew us.

Her cheeks warmed, a hand touching her forehead, "Of course you don't remember... How silly of me. Allow me to re-introduce myself. My name is Artemis. I've been looking forward to our reunion for quite some time..."

Selene looks to me confused, "Reunion?" There was a glow around her head, I didn't know if it was the reflection of the sun, or something clinging to her.

Artemis does not continue, but she does gesture once again for us to sit. We follow her air instructions, her hands take the tea pot, pouring us tea.

"How do you know us?" I try again, watching her carefully.

Artemis places the cups in front of us, sipping from her own. "How much do you know about reincarnation?"

"Reincar–what now?" Selene doesn't touch the tea. She took one glance at it and pushed it away from her, not trusting the liquid inside.

I answer Selene, from my own understanding. "It's the act of being reborn after death, to take in flesh again." A grin grows on the woman's face, nodding her head. "Are you implying that we–" I point to Selene and myself. "Were reincarnated?" Selene's eyes bulge at my question.

"Hmm..." She hums, as sweet as a note. "Your case however, Hecate, is a little different...." She points to my necklace, "the crone...."

"Look miss Artemis, you're going to have to be more straight forward for us. I am a bit of a simpleton, and all this talk is making my head throb." Selene intersects, if this lady truly knew us, she would know Selene prefers straight to the point.

The auburn–haired lady laughs, and déjà vu strikes me.

That laugh in a bright area, near crystal waters... A mighty silver bow in her hands, she looks to me, her mouth moving without sounds. She pulls the bow back, lining an arrow, and shoots it off across the water. The water parts, as the arrow glides across.

"H–Hecate?!" I blink rapidly at Selene who called out. "A–Are you alright, your eyes...."

"In time you'll remember..." Artemis leans back, satisfied about whatever happened in my absence.

White mist bombards the area, from the skies, "SELENE!" I reach forward in time grabbing her hand.

We both jolt awake, panting.

"Whoa, calm down ladies. It's alright." A familiar man's voice soothes us, Marcus steps forward. "Everything is okay, you're safe."

Marcus fetched father, who was checking in on Alastor's state in the other room. They gave us the rundown of what happened and where we were... I couldn't believe we'd been out for four days. Marcus suggested bringing us to his private residence, for safety measures. I guess he knew what we were as well, even without us saying so.

"Thank you." Father and Marcus turn to me, "Thank you for helping my family."

Marcus beams, turning back to father. "This one here is like a son to me, so in some aspect child, I was looking out for my family. Our family." He puts a hand on fathers' shoulder, who nods to him. "And you little lady..." Marcus turns to Selene next, "You took some nasty toxins in your body... Those bandages need to be changed, bed rest for at least two days to stop the toxins from pushing toward your organs." Marcus began flying off orders, father gestures his head to follow.

I shakily get up and follow him through the cosy place, he offers his hand and guides me to the garden. We sit on a bench, watching the bees and butterflies hard at work.

"Is Al alright?"

He puts an arm around me, bringing me in. "He'll be fine, he's triggered his awakening..."

I sit back up, "What do you mean?" Father tells me a story, one remarkably similar to a story I had read at home... "Like the book?" I asked curiously.

He rubs his beard, head moving slightly, "I was wondering where'd that gone, I should have known the book worm herself had it." He gives me that mischievous glint, pinching my nose.

I wasn't surprised to know about our family history, there was something different about my father and brother, and myself for the matter. We were just an odd family.

"Is he going to be alright though?" I needed to know, I had never known a moment of Alastor being down for so long, or even one to sleep in, in the mornings. I genuinely was concerned for his wellbeing.

He smiles a small smile, "Of course he will, we are all going to be alright. We'll get through this together, like we always have." He leans forward on the bench, staring off at a flower. "Your mother was a marvellous woman... Melena was fond of her..."

I stilled, father was openly talking about our mothers, unexpectedly.

"She was there for Melena in her last moments when I hadn't been... I will forever be grateful to her. To you both." He gazed to me, smiling.

"But... didn't the duchess hate- "

He stops me quickly, "Never. Melena loved you like her own. You may not remember much. You were a very poorly child... It was Melena who took care of you, Asteria was too emotional at the best of times when it came to you..."

Asteria... So that's what her name was. "But she seduced you..." All the whispers, all the rumours replayed in my head. I tried to pretend like it never affected me, but deep down, a part of me always believed the horrible words said.

He laughed, shaking his head, "No..." He brings me back into another hug. "This is a story for another time... I'm sure your brother will want to hear it as well." My eyes closed listening to his steady heartbeat.

SELENE

I watched Hecate and the Duke leave, while the old man was blathering on about the damage I had taken. "It's alright child, we are all allies here..." He placed a stool in the middle of the floor, between the two straw stuffed beds.

"I'm sorry if I offend you sir, but in my years, I haven't had many allies...."

"Yes, that seems to be a common thing among our people..." He undoes a wad of cloth, that magically appeared from up his sleeve. One of his hands held out, I presumed he wanted me to give him my arm.

I hold it out so he could remove the old bandage, I was surprised by the lack of pain. I fainted from the impact, remembering the fire surging through my body when they impaled me. I thought I would die, finally. "Our people?"

He unwrapped the first one, the veins in the area, near black. I held my nose from the awful smell that came, when it was revealed. "You know what I imply, it isn't wise to say such words in the most sceptical place in Desdemona." He gives me a look, and I shut my mouth hard, my teeth making a grinding noise.

So, he's a wizard...

"Judging by how well your body is fighting the toxins unaided by ointment... I would say your mana is quite mature." I'm pulled back to the conversation by his analysis. "How have you been doing your incantations?"

I keep my voice low, paranoid of listening ears, "Since I was a child. I've been able to... accidently use it.... It just happens."

His face lights up, "No spells, stones, rituals even?" Those old hands pausing. I felt the warm air on the wound, stinging slightly. I shake my head in response. "Hell... Maybe I am wrong..."

"Wrong about what?" He was beginning to confuse me, why did everyone talk so weird here.

"Witches need spells child. Or some sort of ritual to invoke the magic... An outlet, to allow the mana to flow."

"Shhh you just said– "

He erupts with the giggles, "I was kidding, this house is warded with mana stones, throws off the seekers! I'm a licenced mana-handler you know, they are none the wiser in my case." He slaps his knee like his little prank was the funniest thing in the world.

This senile bastard...

"Aha. All jokes aside, Miss. You hail from north, yes? I am going to assume your mana was activated at a very–very young age... And given from what I have deduced, you too must hail from a race of beings."

I flinched as he wrapped the new bandage, feeling the cotton snag against the wound, "No idea what you're talking about, but sure let's go with that..."

"A race of beings not found here." He gets all serious, "what was your last name before you family dumped you into that orphanage?"

How does he know that?

"I... I cannot pronounce it... We came from one of the continents, a hundred years ago I think... My grandparents settled in Fort Zira..." He nods his head like what I said made sense. "Do – "

"I'd have to dig, if you could write out the name for me, that would make my search a tad bit easier." He finishes the bandage and starts with another, straight after.

Our talk was informative, I hadn't realised how many people hid their true nature. Magic wasn't a taboo thing in the outside world, Desdemona was the only place in the realm that hated our kind. Then he went on about seekers, executioners who hunted witches, wizards, or sorcerers of any kind.

"What do they look like?" If we were to be here, I thought it was good to know what these people looked like, we needed to avoid them as much as possible.

He stood, his robes dragging behind him. Reaching for a cupboard, just outside the room. He slides a few scrolls out, bringing them too me. "See for yourself."

I took the scrolls, unravelling one, the parchment felt fragile between my fingers. A sketch of a bald man with a star painted on his forehead was drawn. "What the..."

A wrinkled finger points to the star, "They carve those symbols into the foreheads.... Similar to the ash smear in worship... These seekers take their roll very seriously, it's practically religion to them..." His hand retracts, playing with an end of his long grey moustache. "We must be very careful around them...."

A shiver took over my body, they were easier to spot considering the obvious features. "Why..."

"Hmmm, why indeed. Witch hunting has been going on since the dark ages. The war Prince Elen started... Jealous of the fact he himself had no magic powers, unlike his older siblings."

"I knew that much... What I mean to say is, why must we be careful? We've hidden well among the others fine, what makes them so different?" I rolled the scroll back up, wanting to spit on the image. Murderers, that's what they were.

"Because child, the eyes are the windows to the soul. Seekers can see things others cannot. That is why they are what they are. King Jonathan adores his freaky pets..."

Hecate wobbled back through, with the aid of her father. "What are you guys talking about?" Her green eyes look my way, questioning.

"I was just warning your friend here," he takes the scroll handing it to Hecate next.

"Seekers." Hecate doesn't even open the scroll when her father growls out. "A bunch of religious lunatics who believe they are god's gift to Desdemona…. A bunch of whack jobs." I was stunned by his fierce attitude- he didn't like them either.

Hecate unrolled the scroll, her eyes shadowing over. "I see…" She hands it back to Marcus, "Thank you." He slightly inclines his head to her. I was curious about her lack of reaction.

"You girls will have to walk around with a little pendant of some sort…" Marcus scurries into the other room, rummaging through things. Clanks and clings resound, the sound of things being thrown to the floor.

"That's why you and Alastor wear those anklets, isn't it?" Hecate sits on the edge of her bed, speaking to her father.

"Yes." He stands at the end of my bed, looking over the new bandages on my arm. I felt skirmish under his intense gaze, his arms folded. Hawk-eyes took after this man.

"Here we go!" Thankfully Marcus joins us again, with little gold chains. Blue rocks embedded between the chain links – each rock had an eyeball carved into it. "Wear these around your ankles, keep them out of sight." He hands one to me, then to Hecate.

As the chain makes contact to Hecate's hand, light flashes throughout the room, and Hecate screams. "Hecate?!" Her father lunges to her.

Her hand is smoking, the chain on the floor. She brings her hand to her chest also rubbing her necklace, or the skin around the necklace. "Whatever that was, felt like I was hit with lightening!!" Her face turns fierce toward the old man, she removed the necklace examining it for damage.

"Defensive magic… Quite powerful enchantment to reject a few mana stones…" I didn't know if he speaking to us, or himself, quietly. He then steps toward Hecate, pointing, "What is that there my Lady? What is that in your hands?"

She defensively covers it – I had watched her countless times, fiddle with that bizarre thing. I found it odd how someone like her would wear something like that.

"My... mother gave this to me..." The duke pulled her protectively to him, angling his head to look at it as well.

The lady from my dream echoes in my mind, as she too pointed at the necklace. *The crone.* Then I remembered the hooded sorcerer calling her a hag, the fae too called her hag or crone. "HECATE!?! THE NECKLACE!!" Everyone stares at me stunned, from my random outburst. "That lady, Artemis, remember she pointed at your – and then said– oh my word! "

"No way..." I was thankful Hecate understood the pure gibberish I spewed forth – I was beyond excited to have figured it out myself.

The necklace was the enchantment, that's why the fae saw her as an old woman!

"Artemis?" The duke asks.

"We had a dream, before waking up here..." Hecate begins explaining it to the men present, her father's eyebrows turn downward, disturbed by this.

Marcus on the other hand looked delighted, he scampered away again, noise banging from the other room. When he returned, he held a book, one that was falling apart from the spine. Pages were hanging from it, thick dust covered one of the leather sides. He flips it open, pages falling out, and abruptly stops. His eyes darting between us, "Auburn hair and silver eyes you say... Artemis... Goddess of the hunt." He flips the book, showing us an illustration.

A woman in white robes, auburn hair braided around her head, and silver eyes. She held a great silver bow, an impressive elk with incredible antlers raised its legs behind her. Hecate slowly raised from the bed, the sound breaking me from my stare.

Hecate whispers, "I've seen that bow before...."

CHAPTER TWENTY-THREE

HECATE

Father was deeply disturbed about the dreams, considering what happened with his wife. He and Marcus left the room, to talk privately amongst themselves.

"Hecate do you think... You know that lady... could she be, the goddess?"

My head rolled to the side – Selene was sitting upright, back against the wall. She was twiddling with her soft white ends. I could see the internal debate she was having.

"To be perfectly honest with you, Selene... I feel like I am not sure of anything anymore..." My entire world had been flopped upside down in the last three weeks. I was beginning to miss the days of lounging and just reading books of suspense, not living them. I missed gardening and my banters with Al.

Her mouth opened and then closed. "I have something to confess..."

"What's up?"

"I... dreamt of you... before..." I barely caught what she said.

"What?"

Her cheeks flushed, "I think... When I was little... I dreamt of your eyes... Something about them... Startles me." I sat up quickly and she stammered, "N–no offense!" She gripped her hair.

"Sorry..." I turned away from her, "I meant to say what do you mean, I never meant to frighten you." I kept my gaze at a seam coming away from the quilt, conscious now, how my eyes made her feel.

"There's something quite different about you Hecate. I don't mean from other ladies... I mean from people in general. You don't belong... here..." I could tell she was trying to soften the truth, but I felt every word she said.

Words from people I knew back home run through my skull.

She's an odd duck, isn't she? Oh, careful now here comes the princess. She doesn't belong here! Their whispers and sneers like flicks to my heart. *The apple doesn't fall far from the tree, hide the men from her! The Crosse family is stained from the likes of her. How could our lovely Katrina hang around someone so weird?*

Alastor's voice begins to overlap into the mayhem inside me. *Stop staring at me with those creepy eyes. Why couldn't father have another son at least, you're useless. Can't you do anything right? I don't want to play with a weirdo like you, find your own friends. You shame our family name, at least use it to defend yourself, it's the only power you have. You don't belong here, why don't you join the circus and fuck off already.*

I got up, careful not to look at her. "I'm going to check on my brother." My heart felt funny. I didn't look back as I used the walls for support.

Father and Marcus were seen out one of the windows, father had his hands behind his back. Whatever they were talking about, he didn't look so good. I continued along the wall to the second room, which was on the other side of this modest home. The place was cluttered. Herbs of all sorts hung from the ceiling, books and scrolls scattered on tabletops and shelves. A fireplace near the faded red door, the mantel covered with bright little stones and vials. I was in no mood to gander at all the interesting items.

The second room door was opened a crack, I pushed the creaky door. Seeing my brother for the first time since we trained.

His face was ghostly, not sun kissed. Sweat shined on his forehead, dark stitches to the left-hand side. Dust sparkled in the air above him, as the sun poured through the little window. There was a small chair at the side of the too small bed for him. I breathlessly got to the chair in time before falling. Alastor never stirred, his wide chest proceeded to steadily rise and fall.

"You know... I was always envious of you..." His hands were at each side, his feet hanging over the end of the bed, prompt up with pillows on a table. I'd never actually seen what his sleeping face was like. "Everything you did, you went above and beyond. Everyone who knew you, praised you, like you were some god..." His lashes never twitched as I complained to him, freckles coloured his straight nose, standing out more with his paled skin. He looked exactly like father in this moment.

"I just wanted you to like me... Even just a little... I never understood why you hated me so much... Our mothers were actually friends, did you know that?" Warm liquid slid down my cheeks. "I will not ask for your forgiveness now... I deserve the hatred you feel for the last two years... I just wish. I just wish I was stronger... like you... I just want to belong somewhere... and not feel so... alone." I pulled my necklace from my pocket, placing it around my neck. Then folding my arms to the side of the bed, I buried my face in them.

I drifted off at Alastor's bed side, my world became dark, that dark mist swirled around. The mist parted and I found myself back at that tree, silver leaves decorated the ground below. I should have been afraid, yet I wasn't. I felt numb, not even the frigid air could shake me.

"YOUUUU!?" I turned slowly to that all too familiar voice. Silver eyes stared at me with such anger. His perfect nostrils flared, a twitching hand rising.

"Why do you hate me so much?" My whole life's injustice began spewing out, uncontrollably. "What did I ever do to you?"

His hand paused, that sculptured chest, wrapped up, heaving faster. "Why does one need a reason for anything?! If you want to do something, just do it!" His face went crazy, "You are the bane to my existence, hag!" His eyes began to swirl, shadows poured from his pupils, engulfing his irises.

I knew the raised hand could kill me – I could not forget the scene of Selene being overpowered by him. Helplessly watching, as her body flew by me. My hand raised too, pulling the necklace from my neck. Those swirling depths, froze, dead in their tracks.

"Y–You?!" Terror crossed his face, a spark igniting with in me.

"If you're going to kill me, at least know who you're actually trying to kill." I studied the stars, taking a deep breath, then studying every groove on the pendant in my hand. If my life ended here, at least I could see my mother again. "Let's get it over with already..." I faced back to the nightmare standing before me.

His hand was no longer up, he had taken a few steps back. His chest continued to heave – confusion written all over his face. "You... want to die... Why?"

VALDIS

That sword came down into the prince's chest, and chaos ensued in its wake. Valdis slipped out of his body and stood in light – light so bright it burned. No wound covered his chest, to think he would be beaten by a relic of the past. Would have been nice if the king informed him, that they still lived among those mortals. Annoyance was an understatement, in his case.

He stumbled blindly, an arm covering his eyes. "COULD SOMEBODY PLEASE TURNED DOWN THAT AWFUL LIGHT!?" Yelling out, frustrated.

White mist swirled around, blanketing him. It ran over his skin, like a warm gentle breeze, causing him to shiver. He removed his arm, that mist congesting the light that blinded him moments ago.

"Uh– Thank you?" Shimmering in the distance, caught his attention. He decided to walk towards it, for it was the only thing visible for miles. His cloak gone, that gentle white mist walked with him, keeping him company. His hands played with the mist, curious as to why it answered. It was warm, and playful, dancing around his fingers.

He eventually made it to the shimmering specks. Tall mountains surrounded a calm lake. He had travelled to many distant places, never seeing this place in the waking world or dreaming one.

"Oh, beloved sister!? If this is your doing, please stop messing with my dreams. I'm in no mood for your games!" He tried to sound aggressive, but his sister was his soft spot, he could never pretend to her. He was curious when she learnt this new little trick, "Are you trying to be like me now?" Softly laughing as the mist nudged him closer to the waters.

He gave in, walking to the shoreline, peeking to the reflection. He was perturbed by what he saw. The hag laid upon a bed, then the water rippled outwards, she sat in a garden next to the man who stabbed him. Anger bubbled throughout him, he wanted to reach in and pull her through by her hair.

The water rippled more, that girl with black hair wept at someone's bed side, the rest of the image was hazy. "I just wanted you to like me... Even just a little... I never understood why you hated me so much..." Her eyes were dull with such sadness. He looked away, feeling awkward.

He closed his eyes, "Why are you showing me all this..." That mist tightening around him, as though arms gently hugged him. He sighed, "I just wanted him to like me too..." He tried to shake away the intrusive thoughts of his childhood. When he opened his eyes again, he stood before the hag. Her hunched back to him, she was staring at the tree. "YOUUU!?"

Her hideous face slowly turned to him, flat and unreadable. Those haunting eyes swirled, this was his moment, his gift from the fates. His hand flew up as her frail voice spoke up.

"Why do you hate me so much?" Her words shook with emotions, "What did I ever do to you?"

His paused, breathing faster and faster, "Why does one need a reason for anything?! If you want to do something, just do it!" The rush of excitement had his heart soaring. "Because you are the bane to my existence, hag!"

He would finally kill her, then no one would stand between him and his mission. Her old hand trembled, ripping something from her neck. Her roots bled black, her skin glowing with youth. She transformed from a hideous old woman to a beautiful young maiden. She wasn't just any maiden, but the child with green eyes and black hair.

"Y-You?!" He recalled the hag flashing and in place stood the girl. He thought it was an illusion, his mind playing tricks on him then, and sceptical now too.

Her voice was as sweet as it was the last time, even if her words were anything but, "If you're going to kill me, at least know who you're actually trying to kill." Her sorrowful eyes found the sky, making peace with something. "Let's get it over with already..." Those eyes met his again, and his believed to be dead heart, ached for some strange reason.

"You... want to die... Why?"

She laughed at his question. "Why does one need a reason for anything?!" He couldn't shake the lack lustre in her eyes. "So, let's finish this, mister." She raised her empty hand to him. "If I'm going down, I'll do them all a favour and at least take you down with me." That same white mist from moments ago, whirled around her, a smell cascading off.

"Who–Wait..." He stumbled back, even more confused.

"My name is Hecate Crosse, Jackass, and today we end this." That sadness swirled into something sinister, shadows darker than his own surged in her green depths.

Eyes are green, as the underworld's flame! The king's words rung through him. Her eyes were the essence of the underworld, a burning damnation.

In that moment, Valdis realised something. "He fears you..." The king needed the child because he knew just how powerful she could be. "W–Wait!" His hands went up to protest when she threw the first attack. A force like hurricane threw him back before he could deflect.

Purple energy flowed up from her spot, straight up to the skies, as his back slammed into a stone wall. Winged creatures flew toward him, spawning from blobs of mist, he threw his hands up, shadowing them with his own power. Her powers were indeed juvenile, but even then, she was strong. What could she become with proper training.

"I NEED TO SAY SOMETHING!" He held his hands up, a shield of darkness stopping the onslaught of creatures and energy from trampling and ripping him to shreds.

Her black hair whipped around her insanely, her veins shimmering purple. "I tire of your voice." Her voice sounded out of this world, as though many others overlapped with hers. Real terror washed through him – he was going to die.

"Hecate..." Someone booms across the area, shaking the ground. "Hecate, please wake up!" The area rocked insanely, white mist rained down from the skies, engulfing everything from sight.

When it cleared the girl was gone, his dream world left in ruins. He slunk down the wall taking in the destruction. The spot where she stood, scorched to ash. The tree behind, still smoking from her explosion of mana.

"Hecate... Crosse." Asteria's promised child, was a weapon. He closed his eyes, giggling. "Fate is a funny thing." He opened his eyes to rise, and one of those winged hell creatures rushed towards him. White teeth snapped for his face – empty soul sucking eyes pinned him to his spot. He yelled before it hit him, turning to white mist.

"Sire?"

Doc stood above him, Arrus too, both looking surprised that he woke screaming.

Sweat dripped off his face, he quickly sat up, considering things around him. Unbothered by the sharp pain in his chest.

"Be still, my Lord!" Arrus tries to hold him down, his hysterical state concerning. "We're back at the castle, you have been hurt, lie still will you!"

Valdis laughs maniacally, "The hag is the child!" His cackling fills the room, sending chills down to all present. Shadows slunk further into dark corners, Doc and Arrus released their hold on

Valdis, giving him space. He sat on the edge of the bench, hands gripping his hair, yelling at the floor.

"Hecate Crosse!"

HECATE

I see the realisation on that bastard's profile, I relished in his fear, witnessing his understanding. Before I could taste my victory, I was ripped from that dream. The room was filled with mist, thicker than smoke, father was shaking me profoundly. "Hecate!" Marcus was standing beside Alastor, shielding him with a translucent wall of shimmering lights.

I shot to my feet, "I was just about to kill him!"

My father's face drops, fearful. "He is your brother."

"NOT HIM!" I screamed my grieve in his face, "THAT SILVERED EYED FIEND!" I saw the veins in my arms begin to glow, throwing off his arms that were holding me. Heat spread along the glow, the fire within roaring back to life.

"He's still alive?"

"I can't believe you would think so low of me, to hurt Alastor while he slept..." I cracked, that rage and fire, crumbling to cinders. "Do you truly believe me to be, that kind of a monster?"

"Hecate dear no–" He reached for me again and I jumped away from his touch.

"Don't touch me...."

"Stinks–" I flew past him, running out the room. "HECATE!?"

I ran outside, making a break for the gate, slamming into some invisible wall. I hit the ground hard, a sob popping from my throat. Marcus crept up behind me, his boots crunching stones. "I've warded the house so we're all safe inside... You cannot leave..."

I rolled onto my stomach, a stone wedging into my cheek. "Stay away from me..." I let myself cry into the dirt.

ALASTOR

"So, you've upset her?" I drank the tonic Marcus had to the side, blue liquid in a vial, extremely bitter. I just felt insanely sore, as though I was experiencing growing pains all over, simultaneously. "You thought she was trying to hurt me?" After his educational story, he went on to explain his misunderstanding with Hecate.

Father runs a rough hand over his forehead and hair. "She screamed about almost killing him... I didn't realise she was dreaming... she was sitting there staring... the room... and her veins were." He sighed frustrated, that hand pulling at his own hair.

"Just like when you thought I'd sell her out?" He immediately glared at my words. "I'm not trying to fight with you... I get it, we're just as bad as each other... Give her a moment to calm down. I'll talk to her."

"No..." His head leant against the wall "You didn't see the pain in her eyes. I did that... I must fix this myself."

I knew where he was coming from, but I too had things to fix. Hecate would forgive father in the end, I had to make amends as well.

"Hecate is dealing with a lot right now. We both just found out, a whole lot of stuff, that has put us into some internal conflict. Let me talk to her... I can understand better from where she is coming from."

Father looked tired, "I've failed as a father."

I couldn't help but chuckle and he turned that terrifying frown to me. "Sorry, it's just" I chuckled more, till my sides began hurting. I clutched them. "Fuck... It's just, we're all thinking we failed each other in one way or another. I just found it ironic, that's why I laughed."

His mix-matched grey eyebrow raised, a small smile on his tight lips. The muscles around his mouth and eyebrows, gradually relaxed.

After some persuading, I was able to leave that stuffy little room, Selene was sitting at a table, poking some hanging herbs. Her hair was tied up, her ponytail swinging with her movements. Her tiny arms practically covered in bandages.

"Hecate could probably tell you about every single herb in here, and every pro, and con to them."

She startled, her head quickly turning to where I stood. "You're... awake then."

I held the walls, limping for the door. "Obviously."

I heard the daintiest snicker, "S-Sorry... It's just you two are similar with your sarcasm." She hid her face, looking down to her hands.

I nodded in agreement, "Recently, I think, we've all come to realise just how alike we really are... and I'm convinced that's why we buttheads so bad..."

She peeked up from her hands, a soft smile playing on her pink pale lips. "You all love each other regardless. It's envious."

I watched her for a moment, she looked back down as if staring too long, would offend me. "Well welcome to our very dysfunctional family. We put the fun in, dysfunctional." I nodded my head in farewell and continued my way to the door. I could hear from behind me, the small white-haired lady, covering her giggles.

The sun was descending in the sky, a brown fence surrounded the home, boxing in, a decent sized garden. Marcus sat on the ground pruning tall green stalks. Hecate laid face first in the dirt by the wooden gate.

I wobbled quickly to her when Marcus stood. "Leave her be... She's alright, why don't you head back inside."

I brushed his hand off, side eyeing him, "I appreciate the help, Sir. Marcus. I know my sister better than that, she shouldn't be left alone in her misery."

"My apologies." His lips pushed out, making a face. "I'll excuse myself then... Lieutenant Colonel." He went through that door I came out from, leaving me and my sister be.

I not so gracefully hit the ground beside her, she grumbled for her visitor to go away.

"You're not one to wallow..." I flicked her white ear peeking out from her very messy hair. "Putting poisonous flowers on my desk, pushing me down the stairs and now trying to suffocate me while I sleep. Damn Hecate, you're really upping the antics!" Her head shot up, frowning. Mud stuck to her face, the whites of her eyes, red. I wanted to laugh at her miserable state, "I'm up now, fight me."

"Piss off." Her head hit the dirt once more. She reminded me of a sulking child.

"He thought I would sell you out... You did not see the look of fear on his face when he found out I knew about you." She stirred but did not look to me. "To be fair, you and I put that poor bastard through hell growing up. I'm not surprised he thinks we'd kill each other. I mean, we vocally expressed it plenty of times." I nudged her, she finally raised her head, and I gave her a smile. We really did put a lot of pressure on our father, I was hoping she too would understand this.

"What's that?"

"What?"

She slowly sat up, she was filthy, still in those training clothes. "That look on your face?"

"Uh I smiled, dummy."

"Pfft, that looked more like you were constipated!" She begins mocking whatever face I pulled.

"Fuck off" I pushed her slightly, and she easily toppled over.

Those eyebrows of hers went batty, a thick chunk of mud was smeared between her brows, and it was my turn to laugh at her face now. She paused, as though she realised what I was doing. Crossing her legs, she sighs, head going down once more. Her hair was tangled, covering her face.

"No one is perfect Hecate, and that goes for families as well. The downs are going to happen, but we'll get back up... Together..." I watched the sun, ducking behind distant trees. Marcus's home was on the outskirts of the capital. I wondered, just how many homes he had, and what his story was.

"Gross, you sound like him now too." Hecate was making weird eyes at me. "Stick to being a brute, that suited you more."

I fought the smile forming on my lips. "Yea that sounded rather cringe, didn't it?"

The air here wasn't as cool as the air on our journey. Even as the sun began to disappear, the air was thick and warm.

"Thank you." Her words were quiet, I tried to get up, pain shooting down my sides again. I didn't want the conversation to turn anywhere else, it was good enough for now, just here. Hecate raised to her feet, stepping toward me with a small white hand offered.

"I'm too heavy." I knew she was trying to be helpful, but the wind could push her over, let alone me pulling her hand down.

"Just... Come on." She stepped forward again, gripping the back of my shirt, yanking it.

"You're going to bloody strangle me!"

"Well, I got to finish the job, and no one's here to save you now!" She snickered, her hold slacking.

I laughed with her, "You're mental you are." Eventually getting to my feet with her help.

CHAPTER
TWENTY-FOUR

ALASTOR

The old man didn't even give Hecate a moment when we entered the house again, grabbing her into a hug. Her arms vaguely hugged him back, a bit embarrassed considering all the eyes on them. She was a daddy's girl, but did not enjoy showing that off, publicly.

Marcus was brewing soup in a massive black pot in the fireplace, Selene sat at the table still, fiddling with different things. I hobbled over and sat at the table too, giving my father and sister a moment. Selene would occasionally glance over conspicuously, I pretended not to notice. She really did remind of a rabbit, easily spooked. I spied Marcus adding carrots and broccoli to his pot, from my right.

"Where's the meat?" I couldn't see any meat chunks from where I sat, nor did I see any animal bones around.

"It's a veggie soup kid, no meat in this."

I ensured to control my facial features, holding back a groan, one needed to be grateful to their host. I turned my attention to Selene, she was staring at my arm, with a very concentrated look.

Hecate and father finally joined us, Hecate sitting next to Selene, who snapped out of her stare down.

"Tomorrow I'll have to go to the castle. I cannot delay the audience with the king any longer. I would prefer if you all could stay here, Marcus has kindly offered us sanction while you recover." Marcus joined us at the table, as father went on about tomorrow's plan.

"What about those seekers..." Selene asked Marcus, who turns a look to father.

"You'll all be fine here. You all need a few days of recovery. Though, you'll need to prepare yourselves, he will ask to meet you." His hand reached out and covered Hecate's. "For the time being, until Marcus can understand the enchantment on your necklace, please only wear the pendants he has provided."

"Enchanted what?" I seemed to have missed something.

Hecate pulled that necklace out from her shirt, the one she religiously wore. "Remember when I told you about the fae seeing me differently? Well after a minor accident, we have reasons to believe, this to be the cause." She removed the necklace from her neck, running her thumbs along the symbol.

"No, she'll be better off keeping that on!" I didn't like this idea – something didn't feel right. "Feed him some bullshit story of how hard of a hit we took, and we are unable to come. That is her defence- "

"He knows..."

Silence fell around the table, Selene's eyes bulged. "W–What do you- "

Hecate dropped the silver necklace on the table, "I pulled it off. I wanted him to know who he was really fighting."

Father sprang to his feet faster than I could, "HECATE CROSSE!"

She didn't flinch, her eyes darkening, "Yes, he knows that as well."

My father's face went pale, even Marcus was disturbed.

"Why the fuck did you do that!?" I was frustrated with her recklessness.

Her attention slowly came to me, her eyes following after, her head moved. "I was going to kill him. I was going to end this nightmare."

Father went mental, shouting about grounding my twenty-one-year-old sister for the rest of her life, he was grumbling still, even as we ate dinner. Marcus calmed him down, pulling him away to speak.

Hecate just sat there staring off at nothing, unbothered by my father's fit. Something had changed with her – I could see and feel it.

That night, no one slept soundly.

SELENE

I tossed and turned all night, terrified to close my eyes. Hecate laid awake as well, the moon light reflecting off her eyes, other-worldly. "Can't sleep either?" I whispered in the dark, the home was so quiet, I was afraid to disturb the others. Marcus had more bed space upstairs, that's where he and the duke were staying. Some sort of converted attic.

She continued to stare off at the ceiling, her hands together on her stomach, tapping. "I think for everyone's safety. I'm going to leave tomorrow, while father is away. I just got to figure out the wards..."

I protested, "No you are not!" Fully understanding now, she was indeed reckless.

"People are going to die..." Her eyes finally found mine, there was such sadness in them. "I won't be able to live with myself if something happened to them..."

"We won't survive long out there."

Hecate's nose twitched to my words, "We?"

I folded my arms, gazing out the window, "That's right, we. We are in this together, remember." I took a deep breath, "I'm not going to pretend to be strong or unafraid because I'm terrified, but I am your lady in waiting. I took this job under the agreement we'd do this together, so deal with it. If we can get back North, I can navigate us around. No one knows us there..." My words were sloppy and shaky, I meant it to be impactful, just like she did when I was down in the dumps.

Something glinted, and my attention went back to Hecate, a tear sliding down her cheek. "Thanks for being my friend."

I found myself choking up. She never seen me as just an employee, or some survivor. Or some ill-fated witch... She saw me as a friend. "Thanks, for being mine." I had to look away again, she always made me feel so vulnerable. I couldn't remember the last time I had a friend, a real friend.

I drifted in and out of sleep, checking on Hecate, paranoid she'd leave to protect all of us. The sun poured into the small-crammed room, birds chirping outside. The sound of boots walking across the floors above had me sitting up. "Morning." I greeted Hecate.

I peered over at her quiet state, her hands still together on her stomach. Her face relaxed, as her eyes were closed. She had such long lashes, resembling dark curtains. Even as she laid there, not as clean or groomed as her usual noble self, she was beautiful. I could see why Coppertop found himself in such a state around her.

My mind drifted to him and the other girl.

A light knock came from the door, I got up and answered, the duke standing on the other side. "Hecate's still sleeping…" I whispered, not wanting to wake her. I opened the door little by little, hoping it didn't creak too loudly. The duke slid around it, tip toeing to her. I quickly averted my gaze as he leaned over to place a kiss to her forehead.

He made his way quietly back out the door, pausing. "Marcus's wards are linked to him, you two won't be going anywhere." Those blues warned me, I gripped the door for dear life. "I know you mean well, but as her lady in waiting, you shouldn't encourage her recklessness."

The heat rose to my cheeks as the duke winked and walked off, aware of our plan. "S–Sir?!" I stepped out swiftly, closing the door behind me.

The duke turned back to me, "Yes?" he was tall too, his face more relaxed than his son's face was. I was still nervous none the less.

I swallowed hard, "As her lady in waiting, I do have some concerns…"

"That is?" I could see worry now on his face– he wasn't shy to show how he felt.

"The g–guard and t–the girl. Miss Smithe… T–They are suspicious of Hecate." I held my breath for some reason.

His eyebrows came forward, "Katrina?"

I nodded quickly, "She knows we can understand their language… I worry who she may tell."

"Hecate and Katrina have been friends for years– "

"Something has happened!" I quickly cut him off, I knew it was rude, but he needed to be aware. His face went blank. "I cannot tell you exactly. Those two have not been the same since the kidnapping… I watched as she told the fae to take Hecate."

His eyes bulged then, but it was another voice that startled me.

"She did what?!" Brown eyes looked on with horror, holding the other door frame for support.

I bowed, "I'm sorry." And rapidly went back inside our room. Hecate was waking up, frowning, swatting the sun on her eyes. I kept my back against the door, listening, two sets of boots stomped off outside, a door creaking open and shut.

"Why do you look so afraid?" Hecate was sitting up now, watching me, still sleepy.

"I–I told them a–about the guard and p–pisshead."

"Oh?" Was all she said stretching. She rubbed the sleep from her eyes.

"Your father is aware of our plan!" I whisper yelled to her next.

"That's never stopped me before." Her hand massaged her shoulders. "What did you tell them about Trevore and Katrina."

"I...." She checked on me, waiting. I had this inclination – I overstepped my boundaries. "I'm sorry. Trevore saw your eyes, and I told them about the wagon... How she..."

Hecate sighed, "Uh that..." She rose, brushing herself off. "Let's get cleaned up, we've got other things to worry about..." She stopped, "Did they say anything about Trevore... is he alright?"

I shook my head. I didn't have the answer to that. I saw disappointment cross her face, regardless of their relationship, it was clear she cared. Hecate came to care for those around her quickly, I noticed, she put up a front but that was her way of protecting herself. The more time I spent with her, the more I realised how similar we were in many ways.

Boots stomped toward my back, then the door shook with the harping on it.

"I want a word with you two!" I could feel those angry brown eyes through the door, burning two holes into the wood.

ALASTOR

The door opened bit by bit. Violet eyes, peered at me, "Y-Yes?"

"You do not need to be worried about him, Selene. His bark is bad, but he won't bite. He was raised better than that." I could hear my sister behind her. The door opened more, Hecate stood by her, hands on her hips. "What's up?"

"What's up? What's up! We agreed no more secrets when we're planning to tell me about that bitch!" I itched for my sword, reaching to my empty side.

Hecate caught my little twitch, "It wasn't worth mentioning."

"I'm going to kill her." I was growling, physically feeling heat radiating from my bones. The white hare stepped away from the door, trembling.

"Calm down." Hecate waltzed up, the top of her head barely under my chin. She pats my chest firmly with three thumps, from her palm. "She isn't worth the drama that comes after it, karma will find her." I stepped back, momentarily surprised. Darkness swirled in her eyes as she spoke. "Are you going to help us get out or are you on father's side and babysitting us?" She walked by me, straight to the table, grabbing some fruit.

"Get out?"

Selene stammered next, "We're leaving... Hecate wants to protect you all. It's the only way."

I snapped at her, "Bullshit, and you know it." My finger pointing to her. "Hecate is quite the drama queen, believe me. She gets so focused in on an idea she loses her common sense." She flinched back at my finger.

"Well good to see you're back to your usual self." My sister bit into an apple she picked out of the wicker basket, throwing one at me. "Then tell me brother, do you have a better plan?"

I caught it last minute, fumbling the apple in a hand. I frowned at her, "Are you actually going to listen to me?"

She was staring at the bitten apple in her hand, "You've tried to warn me before... didn't you... I'm all ears, now." There was such clarity in her eyes even as those shadows whirled.

"Then listen up."

I gave them my opinion on a plan, Hecate listened intently, Selene eventually joined us at the table. She kept a healthy distance away from me, edging herself to sit down. Her white eyebrows jumped rapidly, she didn't seem to agree on things, but she kept silent and listened anyway. Hecate added some input here and there, not that it was bad ideas, but Hecate wasn't used to strategizing. We needed to be patient for this to work. I got them aboard my plan, leaving out some vital information of my own. We need to silence some loose ends, and we needed to know intel from father, first.

We would leave, just not yet.

"Common I'll help you change those bandages." Hecate flicked her head to Selene, something like embarrassment fleeted across those doe eyes.

"N–No, I can do it. I should be the one helping you."

"How bad is it?" I was curious, I remember the pain on my fingers when I tried to remove the dark shadowy blades that pinned her body. I couldn't imagine the pain of having multiple blades impaling me.

Her hands flew up, waving around. "There's no need for concern, I'm fine, truly."

"Marcus gave her some elixir to aid the healing and pain, but the bandages still must be changed. They are soaked in ointments that helps pull the toxins out." Hecate informed me, I caught from the corner of my eyes, red raised to Selene's cheeks. I didn't know she could colour that way, her skin seemed painted white.

"No more secrets." I turned to my sister's lady in waiting. "That also goes for each other's well-being. As a unit we need to be able to trust each other, information should flow freely, if we are to make it out there." I tried to soften my words – this woman was extremely fidgety in my presence.

She seemed stunned, I knew she was an orphan, but that was all I knew. On top of the information Hecate provided, I was curious about her background, what exactly happened to her. I could see the trauma responses that occasionally slipped from her. It was clear she wasn't educated as a lady of society would have been, easily showing those around her what's on her mind. Companionship seemed foreign and sceptical to her as well.

"They're sore..." Her head was down, still seated between where I sat, and Hecate stood. "But I really am okay, I wasn't lying."

"Then go get cleaned up, I have no idea when those two will return, but it gives us time to snoop."

Hecate's face lit right up at my words. I knew she was itching to get her hands on things, in here.

After we all cleaned ourselves up, we began rummaging carefully through Marcus's items. I knew truly little of the things I found, the girls would pipe up, telling me what exactly was in my hands, whether it was useful or not.

"Are you two wearing the pendants, Marcus gave you?" I noticed Hecate didn't have anything around her ankles. She was bare foot on the wood floors, Marcus had retrieved our belongings that were not ruined, thankfully. Hecate was in one of her humble dresses, a dark one, as were most of her dresses. This one stopping just at the knees.

"I've got mine!" Selene chirped up, skimming through a book. She wore one of Hecate's humble dresses as well, this one a dark purple, loosely clinging to her.

Hecate just nodded, smelling a few bundles of herbs. "Hecate?" I knew she wasn't listening.

"Yup mhmm..."

I walked to the room the girls were currently occupying, and just as I thought, a little gold chain gleamed on her bed.

"Oi!" Hecate turned back – I flung the anklet to her. "At. All. Times."

She failed catching it, scrambling to pick it up and put it on. "Thanks dad!" I caught those green orbs rolling.

"Hey... you guys...." Selene murmurs, "Take a look at this..." She carefully brought the book she was skimming toward us, paused on an illustration, a hooded figure with silver eyes. Her face going between Hecate and me. "It's him."

Hecate scowled fiercely – unlike any look I'd seen before. Worse than that look in her eyes as she stared down Katrina. She stiffly took the book from Selene, running her finger along silver writing. The weird symbols began swirling, changing.

"Whoa– Whoa, how are you doing that?" I was startled witnessing my sister do magic.

The girls both look at me in question, "I'm not doing anything?" Hecate blinks.

"Yes, you are, those symbols are changing!" My stomach started doing flips, the swirling felt like I was aboard a ship on the sea.

"Can you read it?" Doe eyes surveyed me carefully.

I focus in on the whirling, the letters appearing. "What the fuc–" I staggered back, my back slamming into a wooden post.

The girls then shared a look, before Selene piped up, "Can you understand the fae as well?"

Could I understand them? I never spoke to the creatures, too busy killing them. *Retreat!* I remembered hearing one yell out to the others, in human form, "Maybe... I'm not sure..."

"Well, you're not a sorcerer or a wizard, father would have said something, or Marcus for that fact." Hecate critiques trying to analyse the situation.

My father's words replayed in my head, "My mother descends from the Ortu-family..."

My heart shook, at the look on Selene's face, "You descend from the commanders of light?" Those eyes sparkled with hope. A smile that reminded me of flowers blossoming, after a harsh winter, crept upon her lips. "That's amazing..."

"Father said he descends from the Crossidius lineage, and now your mother..." Hecate's voice faded off. She looked back to the book, "Have they returned to finish what was started?"

We all went silent in thought, my father's words echoed in my mind.

War is coming...

CHAPTER TWENTY-FIVE

VALDIS

Music filled the room, soft notes played from a woodwind instrument. The lovely melody echoed down the empty halls, outside the room. Valdis laid upon his dark-red silk sheets, playing away on his too-big bed. The song he played wasn't anything fast, nor too slow, the tempo just enough that made one sway. His foot tapped in air, keeping to its rhythm.

"I love this song." A little voice stops his tune, "You've always had an ear for music, no matter what instruments you played."

He sits up smiling at his visitor, "Yes, I enjoyed writing this one. What brings you, tell me, the tune didn't summon you did it?"

A woman with short black hair, that stopped just under her pointy chin, stood at his doorway. "I'm told you are recovering. How can I be of help, to you?"

Valdis laughed at her ridiculous words, "No-one can help me, I am but extra-parts." Flopping back onto the bed, he tosses the piccolo he was playing with. Sending it crashing toward his dark slate dresser-drawers.

"Don't say that..." The woman glides across the room, white eyes squinting at him with concern. "What is wrong, tell me? It

246

hurts my heart seeing you like this..." She sits on the edge of the bed to his side, her dress flowing behind her. "What has he done to you now?" She whispers, a long fingernail dragging up his arm.

Valdis brushes her off, rolling to the opposite side. His legs kick over, sitting with his back to her. "I do not wish to soil my down time with talks of him..." He didn't want to be moody with her, he knew she was just concerned for him. "I'm sorry sister, please excuse my terrible manners..."

She stands, gliding around, dark mist following her. She gracefully sits next to him, rubbing his back. "He's an ass at the best of times Val..."

Valdis gives her a look, "Careful now, that's considered blasphemy."

"Let him try!" She stood quickly, stomping to the little slate table. "I'll knock his block off to Tartarus!" She spun, her dark-sequenced dress fanning out all around her. "Don't give me that look, you know I can, and I will, just say the word."

The wicked prince knew it wasn't wise to whined her up, but he found her defensiveness for him adorable. "I didn't say anything, I just don't want to see your name on his punishments list." He rose, strutting to the table. "Care for a game?"

A beautiful smile exploded on his sister's face, "I thought you'd never ask!" She quickly claims her seat, smiling at all the little pieces. Her smile glimmering like the stars.

Valdis sits, setting the board, "I got my backside handed to me few days ago, I was unprepared by the power that still lurked..."

White eyes enlarged, then swirled. "By whom, tell me?!" Her mist whirled around her violently, a bird of mist with big eyes materialized on her shoulder.

He snickered at her, "A warrior of light."

Her mist dissipated at once – shock replaced the anger. "That's impossible... Eru–"

"LIED!" Valdis gripped a dark marble piece in his hand, the wings groaning under his might. "He lied about them all being slayed." He showed his chest, a red blotted bandage appeared before her. "That soul sucking sword, Wrath, was driven into my chest..." Her head twitched, taking in the damage. "Then there is Asteria's child..." He flicked his button up shirt closed.

She stood abruptly, knocking over some of the set pieces on the table. "What?!"

He hummed to himself. It seemed the King with-held information from her, as well. "Yes, our little missions have always been about her child...." He assessed his sister, boiling with anger, her mist spinning around her like a whirlpool. He just needed to probe a little more, "He wants her." He examined the wings on the piece in his hand, noticing cracks that had appear. "What for – I'm not sure... But he'll kill them all, just... for... her."

Her nostrils flared, she was beautiful and terrifying, like the night itself. "How dare he!" She spun on her feet, gliding quickly for the exit, not bothering to say goodbye to him.

Valdis let his sinister laugh out, after he knew she was indeed gone. Placing the angel of death piece down, checking the king piece on the board. He lent back in the chair, smiling down at it. The king had his tricks, but so did he...

He snapped his fingers, shadows swirled near the great red doors that matched his sheets.

"You summoned me, my liege?"

His silver eyes watched the shadow, the swirling not as impressive as he used to find them. "Where is that travelling company now?" He tapped a nail to the table.

"They have reached Ortusolis..."

"Is that so... Have the shadows found the girl?"

The shadow shook its humanoid head, "I'm sorry my liege, we cannot find her, the knight, or the white-haired-witch... The red-haired mortal is recovering in the castle, but we discovered the blonde one!"

He pulled an uninterested face, "Who?" His fingernails looked more fascinating.

The shadow eagerly scurried forward, "The one that was taken alongside the child! Whispers say they are friends.... good friends!"

Valdis raises his hand, tapping his lips now, "Do we have a name?"

It bows deeply before him, "Katrina Smithe, my liege."

A smirk forms behind that tapping finger, a sharp fang peeking. "Well done."

HECATE

Al was disturbed with whatever he realised. "The king needs to know... the people need to know." I didn't envy the sense of responsibility he carried on his shoulder. Which is why I decided to play along with his plans for now, Father needed Al, I wouldn't take them away from each other. Alastor suspects we'll be summoned before the king, and we'd slip away after the audience. I would indeed slip away, I looked to Selene who was watching Al with concern and caution. I would slip away alone... She had been through enough already, she would be safe with my family, and taken care of. I made the decision this was something I needed to do alone. I wouldn't drag anyone else into it.

"Surely Father has already told him, that was part of the reason we were subpoenaed, wasn't it?" I inquired, looking back down at the jackass drawn on the page. Prince of Darkness and Shadows. Seemed like a fitting name, but if he was just a prince, who was the king?

"Hecate, we are dealing with beings who could be hundreds, maybe even thousands of years old..." I looked back to Alastor, his brown eyes serious. "Powers we can't even begin to fathom."

I crossed my arms, looking down to his lowered head, "Father kicked his ass, I nearly kicked his ass. Seems like it is them who cannot even fathom, our power."

He stood, challenging me, "Don't get cocky... What else does that book say?"

I push the book toward his direction, "Why don't you just read it?"

He shook his head, refusing to look at the book, "I don't like this..."

Sounds of horse hooves hitting the dirt, alerted the three of us, scrambling moments later to put things away. Alastor picked up a knife from the kitchen work tops, peeking out a curtain.

"Are they back?" Selene was trying to put the books back as she found them.

Alastor's voice was grave, "No, they shouldn't be returning till late this evening..."

I grabbed a butter knife from the work top, sliding it up my sleeve, I then positioned myself in front of Selene. "Stay behind me." I whispered over my shoulder. "Who is it, Al?"

He was squinting, "A carriage approaches... A royal carriage." He flings the knife out of his hand, opening the door.

I walked to the door, going no further than the threshold, Alastor stopped by the little wooden gate. Any further and he would slam into the invisible wall.

"Why would a royal carriage come here..." Selene was peeking over my shoulder. I shook my head, I had no idea either, I grip the end of the butter knife.

The carriage came to a stop, a small entourage of soldiers surrounding it. A lanky man leaps down from the front, unrolling a scroll. He wore a funny pillow hat, a tassel swinging in front of his extremely freckled face.

"Hear ye, hear ye! All occupants are to present themselves before Her Royal Highness Princess Cecilia! This is a royal decree!" He stomps his foot, finishing his loud proclamation.

Alastor flicks his head to us. I grab Selene's hand with my free one. Walking out to where Alastor stood, I made sure the knife handle was well secured within my closed hand and sleeve.

Two soldiers stand at the painted door, a great golden sun with a gold crown within it, proving it to be the royal carriage. Alastor bows, I curtsey, signalling Selene to do the same. I could hear the door open, heels tapping the steps, those steps softly touching the gravel.

A soft voice spoke, with firm words. "Rise."

Alarmed when I rose, to the woman standing next to the soft-spoken princess. Katrina. She was dressed as usual, bright clothing. I noticed an extremely valuable jewel on her sun hat.

"Well met, Lieutenant Colonel Crosse of Newmont and Lady Crosse, daughter of the Duke of Newmont. I heard of your injuries and come with good will. I hope you do forgive me for not sending prior notice." The brunette princess slightly curtsies in return to us, her white and gold dress flowering around her.

"Tee, I've been so worried about you!" A sickly-sweet voice tries cooing my attention.

I keep my eyes on the princess, face neutral. "Well met Your Highness, we are honoured you would travel so far on our account." I incline my head slightly.

Alastor agrees next to me, "We are honoured and humbled by your generosity, a princess of your stature finding time for us... mere people."

Now anyone who didn't know Al would think he was being nice and respectful. However, I could tell by the slight tone change he was sneering at her. Alastor hated the royal family, hated them for their lack of responsibility and accountability. He knew though father would have his neck if he disrespected them, without reason, so he learnt sneaky tricks to still have it his way.

She smiles, sizing up my brother, "You are as charming as your father, Lieutenant Colonel. May I call you, Alastor?" I noticed Katrina's hand twitch while the princess addressed him.

"I would be honoured, Your Highness." Alastor bows slightly once more. He appeared much stronger today. Colour had returned to his face, not as ghostly white as he was in that bed.

I decided to stir the shit pot for someone, make her anxious even more. "If Your Highness would be as so kind, to address my brother as Al, he would appreciate that more. You see..." I wave my hand up, fanning myself with it, smiling. The knifed one, tucking behind my back, "Only father calls him Alastor, when he's in trouble." I paused just near my mouth, giving her a sly wink.

Her smile beams, wide, "Very well, Al and Tee. Is that alright?"

I smiled genuinely at her, "Ah you already know my nickname, I am honoured." Careful my tone didn't come off as mocking. Katrina shifts on her feet, I could tell she didn't like how friendly I was being. She was used to the Hecate who preferred to avoid people, and only cared for her company.

Cecilia pulls out a fan, fanning herself, "Yes I have heard so much about you both, from Miss Smithe here." She gestures the fan to Katrina – I could see Alastor nostrils flare at the side.

Selene tensed, Katrina smiling deeply at her, I knew she noticed that too. Cecilia continued to talk despite the little moments happening around her, "Your father too, has said a great many of things, about you both."

"We would offer you a cup of tea Your Highness, but this is not our residents." Alastor thankfully cuts in, Katrina's attention whips back to him. "I ask that you forgive us for our poor hosting manners."

Something dark walks around the carriage, a bald man in deep brown robes, appears from the side. A star scarred into his wrinkled forehead, his eyes dull and lack lustre. There was a thick rope tied around his waist, weird trinkets hung off the rope.

I break out in sweat. *A seeker...*

CHAPTER TWENTY-SIX

HECATE

"**H**ow kind of you, I've come to see how you both were faring myself. The fault is mine, for no notice. Since you look well, perhaps you would do me the honour of joining us tomorrow?" Cecilia's blue eyes remind me of calm waters, I couldn't read any further into her. Her body language was impeccable, other than her sizing my brother up, she was a blank book. It was clear she wanted to check on us, but I didn't believe it was for our wellbeing.

Alastor and I say in unison, "We would be honoured." I curtsey once more, holding, Alastor bows too.

"Then I shall see you both again, until tomorrow." She inclines her head and leaves us. Katrina stands there her feet unmoving. "Come along Katrina." The princess beckons for her to follow.

Once the carriage begins pulling away, Selene lets off a shaky breath, while Alastor grunts. "Bunch of royal pricks."

"They brought a seeker..." I watch the horse ride off, zoning in on the seeker's shining head.

Alastor grunts again, "There is always a seeker with a member of the family, for protection." He rolls his eyes, making big strides for the house.

Selene stays, also watching as they depart, "Do you think she told them?"

"The royal family wouldn't have allowed the princess near us if she had, and I'm sure we would have been dragged from here." I pat her shoulder. "You did really well though."

She gives me a twitching smile, "I wanted to vomit..."

We made a light lunch, no one particularly hungry after that surprise visit. We informed Selene how she should act while in the capital, I decided to give Selene a crash course on etiquette here, which was slightly different than ours. They would be watching her, if she fumbled around too much it would draw far too much attention to the two of us. Considering my emotional outbursts, I wondered if Selene too would be consumed by her emotions... We were in the wrong place for any accidents to happen.

Father and Marcus returned earlier than expected, they had heard the princess came unannounced. Marcus was fuming, few people knew this was his private residence, which meant someone was flapping their lips about his private affairs.

"What is going on with you and Miss. Smithe?" My father pulls me aside, we walked out the side door, to speak.

"She freaked out when I was speaking to the fae, Selene witnessed her shouting for them to take me away... It hurt to find out..." Everything just poured out. "But even while I was unconscious, no one told me she visited the house... Then I find out she had been, but it wasn't to see me..." I took a deep breath, keeping my eyes down, I wiggled my toes. *Oh my god, did I greet the princess bare foot?!* I physically wanted to face palm myself.

A deep hum comes from father, "I did find it odd she never visited you... I try not to pry in your personal affairs. I understand my children need at least a bit of privacy considering their whole lives will be critiqued everywhere else..." He rubs both my arms. "I am sorry, Stinks. Friends will come and go. Good riddance to her, even if she was afraid, friends stick up for each other. I'll deal with her, do not worry."

I scoffed, "She is no friend of mine. I could have forgiven her for that, but what she did to Al is unforgivable!" Anger festered again, just thinking about it.

My father's rubbing stopped, his hands pulling away. "What did she do to Alastor?" Those deep blue eyes giving me a pressing look.

"Shit!" I covered my mouth. Father storms off, head bobbing. He was looking for my brother, I chase him, "Wait, I wasn't supposed to say anything, please don't ask him! He'll be mad!" I got in his way, arms out, keeping my voice low.

"Mad about what?"

Double shit. I didn't want to turn around – I could feel his scrutinizing stare.

"What did Katrina Smithe do to you, boy?" Father's tone was flat, this was going to go one of two ways.

"You couldn't keep your damn mouth shut?" Alastor's own tone – harsh, spitting at the back of my head.

"Don't you get nasty with her, young man!" My father side steps me, marching up to Alastor. I spun at once, trying to stop this, just able to grab his coat sleeve. Father gripped Alastor's ear at the same moment. "Your sister refuses to forgive the only friend she ever had, because she did something unforgivable to you. She was willing to forgive her for the insult upon herself, but you... You, my son. Future Duke of Newmont. What monstrosity has she committed that would merit such hatred from your sister?!"

"Papa please, remember... privacy." I glanced to Al, who was furious. "We are grown up enough to handle our affairs..." I looked back to my father tugging on his sleeve. He doesn't budge, his attention locked on Alastor.

"She molested me." Alastor said through gritted teeth.

My father instantly let go of his ear, "What did you say?" His voice dangerously quiet.

Alastor was still staring at me – I was slightly shaking my head. *Do not repeat that, do not!* He turned to my father, "She– "

Slap

My hands flew up to my mouth, from the crisp sound of father's hand connecting to Alastor's cheek. My brother's head inclined completely to the side from it.

"Some one dares to lay a finger on you, without consent. You waltz around, allowing such a crime to go unpunished? What if she had done that to your sister? Huh? What about a member of our estate?" He grabbed Alastor by his shirt, shaking him. "Do you have no honour… Do you care, so damn little about yourself?!"

Alastor eyes were wide, I felt my own burn from how open they were.

"No one would believe a man being– "

"AM I, NO ONE?!" My father bellowed into his face.

My knees clacked together, the vein in my father's forehead pulsing. He was beyond pissed. He let go of Alastor, facing me, that frown now directed my way. "How will you punish her, Hecate? She insulted you," his finger pointed to Al. "Attacked your family, committed a crime so heavy against your brother. What. Will. You. Do?"

I didn't know how to answer, I had never been on the receiving end of such fury. It had me scared stupid.

"Don't be like that with her… I told her to keep quiet, we have been discussing how to deal with it." Alastor grips his arm. For the first time in my life, it was Alastor I wanted to hide behind. "We were taking your friendship with Harold into consideration."

"THE HELL WITH THAT!" He turned to Alastor again, "He failed to teach that tramp decent manners, your wellbeing should have been priority boy!"

"W–We're sorry!" I felt like I was slurring my words, "With everything happening, we were just so - so caught up! He was going to tell you..."

"When?" He was growling again.

"I told Hecate after we– "

"No... WHEN, DID THIS HAPPEN?!"

Alastor looked him dead in the eye, "Her coming of age. That night." He swallowed hard. I could see how difficult this was for him, to continue talking about.

Father faced away from us both, a hand messing his hair. "I want her hanged."

Both Alastor and I made a noise, I choked on my own saliva.

"She practically hands my daughter over to those demonic bastards and laid a finger on my son. Only her death will satisfy me." He marched off, back into the house, slamming the door behind him.

I flinched from the noise, Alastor put a hand on my shoulder, and I jumped again.

"Well... That went well." He was still watching the door with a welting red mark on his cheek.

ALASTOR

Hecate was too nervous to go back inside, I had been on the receiving end of his temper, time and time again. Father would be angry for a few days, but he would calm down, only after causing a scene. Tomorrow was going to be interesting day. "Let's go in."

She shook her head quickly, her cheeks jiggling.

"You know what his temper is like."

"Al... we hurt him." I paused my steps, at her words, "He wasn't just angry... That was his heart breaking." Her hands went back up to her mouth, tears began falling down her face.

I failed as a father. His tired face flashed through my conscience, his words following Hecate's. All those times he lost his shit on me when I got injured... *That was his heart breaking?*

Selene popped out through the door, tight lipped, pity in her eyes when she glanced to me.

Oh god, she heard it all.

I stormed past her, straight to my little room. Marcus was minding his business, moving forward and back, in a rocking chair, glaring into the fire. Father nowhere in sight. I got to my little room, closing the door quickly.

My cheek stung, but my heart strangely stung even more. *That was his heart breaking.*

I looked back on the time I was seventeen, I'd taken a brutal beating from some thugs. I decided to take on an investigation, intel telling where and when they would appear. I got out narrowly. Father lost his shit on me, I assumed he was angry with my incompetence. There were so many times he got that way with me...

"*Your mother would be furious with me, for the way you turned out.*"

"*Don't start this now, of all – *"

"*You're a lot like me in my youth, hard-headed, and always trying to take the world on alone. You're not alone though my son, we're all here for you.*"

Hecate was right, he was angry, but hurt. "Fuck..." I got up from the bed, exiting my room. Marcus still sat scowling at the fire. "Know where my old man is?"

He pointed up, I made way for the stairs. "There's a bottle of bourbon under the stairs, take some up with you." My hand paused on the wood railing. "That man needs a damn drink."

I listened to his advice, taking the half bottle of liquor I'd found. The steep stairs made awful noises as I went up, the ceiling low, I was leant over walking across the floor. There was a corridor and two rooms, the ceiling angling down on both sides. The first room door was open, a messy bed in the corner, but nothing else. I continued to the second, the door was opened as well.

Father sat, front facing the entry, head down in his arms, at the end of the bed that was made on the floor. I found it unsettling seeing him like this. I knocked on the door, his hand raising to dismiss me. I invited myself in regardless, closing the door and sitting on the floor.

I was twirling the liquid around inside the greenish glass bottle, "Want to drink?" He made a sniffling noise as his head rose – the whites of his eyes, red. Guilt slashed my conscience open. "I'm sorry." I understood why Hecate got so emotional, it was not a nice feeling, paining the strongest man I know. "I truly am sorry..." I had to swallow down the thing stuck in my throat.

"Have I failed so badly as a father, that my own children could not confide in me for protection? For justice?"

My head wobbled– *don't you dare cry.* I was mentally repeating to myself, I couldn't cry.

"Then why have you two, shut me out? I am your father, your protector. Everything I do, everything I have done, was so you both could have bright, better futures..."

"We never meant to hurt you." My eyes were burning. I failed, something warm ran down my cheek, my vision blurring.

"While I was doing what I thought was right by you two… Was wrong. I missed so much, failed to see the real danger. The greatest threat, was my children, growing up thinking, I wouldn't have had their backs too." He sniffled again, hand out for the bottle. "I've been too hard on you, while being too easy on her… Parenting has been the toughest opponent, I have ever tackled." I handed him the bottle gently, terrified he would crumble. He took it, popping the cork with his teeth. "But I would do it all again…" He smiled gently at the bottle, the same smile I watched from afar countless times, when he was with my sister. "This is the feeling of realising, your children truly are all grown up, and don't need you anymore. The truth hurts." He took a long drink, smacking his lips.

It came out breathy, "We'll always need you…" I was finding it hard to breathe.

He handed the bottle back to me, gesturing me to drink too. We sat there, drinking in silence, the room was getting darker, evening had come. A part of me would have been so humiliated to cry in front of him, yet here he was, the greatest man I knew, crying in front of me.

It's okay to cry Ally, tears are just our bodies releasing all that forced down energy. Good or bad, emotions remind you that you are alive. Whether you laugh, cry, get angry, be kind. Never forget to let yourself feel these things. Let it flow, acknowledge it all, and then release it.

I could hear my mother's soothing words, as I stared at my father. Creaking sounded down the hall, toes soon appeared through the big gap, under the door. I scooted over opening the door before those toes could chicken out.

My sister stood fidgeting with her fingers – her eyes as red as the old mans. She slowly stepped in, sniffling too. She said nothing as she plopped herself next to him, head on his shoulder.

He put his arm around her bringing her in tightly, "Boy don't you say a word, get your ass over here. I deserve at least, one damn hug from you both... before you go off and start being all grown up again."

I didn't object, I awkwardly placed myself on his other side, allowing him to bring me in too. We gave him as much time as he wanted, to just hold us, as we were.

CHAPTER TWENTY-SEVEN

KATRINA

"You know Miss. Smithe..." Katrina jerked to the princess, who was combing her long brown hair. "For someone so close to the Crosse family, I find it particularly peculiar they did not seem so thrilled to see you. As you were, them." She placed her ivory comb back inside its wooden box, her calm eyes dragging to Katrina.

The capital was bustling with noise, the inside of the carriage, quiet. Katrina smiled shyly, "Well Your Highness, we have all had a terrible time coming here..." She pouted her lip, "Tee can be quite... Tempered. We had a little squabble before everything happened..." She kept her pout on, pretending to fidget with a frill on her dress.

"Yes, I heard the beauty of the south was quite a handful. I must admit, even as she stood bare foot in those rags, she was quite stunning. It must be hard on you to be compared to such a lady?"

Katrina's face dropped, appalled by those words, the princess was smiling coyly at her. She only sucked up to this princess because she was higher ranked than Hecate. She knew if she spun her sob stories the kind-hearted princess would fall for it, and she did... Or so she thought. "C-Compared?"

Cecilia's head drifted – the outside scenery much more interesting than Katrina. "Yes, I had heard from the Newmont guards plenty of times during the social seasons... The no name girl, in the shadows of the Crosse princess. After years of being compared to your sister, only to be compared to your dear friend... It isn't easy, is it?" She deliberately jabbed the country bumpkin.

She found it odd this no name lady, approached her, pretending to be shy. Cecilia knew the act – it was one she was well versed in. She noticed Katrina grip the frill she played with – she was also poor at hiding things.

"Oh dear. I'm sorry Hun." Her laced gloved hand came up, resting on her lips, "I didn't mean to bring up Miss. Coralline. That was insensitive, your sister truly was a star in our society. I just admired her so..." She analysed her little frets, aware of what triggered Katrina.

Katrina was at the end of her rope with the princess, but she needed to hold on until after they reached the castle again. "It's quite alright Your Highness... I too adored her and miss her so."

"On a lighter note, Alastor Crosse..." Katrina sucked in a sharp breath, Cecilia secretly smiled, this girl was an open book. "What a fine specimen he is, I envy the years you spent with him."

Katrina genuinely smiled thinking about Alastor. "Yes, he is so kind, and a hard worker. Newmont is blessed with our future Duke."

"He's twenty-four, twenty-five now? I'm surprised I haven't heard any marriage agreements yet?" The princess watched Katrina's movement from the side. She was possessive when the young master was mentioned.

"Lord Crosse doesn't believe in arranged marriages. He wants his children to find love in their own time."

Cecilia smiled, "Duke Crosse really is a lovely man, and a wonderful father to those two." She would stop here – she got what she wanted from this girl. Her next target would be Lady Crosse herself, it was amusingly obvious to her, the game she was playing earlier. Her sly wink to her, nearly cracked her with laughter.

Meanwhile, Katrina held her seething anger. The princess was the same age as Hecate but was on a whole different social level than herself, she would have to try a different approach tomorrow.

The carriage finally rolled through the palace gates. Katrina waited until the princess was escorted out before rising herself. Her father helped her dismount the carriage steps. "Welcome back my dear, how is Hecate? Did you find comfort in seeing her?"

She wanted to scream at her father too, but held it in. "Yes daddy, Tee was looking healthy, I'm so glad the princess took me along."

She jumped realising Princess Cecilia hadn't left yet. She curtsied quickly.

"Lord Smithe, I hope it isn't an inconvenience, but I would love Katrina's company tomorrow. I am hosting a small tea party. The duke's children will also be in attendance."

She watched her father bowed deeply, "It is not an inconvenience at all, Your Highness. My daughter is quite the social butterfly, I'm sure she too is honoured to be of company, for you."

"You may both rise, until tomorrow, farewell."

Katrina raised, her face twitching.

"Coralline would have been so proud of you." Her father rubs the back of her head. She smiled bleakly to him.

Coralline this, Coralline that...

Her father escorted her back to their residence, because of his friendship with Duke Crosse, the king was gracious toward them. Giving them a humble place near the palace, within walking distance of the gates.

She had always wanted to see the capital, something about it wasn't as dreamy as she imagined it to be. The people here were far more intimidating than what she was used too, and much harder to toy with.

She stomped into her room, throwing herself onto the bed.

Alastor and Hecate barely spared her a glance today, Alastor was no surprise.... She remembered Hecate's strange attitude toward her, before the attack. Hecate had never looked at her like that before.

"What exactly did he tell you..." Anxiety exhausted her. She was thinking how she could use this to her advantage. The stage was set, the princess fell right into her act, she just needed to set Hecate and Alastor up as well. One that would benefit her, even secure her seat as the future Mrs. Crosse, Duchess of Newmont. She would no longer live in anyone else's shadow. They would live in hers.

My lady in waiting will ride with me.

Made up scenarios of the northerner and Alastor together, began playing out in her mind. She grabbed a pillow, screaming into it. The white-haired bitch was standing right beside Hecate, spending time with Alastor, being showered with gifts from the Crosse family. She felt replaced, Hecate traded her in for a nobody, weirdo. She thought about exposing the northern savage, then she thought about the vital information she knew... Information that would have all three of them, sucking up, unless they wanted to be exposed.

She dosed off, thinking about her clever little plans for tomorrow and how she would carry them out. She was seated at a massive table, with tea and fine delicate dishes. Sun was pouring down on her, the air was just right. She had poured tea all over the white-haired nobody, making her cry, exposing her. Guards came dragging her away. She felt triumphant, sitting there. Shade casts over, she turns in a huff.

Alastor looked down, smiling to her, "Would be a shame if the sun burnt your lovely skin." Her heart leaped into her throat – he was holding a parasol for her. "Thank you, you have made Desdemona safer, exposing that demon."

Everyone at the table applauded her, but Hecate.

She sat their staring daggers at her. That same look, before the attack happened. Her hair was down, leaning back in her chair, finger tapping her small bicep. Her pupils pinpointed on her.

The shade covering Katrina started to grow, covering more. The sun blocked out next, by a dark menacing cloud. She reached behind her, "A–Ally" holding him, an arm wrapped around her protectively.

"What is it, dear?" A very distinct voice replied instead of her Alastor, her head shot back, to the intruder. A beautiful man with black hair and silver eyes, held the parasol in Alastor's place suddenly.

She found herself breathless from his beauty, "Who…"

"Hello pet." His charming smile changed to a sinister sneer, darker shadows growing and covering the courtyard, devouring it. Dark mist like the one from the attack pushed away her dream. She kneeled before the man, that mist shackling her in place. "Katrina Smithe, is it?" She had no voice to scream, no control to cry out. "Oh, are you going to cry?" He leant down laughing in her face. "Come then, cry for me." Her tears did fall, her vision shaking from how much she was trembling. He sniffed the air around her, "You reek of fear." He stood, snickering more. He disappeared into mist, or his body did, his eyes continued to circle her. His threatening voice like knifes, dragging along her skin, "Where is she?"

She felt her diaphragm loosen, warm liquid pool down and around her legs. She had no way of replying to him. He continued his laughing assault. She was far to terrified to be embarrassed.

His face rushed towards her, "Where is she?" Exploding into mist before hitting her in the face. She launched backwards from the force, free from the shackles.

A scream ripped from her, "Who?!?!" She tried to stand and flee, falling over nothing but herself. The further she ran, the longer the narrow dark passage became. "What do you want from me?!" She fell to the floor again.

"You mortals and your questions. Just tell me where she is?" Mist swirled around her – a figure stepped out from the swirls. "Where is Hecate?"

Katrina shook, staring at the feet of the intruder. Her father mentioned a sorcerer who was behind all the attacks. Was the sorcerer after Hecate? She shook, daring to look up. Silver eyes smouldered through the darkness of the hood. "I'm growing impatient." Red eyes glinted all around them, snarls echoed.

His white hand came near her face, she couldn't move, his fingers materializing a dark liquid. It moved as if it were alive, jerking in different directions as it closed in closer, to her.

"SHE'S ON THE OUTSKIRTS OF TOWN!"

HECATE

When morning came, father was in better spirits. We all talked long into the night. I fell asleep in his bed, we all did. No one made jokes or teased each other about it, there was a silent understanding between us.

"Make sure your pendants are on and out of sight." Father was warning Selene and I, at the table. I was stuffing a bowl of porridge down – Marcus threw bits of apples into mine. We would be leaving soon for the palace, I wanted to eat something as I knew I would lose my appetite there.

Selene played with her bowl, spacing out. "You going to be alright?" My brother asks her, watching her closely.

"Yea, I'm just praying..."

"You pray?" I was surprised, Selene didn't seem like someone who did.

Her doe eyes looked up to Al, then to me, "I pray to the moon... My cousins taught me the prayer when I was small." She took a deep breath, closing her eyes as her cheeks flushed. "We honour the moon, and thank you for thy generous light..."

Marcus stopped his rummaging in the kitchen, "May the sun protect the day, while you protect the night." He turned – eyes closed as well. "From the earth, the sea, the stars, the sky. Keep us from worries and bring us thy lullaby. Your gift to us is kindness, and we praise you for your benevolence. Lead us from catastrophe and shield us from maleficence."

Selene's face lit up, "You know it?"

When Marcus opened his eyes, he looked at peace. "It's an old prayer... Incredibly old. One not originally in our language." He stepped toward us, even father stopped eating, scrutinizing Selene. "That prayer... Phanaik..." Marcus looked to the floor, lifting ends of the rugs with his foot.

Father blinked, "You mean, Phanaikeluth?" His mouth was still full of food, porridge on some of his beard. He considered Selene, his eyes growing larger. He seemed to have realised what Marcus was saying.

Marcus plopped a massive book down on the table, dust flying into our faces. He pulled it from under the floorboards, near the stairs.

Damn, so that's where the good stuff was hiding.

He was flipping through the dusty pages, his finger stopping on a page nearer the back. He hummed, "Your family comes from a race of High-Elves..." He turned the book, pushing it toward Selene. "These elves worshipped the moon as we do gods. Each god to us, for them, is each element. Moon, sun, earth, light and so on." He was gesturing his hands a lot – this man really was highly educated with world knowledge. We all learned, listening as he went on about the houses of High-Elves, it was like the houses and courts of fae. "Your families spelling was slightly off, but it matches, and it explains the unique features." He pointed at Selene's eyes and hair.

She sat there in awe, occasionally glancing down at the book.

"Uh that's awesome!" I excitedly grabbed Selene, peering down to the book as well. Tall-lean folk with pointed ears and long white hair, some with the same-coloured eyes as her, surrounded a moon. It looked as though they were dancing around it, hand in hand.

Father ruined my little moment, "Which means you young lady, need to be extra careful... You think the North was bad for its welcoming to outsiders. You've not walked the castle halls." He leaned back hands clasped together.

"What do you mean?"

Alastor answered her instead, "They have paintings, huge paintings... Killing beings of all kinds." He played with his spoon.

"Elves were like trophy kills for the royal family... Their hair... Made into wigs."

I immediately lost my appetite, "No..."

Marcus nodded slowly, "Unfortunately. People fear the unknown, and that fear makes people do stupid things..."

I stood up, pushing away from the table, "I absolutely hate people!" Wind rustled around me, things rattling from it.

"Hecate, calm down!" Father pounced to me, pulling me into a hug. "You cannot act like this in the palace. You mustn't!"

White mist swirled around us, Marcus crept around, examining it. He poked it, playing with it. "This again... when did this start happening..." His words were drowned out, father's heartbeat like a steady drum, bringing me back down from soaring. I could briefly hear them mumble, listening to father's chest. Another warm hand found the top of my head, I opened my eyes, to violet eyes.

"I'll be alright..."

I launched myself to her, hugging her next. "I promise, I won't let anything happen to you."

CHAPTER
TWENTY-EIGHT

HECATE

Alastor and Marcus began packing up, a carriage would be arriving for our company. Father jumped into a lengthy lecture for us to control our emotions. We would be separated for a time being once we had our audience, guilt crawled through me, listening to him talk about our plan to return here again. Selene was holding my hand, and she squeezed it, I believed she too was feeling guilty.

We changed afterwards, cleaning up, it had been a while since I wore an elegant dress. It felt foreign, I became easily accustomed in being dressed down. Selene changed into a more sophisticated outfit, playing her part as my lady-in-waiting. I did her hair for her, braiding it, then crossing those braids and attaching them further down. Once I was satisfied with the different crossroads, I twirled the rest of it into a braided bun. Wishing I had more clips from home, I attached gold links here and there.

She wore a dark blue dress top, tucked into her black floor length skirt, black boots underneath. Her hair was up, and her top covered her bandages. She was ready. My dress was dark, shining green in the light. It was loose in areas, which shouldn't be, it was a tight fitted dress that flowed after the bosom.

"You lost some weight..." Selene pointed out while I was pinching loose fabric.

I decided for my hair, I would braid two semi crowns at the back. Loosening the braided loops, leaving the rest of my hair down and free. I slipped into ankle tall boots, tucking the anklet into them.

How was I to bring my necklace? The necklace laid on the side table between the two beds, I didn't want to attempt to smuggle it lest it reacts once more with the stones on my ankle.

"GIRLS, IT'S TIME TO GO!" Father's voice booms into the house, Selene and I nod to each other and exit.

...

The capital was glorious looking, but after learning about how they acted and treated outsiders, I didn't find it as pleasing as I thought I would. I would occasionally glare at people passing by, it was a good thing they couldn't see within the box. Alastor rode with us inside the carriage, his face well known among the streets.

"You seem to have many admirers, my Lord." Selene slid right into her role, careful how she was addressing us.

Alastor didn't look so happy, "Materialists that's all they are... For the record, Miss. Don't address me as lord when it's the three of us. It's.... weird." He made a face out the window, leaning against it. There was something satisfying, seeing them sat together, their outside contrast was pleasing to my eyes. Alastor was in his usual suit, father told him no armour, I think that's why he was grumpy. He did look charming, the same way father did. Alastor combed his hair back, few strands near his eyes. My mind drifted to Trevore.

"Do you think we'll be able to check in on Trevs?"

"TREVS?!" They were both spoke, confounded.

"Well, it's better than calling him Coppertop!" Warmth took over my cheeks.

Alastor looked to Selene, "Coppertop?"

She nodded, "Yup. Don't think he's fond of it but tuff, I'm sticking with it."

Alastor nodded in approval, then frowning at me, "Your guard or Lance Corporal Barnes, I don't want you giving him weird nicknames... The kid's head will swell." He shook his head to me, scowling out the window.

Uh what? I chose not to refute, Selene seemed to agree with my brother. I was feeling a little sour with it, I decided I no longer found it pleasing, them sitting together. "Selene, come sit here." I scooted over, directly across from Al, who gave me the eyebrow. I stuck my tongue out when she was seated next to me, no longer by him.

ALASTOR

Hecate brought Trevore up, my mind began looking forward to going into that hell hole. I too wanted to check in on him and Gregory, even if we had to suffer listening to that stupid king for a time being, seeing them sweetened the deal.

We proceeded through the golden gates, "Ready yourselves." I fixed my collar and sleeves, then fixed my sword at my side.

"We never got any more practise time."

I glanced to Selene, who was staring at my hand on the hilt. "We'll have loads, don't worry." Something shifted in her eyes, and I glanced to Hecate next, whose lips tilted downwards. "If you two have schemed some elaborate plan to ditch me and take off on your own, I will hunt your sorry asses down."

Those doe eyes went wide in surprise, and I knew I hit the nail on the head, frowning at Hecate. *Predictable as ever.* She conspicuously observed the overly polished guards outside, her hands occasionally reaching for her neck. The carriage stopped and I rose first for the door, stepping out.

We were stopped at the carriage point, just below the hundreds of stairs leading up to the ginormous white and gold palace. Guards positioned on each step at each side, going up. Flags gently swayed with the breeze above the doors, leading into the royal hell.

I helped both girls out, their faces astonished. I too was once like that, here.

"Greetings Duke of Newmont and your kin, Welcome back Sir. Marcus." One of the king's aids greeted us.

We all exchanged formalities, being escorted inside. I kept my attention forward, watching everything and everyone.

"Easy boy." My father whispered next to me. I hated coming here, these walls felt off. I could feel many eyes all over us, the pictures seemed alive, their eyes following our every step.

We made it to the grand audience chamber, King Jonathan and Queen Alice sat upon the two gold thrones. Smaller gold chairs positioned a step down, to each side. Princess Cecilia to Queen Alice's side, and Prince Richard to the King's side. Seekers hidden around the white pillars as we approached.

The fat man rose, arms out, his belly hanging over his belt. "Vic, Marc, welcome back my friends!" His face gleamed when it reached me, "Little Lord Crosse." He laughed, that belly jumping with it. "Well not so little, anymore... I commend you for your efforts against this demon who has been plaguing our kingdom. I have heard stories, you're just like your father. I look forward to hearing your side of the stories, later as well." I bowed low as he addressed me.

That smile of his bloomed even bigger when his eyes settled on my sister, my hand twitched for my sword. "By the realms. The rumours do you no justice." He stepped forward, away from his throne, down the red carpet that covered the stairs. "Vic, you said your daughter was lovely, not devastatingly beautiful." I caught the eyebrows flinch forward.

This was why father never wanted Hecate in front of the creepy king. Queen Alice was no ugly duck, she had thick gold hair, and hazel eyes. She was the queen of natural beauty, yet the king still took concubines to his chambers. Which was no surprise, Queen Alice, was once upon a time, one of them.

He stopped in front of Hecate – she curtsied in respect. "I greet the Sun of Desdemona. Long may he shine upon us. I am Hecate Crosse, daughter of Victor Crosse, Duke of Newmont."

He nodded, examining every inch of her, it took everything in my self-control not to spit at him. His attention slid to Selene behind Hecate, "And who is this beautiful young lady?"

Selene curtsied stiffly, as my sister answers him, "This is my lady in waiting, Miss. Selene, Your Majesty."

His hands clapped together, then rubbing, "Vic you lucky bastard!" Jonathan waddled back up the stairs sitting in his throne. "We welcome you to Ortusolis, my Ladies."

My attention was next snagged by Prince Richard, who ogled at my sister with wide blue eyes. *He is far too young for that.*

King Jonathan enjoyed hearing himself talk, flipping his shoulder length brown hair back whenever it came forward. The princess was strikingly like her father, the young prince similar to his mother, all but his eyes. Shining gold hair like the queen's, and bright blue eyes like the king's, those blues – never once left my sister.

"My Prince, has your heart been captivated?" The king's annoying laugh bounced off the stone walls around us.

The young prince rose, still watching Hecate. "I would like to invite Lady Crosse for tea after this." His young voice gentle.

Princess Cecilia spoke up next, "My dearest apologies, Prince, but Lady Crosse is here for me today." His eyes broke off my sister, looking left to his big sister. He seemed upset but said nothing as he sat back down.

"I'm sure Lady Crosse can find a few moments for you, my son." Jonathan's tone changed serious, interjecting between the siblings.

I warned Hecate this would happen, there was rumour the princess was gathering power, I had a feeling she was aiming for my sister. Father's allegiance was to the king, so whoever the king supported for the crown, so did my father. As future Duke, I too had to support the king's decision, everyone was aware Prince Richard would be crowned king. His sister was not even a competitor for the throne. That was why Jonathan remarried after the first queen died giving birth to a girl, they wanted – needed, a male successor.

"I would be honoured to join you before the late afternoon's tea party, my Prince." My sister was doing better than I imagined. Her attitude was commendable, a clean face, unreadable.

Even though Richard's lips did not move, his eyes shined with delight.

"Brilliant!" King Jonathan rose, "Come gentlemen, we have much to discuss."

I glanced to Hecate and Selene, this is where we would separate, until later. Selene was the only one who acknowledged my glance, ever so slightly nodding.

We walked to the council room, many lords already waiting. We took our seats, as I quietly watched every interaction. As expected, many disagreed to a war coming, the other half sceptical.

Marcus stood, that book we were snooping through yesterday in hand. His face solemn, "I'm sorry to disappoint my Lords, however we have concrete evidence the bogeyman himself has returned." He opened the book to the page we had stared at, silver eyes under a dark hood. "Valdis, Prince of the Dark Fae."

The room fell deathly silent.

HECATE

I walked behind the prince, guards all around us, Selene walked behind me, a seeker behind her. We were being escorted to the prince's palace, where we would have tea before we joined the princess later for her party.

It was just as we were told, massive paintings decorated the halls. Thick gold frames around earlier rulers, as well as battle scenes depicted. I recognised a few from my early education, as well as the beheaded white haired – pointy eared paintings. I was extremely careful of my facial features, keeping them as blank as possible. I slowed down here and there, pretending to be amazed, pointing at things so I could check on Selene. To my relief she showed no fear, and she played along well, to my little act.

We walked through a stunning garden that led to the prince's palace. The smell of roses thickly carried on the breeze. Selene's nose would twitch, rose was her least liked flower. I fought the smile at her twitching, just like a rabbit. Rose bushes narrowed us toward the great blue doors, guards in golden armour and giant spears. The golden spear blades were shaped as giant arrow heads, the base before the long staff, carved with the royal insignia. The sun's rays spear out sharply, below the blade itself. They raised the crossed spears, allowing us entry.

The young prince kept quiet until we reached a sitting room, where all others were asked to leave, including the seeker. The room was the same as the family colours, gold, and red. Nothing screamed individuality.

It was just him, me, and Selene, who stood behind the red sofa, that remained.

He often, tucked his golden hair behind his ear, those ears red. His hair was short on the sides, the top few inches longer, combed down – hanging by his red ears. His lashes and eyebrows were slightly darker than the hair on his head, his bright blue eyes like the sky. I tapped my knees in rhythm, the awkward silence was unbearable.

Those orbs would sometimes meet mine, I offered a smile, and his attention would shoot elsewhere. I didn't know what or how to talk to children, let alone a child prince. Tea was brought in and served, luckily, I had something to drink while I sat.

"Are... you really the duke's daughter?" His voice was so young, so innocent.

I tried not to laugh at his question, I was trying to avoid a trip to the dungeons. "Yes, Your Highness." I kept my eyes on the tea, careful not to fluster him further. A sweet aroma wafted into my nose, vanilla and almond.

"I'm sorry if my question seemed rude, it's just, you don't look alike..."

I inclined my head, placing the hot cup down. "I hear that often, Your Highness, it's quite alright."

He was fidgeting with the bright red sash that angled across his tiny torso, I felt sorry for the boy. Rather than being outside playing like most his age, he probably spent more time in that suit, studying and training more than any other boy his age. "It's Richard... Y-You can call me Ricky..."

I honestly wanted to tease the little guy, but I refrained. "I am sorry Your Highness, it is considered a crime to address the rising sun by his name, let alone, a nickname."

His cheeks puffed up, reminding me of a golden lynx-squirrel. His hair and cheeks, strikingly similar. "But it's just us here... I-I would feel more c-comfortable."

I leant back, angling my head to check with Selene, her hands behind her back, she shrugs to me.

He was intensely staring, waiting for my answer, his eyes were large compared to his little head. "Very well Your High-... very well, Ricky." He smiled so wide- all little teeth were displayed.

CHAPTER TWENTY-NINE

HECATE

The conversation picked up from there, or more so, the prince drilled me with questions. Odd questions about me and my likes, I tried to counter and ask him what he liked... He would tell me it was not important, moving on to ask more about me. *Did young children converse this way now a days?*

"How old are you, my Lady?"

My cup was now empty, sipping between his questions. "Twenty-one, Your Highness."

"You said– "

I raised my finger, "On the contrary, as I have addressed you as Ricky, you continue to address me as, my Lady."

His cheeks were permanently red during our conversation, I deduced he was just extremely shy. "My apologies, H–Hecate." I offered a smile for his correction. There was a moment of silence that followed.

He took a deep inhale, "I used to dream about you." My smile was wiped clean, as his little voice proceeded on. "I saw you, dressed in an all–black gown, that sparkled like stars. Your eyes like the green forests smiling down at me. Those... elegant, white hands..." He shyly pointed at my hands, and my fingers tightened around themselves. "One was offered out to me, the other holding a flaming torch, lighting up the... darkness." Selene gasped behind me. "You wore a crown on your head, as brilliant as your gown." He peered above my head, as though that crown he mentioned, was there.

"Your Highness, surely you jest!" My heart was pounding in my throat.

He shook his head, "You are here to liberate us, aren't you? If we wed, I could help you."

Selene spoke up from behind, "Pardon my rudeness, Your Highness, but we– "

His little hand raised, stopping Selene from continuing. Those eyes locking me in place. "Someday, I will be king, and if you would have me. I can help you. M–My Q–Queen." His brave bravado slipped away addressing me with some ridiculous title.

"I'm extremely flattered, and honoured Your Highness, but I am far too old for you. I am not sure what this dream is you speak of, but you should be careful who you tell this too." I was sure everyone could hear my heart thumping violently. I looked around for anyone else in the room, eavesdropping on the conversation.

"I'm eleven and three quarters, nearly twelve!" He missed everything important and chose only to listen to the part about our age gap.

"I think it's time for us to go." I rose, nodding to Selene, who was pale. "I enjoyed our time, Your Highness."

He shot to his feet, "You'll wait for me, won't you?" His eyes searching my face.

My mouth flapped open and closed.

"In six years, I will be of age, you won't even be thirty yet!"

I curtsied quickly, "Excuse us." Turning and fleeing, Selene quick to follow. Once we were out of the prince's palace, and was certain he wasn't following, I slapped my cheeks a couple times. The guard walking with us, double taking.

Selene let a laugh slip, whispering, "An eleven-year-old proposed to you. Wait I'm sorry, twelve."

I glared at her, "That's not funny!" Eyeing up the guard with us. "No, I suppose not... Your Highness."

Before I could say something snappy, another lady approached curtseying. "Princess Cecilia asks that I escort you, to the party."

I nodded my head and followed her lead. The walk didn't help my nerves, every person who looked our way, I presumed they were suspicious of me. Selene stepped forward to my side, gently grabbing my elbow. "Careful now, my Lady." She spoke a little louder to the lady leading the way, "Excuse me Miss, could we walk slower, my Lady is still recovering since the attack." She pulled a pitiful look. The lady apologised slowing her steps. Selene whispered near my ear, "Calm your emotions..."

"I'm trying..." The walk was long, the princess's palace was on the other damn side of this huge place. We passed by the medical wards, and I stopped, walking backwards to read the sign correctly.

"My Lady?!" Selene grabbed my arm, the lady ahead alerted.

"Do you mind if I pop in there?" I pointed, asking the escort. "My guard was gravely injured... I'd like to see first-hand, how his recovering is going."

She smiled, nodding her head. I entered the ward with them both, looking round to the many healing personnel.

"My Lady!?" A few of the guys burst out, surprised.

I bowed to them, "Thank you all for your services, and thank you for your efforts during the attack. My family will always be grateful to each and every one of you."

A few awes and light sighs replied to my words, but one voice primarily caught my attention. "It's part of the job, my Lady. You shouldn't be thanking us for the bare minimum." Copper hair shined in the corner, near the massive windows, his whole top bandaged up tight.

I made quick steps to him, "By the realms..." I didn't know where to look, there was so much wrapping.

"It's alright, I should be discharged today and back to duty, my Lady." A small smile tugged on his lips. He was pale, I could see black veins peeking over areas wrapped up. The man in the streets flashed through my mind. My attention went to his neck, luckily no nasty scar, but many scratches on every inch of exposed skin. His large hands covered himself, "Are ladies so brazen now these days, to openly stare at an indecent man?" That signature smug look on his face.

I pointed a finger at him, "Shut up you, I'm assessing your damages, there's a thing called worry!"

That smug look disappeared – Selene chirped up next to me. "She mentioned checking in on you a few times since she woke up, Trevs."

Warmth exploded on my cheeks, and I glared at her next.

"You were worried about me?"

I faced back to Trevore – he was blinking blankly at me. "You are my guard. Mine. Which means an injury to you, is an injury to me." I gestured to everyone around, some watching on curiously, others averting their eyes. "You are our people, an attack on one of us, is an attack on all of us." Many looked down, stunned. I looked back to Trevore, just not his eyes, focusing on his forehead. "Of course, I was worried..." The heat in my cheeks burning. "Would be a pain in the back side replacing you." I closed my eyes, pinching the bridge of my nose.

I sounded so cringe...

Laughs – one by one, began sounding around me, even Selene was covering her mouth.

"Don't worry, I'll be back at your side before you know it." Trevore wasn't laughing, his neck and cheeks as red as I felt. "My Lady."

"Good." I put on airs again, trying to recover from the embarrassment. "That goes for all of you." I marched back to the door, where our escort waited, her eyes wide. I spun around, surveying them all, "Please get well soon, we're thinking of you." I bowed my head once more, leaving.

Selene was smiling at me, the escort, dazed still.

"Sorry for the delay, lead the way please."

ALASTOR

After the council meeting was over, I excused myself to father, making my way to the medical wards. People of all sorts tried stopping to talk to me, I pulled a Hecate, aloofly looking away and continuing. I recognised a few of the local smaller Lords and Ladies, but didn't deem the conversations worthy enough, I had priorities to take care of. I was glad when I saw the great white doors, knowing our people were just inside.

Thirty were still recovering in the wards, we'd only lost a handful in the attack. Informing their families was going to be hard, it was the least favourite part of my job. I entered and immediately noticed many lively faces, I seen one young man, who had the worst among them. "You alright soldier?"

"Sir!"

I nodded at his partial amputee. "We still have plenty of jobs to do that don't require your foot, don't worry about a job once you've recovered, focus on you."

John, one of the older senior staff barked up, "Aren't we spoiled lads, our duke visits us yesterday... Then our young lady, and now our Lieutenant Colonel." He was genuinely smiling, not mocking nor sneering.

"My sister visited?" My eyebrow shot up, was she not with the prince?

I heard Gregory next, "She gave a speech, kind of made me, emotional." I was taken back, *my sister?* "She also told Trevs over there, replacing him would be a pain in her back side!" Gregory spilled with giggles, others following with their own.

Trevore was as red as a tomato, his eyes not meeting mine. "Did she now... What else did she say to you, Trevsss"

His hazel's wobbled to me, "Why are you doing that? Even Miss. Selene was doing it."

My mouth pulled, "My sister recently called you that." Oh boy I did not think his face could go any more flushed, but I was wrong, a deep red exploded all over. A pillow came up covering himself, from eyes watching him. "You know Trevs, if you weren't such a playboy, I might have rooted for you." His face reappeared, and once again I hit the nail on the head. "But unfortunately, my sister doesn't like playboys...." I stepped away, he was looking good, my conscience felt better. "That's why I recommended you in the first place." I threw him a wink, marching over to Gregory who was shaking his head, still laughing.

"Right for the jugular!" We exchanged arms, firmly.

"Go straight for the kill."

He was shaking still from laughing, "It's good to see you sir, we didn't see you here and thought the worst."

"It'll take much more than that to keep me down." I noticed the arm I wrapped, cleaned with a new one, cuts all over him as well.

"Whatever happened, that blast sent us all soaring. Was that your father?"

I nodded, everyone else had minor injuries as well, this was good.

"Damn your old man is a bad ass. I'm thankful he's on our side." I sat down on Gregory's bed. His face dropped when he appraised mine. "What's up Lieutenant Colonel, you only make that face when you have something up your sleeves."

I leant in, he came closer, "I've got to get my sister and Selene as far away as possible..." He shot back looking at me, I grabbed him forcing him back, "Help the old man in my absence, I got to get them somewhere safe..."

Our whispering raised many alarms, "Oi, sir!" Steve was next to Gregory's bed. "An attack on one of us, is an attack in all of us... Share your intel we've got your back."

Before I could dismiss it, Gregory spoke up, "Code green." I glared at him. "I'm coming with you. You'll need another set of hands."

Trevore spoke up next, "As am I!" Other voices murmuring in agreement. A finger flew up to my mouth. Everyone quieted down, I quickly trotted to the doors, closing them, when I was sure, no one lingered outside.

Their faces dropped noticing my suspicious behaviour.

"Code Green..." I repeated, making eye contact with all those at attention. "I cannot give any details at this present moment, but I ask that you have faith in me and my family during this time." Their looks are serious, many raising a fist to their chest, I too give them the Crosse salute.

Trevore stood, stiffly limping to where I stood by the doors. "I told you, I'll protect her, from anyone."

Gregory stiffly got out of his bed as well. "When?" Stretching his limbs with many grunts.

"Tonight, if she doesn't run off without me." I poked my head out the door.

He rolls his shoulders, "Then let's suit up."

I nodded, thankful for these loyal bastards.

The staff were a handful, not wanting to sign them off. It took some persuading and Trevore's serious flirting, but eventually their sheets were handed to me. We were on our way to the armoury, they needed their weapons and some proper kit, when we noticed a lady approach.

She curtsied, "Greetings Lieutenant Colonel, Princess Cecilia has asked that I escort you, to the party."

Fuck, I forgot about that. "I appreciate it... however, I will be late arriving." I flicked my head to Gregory and Trevore. "I have duties to attend to first." I made sure my tone was harsher, knowing it would startle her.

"O–Of course! I will send a message to Her Highness and return later." She scampered off, quicker than she approached.

"Scared the poor woman..." Gregory points out the obvious.

I roll my eyes, "We don't need eyes and ears on us, no one here is to be trusted..." I sighed running a hand through my hair, "I forgot about that stupid tea party..."

Trevore whistles, "Here we were recovering and you're out here wooing a princess off her feet..."

I was in no mood to joke, too much to do.

We reached our destination – the guys were quick to get armed and ready. I gave them a run–down of the plan, listening to anybody nearby. I would tell them later about my sister's gift... and my own for the fact. They just needed to know she and Selene were in danger and getting them away from here was the priority.

We were leaving when I bumped into Lord Smithe. "Alastor, are you not attending the party?" He looked between the guys behind me.

"Just heading over, two of my guys have been signed off, my sister needs her guard."

He gave me a strange look, "She doesn't need a guard here, this is the safest place in Desdemona... I understand the events as of late have left you extremely defensive, it's lovely to see you two get along so much better."

Naive cunt. I grunted in response. We said our farewells and I paused mid-way.

"What's wrong sir?" Trevore's on alert, scanning our whereabouts. Gregory too begins evaluating the situation.

I slam a hand to my face, "I forgot to ask where this fucken party was..."

CHAPTER THIRTY

HECATE

The tea party was in the major courtyard, a long table decorated with fine cutlery and fancy dishes. I found it hard to focus, my attention pulled around me. I kept small talk with the other ladies around, Selene was seated at another table with other ladies in waiting. She kept posed, drinking her tea silently, the others seemed eager to speak to her.

The area was full of diverse types of herbs, unlike the other courtyards with the flower gardens, I itched to check them out. Someone had sat next to me. It wasn't until they started putting things on my plate, that I noticed her. She gripped my hand, "Tee... we need to talk." Katrina didn't look well and smelled off.

I tried to remove my hand from hers, her sweaty grip tightening. "I am the daughter of a duke, remove your hand or there will be consequences." I spoke low to her, warning her if she did not listen.

"Ladies, is everything alright?" The princess was seated at the head of the table to my right, she placed me next to her to chat. She asked earlier what the prince and I talk about, I told half-truths, saying he was just wanting to know more about me.

I smiled plainly, my other hand tapping Katrina's, "I don't think Katrina is feeling the greatest."

Those calm blues dragged to our hands, "Miss. Smithe, you shouldn't have burdened yourself on my account. LYNDA COME!" She snapped her fingers to an attendee, "Lynda will escort you back to your residence."

Katrina's head snapped to her, inhumanly, her eyes insane. "He's coming for her." The giggles and chats around the table died down, their attention our way.

I tried to pull my hand from hers again. "Katrina Smithe, you're hurting my hand." This time I pulled harder and not so subtly, so everyone could see.

She yanked me to her, "He knows your name..." her teeth chattering near my nose. "He's coming for you." I heard the princess shout for someone, as Katrina began shaking. "He says, he'll see you soon." Her eyes rolled, going limp in her seat.

I barely caught her, half her body leaning away. "WE NEED A DOCTOR!" I screamed. Her body was cold, that's when I noticed the veins on her chest. "Oh my god..."

I don't know when my brother arrived, as he dragged me away from her body. Other people swarmed the moment I let her go, all the sounds around me muffled. Her words on repeat in my head.

He's coming for you. He says he'll see you soon.

"Hecate?" My vision was blurry when Alastor's face came into view, "It's okay, it's alright." He was wiping the tears from my face.

The party was cancelled, the King giving us a residence on site for the night. An investigation opened for Katrina's state. Everything was passing by me in a blur, I didn't know where I was or who I was with. Those words kept repeating on and on.

"Stinks?"

I could hear the voices around me, but I couldn't see clearly, I felt so exhausted.

"She's been like that since Miss Smithe collapsed."

"Is she sick?"

"Just give her space!"

"Summon Marcus!"

The voices overlapped with each other, a sinister laugh weaving them together. Then there was silence, and darkness. A steady drumbeat started – I listened as it chased away the chaos in my mind.

When I opened my eyes, I was in a room. A lounging room by the design of it, lit only by candlelight. Warmth secures me in place, something rubbing the side of my head. "Hey Stinks... are you alright?" My father, soothing me. I felt weak trying to pull away, "No, no, just stay as you are. You've overexerted yourself. The others have gone to bed, it's just you and me here, relax."

"Papa?"

"Yes?"

"Why do I feel so weird?"

I swear I heard him fight a sob, his chest constricting, "Marcus had to give you some medicine. You're probably feeling a bit drowsy from it, you just rest right here, I'll stay with you." He kissed the top of my head. "Everything is going to be okay..."

I weakly nodded, rubbing my cheek against his chest, that sounded like a good plan. My conscience spilled forth, like I was drunk, "I was going to leave today..."

"I know, my darling." I felt the warm liquid, drip onto my scalp.

"I just... want to protect you, the same way you've always protected me..." My eyes closed again, as my father began rocking me.

"That's a very you thing, to say." He laughed, sadly.

"I love you... you know that. Right Papa?"

His shoulders shook, "and I you, Stinks. I was blessed the day your brother was born, and when you arrived. I don't know what

I've done to deserve you both. I'm the luckiest man alive, you have no idea, my girl." His words faded away as the darkness swept through.

That women whispered to me, "Si haras ellath." Then only the sound of a beating drum, kept me company.

ALASTOR

Hecate was completely out of it, when we arrived at the party, people stood far, but circled around. Selene was trying to get through, worried. I barged my way in, pushing people alike away, my sister held a sickly Katrina at the centre. She was sprawled across Hecate's lap, dark veins creeping up her neck.

Hecate was dazed out, tears spilling down her face. I pulled her away so the doctors could get to Katrina. My sister's eyes were empty of emotions, even as her tears continued to fall. I picked her up, rushing her from the courtyard.

The palace was put on lock down, the seekers alerted from the essence of magic. Tonight, they would sweep the palace for intruders. We were given a guest ward, many bedrooms for my family, Selene, and a few guards. Trevore and Gregory were some of the guards staying with us. Each of us had to give statements to the officials, all guests locked down in their respected areas.

As we were sat and the bells to alert the residents of the sweep beginning, father called a meeting, questioning all of us next. My sister was physically there, yet she was mindlessly far away. She stared off at nothing, her head swaying side to side.

Father tried speaking to her and got nothing. Selene came forward, notifying him, "She's been like that since Miss Smithe collapsed."

"Is she sick?" Trevore stepped forth, trying to look at her. Gregory pulled him back, "Give her space!"

My father flew into a fit from Hecate's lack of response, "Summon Marcus!"

Marcus had returned home after the council meeting, we waited awhile for him, after sending word. Father never once let go of my sister, waiting for the only person he trusted, to examine her.

Marcus sceptically looked around at us, eyeballing Trevore, and Gregory. "She's alright but she isn't..."

"No secrets. I trust those two, you can too." I encouraged Marcus to continue.

"Her mana needs an outlet..."

Gregory's eyes went wide, Trevore didn't even flinch. Which told me, he knew somehow.

"What do you mean?" Selene quickly asked, she was in pieces since the tea party as well, pacing around.

"If those of..." Marcus squinted around at the walls, "You know. Don't let the mana out, it builds up... Draining them. I noticed back at my home, your daughter's mana Vic... It isn't normal..." His words were just above a whisper.

"So, your saying, if we don't let it out, it hurts us?" Selene was chewing on her nails, nervously on looking.

Marcus gravely nodded, "Not just hurt child.... It can kill you. Once it's been activated it's a do or die sort of bargain..."

Father whispered, "It's why your mother died..."

Everyone gasped, Marcus put a hand on father's shoulder, "I have a tonic in my bag to ease the pain... Unfortunately, I've only got one. I'll have to return and sort my place out, someone or something has hit it, in my absence."

Katrina's rambles echoed in my mind, father spoke, mirroring my thoughts. "We have to get her out of here..."

I confessed everything to my old man, he was upset but surprisingly understanding. I knew Hecate would be crossed when she woke and heard, but I needed him on board too. He reluctantly agreed, Hecate needed to go, far away. That sorcerer wanted her, but we did not know why. Katrina's insane whispers had my father fearful, and Marcus reporting his home being hit confirmed it.

He was coming for her, he got to Katrina, provoking us.

Everyone was dismissed to get some sleep for the night, I lingered, watching my old man and sister.

"Take Wrath with you."

I took a sip from the whiskey glass, "Wrath is yours. You'll need it while were gone."

His red eyes found me, clutching Hecate to his chest, "Wrath's power in embedded to me, I can easily fight with another sword... It is time for you to take on this burden, you will need all the help you can get, out there."

"We'll come back." I did not like how this sounded like a goodbye. "We'll send letters, letting you know where we are."

"No, you get her away from here, as far as possible, Alastor. You protect each other, do not send word, I will not take the risk of anyone finding out." I filled my glass again, noticing his untouched. "Go to the continents, there she can learn freely..." He kissed the top of her head.

"Why didn't you take mom away?" I wasn't trying to fight, but I needed to know.

"Your mother loved Desdemona. She would not abandon her home... I tried to convince her... Asteria tried to convince her."

I growled out when I heard that gypsies name, "That's because she wanted that fucken place."

His face turned fierce. "Watch your mouth boy, your mother loved that woman like a sister. Loved your sister like a daughter, even when you were difficult, who do you think folded your clothes so neatly? Asteria did. Who woke early to learn how to cook your favourite meals? Asteria."

I sat back, stunned from his attitude. "She was seducing you, playing the role of a dutiful stepmother."

"She did no such thing. I loved your mother, and respected Asteria. Asteria loved her deceased husband, she fled with Hecate to protect her after he died!"

I was confused now, she fled with Hecate... "So, Hecate?" I couldn't say a coherent sentence, my brain felt jumbled.

His voice was so quiet, compared to his fierce attitude a second ago. "Isn't mine..."

I didn't think I heard him right. "Wait, say that again?"

"She must never know Alastor..." He doesn't repeat himself, but his words confirming what I thought I heard.

"But she deserves to know the truth?" I found myself getting angry on her behalf.

"She doesn't need to know, Alastor." His eyes stare daggers at me. "Your mother dreamed of the child before her mother appeared on our doorstep. With Hecate wrapped in a small, bloodied bundle, dying. Your mother believed Hecate was a blessing from the moon herself, come to right all the wrongs. We took them in... loved Hecate as our own... She will always be my little girl, regardless of the truth. You will not tell her!" His hold on her tightened, as if the truth would make her disappear.

I was speechless... My whole life was a lie, our whole history a lie upon lies.

"Hecate was born outside Desdemona... she came from one of the continents... That's all I know."

"She should know the truth." My heart broke for her, whose whole life had been a lie as well.

"The truth would break her..."

I had to walk away, leaving my father and sister sat there in the dimly lit room. As I was going up, Selene was frozen on the sixth step, tears in her eyes. Her hands covered her mouth, she heard it too.

"Say, nothing. Understood?"

"But– "

"When Hecate is more stable. Then, we tell her." I pulled the handkerchief from my pocket, handing it to her when, I passed by her on the stairs.

I sat on the bed, head in my hands, reminiscing about my childhood. Mother was always happy before she fell sick... That woman was always near, helping her with everything. I convinced myself it was an act, that woman was trying to replace my mother...

Hecate had her long dark hair, but the woman's eyes were like stars, the constellations dazzled in them, changing every season. I convinced myself her beauty was a devil's spell, to reel in my old man. She was kind to me, even when I was horrible to her. That night I dreamt of the woman, dreamt about every horrible prank I played on her, her sad – starry eyes. My mother, rocking the small black-haired baby.

"Be calm Asteria, Hecate will feed off your energy." I was peeking into the nursery room. My mother spots me, spying, and smiles, "Ally, come meet your baby sister."

I wobbled to her, watching the sad woman to the side. "When did you have her mommy?" I can't remember seeing mother walking around with a big belly. I woke up one morning to baby cries.

"She's lovely, isn't she?" She brought the little bundle down from her shoulder, thick fluffy hair stuck out the top, wrinkly skin, and hands.

"She looks like a hairy potato."

Both the women, giggled with laughter at my childish words.

Everyday mother tried to have me around the baby, every day she called her my little sister. When I heard the gossip from the other lads I used to play with, anger fuelled my heart whenever I looked at my little sister.

I tossed and turned all night long – the bells rang again. I sat up to the signal, the sweep had ended. I got out of bed, throwing a shirt on. The sun was just rising, the sky purple and shades of orange.

I walked down the hallway to the stairs, Selene was sitting on that step still, leant against the wall, handkerchief in hand.

Was she here all night?

I was careful stepping around her, her eyes closed, breathing softly. She was asleep, I carefully scooped her up, taking her back up the stairs. She was lighter than my sister, and thinner too. I hadn't noticed when I tossed her on my horse that night, surely it wasn't healthy to be so light?

I didn't know which room was hers, so I opted for placing her in mine. I laid her down, covering her with the thick blanket. Her head rubbed into the feathered pillows behind her head, then her cheek rubbed deeper into them.

She had thin white lashes, another thing I hadn't really noticed. Her facial features were extremely feminine, a button nose accompanied those doe eyes. Were women from the continent just blessed with beauty? I caught myself staring too long, if she woke, she would have been disturbed, so I made quick steps to the door. That's when I realised, I was walking around in a shirt and shorts, nothing else.

"You fucken idiot…" I mumbled at myself, scanning the floors for my pants. I found my trousers back by the bed and quickly slipped them on.

I was making my way down the stairs, again, when Trevore popped up. He was leaning against the entry way, looking out to the lounge.

"Everything alright, Lance Corporal?" I got to his side, seen what he was watching. My father had stayed down here all night, holding my sister, both fast asleep.

"Before the attack happened, I felt it." He whispered next to me. "Her eyes glowed unnaturally, but I wasn't afraid. I was confused, I could smell her changing somehow… I should have been afraid…"

Trevore came from a family that used stories of witches to scare them, Trevore was forced by his father to join and learned to fight, to hunt them down. Most people in Desdemona were taught to hunt down anything considered, not normal.

"I always suspected she wasn't like the rest of them." I leaned against the opposite entry way wall, beside Trevore. "My sister…" A laugh slipped from my lips. Trevore was curiously watching me. "My sister loves the eerie dark library. She has a fascination with anything opposite what other young ladies did." I thought back to a lot, "She was also shunned by society. I used to think that was why. It was only recently that I remembered an incident when her mother died… that brewed my suspicion."

"What happened?" His hazel eyes went back out, watching her.

"Hecate ran away from home, when she was informed of her mother's passing."

His face shot back to me, his folded arms tensing.

"The guards nor the soldiers could find her. My father was a wreck… I found her though, Hecate had a list of favourite places to hide." The docks flashed through my mind, Hecate's little face crying into her hands. "I admit, I wasn't the picture–perfect brother

I could have been for her..." I inhaled deeply through my nose. "I was trying to get her away from there before the tide came in... She wouldn't listen to me, and I lost my temper on her."

"And then?" He was listening, intently to me. I could tell he sympathised with our sibling dynamic. I had seen first-hand his sister scream her hatred for him, to his face.

"Well, she fed off my energy, and yelled for me to go away. As her head came up, a strong gust of wind and some weird purple light – rocked my shit." I remember the fear that also grew in my heart. "At first, I thought nothing of it... but now... it makes sense."

"How old were you two?"

"Asteria died when she was seven, I was eleven."

Trevore pushed off the wall frowning, "Didn't the old geezer say, once the magic is activated it's do-or-die..."

It took me a moment to click into what he was implying, "Oh shit."

I stood up straight, bee lining for my sister. My finger flew to her neck, checking for a pulse. My father stirred awake from the racket. "What's wrong?" He flipped Hecate over to look at her face, her head flopped back.

Green eyes snapped open, pupils dilating upon focus.

CHAPTER THIRTY-ONE

HECATE

I opened my eyes to father staring down to me, Alastor leaning over us and Trevore looming over as well, all apprehensive. "Morning." My words sounded rough with phlegm, I cleared it trying to move, father tightened his hold on me.

"What was that about, you've woken her up now!" Father was grumpy with Alastor for some reason.

"Give me a minute." He had his hand on his chest. "I nearly had a heart attack..."

I was insanely confused – I was at the party moments ago...

"We apologise, my Lord." Trevore bowed, "Marcus said yesterday about the mana being activated and Lieutenant Colonel mentioned an incident years ago... We thought the worst."

He knows!? I tried to squirm out of his hold, but father had me tight, cradled like a baby. "Sh, calm down my dear everything is alright."

Alastor was staring at me, "We thought you..." That look I had seen before back at home, returned to those browns.

"UH... Can someone please tell me what's going on?"

Father eventually let me go, still holding my hands, as they ran me up to speed. I could not remember anything, the last was sitting at the table, my memory foggy with white mist. "That happened?" I was there, so why couldn't I remember.

"Hecate used magic fourteen years ago." Alastor was telling my father. My eyes went to him, *excuse me?*

"If what Marcus says is true... shouldn't she be..." Trevore's words fade off, not finishing.

Even father seemed perplexed.

"Wait. So, you're telling me, Katrina collapsed from sickness at the party? I used magic when I was a kid, and I should have died because of it?"

"No, you activated your magic young, which means without an outlet, there should have been signs..." Father was making no sense, but I nodded anyway.

"I didn't go crazy at the party, did I?" I had no idea where we were. Did we have to flee, are we being hunted?!

"No, you were out of it though. I rushed you away just in case." Alastor was now pacing back and forth, behind Trevore.

"Young lady, if you ever scheme again, making plans on your own I will put a whooping to your backside." My father gently squeezed my hand, eyebrows frowning at me.

"Uh–wait–"

"He knows Hecate." Alastor stops briefly, telling me.

"You told him!"

Father squeezes again, "You also told me last night." My head was spinning now, I was beyond confused, and annoyed. I pulled my hands from his so I could rest my head in them. "Stinks?" He scooted closer, his hand now on my head.

"I'm okay... My memory is just, foggy."

Selene and Gregory were now downstairs with us all, talking about the sweep ending. Another thing I had no idea had occurred...

One of the king's aids visited after breakfast, summoning my father and brother away, a basket of goodies in his hands.

"And this is for Lady Crosse, the prince hopes you are doing well." A bouquet of flowers was also handed to me, an assortment of roses.

Everyone but Gregory gave me a look, but it was Selene who giggled, "He's really trying, isn't he."

Father and Alastor were escorted away before they could fly off with questions, Trevore stared at the flowers, like they were a threat to me. I placed everything aside, sitting down for a cup of tea, catching my breath. "It's good to see you both again..." Gregory offered me a smile. Trevore was still staring at those flowers.

Selene crept next to him – hands tucked away in pockets. "The prince proposed to our Lady."

Gregory and Trevore asked in unison, "He did what?"

I pinched the bridge of my nose, I wished of all things I couldn't remember, that would be one of them. "Relax, he's just a kid."

"That kid, my Lady. Is the future King of the South." Gregory's face lately was anything but stoic, this version of him was unfamiliar to me.

"Younger guys aren't your type, are they?"

I looked to Trevore, aghast, "He's a boy! Do I look like some creep to you?" His head shook quickly.

Selene was clearly enjoying this, "Oh come on, he was pretty cute the way he went about it." She enlarged her eyes and went to her knees before me. "Y–You'll wait for me, won't you?" She titled her head, trying to mimic him.

I laughed at her, "You're not funny!" She too laughs with me.

"Careful now. It is blasphemy to mock the royal family." Gregory kindly warned us two.

Meanwhile Trevore just stood there, staring stupidly.

My father and brother returned within a few hours, servants with them, clothing in hand for us, Selene helped me change. The king was holding a dinner party tonight, showing those around that we were unaffected by the incident. Father was cursing, the idea of all of us in a big space together during this time sounded ludicrous to him. The seekers found nothing through the night, only dark mist wisped in the streets. A cleansing was preformed, and everyone was none the wiser.

"Do you think anything will happen tonight?" Selene was brushing my hair.

"I think if we are to slip away, tonight is the night..."

She shook her head, "I think we should leave after, if you're not there to say farewell upon your father's departure, it may raise suspicion."

My plans were completely screwed, returning to Marcus's wouldn't be a terrible thing, I needed my necklace. I tried to see the positive aspect here.

Selene was dressed in a creamy yellow gown. "I think you can pull off any colour." I said mindlessly to her.

Her nose turned up, "To be honest, I understand your love for dark shades... There's something more comfortable about it."

"Yes! You have no idea how much I was critiqued growing up for wearing darker clothing. There is just something more appealing than walking around looking like a cupcake." She laughed, bringing a weird tool to my hair. "Whoa" I stopped her, "What is that?"

She explained to me the servants said it was a curling tool, she wanted to try it out on my hair. I agreed if my hair was staying down. I dressed next – the queen had sent a deep purple gown. It went up covering the neck, sleeves long and tight, exploding out, around the wrists. The waist around flowed out, a bodice and crinoline were giving as well, but I refused to wear them. I felt caged with all that unnecessary equipment underneath, my clothing. The princess too sent jewellery for us, massive green earrings for me and small purple studded gems for Selene.

After I was dressed, I decided to visit Lady Grace, regardless of what Katrina had done, I felt sorry for her family. Lady Grace had lost one daughter years ago, and now another was ill. Father accompanied me, the idea of me walking the palace grounds alone, unsettled him. Gregory escorted us along the way, their guest residence was a detached building just near the golden gates. I brought flowers for Lady Grace, as father went off to talk with Lord Smithe in a study. I waited with my guard for her.

She entered, her hair down, dressed in humble attire. I rose from my seat flowers in hand, her face broke when she saw me. She covered her face with her hands, "I'm sorry darling, please excuse my terrible manners." I put the flowers on the coffee table and rushed to hug her. All etiquette was gone, Lady Grace wept into my shoulder, I rubbed her back allowing her to lean on me for however long she needed.

The doctors say Katrina will be alright after rest, somehow her body was infested with toxins, the madness they called it. She would be heavily medicated for the days to come, with a nurse always at bed side. I couldn't help but feel guilty.

We left late in the afternoon, returning to our ward, only a couple of hours until we had to go to this dinner. Lord Smithe never came to bid us goodbye, like he always did whenever we visited. Father was oddly rubbing his knuckles a lot, during our quiet journey back. When we returned, father returned to his room, mumbling about freshening up. I sat in the lounge, thinking about everything.

"It's not your fault." Alastor seated himself across from me, he was looking exactly like father. Suited up, hair combed to the side. That sun-kissed skin bronzed once more, he was in fancy dress, his sword in a white sheath at his side.

"He targeted her because of me..." My bottom lip betrayed me as it quivered. "Who next will he go after... You understand now... why I must go."

"Yes, and I'm coming with you."

"So, you can be targeted next? Al..." I swallowed hard, "We may not have seen eye to eye, or got along most of the time... But I would never, ever, wish harm upon you." I had to keep my attention down, I didn't want to weep.

"I know... But who's to say he doesn't come after us anyways in your absence. I'm coming with you. We leave tomorrow, we'll depart from Marcus's, head to King's Port, and jump aboard a ship." I just nodded, whatever I say or think, Alastor would disagree. "Don't cry, you'll ruin your make up and look ugly."

I made a very unlady like snort, "I'm not wearing any make up."

Alastor's eyebrows were sky high, "Seriously? No powder, not even mascara?"

I shook my head, "I've never worn makeup, I don't like all that unnecessary stuff on my face. I only carried some for... someone else."

He blinked numerously, scanning my face. "Well, you've got phenomenal skin, I always thought it was the makeup." He rose, ruffling my hair with his white gloved hand, as he walked off.

I ran my fingers through my soft curls, I wasn't a fan of them, but Selene worked hard so I would keep them for tonight. Someone cleared their throat, I found Trevore entering, all done up as well. "Everything okay?" I asked.

He couldn't keep his eyes long on anything, darting around all over the floor with every step toward me. His boots were polished clean, his suit was darker, almost black, large gold buttons sparkling from the light. Our family insignia on the top button on his neck collar, even his belt was fancier than usual. His hair was sleeked back, not a hair out of place.

He cleans up nicely. I thought.

He had a hand behind his back, "I uh…" His smug face and confident self nowhere in sight, "I got you this." He shoved a purple flower toward me, his other hand on the hilt of his sword. "To… Put in your hair, for tonight." He bowed completely, hand still out.

I leaned back so I could see the flower, he had nearly shoved it up my nose. It was three Calla Lilies bundled together, weaved smoothly into a hair clip. I took it from his outstretched hand, "Thank you Trevore, they're stunning." They were real flowers. From a first glance, I thought them to be artificial. I smelled the lily sent off them, a clean refreshing smell.

"You're most welcomed, my Lady." His head was still down, bowed, looking toward the floor. I rose, a hand on his shoulder, guiding him to stand straight again. He looked between me and the hand that touched him. I picked one of the flowers off, and his eyes shook. "Do you prefer– "

I stepped closer to him, and he silenced, as I placed the flower in his chest pocket. I then clipped the remaining two flowers just behind my ear, tucking the hair back. Trevore was crimson red at this point. "There," I gave him a spin, showcasing my dress with my new hair accessory.

As I spun, I noticed Selene peering around the stairs, thumbs upping Trevore. I played it off, that explained how he got the clip in the first place.

SELENE

Hecate and her father wanted to do a wellbeing check on Katrina's parents. I was once again in awe of Hecate, even Alastor seemed sullen. Considering everything I had found out, if I had been in her shoes, I wouldn't have had the kindness in my heart to care at all. No, I couldn't care less. A part of me believed Katrina deserved what happened to her, karma ran its full circle. For Hecate's sake, I chose not to voice my opinion. She was blaming herself for all of it, I understood why Alastor wanted to wait to tell her the secret. I froze on that step when I heard the duke talk about their family. Even though Hecate wasn't his, he loved her immensely, my heart hurt for her, for all of them.

When they left, I ran about looking for Trevore. I wanted to do something for her, make her smile. Luckily, I found him in his room, changing his bandages, alone.

"BY THE REALMS!" He jumped scared as I crept in, closing the door slightly. He was covering himself next, not looking too pleased.

"Oh please, I have seen a man's body before. I'm not interested in boys."

Now he was full on frowning. "There's a thing called knocking, Miss. It's shameless barging into a man's bedroom."

I shrugged it off, peering at his chest. An old wound still healing, as well as his new one. "Those suck...." He stood up, turning from me. The kid's back was riddled with scars as well. "You know, I can still see the other end of the wound on your back."

The back of his neck reddened, as he pointed to the door. "Get. Out."

"Fine, fine." I raised my hands in protest, waltzing away. "Here I was coming to give you advice on how to woe our fair lady off her feet." I reached the door when he shouted.

"W–What do you mean?!"

I spun back very slowly, "Exactly as I said. You're obvious, Coppertop."

CHAPTER THIRTY-TWO

He was gripping the bandages, reminding me of a kid caught with his hand in the cookie jar. "I'll help you change that and give you this." I placed a clip on the table he was sat at when I first walked in. His eyebrow went up in question. "After I wrap your new bandages, we'll go pick some flowers, I'll show you how we northerners turn the nature around us, into something better than a bouquet of flowers."

"Why?" He really did look confused.

I shrugged, "I really like Hecate..." I turned the tips of my feet in and out, "And you're not so bad, you accepted her immediately. People like us... need people like you in our lives. So, with that I decided to root you on!" I slammed my hand to my other.

His hazels blinked and blinked.

"Come now." I patted the seat, "We have some wooing to do." Wiggling my eyebrows.

Coppertop did as he was told, when it came to Hecate, he reminded me of a dog. I imagined if he had a tail, it would wag back and forth whenever I mentioned her, he even had the puppy eyes to go with it. We got him patched up, and then made our way outside to pick some flowers.

"These are the royal family flowers!" He was whisper yelling at me, while I snooped around.

"I know, and they are being wasted out here with no one to look at them. Do you honestly think they're going to notice a few missing?" *Man, this kid,* I thought.

"We shouldn't."

"Hey now." I stood up, staring him down. "Do you honestly want to lose to a nearly twelve-year-old boy?" His mouth flapped, but nothing came out. "Listen, I was there, Prince Richard was serious on marrying her... He genuinely believes she's to be his queen, regardless of their age gap."

"He's a young boy. Feelings change." I respected he was trying to rationalise the prince's heart.

So, I pushed it further.

I looked around carefully for any imposing ears, whispering, "He dreamed of her... A crown and all." Coppertop looked disturbed, "Hecate, and me, dream of things and somehow, they happen. Who's to say the kid too was dreaming of a future to come?"

He shifted while crouching, "You have visions?"

I nodded gravely, "Unfortunately so... and believe me, some of them have been horrible ones, a few have already come to pass." I picked a flower, tossing it, it was brown and yellow, dying.

That was enough of a push for him, we spent an hour discussing which colours looked best on Hecate. Coppertop wanted to go with red, I had to educate him on the colour wheel. So, we decided a colour similar to her dress would suffice and went on a hunt for the perfect flowers. He found a lily, stunning deep purple lilies that faded a lighter purple toward the ends of the petals.

"This one." He caressed the petals.

"Do you know what they mean in the flower language?" I was curious, it was an interesting pick.

That punch-able smug look returned to his face for the first time, "Flowers have languages?"

My tongue clicked as I educated him next on this too, he listened, sometimes asking questions. "So, what exactly does the lily represent?"

I pulled a face, "Well lilies and calla lilies have two different meanings."

"Calla?"

I pointed, "Those ones there, the ones you picked are Calla Lilies... They express the idea of life and fertility..." His ears reddened slightly, "While on some accounts, it is seen as a symbol of death." His jaw dropped, I nodded slowly, "And in other cultures, it symbolises magnificent beauty."

"Why can't people just pick one for its meaning." He stood brushing his laps off.

I countered his complaint, "And why can people not all speak one language or pray to one God, or none. It's just the way the world is, we all feel and comprehend things differently. It's diversity."

He continued to look at the flower, mumbling, "I like the magnificent beauty aspect..."

"That's good enough for me!"

We picked only the biggest and most vibrant ones, sneaking off with them, when shouting stopped us. "You there, stop, in the name of His Royal Highness!"

We both stopped with the stomp of our heels, as a guard in golden armour approached. Coppertop gave me the – told you so face – when a little golden head appeared next. I curtsied quickly as we spoke to him. "We greet the rising sun of the south."

"Rise." Soft words like the summers breeze greeted us. "Greetings Miss. Selene and..." His bright blue orbs looked Coppertop over, pausing on the flowers in our hands.

Coppertop bowed again, "I greet the rising sun. I am Lance Corporal, Trevore Barnes, soldier, and guard from Newmont."

"You are Lady Crosse's guard." He scanned the gardens, "Yet, I do not see her."

How did he know?

Coppertop continued, "Sergeant Gregory Thorpe, is on duty today, Your Highness."

The prince inclined his head with acknowledgment, "Picking the former queen's flowers is a crime against my family." Even with that innocent tone, I shivered.

I curtsied again, "I ask your forgiveness Your Highness, I was not aware. I just thought my Lady would– "

"It's for Hecate?" I got him. I nodded my head, still curtsied before him. "Rise." His little face was still looking out the garden, as he pointed to a red flower in the distance, one Coppertop originally wanted to go with. I noticed his auburn eyebrow twitch. "They are Camellias... They mean love, affection, and admiration."

I was surprised this young prince even knew the language of flowers. "Our Lady will be wearing a purple gown this evening, which is evidently why we chose purple, Your Highness."

He glared at the flowers in our hands, and then to Coppertop, intensely glaring. "Fine. I will let this pass, for her. Farewell." He spun before we could properly bid our farewell, the golden guards hot on his little tail.

"Did that little punk scowl at me?" I could not stop myself from laughing at Coppertop's rant, the drama between them was real.

I watched from the stairwell, waiting for Coppertop to return and carry out our plan. Alastor approached the steps, scrutinizing, "What are you doing?" My finger flew up to my mouth, I signalled him to pass me, quickly. I tried to keep focused, waiting for everything to unfold. Alastor leaned against the wall behind me, his warmth fell on me like sun rays. "Why are you spying on my sister?"

That's when he entered, all spruced up after visiting the palace's boutique. He was so terribly awkward, I wanted to go in there and kick him. "What have you done..." That deep voice sounded off next to my ear, but I was mesmerised as Hecate spun, giving a thumbs up to Coppertop. My work for today was done. I turned to go up the stairs, head butting a solid chest. Alastor's arms shot around me, keeping me from falling. He was frowning, deeply.

"Sorry, if I could just." I removed myself, trying to sidestep him. He continued to block my path. "My Lord, could you please move?" He frowned even deeper, not moving. I heard Hecate laugh behind me, and shot under her brother's legs, straight up the stairs. "Oi!" The sounds of boots chased after me. I ran straight to my quarters, about to slam the door, when he slid in. I nearly slammed the door on him.

"You almost– "

"SHHH!" I listened to see if Hecate was coming up or not.

"Why are you meddling between those two?" Hecate's brother was dressed sharply, pushing his now messy hair to the side.

"Why not, don't you want nieces or nephews?" His eyes went huge, those cinnamon orbs upset. "Obviously not right now, but in the future I mean." I corrected myself.

"I don't approve of Trevore."

"Why not?!" I pushed off the door, standing my ground.

"He's a playboy, he'll break her heart." He stood taller, towering me by a few heads.

I wanted to step back, but planted my feet, "And people change, look at you and Hecate." I pointed out.

"That's different."

"Oh, is it now? It's only conveniently applied amongst oneself? No one else could possibly change for the better?" I wanted to yell at this selfish guy. His thick eyebrows frowned further, the t-section between them, sunken in. He was handsome but a big jerk, I could see why he and Hecate fought so much. "Or are you afraid something will happen to her, like what happened to you?" I walked away from the door.

Boots scoffed behind me, "How dare you."

I turned, my dress swaying around me, real anger looked upon me. "You are not her father. You cannot keep her from things just because you are afraid."

He growled like an animal, "How dare you speak to me about something you haven't got the slightest clue about!" His hand flew up and I flinched back hard, closing my eyes. Silence filled the spacious room, I peeked, shaking a bit. His face flabbergasted, that finger pointing to me. "Did... Did you think I was going to hit you?" Pity washed over his features as he quickly withdrew his hand.

Now I was angry. "No your right, I have absolutely no idea!" My arms went cold. "Not like I had to sell my body for chump change, let people touch me, use me, just so I could buy something to eat!"

He stepped back, "I'm... sorry."

It flowed forth, "Why are you sorry huh? Why because daddy always paid for your food? Huh? Daddy always made sure you had a roof over your head and clothes over your skin!" I was yelling, for the first time in my life.

He wobbled, his mouth flapping.

"Get out."

"Selene..."

I yelled again, "GET OUT!"

He made large steps for the door, and as he opened it, Hecate was running for it. Her eyes dart between the both of us, Coppertop right behind her, he too looked worried. I ran up pushing the jerk out with everything I had, closing the door quickly.

I could hear Hecate lose her lid outside, but he didn't fight back, he was quiet. Footsteps left from behind the door, and I allowed myself to cry then. My forehead against the door, I allowed myself to feel it all, everything I thought I had healed from. Those old scars, ripped open, reminding me just how damaged I was.

CHAPTER
THIRTY-THREE

HECATE

Trevore took Alastor away, I sat against the cold wall, next to Selene's door. Sniffling and sharp gasps sounded from under it. *She's crying.*

I was fuming, shocked first when I saw her terrified face, after screaming at my brother. I had no idea what transpired, what confused me more was Alastor's face. Even while I yelled at him, he didn't fight back, no, he looked remorseful.

After some time, the door opened, I stood quickly in my heels. Selene seemed shocked to see me on the floor. I didn't give her a second to speak, hugging her. "I won't ask unless you want to talk about it. But I'm here."

Her thin shoulders trembled slightly, "Thank you..."

I dragged her to my room to freshen her up, her eyes were dimly red but noticeably puffy. She didn't protest, allowing me to silently comfort her, in my own way.

"We had... a disagreement. I lashed out on him, unfairly..." She was still quiet but talking. Her eyes casted down when I glimpsed in the mirror.

"We do that a lot, it's a family thing."

"I don't have a family..."

I paused fixing her hair, "Are we not your family?" Her head came up, such vulnerability in her eyes, "You're part of my family now. Get used to the fights... It's better than bottling it all up and exploding later." I squeezed her shoulder, then I continued to fix the braids in her hair.

"I used to sell my body... for... money..." I kept my emotions in check as she opened–up more about her past. I knew bits and pieces, of what she allowed me. "Some of them... used to be violent..." My jaw was clenching but I proceeded to fix the hairs sticking out here and there. "Sometimes... that fear returns in some situations."

"What did my brother do?" I flat out asked.

"N–Nothing... He pointed a finger and those memories just surfaced... I provoked him." That happiness and light faded from her healing eyes. I didn't like this broken version of her.

"I won't tell you I'm sorry." Her attention found me in the mirror, "I know you don't want people's pity. You did what you needed to do, in order to survive. I respect that, the guts. I cannot even begin to imagine what that was like, but... I can imagine that it'll never happen again." I swallowed the lump in my throat. "You do not have to do it alone anymore. We are in this together." I wiped the tear that escaped from her eye, with my thumb. "Now, no more of this. We are to be the beauties of the ball." I spun out, exaggerating how people dance, my arms high above me.

A smile cracked out of her, and the rest was smooth sailing. She picked back up after, her wounds were still healing, I knew it would take time.

"How long did it take you to help Trevore find these flowers?" I played with a petal behind my ear, lying in bed.

Selene stared, "What do you mean?"

I laughed at her state, "Magnificent beauty? No offence to Trevore, but he doesn't look like the type to read a book on the language of flowers." I raised an eyebrow at her, half smiling.

"He didn't?" – "He did." Her eyebrows bunched, "I told him not to say that…" Her hands went up, massaging her temples.

"I also saw you giving him the thumbs up, downstairs."

Her mouth opened wide, "Oh my goodness…"

I erupted in laughter, she sat at the end of the bed upset, with her not so subtle give away.

Knock – Knock – Knock.

I stopped laughing, Selene slowly got up to get the door. "I can do it." I scrambled off the bed.

"I am your lady in waiting, it's my job." She smoothed out her dress and answered. "Oh, my Lord, come in." Her head inclined as she quickly stepped back.

My father stepped in smiling to her, his attention slid to me, "Dare I ask why your brother has such a long face?" I shook my head, and he nodded, "Well in any case, it's time to go."

Selene kept her eyes trained forward the entire time, I caught Al occasionally looking to her, when we were all finally together again.

"Don't you look nice." I stopped in front of Gregory – he inclined his head to me. "Very smart." I flicked the tassels on his shoulders, both my brother and father had them as well.

I caught my father looking back and forth between Trevore and me, or more so the flower still in his chest pocket. He frowned, "Where's mine?" Selene cracked again, covering her mouth from giggling.

The five of us met up with Marcus along the way, there were three other guards with us as well, but I didn't know their names.

Father wouldn't let me close to them, grumbling about them possibly getting flowers as well. Alastor was visibly rolling his eyes, to father's fits.

The party was being held in the oldest hall in the palace walls, the hall where the first treaty was signed among the warriors, one thousand–three hundred–fifty–three years ago. I was ecstatic to see the historic hall, the rest of the castle was clearly remodelled, taking away the historical background of the place. This hall was untouched, sacred in some sense, father told me. The place was located east of the palace grounds, close to the cliffs. We had to ride a carriage, as it would have taken far too long on foot.

"You seem excited?" Father sat next to Alastor, and across from Selene.

"Do you think they have original tapestries still hung in the hall?"

Father smiled shaking his head, "No, but the place feels old, the courtyard is where the history is." That mischievous glint speckled in his eyes.

The carriage pulled up, lords, ladies, knights, and guards scattered all over. The air was nippier over here, the smell of sea air stronger, we were on the very edge of the country, near the eastern sea. The building was indeed huge, as if it went on for ages, there were ruins around it, once as side buildings.

"Incredible..." We entered all together, many people greeted us, I was anxious to get to the hall. Feeling my patience run thin, every time someone stopped to talk to my father or brother, or to introduce themselves to me.

I had the opportunity to meet the other lords of the other towns, who looked extremely old in comparison to father. One of the lords even introduced their sons to me, each eager to kiss the back of my hand. Unfortunately for them, I was one of the strange women who left the hands empty, when they held theirs out for me. "My apologies, my father has a knack for... hunting those down for touching me." I told a half-truth again, each falling for it. I was beginning to feel uncomfortable from the attention, sliding closer to my brother's side. The young men kept a good distance, after that.

We finally reached the doors leading in, my steps slowed. An old chandelier hung in the centre of the hall, white candles dripping. Pillars too had candles dripping down, painting the stones white. Tables were scattered all over for those attending tonight. At the furthest wall, leading up wide stairs to a stone platform, a long table and four golden chairs were placed in front of the massive stained-glass window. Twelve people coloured into the glass, stretching that whole wall.

"See." My father elbowed me.

This place didn't just look old, it felt old, just as he said. The decoration put up stole away the authenticity the hall provided. Huge pillars reaching high, I looked up twirling, circular patterns high in the ceiling beyond the grand chandelier.

We made our way to a table labelled for us, closer to the stained-glass window. The other Lords and Dukes from other towns finding their seats as well. Lady Grace and Lord Smithe chose not to attend, staying back with Katrina, three empty chairs left at our table. My mood took a turn, thinking back to how Katrina and I would stay up chatting late into the night about this place. We dreamt of coming together... We made it finally, but how different things were since our dreaming days.

The royal family entered, and we all rose for them, as they took their seats at the long table. The prince smiled brightly waving at our table, Selene yet again cracked, Trevore, my father and Alastor frowned. I hesitantly rose my hand, waving back.

"GREETINGS FRIENDS OF THE SOUTH!" King Jonathan stayed standing as the rest of his family sat, and he began a long speech of kindship and glory to our kingdom. I fought hard not to yawn the whole time he blabbered, understanding all my father's past complaints about him...

After the speech we were finally able to dig into our food, dishes were brought out on silver platters, gold for the royal family. Duck, chicken, roast beef, meats of all sorts were served. Potatoes – roasted and mashed, a variety of boiled veggies too, my mouth watered.

"You're drooling." Alastor said digging into a pile of meat. His pupils were huge going through his piles.

"So are you." I countered.

The hall was filled with chatter, wine served to each of the tables. I had to be careful, I was a light weight compared to my brother. I didn't want to make a fool out of myself, I chose not to drink with my meal.

Someone approached our table, I was too busy eating broccoli smothered in gravy, when my father's voice got my attention. He flicked his head to the individual, "Greetings Lady Crosse, His Royal Highness asks if you could spare a moment."

I wiped my mouth with the red napkin placed, rising. Selene raised as well, the attendee stopped her, I was summoned alone up to the table. I blinked to my father who nodded once, carefully. I shifted from the table, following the attendee to the stairs, he gestures that I walk up them and stand before the prince.

I curtsied, "I greet the rising sun of the south."

His little face was beaming, "Are you enjoying your meal?"

Before I could answer, Queen Alice spoke next. "My prince how is the lady meant to enjoy her dinner when you have pulled her away from it." She smiled toward her son. I curtsied to the other royals, looking over.

"Ha! That's my boy. Lady Crosse, you have captured our prince's heart, how will you compensate for that?" I didn't know how to answer the king, even the prince went tomato red from his father's words. Princess Cecilia sat there quietly watching, King Jonathan roared with laughter. "There is no need to be nervous my Lady, go, enjoy the night!"

I was mid curtsy when Queen Alice spoke again, "You look marvellous in the dress I sent you, dear." I noticed Cecilia's face twitch.

"You honour me, Your Majesty. Thank you." I was escorted back to the table, appetite gone.

I knew father and Alastor had questions, but I needed air. I excused myself, Selene and Trevore rose to join me. There was red rope on golden poles, guiding us to the courtyard, so guests didn't wonder into dangerous sections of the place.

"You, okay?" Selene lightly linked into me. Trevore kept few paces behind us, following quietly. I too kept quiet.

We finally made it outside, the sky shades of pink and orange. I took a deep breath, taking in the beautiful setting scene.

"No way..." Selene breathlessly spoke next to me. I turned my head to see what she was looking at when a tree caught my attention, the same thing she too was looking at. "The tree of Ortusolis!" She was smiling in wonder, even Trevore was dazed.

My food began to flip in my stomach at the white bark and gold leaves... "No way." They both glanced to me, double taking.

"My Lady, you've gone pale." Trevore's face morphed into concern.

The yards ground beneath the tree was soft mossy grass, broken up by stone pads leading away. The cracked stones had dandelions shooting up from them. My body broke out in a cold sweat.

"Hecate." Selene tugged my arm, but I was transfixed, it was exactly as I dreamt it.

"We need to leave. Right now!" I turned making quick steps back inside, Trevore and Selene's words muffled behind me.

"I said to that girl, to pass my message along." That distinct hoarse voice echoed off the stone walls. "What did I say too you then hmm..." Trevore grabbed me, his sword unsheathing. I grabbed Selene, pulling her closer to me. "You were crying then... An old face so terrified." He laughed, the place shaking, crumbling stones began falling, dark mist whirled around. Yells and screams from inside the hall reverberated toward us, then came the roars.

"We leave now." Trevore began pushing back.

"My family– "

Selene grabbed my arm, pulling me away. "He's in there Hecate..." Her eyes certain, and terrified.

"You're suffering will cease to exist! All I ask, is the girl." More screams and roars echoed from the hall. "Bring me, Hecate Crosse!"

"Run." Trevore turned grabbing a handful of my fabric, running back outside. The hall exploded into darkness – the mist thick like sand. We were swatting it away, running. Trevore held the fabric at my shoulder, I gripped Selene's hand, running back toward the front of the hall, around the building. Seekers were everywhere, glowing electrical balls flying out of their hands, fighting those big black beasts.

"This way!" Trevore docked. I was running to whichever way he pulled us. More creatures appeared, creatures of flesh and claws crawling around the building, their eyes void of any life. "Go back, go back!" Trevore pushed back.

"Where are you Hecate?" The hooded prince's voice booms across the sky, silver eyes replacing the moon. "Dearie me, a fancy little party, where was my invite?"

Trevore didn't stop running, I fell, my heel lodging into something. I cried out from the pain gripping my ankle. "Get up, Get up!" Selene was shaking helping Trevore pull me up, I pulled the heels off discarding them.

We ran right back to the tree, "Wrong way!" Selene screamed at Trevore. Mist circled around us, trapping us to the area, our backs to the tree. Trevore positioned himself in front of us, sword up and ready.

A blob of mist grew towards us, smouldering silver eyes, breaking through the wall. The prince of shadows, stood before us once more. A fanged smile reached his feline eyes, "Good evening."

"Come any closer and you die." Trevore warned.

The nightmare removed his hood, uninterested in Trevore, "Last I checked, you were the one who nearly died." His eyes never leaving me. "If you come with me now, no one will get hurt."

"No!" Selene threw herself next to Trevore, her hands up. "She goes nowhere!"

His white hand raised, something dangling from in it. A silver delicate chain, my own necklace. I fell back into the tree, my breathing becoming laboured. *He was the one who ransacked Marcus's...*

"No one has to die Hecate, the choice is yours, and yours to make."

Selene's palms radiated with light, and time slowed. Trevore's sword moved little by little, their breathing chests, inching up.

"You have the gift of time manipulation, I see..." The dark prince was the only one, other than me, moving at real time, analysing the three of us.

"N–no, this is your doing!"

He shook his head, "I thought you were a clever little thing... but you haven't got a clue about the reality of these worlds, do you?" He hummed, "Make your choice, Hecate. I'm being quite patient with you."

Screams continued to assault my mind, Katrina's state, the sick man in the streets, the girls in the wagon. An onslaught of memories resurfacing, a sob slipping from my lips. "Do you promise... No one else will die?"

He placed the hand holding my necklace up to his chest, "You have my word." Grinning that sinister smile.

I wobbled by Trevore and Selene, placing a kiss to each of their cheeks. Their eyes begin to gradually move to me, widening.

"Thank you both, for everything." *I would go down fighting, I would drag him to hell, with me.*

His words, shatter my mental plan. "Try any tricks girl, and everyone in that hall dies. Your father and brother, first."

I spun back to the being, his eyes watching me, carefully. "If I come with you... And play no tricks, you must not harm a single hair on a single person." The food I ate earlier was lodge in my throat.

He nods his head once, "Fine."

CHAPTER THIRTY-FOUR

HECATE

"**F**ine."

"I WANT SOMETHING MORE CONCRETE!" I screamed at him, my tears felt like icy water, running down my face.

He leant back, his eyebrow twitched, "A bargain then..." His empty hand reached out, open to me. "This bargain will seal the deal." His knee-high boot stepped forward. "I – Valdis, Prince of the Dark Fae and Lord Commander of the Legions..." Shadows crawled from his chest, his eyes swirling. "Swear to you, Hecate Crosse... In exchange for your cooperation, should you come along willingly, without fighting back!" He raised his hand, gesturing to himself, "I will not harm, a single hair on a single person, here." His hand was back out waiting for me. "Whoever breaks this bargain, shall therefore forfeit, their own life."

"How d–do I not know this isn't some trick in itself..." My hair whirled around my neck, as the mist and shadows continued to circle us.

His smile turned serious, "Your mother died because she broke a bargain with someone far crueller than I."

"What?" My vision went hazy, I wondered how this man knew my mother.

"Quickly now, time is of the essence."

My head was throbbing, I had so many questions slamming into me.

You have and will always be the light of my life, Hecate. Guide others with it too.

I reached forward, hand in hand with Valdis. *I'm sorry Papa, I'm sorry Al.* His long fingers enclosed my hand, pulling me to him, his nails pricking my skin.

Pain exploded up my arm, the area shifted. "Uh, I forgot to mention, the sealing part of the bargain is incredibly painful, sorry." A laughter broke out from him, as my whole existence descended into darkness, I screamed plummeting into it.

ALASTOR

I was shoving food down my gob, savouring the piles of meat, I hadn't had in a while. Marcus was spewing the stories of the warriors on the stained-glass window to Gregory.

"Your sister has been gone too long... I should go check on her." Father was fidgeting, watching the side door she left out of.

I swallowed down my food, "She just needed some air, that entire family just put her in the spotlight. You know how she feels about that."

He looked to me – his eyes full of worry. I lowered my voice, leaning in, "I told her, I'd hunt her sorry ass down if she tried anything, relax please." I sat back, passing him, his wine glass.

Clatter at the Scarbra table, caught all our attention. The mayor face first in his dinner plate, his attendees shaking him. "Sir? SIR?" Others begin dropping or face planting into the tables. That's when shit kicked off.

That voice bouncing off the walls around us, "I said to that girl, to pass my message along." The stained–glass windows rattling. "What did I say to you then hmm..." Those still standing shot to their feet, swords drawing out. "You were crying then... An old face so terrified." Malicious laughter rumbled through, the chandelier above, swinging violently. That's when the dark mist whirled around us. Seekers appeared everywhere, all along the walls, a unit explodes before the royal family.

It was all happening, rapidly.

Then came the roars, those hellhounds appearing out of nowhere. People were scattering, the creatures growling.

"Find her!" My father grabbed my arm, pushing me toward the exit.

"Your suffering will cease to exist! All I ask, is the girl." The women's screams had my ears ringing. That bastard's voice continued. "Bring me, Hecate Crosse!"

I froze looking to father, many eyes darted to my father as well, human and beast alike. *No...*

The mist sealed off all exits, covering the walls like a shield of darkness.

"Where are you Hecate?" He continued to coo for my sister. "Dearie me, a fancy little party, where was my invite?" A burst of darkness appeared behind the king, grabbing his throat. "Where is she?" Hissing into his ear.

King Jonathan was going blue, thrashing at the hold on him. Guards and seekers were thrown, with a flick of the sorcerer's wicked wrist.

The princess stood firm, "She went outside for air, release him, immediately!"

I tried to run for the sealed door, new creatures crawled down. Empty eyes and jaded teeth dragged toward me, from above.

"You have my thanks." That bastard dark prince bowed his head, vanishing as quickly as he appeared.

I started hacking at the mist, as it absorbed the impact. Then everything slowed, I check behind swiftly, as every person and thing moved at snail pace, even Marcus somehow was slowly moving. "Hecate!" My father and I the only ones in real time motion. He sprinted to where I was, his sword began hacking as well.

That's when I heard it, my sister's scream as the entire world rocked, with an earthquake's force. Everything and everyone resumed to real time again, screams, and roars. The glass window shattering, exploding, as pieces sliced and stabbed many nearby. As my sister's scream faded away, everything disappeared.

The creatures, the hellhounds, the mist – gone.

"HECATE!!!" My father scrambled from the floor, dashing out the revealed door, at last. I sprinted after him, climbing over fallen bits of the crumbled building.

Seeker's bodies littered the floor, and creatures too. We vaguely recognised two figures by the golden-leafed tree, running to them. Trevore and Selene sprawled out - eyes opened. Father was doing circles, screaming my sister's name, again and again. "Hecate... HECATE!?!"

I checked their pulses, both still breathing. Selene gripped my forearm, her body ice cold. "She's gone." Her eyes rolled back as tears rolled forth, and her head hit the grass.

TO BE CONTINUED

PAIN

HECATE

The last thing I dreamt about was pain and darkness. Those pompous silvers looking down to me, sneering with triumph...

I rolled to my side, my nose brushing against solid warmth. I nuzzled closer to it, wanting more, a chilly draft drifted up my legs. My knees came up, and they too knocked against that warm wall. Then a scent came to me, dark and sweet, my mind and body, feeling a moment of peace. My awareness steadily returning, that scent making me hungry. I rub my cheek against silk, the thing I was laying on, warm and soft.

"Ah, you are awake now." That distinct voice sounds from overhead.

My eyes shot open, that thing I was nuzzling, a leg.

"You wouldn't be so cold, if you had stopped kicking the quilt off, all the time."

I thrashed back, falling off whatever I was lying on. Hitting solid – cold floor. I sit up, pain spreading all over. I fell off a bed, silk sheets covering it. I can see him, sitting there, reading a book.

Those silver eyes not leaving the pages, his black hair tucked behind a long-pointed ear.

"I imagine it's much colder down there, than it is up here." That white hand - pats next to him. Those damn eyes looking at me now. "Especially, dressed like that."

My attention rapidly fires down, immediately covering myself. I was in a night gown of creamy silk, stopping mid-thigh, my arms and legs exposed. A sick feeling of dread spreads through me. Every vein in my body begins shimmering, the heat spreading with it. "You bastard!"

His dark eyebrows shoot up, a finger shaking at me. "Nuh Uh, none of that, remember the bargain?"

As if that word was the key to the lock, my memories flood in. It was no dream, no nightmare, but my life.

"Take a very deep breath and ground yourself." He leans over the other side, standing to his feet. Placing the mosey -green book on a side table, next to the bed. "I have places to be, seeing as you haven't died, then the bargain is sealed." He makes quick work for the arched door, his cloak nowhere in sight.

I can –

He cuts my train of thought off. "This room is warded, no one in, and no one out, other than me." He reaches the door, closing it quickly behind himself. "Food will be along shortly!"

I wobble to my aching legs, watching the dark door, expecting him to return. I could not hear anything, the candlelight flickered around the luxurious room. There wasn't much inside the room.

A bed, one large wardrobe, and a little table with two chairs. The windows barred down. "Where the hell am I?" I touched the cold iron bars.

ACKNOWLEDGEMENTS

I would like to express my deepest appreciation to Dolman Scott and all the people behind the scenes. To Rosemary and Richard, who corresponded with me, for making this very scary starting point, smooth sailing.

Writing the story was the fun part, but getting it physically out to the world, seemed like a daunting task. Dolman Scott's admin have been a wonderful support, as well as super informative whenever I had been unsure about anything. I appreciate every single person who has helped get this book launched!

I started writing back in January 2022 after a conversation with my sister, Rizzie. I would like to extend my sincere thanks to her, for getting this idea festering in my mind. Even if it came about jokingly, in our texts, sometimes that's all you need. To plant the seed.

"maladaptive daydreaming disorder lol now you have a name for it."

"sounds like we got a lot of issues"

"Yup. I'm going to start writing books, at least make money off mine."

"What would you make the title?"

"How I learned to put the fun in dysfunctional? Lmao kidding"

Yet here we are!!

Ever since I was a little girl, I thought everyone day–dreamed constantly. It wasn't until late December 2021, that I learned, it was actually a disorder. Disassociating from reality and just shifting yourself mentally, into a make belief world of make belief situations. Whether I'm showering, cleaning, listening to music or even going to bed! There is literally a whole other universe inside my imagination playing out. It's been a crazy – and hard to stay focused ride – seeing one of them come to life on paper!

I'd like to give my warmest thanks to my husband, Sean. For his unwavering support these last 8 months. For being the voice of reason whenever my intrusive thoughts began doubting myself, and my work. Your faith in me and my talents, has gotten me this far. Thank you for believing in me, even when I didn't believe in myself. ♥

I would also like to acknowledge the help and assistance from Cassidy H, Alishia C, Kaylee M and Scott S. I know each of you have your own lives and sincerely appreciate that you took the time out of each of your days, to read through. Thank you for giving me advice and honest feedback about some of the material. I appreciate the lovely words and constructive criticism given to me.

Last, but certainly not least, a huge thank you to all my readers! Creators from authors – musicians – to artists, would be no where without your support. So thank you for getting this far, and making one of my dreams, come true.

"Don't be pushed around by the fears in your mind. Be led by the dreams in your heart."– Roy T. Bennett, The Light in the Heart.